STOLEN ENCHANTRESS

Forbidden Forest 1

AMBER ARGYLE

First Edition: March 2018
Library of Congress Cataloging-in-Publication Data
LCCN: 2018902825

Argyle, Amber
Stolen Enchantress (Forbidden Forest) – 1st ed
ISBN-13: 978-0-9976390-3-2

TO RECEIVE AMBER ARGYLE'S STARTER LIBRARY FOR FREE,
SIMPLY TELL HER WHERE TO SEND IT:
http://amberargyle.com

For all my sisters from other misters.

You know who you are and what you've done.

As well as the retribution coming your way.

(It's tacos. The retribution is tacos.)

CHAPTER

THE BEAST

Mud squelched between her toes as Larkin shoved the hoe into the ground, lifted a sodden lump of earth, and dropped seeds from her belt into the hole. Rain dripped from her damp wool hood, and her back clenched in one big cramp. But she didn't let the ache or the rain slow her. Bane had promised to come for her after her work was done. They were to go fishing at the river. With any luck, her family would have fresh meat for the first time in days.

She dropped the last seed into the ground and straightened with a sigh, rolling the kinks from her neck.

"Sela, time to go."

She pulled back her hood and turned to look for her little sister. Instead, she came face-to-face with Crazy Maisy, jagged lines of mud painted across her skin, her wet hair plastered over her face. Larkin jumped back, heart pounding. She forced her spine straight. Best not to show fear around the girl.

"The forest take you, Maisy!"

How long had she been stalking her? And what nasty tricks did she have in mind? Throwing rocks or insults? Making one of her gruesome predictions?

"Within the shadows of the trees," Crazy Maisy recited in a singsong voice, "the beast doth live and the beast doth breathe."

Gruesome predictions it is. Larkin cast an uneasy glance at the forest. She'd strayed too far from her home. The muddy fields were surrounded on three sides by the Forbidden Forest and the fourth side by the river Weiss. The wind picked up, and the forest's enormous trees groaned, branches straining like arms eager for her to come close enough to strangle the breath from her body.

Only her parents ever risked coming this close to the forest. She stepped back, grabbed the hoe, and held it like a spear—a dull, mud-caked spear. It was laughable, but she felt better with it in her hands. She searched the shadowy stillness for signs of the beast.

Maisy circled Larkin. "When day dies and shadows grow, the beast without his kingdom goes." She was nothing if not cruel.

"Shut it, Maisy!" Larkin searched for a puff of tangled blonde hair, a flash of pale skin. She saw nothing. "Sela?" she called again. Even to her own ears, her voice sounded hollow. With her father at the tavern and her mother attending a birth, Larkin had been left in charge of her sister. How long had it been since she'd heard her little sister playing? She couldn't remember.

Pushing damp strands of copper hair out of her face, Larkin whirled in a circle. On this side of the river, the fields were fairly flat. She should have easily spotted a muddy four-year-old girl. But there was no sign of her.

Maisy circled closer, stalking Larkin. "Shadows his cloak, magic his staff, his snaggily claws reach 'n grasp."

Larkin's heart squeezed violently. The last thing she needed was the druid's mad daughter taunting her. She shot Maisy a glare and ran to the last place she'd seen her sister, mud clinging to her soles and splattering her back. Her skirt tugged free of her belt and dropped around her hips, hampering her every step.

"Sela?" she called again, louder. Only the steady patter of rain answered.

Larkin swept the muck for Sela's tracks. There was a general mess, like Sela had decided to swim in the mud, then perfect little footprints, the toes digging deep as if she'd run. Larkin hiked up her wayward skirt and followed the erratic footprints past mud mounds, mud cakes, and finally, partially melted mud balls. The path took her closer to the smear of trees, but then the tracks went from zigzags to a straight line—directly toward the Forbidden Forest.

"Snatching the virgins from their dreams, never a chance to voice their screams." Maisy squatted, her head cocked to the side as her ragged fingernail drew an *X* through one of Sela's tiny footprints.

"Go away, Maisy!"

Dread wrapping a poisonous cloud around her, Larkin followed those tracks to the outer edge of the outstretched boughs. She stood there, the wind pressing her ragged, damp skirt against her legs. The trees whispered dark secrets to each other. If she strained her hearing, she might be able to understand the words, but she was quite certain she didn't want to.

Beside her, Sela's tracks had also paused—she could tell because they were deeper and nearly perfectly formed—but then her baby sister's footprints crossed into the Forbidden Forest.

"Ancestors save me," Larkin whispered. The sun chose that moment to peek out from behind the clouds, though the rain continued drumming against her head and shoulders. The trees' shadows stretched toward her toes, ready to infect her with their inky darkness.

Maisy stood beside her and faced the trees. "Back to the

forest, he doth go, to nibble and dribble their bones just so."

"You saw her go in!" Larkin whirled on Maisy, grabbed the girl's sodden shift in her fists, and brought her muddy face close to her own. "Why didn't you stop her? Why didn't you tell me?"

"I did tell you."

That idiotic song! Maisy closed her eyes and tipped her face to the sky. Rivulets of water exposed streaks of pale skin.

"The forest called to Sela," Maisy said. "She heeded the call."

Maisy was as bizarre and unwelcome as a midsummer blizzard. Not worth beating to a pulp. Larkin shoved Maisy so she landed hard on her backside. "She's a child!" The forest often sent its beasts to take virgins as sacrifice—the Taken—but never a girl younger than fourteen. Sela must have wandered in on her own.

Larkin was furious. Sela might be only four, but she knew better.

Larkin pointed back to town. "Go get help!"

Crazy Maisy lay back in the mud with a plop. "The men won't risk the forest—not for *your* sister."

"Get your druid father. He serves the forest! He can make it spit her out again."

"He would praise her sacrifice."

Larkin wrapped her arms around her middle, partly to hold herself together and partly to keep from strangling Maisy. Every year, girls went missing—sacrifices taken from their beds by the beast. They disappeared in the night. No one ever saw them leave.

And no one ever saw them again.

Now her baby sister was gone, and it was Larkin's fault. She should have watched her closer, should have reminded her— again—to stay away from the forest. She looked back at her home, situated on a little rise beside the river. The conical hut rose from the ground like a beehive. Beyond the river was the town of Hamel. Blue-gray smoke rose from some of the roofs. For half a thought, she considered going back for help. But Crazy Maisy was right. No one would risk those shadows for Sela, not even Papa. He'd give Sela up as lost, or worse, devoured by the beast—one less worthless girl's mouth to feed.

To never again feel the solid weight of her sister in her arms, to never come home from the fields to find a cluster of flowers on her sleeping mat ... Larkin couldn't bear to lose her sunshine.

"Once to the forest she hath gone, never again will she see the dawn." Crazy Maisy had slipped away to twirl through the fields. She'd made that last part up; it wasn't part of the song.

Larkin couldn't go back home. She had to go in after her. Clenching both hands around the hoe, Larkin eased into the forest.

Rotten leaves and naked branches closed in on her from every direction. She had the immediate sense she'd stepped into some vast being; the forest was aware of her presence, and it didn't want her there. Perhaps even more frightening, the beast could be hiding right beside her, just out of sight, and she'd never know.

With every step she took, the animosity bearing down on her grew. She glanced back. Between the massive trunks, she could make out the field that shone behind her, a rainbow arching over her town. She could still go home—and tell her mother that her youngest child had been devoured and that it was Larkin's fault.

Not really a choice at all.

Larkin willed herself to keep moving, to keep her attention on her sister's fading prints as the forest's anger grew into a living thing that gnashed and clawed. The ground here didn't take tracks as well as the mud of the plowed field, but she saw enough signs of Sela's passage—a freshly broken stick, a stray footprint, more little mud balls—to believe she was headed in the right direction.

And then a giant picked up the forest and spun it—at least that's what it felt like. She grabbed the nearest tree and held on, the bark biting into her hands. Anger and hatred stung like a thousand hornets. She had a sudden urge to do *something*. Some nameless word rested on the tip of her tongue, but she lost it in her desperate attempt to hold on to the tree.

"You think you can frighten me," Larkin gasped. "I've known hatred and pain my entire life. You can't scare me!"

Finally, the rolling slowed and stopped. She concentrated on holding still, though her head continued to spin. She blinked a few times, eyes watering, to keep from bolting away from an animosity so strong it made her stomach heave. Was this what they called the stirring?

She glanced around and tried to get her bearings. The town had been behind her, but she wasn't sure of that anymore. Her legs shaking, she bent to retrieve the hoe she'd dropped when she grabbed the tree. Gripping it so hard her hands hurt, she clenched her teeth and kept going.

She hadn't taken more than a dozen steps before another stirring caught her. Everything blurred, the trees melting in the sun. This time, she had nothing to hold. She collapsed and dug her fingers into the bleeding earth. She tipped her head toward the boughs dripping hot, burning wax onto her. "I will not leave without my sister," she said firmly.

The feeling faded, but it was only pulling back into a crouch, ready to spring at any moment. She bolted, and the stirring struck. The world swirled around her, melting branches dripping on her, forming blisters that popped, clear fluid running down her skin.

With a cry, she slammed into a tree, fell into a patch of prickle weeds, and promptly lost the contents of her stomach. She rested her forehead on a clean patch of dirt. Had Sela endured this stirring? It hurt to think of her four-year-old sister facing this.

She threw back her head. "I will not leave without my sister!" She pushed herself to her feet. She'd lost the trail, but she couldn't stop. She limped away from the patch of prickly weeds and plowed doggedly forward.

When the stirring came again, she did her best to ignore it, forcing herself to stumble through the whirling shapes all around her, hatred pelting her. She tried to avoid the roots that snatched at her feet. The stirrings came faster and faster, one on top of another. Clenching her eyes shut, she felt her way forward. Sometimes she ran into things. When she did, she carefully felt her way around and kept going.

Something growled behind her. The beast? She took off running and slammed into another tree. She cried out as something pierced her palm. On her hands and knees, she crawled. And then the stirring stopped. She looked back. The trees were whole again, glowering as if furious she'd escaped. If the beast had been there, she saw no sign of it.

She collapsed and lay still, panting. Her feet stung with thorns, but though welts and scrapes covered her arms and legs, there were no burns, no blisters. She lifted her hand. A splinter the size of her pinky had pierced the meaty part of her palm opposite her thumb. Bracing herself, she yanked it out, though a sliver was left behind. Fresh blood welled, dribbling down her wrist. She squeezed her palm to slow the blood flow.

With a groan, she sat up and pulled stickers from her feet and backside. In the relative quiet, she heard a child singing. She tipped her ear toward the right, where dark shadows lightened to emerald.

"Sela?" Larkin whispered, the sound of her voice loud in the stillness. She pushed to her feet and hobbled through the thinning trees and into a meadow filled to the brim with wildflowers. She squinted in the bright light streaming down in shafts from the clouds, the colors so sharp it was almost painful.

In the middle of it all, next to a burbling stream, sat Sela in her simple ankle-length tunic. She was surrounded by flowers. She'd stuffed them into her collar, her cuffs, and her wild, strawberry-blonde hair.

"Sela!" Larkin cried as she ran toward her.

Sela's round face lit up, her bright green eyes a stark contrast to her muddy face. "Larkin! Look, pretty flowers," she said, lisping the *l* and *r*. She held out a fistful as proof.

Larkin dropped to her knees and took her sister's too-thin face in her hands. She really was fine. Sela smiled brilliantly back. Larkin bundled her sister into her arms and rocked her back and forth, tears streaming down her cheeks. "Sela, you know you're not supposed to go into the Forbidden Forest! The stirring—how did you even get past it?"

Sela rested her hands on Larkin's shoulders, her little brow furrowed in concentration. Something broke free inside Larkin— a burst of light where before there had been only darkness.

She realized her eyes were closed. When she opened them, the last vestiges of the oppressive hatred were gone. In its place, warmth and life spread through her, growing and enlarging until her limbs tingled with energy and power. She took a free breath. She felt alive, more alive than she'd ever felt before. The sensation was familiar, and yet foreign at the same time—like the stories her mother used to tell of her privileged childhood.

Larkin looked at the forest with new eyes. It no longer seemed a dark and foreboding place. Instead of sinister, the shadows seemed cool and inviting, promising protection and safety. The rotting leaves smelled spicy and fresh. Birdsong sounded in the distance. The new sensation was so strong it overwhelmed Larkin's fear.

"All better," Sela whispered as she patted Larkin's cheek with a hand that smelled of crushed plants and dirt.

Larkin gaped at her sister. "What did you do?"

Sela shrugged. "The trees are our friends." Her big green

eyes full of concern, Sela thrust the flowers into her face. "Picked flowers for you."

Remembering where they were, Larkin brushed the tears from her cheeks as her nervous gaze swept over the meadow. It now seemed a pretty place, but it was all deception. This was the Forbidden Forest. And Sela might have escaped its stirring, but she wouldn't outrun its beast, with its terrible claws and insatiable hunger. If it found them, they were as good as dead.

She forced herself to be calm. Running for safety would do her no good if she went the wrong way. "I'm lost, Sela. I don't know the way back."

Sela patted Larkin's cheek again. "Larkin, don't cry."

Larkin gave a wobbly smile and looked around again, trying to remember where she'd come into the meadow. Something out of place caught her attention, and her gaze snapped back.

In the shadows of a tree, a man watched them. He stood far enough away that she could cover his form with her outstretched hand. Her heart lightened with hope. Had one of the villagers come for them after all?

The man stretched back a bowstring in one fluid motion, the arrow flying directly toward them. Larkin could do little more than let out a squeak of surprise and hunch protectively over Sela, her eyes squeezing shut. Behind her came an inhuman scream of pain and a crash.

Holding her sister tight, Larkin whipped around and leaped to her feet. She staggered back from a writhing, monstrous lizard the size of a man, an arrow sticking out of its eye.

The beast had found her.

With another scream, it clawed at the arrow until it broke off. Its remaining eye fixed on her, and its tongue flicked out to taste the air. It charged, mouth full of curving teeth. Larkin jumped back. Its maw snapped shut over empty air. It gathered itself to lunge, when another arrow bloomed from its gaping mouth. The creature gave a roaring shriek.

"Run!" came a cry from behind her.

Move, she screamed at her sluggish body. Gasping a breath into her starving lungs, Larkin held her sister tight and sprinted away from the creature, toward the man running in their direction. He hauled an ax and shield from his back and charged the creature. The lizard lunged, its massive tail launching it forward. The man braced himself behind his shield, ax swinging up and under. They collided in a heap.

Clutching Sela to her, Larkin panted and waited for one or the other of them to move. If there were more beasts, she would need this man. If he didn't rise ... she didn't know what she would do. Sela lay still in Larkin's arms, her hands fisted in Larkin's hair. Larkin rubbed her back, trying to emit comfort she herself didn't feel.

A groan made Larkin tense—was it man or beast? The beast's great body shifted and rose, then flopped to the side as the man pushed himself out from under it. Relief flickered in his eyes when he saw her. He pushed to stand, planted his foot on the beast's side, and yanked his ax out, scanning the clearing.

"Did its teeth so much as scratch you or the child?" He had an oddly formal accent.

Larkin shook her head, but he wasn't looking at her. "No," she managed. His head was shaved, except for a long braid behind one ear. He was beautiful, his body muscled and his skin dark, though as he came closer, she noticed pock scars on his cheeks. His clothes, though finely made, were worn thin and bloody.

She didn't recognize him, and she knew everyone in town by sight. Perhaps he was from one of the other towns or cities that made up the United Cities of Idelmarch?

"Who are you?" Larkin asked.

"My name is Denan." He rinsed his blood-soaked ax in the stream, dried it, and reattached it and the shield to his back.

"I'm Larkin. This is my sister, Sela. Thank you for helping

us."

He strode over to where he'd dropped his bow and picked it up. "What are you doing inside the forest? Don't you know how dangerous it is?"

She stiffened. "Sela wandered in. I came looking for her."

He approached her, brows drawn down disapprovingly. She forced herself not to back away from him as he paused in front of her. "You should have watched her better."

She ground her teeth and reminded herself that this man saved their lives. "Yes. I should have."

He gave her a long, appraising look, noting the sharp bones of her wrists and the threadbare state of her skirt and her father's too-large, tattered shirt. She was suddenly aware of how fine Denan's clothing and boots were. And how strangely cut. He wore a pair of close-fitting leather trousers, a tunic that came to points in front of his thighs, and a cloak—all a mottled green that mimicked the dappled shadows. She shifted her dirty bare feet, embarrassed by her ragged hem.

He stepped past her, toward the tree where she'd first seen him. "You've made too much noise. It will attract more of them."

"More beasts?" Sela whimpered. Larkin heartily agreed with her. She shifted her sister's weight and hurried after him. Even if he was brusque, he had the weapons.

Denan rummaged through his pack and pulled out something bundled in cloth. "They're called gilgads. They're venomous, and their hide is like armor. You have to go for the eyes or their soft underbelly with arrows. Axes can pierce them if you put enough momentum behind it, but you have to keep clear of their teeth, which is where the shield comes in."

Sela whimpered.

"You're scaring her," Larkin chided.

Denan's expression softened. He held out a bit of hard bread to Sela. "They can't hurt you if you know how to kill them, Sela."

Her sister took it—Sela never turned down food—and began nibbling a corner.

"We're lost," Larkin said. "Can you show us the way back
to Hamel?"

Denan held out another piece of the bread for Larkin. His
cuff pulled back to reveal raised scars on the inside of his right
wrist. Realizing she was staring, she took the bread, but hesitated
to eat it, pride warring with the hollow ache of her stomach. She
settled for stuffing the bread in the pouch at her waist, the one
she used to hold anything edible she gathered during planting.
She hoped it wouldn't get too much dirt on it from the roots
she'd dug earlier.

Ignoring the protest of her watering mouth, Larkin asked
again, "Can you take us home?"

He started into the forest. "This way."

Larkin looked back and noted the storm coming from the
other side of the meadow. It had been raining when she entered
the forest. "No, it has to be back that way."

"It isn't." He pulled out something from inside his cloak—a
set of panpipes.

"You don't understand. It was storming when we left. And
the storm is that way." She tipped her head in the direction she
thought they should go.

"My people are known as the pipers. Would you like to hear
me play?" Without waiting for her to answer, he rested his pipes
on his bottom lip. A melody, haunting and full of longing,
poured forth. A melody that reminded Larkin of a lullaby her
mother had hummed long ago, back when she used to smile.

An old remembrance roused within Larkin—a memory
deeper than memory. A place her soul knew, even if her body
didn't. Her injured hand buzzed, and she drifted into another
time and place.

She was in an elegant boat, her hair long and wavy down

her back. She wore white, a golden headdress crowning her head. Before her, an enormous tree glowed silver. A crowd dressed in finery stood by rank, waiting for her.

Denan continued to play, and she followed, stepping where he stepped, moving when he moved. He glanced back and smiled. She smiled too, eager for him to keep playing. She would follow that song wherever it willed her.

"The Song of the White Tree," Denan said, bringing her back from wherever she'd gone.

Larkin shook herself and glanced back. She couldn't even see the meadow anymore. Sela slept in her aching arms. How far had they come while she'd been lost to the sound? "Where is this tree?" she sighed.

"In the Alamant." He gestured to the south.

She staggered to a stop. "But the only thing south is more of the Forbidden Forest."

Denan reached for Sela. "Why don't you let me carry your sister? You look tired."

Unsure, Larkin stepped back. The haunting melody echoed through her, but as she peered into the towering trees, a sliver of fear writhed inside her. "Shouldn't we be there by now? How long have we been walking?"

Denan stared at her like a cat watching a sparrow, waiting to see where they might land. She took another step back. "Wh-who are you? Why are your clothes and hair so strange? And that music ..." She couldn't remember anything from when he started playing to when he stopped. She took another step back. "What did you do to me?"

"I'm taking you somewhere safe." He lifted the pipes to his mouth and started playing. The song reawakened a river of longing inside her, the current threatening to pull her under again. She hefted her sister higher, the edge of the wound on her palm catching on her sister's tunic. Pain flashed up her arm. That pain brought with it a moment of clarity even as the first raindrop hit the back of her head and skidded down her neck.

For a moment, it was Larkin's will battling against the song's pull, and she was being swept under again. She focused on the pain in her hand. On her sisters and her mother. And Bane … She was supposed to meet him at the river later.

This man was as dangerous as the beast he'd slain. Only, instead of tooth and claw, Denan was using magic. She needed a weapon, a shield, or—A buzzing tingle spread from her hand, shot up her arm, and rooted through her body. The song's hold over her shattered. She gasped and staggered back.

He stopped playing. His face shifted from shocked to grim. "Don't run."

Clutching her sister to her chest, Larkin whirled and sprinted for the meadow, her injured hand pounding in rhythm with her frantic heart.

CHAPTER

VENOM

L arkin ducked a branch and broke into the meadow.

"Larkin?" Sela asked, her hands wrapped tight around Larkin's neck.

Ignoring her sister, Larkin leaped over the stream that bisected the meadow, stumbled to one knee on the other side, and nearly dropped Sela. She glanced back, sure Denan would be on top of her, but he'd paused at the meadow's edge. He lifted what looked like a hollow stick to his mouth and blew hard. A dart impaled the ground next to her.

"Larkin?" Sela whimpered.

What was on the end of that dart? Poison? Bile rising in her throat, Larkin scrambled to her feet and sprinted across the last half of the meadow. She looked back as she passed beneath the tree's shadows. Denan vaulted over the stream, his attention fixed on them.

Larkin stared at the clouds in the distance and silently promised her sister to head straight for them, to not get lost, to keep them both safe. She wasn't sure if she could keep those promises—not when she faced the stirring again.

Sela's hands wrapped too tight around Larkin's neck. "I want to go home!" she demanded.

Larkin loosened her sister's grip. "Shh, the piper will hear you."

Sela whimpered. Trickles of sweat ran down the sides of Larkin's face. She didn't bother to wipe them away. Breathless, she waited for the stirring to happen. Instead, her legs buckled, air sawing in and out of her burning lungs. She couldn't run much longer. She searched for a place to hide. She caught sight of a small incline, a fallen tree covering it like a makeshift roof. She glanced around for Denan, relieved that she didn't see him.

She changed course, scrambled over the fallen tree, and crouched on the other side, holding Sela close. Kneeling to ease the cramping in her legs, Larkin tried to quiet her breathing. Through the trees, she saw a sliver of her family's home, the black rock walls slick with rain. So agonizingly close. But to reach it, she would face the stirring.

She peeked over the log, catching sight of Denan searching for them—close enough she could make out the scars on his cheeks. She ducked, her back between the log and the tree.

"It would be so much easier if you came with me freely, Larkin," Denan called. "I promise I won't hurt you."

Sela started crying softly. Larkin held a finger to her lips. Her sister nodded solemnly and buried her head in Larkin's neck. Holding Sela tighter, Larkin tried desperately to come up with some way out of this. She longed for her hoe; she wasn't even sure when she'd lost it. Not that it would do any good. She didn't stand a chance against someone twice her size, armed as he was, and she'd never put her sister at risk.

Maybe he wouldn't find them. Maybe they could hide until he left and then make a run for it. She strained to listen but heard nothing above her sister's ragged breathing. Steeling herself,

Larkin peeked out again.

He had halved the distance between them, every step bringing him closer. "Let me take you somewhere there's always food and a soft bed and someone to care for you." He was close enough now that she could make out his obsidian eyes beneath the hood of his cloak. He searched for her with a hunger that made her heart leap in her chest.

Sela gasped. Denan's head whipped toward the tiny sound. His gaze locked with Larkin's. She bolted, half expecting the stirring to attack her, knowing she wouldn't be able to fight it again. Instead, something pricked her right shoulder, and pain shot up and down her arm. Something hard and foreign lodged inside her.

She staggered and craned to look back—a dart protruded from the center of her right shoulder blade. She yanked it out and stumbled sideways, bumping into a tree. At the touch, déjà vu washed through her. She shook her head against the strange sensation and stumbled on.

Within ten steps, numbness spread from her shoulder, sinking deep into her muscles. Her right arm stopped working and dangled uselessly at her side. She held on to Sela with her left. Her legs grew heavy and sluggish. She was almost there. She could see the bright blue sky through the trees. The mud of her family's freshly plowed fields. Her home. The town of Hamel on the other side of the swollen river. Denan's steps pounded right behind her. She reached the forest's edge, took the first step into the open.

His hand closed around her shoulder. She wasn't going to make it, but her sister still might. She dropped and hit her knees hard. It should have hurt, but all she could feel was the impossibly heavy weight of her body.

"Run, Sela!" Larkin gasped, tipping forward. "Get help!"

The little girl sprang from her arms like a sparrow loosed from a snake's mouth. Larkin felt a moment of exquisite relief as her sister crossed the muddy field. She had escaped the forest, even if Larkin hadn't.

Arms grasped her ankles, dragged her behind a tree, and flipped her onto her back. She found herself face-to-face with Denan. She tried to kick free, but her legs refused to obey her frantic demands.

"I told you not to run," he said matter-of-factly. He pulled a vial from his bag, bit off the cork, tipped her head up, and pushed it between her deadened lips.

Liquid seeped into her mouth, tasting of pepper. She tried to spit it out, but she barely had enough dexterity left to choke down a swallow. He looked her over quickly, scooped her over his shoulder as easily as if she were a newborn lamb, and loped into the forest.

She tried to writhe, but all she managed was a feeble twitch. The trees slowly snuffed out the town, the fields, her home. She'd never see her family again. She couldn't hold her head up anymore. Her body swayed helplessly, as helpless as she was during her father's beatings.

But after, I always get up.

She glared at Denan's back. The textured feathers of the darts in his belt caught her eye. She strained to reach one, but her arms were little more than dead weight.

Denan shifted to avoid something in his path, and her left hand brushed the fletching. With the last of her dexterity, she pinched it. Denan's next swing pulled it free. It didn't take much to add a little strength to the natural rhythm of her swaying arms. The dart sank into his right side. Denan jerked to a stop.

He pulled the dart free, releasing a bead of blood that streaked down his dark skin. He shifted her from his back into his arms. "Do you have to do everything the hard way?"

From far away, the town's warning horn sounded. Relief washed through her. Sela had made it to safety, and she'd summoned help. Denan's head jerked toward the sound. He eased

Larkin onto the ground with a look of profound annoyance, took another vial from his belt, and tipped the contents into his mouth. She noticed with some satisfaction he was already listing, as if the muscles on the right side of his back weren't working.

Frantic shouts rose in the distance. Denan glanced toward the sound and then back at her. Right arm now dangling uselessly from his side, he tucked her against the same fallen log she'd hid behind before. His movements grew more and more sluggish as he swept up branches and leaves, scattering them all over her. His dark eyebrows drew down in frustration. His fingers brushed the back of her cheek. Her whole body was numb, but somehow, she felt it. And she couldn't even shudder in revulsion at the intimate touch.

He stared at her as if committing her face to memory; the mere thought made her want to scream. He leaned forward and whispered in her ear, "You should be safe until I can return for you." He covered her face with leaves so she could only see a smattering of the world beyond, then turned and limped back into the Forbidden Forest.

Unable to turn away, she watched as his movements became less and less graceful until the trees swallowed him and she could see no more.

On the inside, Larkin writhed and kicked and screamed. On the outside, she was still for so long she wondered if she was dead. But no, she could still feel her heart pounding in her chest—a chest that rose and fell with each of her breaths. She could even smell the spicy decay of the leaves that cocooned her.

Had Denan forever trapped her inside this helpless body? But no, she'd pricked him with the same poisoned dart, and he'd promised to come back for her. Whatever he'd done to her, it had to be temporary. She willed her fingers to move, her nose to twitch. Nothing happened.

Rain began to fall. Though she couldn't feel it, she could hear it tapping against the leaves before dripping into her eyes. Her vision blurred, and she couldn't even blink the moisture away.

From the direction of her town, the warning horn sounded another long, hopeless note. She imagined women snatching their children and running for their houses, the men lifting their hoes as weapons. Another sound wove through the trees: footfalls squelching through mud.

"Larkin!" her papa cried.

I'm here! she tried to call back, but no sound left her dead lips.

"Tracks. She must have come this way." She recognized Lord Daydon's careful way of speaking.

Sela must have gone to their father first. He'd crossed the river to the manor and roused Lord Daydon, who'd sent someone—probably Bane, his son—to sound the alarm. The footfalls stopped, and she imagined the men crouching to study the prints at the forest's edge, much as she'd done earlier.

Please, she silently begged. *Notice the third set of tracks. Realize that this was not the work of the forest and its beast, but of a man.*

"What was she thinking coming this close to the forest? She knows only her mother or I are to work this close to the trees." Harben's voice sounded angry rather than sad. Papa was right. She should have paid better attention, should have focused on her planting and watched her sister instead of daydreaming about escape. Humiliation burned Larkin's cheeks.

"She's one of the Taken now," intoned a third, nasally voice—the druid Rimoth. So, Crazy Maisy had gone for her father. "Your youngest is still alive. Praise the miracle and count yourself blessed."

"Blessed?" her father said, voice pained. An unfamiliar

swelling of hope started in Larkin's breast. "How can I call myself blessed? Her mother is due any day. Nesha is a cripple, and Sela is only four. I need Larkin for the planting."

The swelling died, bitter rot seeping into her veins instead. More steps and ragged breathing. "I sounded the alarm. Where is she?"

Bane! Hope rushed through her. Bane would never give up on her—not without a fight.

"In there." Larkin could imagine her father running his hand through his hair, curly and copper, just like hers. "There's nothing we can do."

Even her father's slaps didn't hurt nearly as much as those words.

"Her sacrifice will not be forgotten," Rimoth said. "Tonight, we will place a candle in the river, as we did for your sister, Caelia, when she was taken."

"No!" Bane cried. She heard a struggle, the impact of fists, and then someone tearing through the underbrush. "Larkin!"

"No, son! You can't go in there," Daydon said.

The suck and release of mud was replaced with the crack of brittle branches and the shush of soggy detritus. Larkin detected motion through the smattering of leaves blocking her vision. Though her eyes couldn't shift to focus on him, she recognized the way he moved, the determined set of his shoulders.

I'm here!

Behind Bane came more motion, Papa and Daydon chasing after him—she could tell which one was her father by his slight build—but her friend pulled quickly away.

"You will make the forest angry!" Rimoth cried from farther away—the coward wouldn't risk the forest for any of them. "It will visit destruction down on all of us. The beast will be unleashed!"

Bane's sure steps faltered. He stumbled, tried to right himself, then his back arched, and he fell hard. "The trees are poison!"

The stirring, Larkin thought in dismay.

A half-dozen steps behind, Daydon and Papa dropped as well. "The whole forest burns," Daydon said.

The trees around them stood silent and still, though the men cowered as if the boughs had come alive and were attacking them. Larkin suddenly understood. There was no stirring. The forest, like the magic of Denan's pipes, made them see things that weren't there.

It's a lie! An illusion! she wanted to say.

"The stirring has taken you," Rimoth said in his superior tone. "The forest will call her beast to devour you for daring to disturb her."

Bane pushed himself up and took a few staggering steps. He was almost directly in Larkin's line of sight now.

"Son, she's gone. It's too late," Daydon implored. "Come back before the beast takes you too."

"I won't leave her!" Bane squeezed his eyes shut, held his arms in front of himself, and staggered forward. Papa and Daydon came after him. One took hold of Bane under his arms. The other reached for his legs.

"No!" Bane cried as he struggled to fend them off.

She seethed at the irony. For Bane, Papa would risk the Forbidden Forest—for another male, but not his own daughter. *Not me.*

Bane shoved her father back. "You all heard Sela. If a little girl can come back from the forest, so can Larkin. Help me."

"No," Daydon said firmly. "I'll not lose you like I lost your sister."

She wanted to call out to Bane, tell him the truth—tell all of them the truth about Denan. But then, from somewhere deep in the forest, a growl reverberated with enough force to make the leaves covering her face tremble and shift.

The gilgad Denan had killed—there had to be more. Her

heart pounded out a frantic rhythm. If any of them would look down, they would see her lying silent and still, little more than a dozen paces from them.

"It's the beast come for us all!" Papa said.

"You will visit destruction down on all our heads!" Rimoth said.

"Quickly, boy, or we're all dead," Daydon said.

At that, the fight drained out of Bane, and Larkin knew she was lost. Her father hadn't bothered to fight for her. Even Bane was giving up. If she didn't do something, they would leave her for the beast or Denan or both. Larkin gathered everything she had, pushing air through her throat. A strangled moan slipped past her vocal cords.

Bane whipped around, and his eyes locked with hers. He gaped, then jerked free of Papa and Daydon, lurching and staggering toward her through the illusions that bound him. "She's here! She's here!"

He ducked under the log and clawed at the leaves, scraping them away from her. He was touching her, probably even scratching her, but she couldn't feel it. His hands cupped her cheeks. "Larkin? Oh, don't be dead. Please don't be dead."

She couldn't meet his gaze, couldn't answer.

The growling came again. The trees trembled around them.

"Bring her! Quickly," Papa cried, hurrying toward the fields.

Bane lifted Larkin into his arms, detritus falling away from her. Her head dangled and bounced as Bane carried her from the forest. Though she could only focus on what was directly in front of her, she was surprised how much she could make out from her peripheral vision.

At the edge of the forest, Rimoth stepped in front of them, hand out. "Put her back!" he puffed. "Put her back or risk the beast's wrath!"

Bane shoved past the older man, Rimoth calling threats after

23

them. Ahead, men rushed toward them through her father's fields, carrying scythes and axes.

"Stop them!" Rimoth called. "Stop them now!"

With looks of confusion, most of the men staggered to a halt. Kenjin, Horace, and his son, Horgen—the richest, most powerful men in town, next to Lord Daydon—pushed through the others to block Bane's path. "What's the meaning of this, Druid Rimoth?"

Gasping for breath, Rimoth lurched to a stop beside them. "The beast will not be denied its price. Larkin belongs to the forest now."

Daydon stepped between her and Rimoth. "Nonsense. The girl will go home to her family."

Larkin hated her father for his silence.

"The last time you defied the forest," Horace said, "we lost five good men and dozens of girls." His brother had been one of those men.

Daydon stiffened. It had been his idea to start the fires in the first place. Seeing his advantage, Rimoth pushed past him.

"This is different." Bane held her closer. "The beast didn't take her. She went in after Sela. Now, let us by."

"Is it different?" Druid Rimoth's voice went husky and deceptively soft. Larkin would have folded in on herself until she was as small as a field mouse if she could. Instead, she lay helpless in Bane's arms as Rimoth scrutinized her, making her skin itch and crawl. The crowd grumbled. No one really liked Rimoth, but those who paid for his protections didn't have daughters go missing as often.

"Why did you go into the forest, Larkin?" Rimoth's rotten breath washed over her. She caught a glimpse of his pale thumb as it brushed over her brow—he was touching her! She wanted to recoil from the man's damp, corpse-pale skin and lean into Bane for support. Instead, she was imprisoned in this frozen body.

"You will step away from my daughter, Druid!" Even with her enormous pregnant belly, Larkin's mother, Pennice, shoved past Rimoth and the powerful men like they were errant children. As the town midwife, Mama had plenty of experience dealing with emotional men. She rested her hand on Larkin's chest, and her eyes fluttered shut in relief. "Bane, bring her to the house."

"Get inside, woman," Papa said, the first time he'd spoken during the entire exchange.

Mama shot him a glare that would sizzle bacon. Bane pushed past Horace and Horgen.

"Now see here, Mother Pennice," Horgen began.

Mama rounded on the young man's father. "Horace, I brought all your boys into this world, naked and screaming. Now control your oldest, or I'll hand him back to his mother the same way I found him."

Horgen stepped back. The rest of the crowd parted for Mama without another word.

"Men, spread out around the town," Daydon said. "If anything comes out of the forest, kill it."

"How can you defend against a creature no one has seen and lived to tell about it?" Rimoth called out to the men. They ignored him as they moved toward the forest.

"Until now," Bane said, his voice rumbling in his chest.

"Move it!" Daydon shouted at the townsmen. They picked up their pace.

"I speak for the forest!" Rimoth raged after them. "I alone can calm her anger. You would do well to obey me!"

Larkin wanted to warn the men; it wasn't a beast they should be watching for, but a man.

Bane shifted so Larkin's head settled on his shoulder. He rubbed his scruff against her forehead. "I won't let them hurt you," he whispered. "You're safe now."

Warmth enfolded her as his familiar smell washed over her, like night mist off freshly tilled earth. She couldn't tip her chin back to look at him, but his features were burned in her memory —his broad chest and narrow waist, his beakish nose and raven black hair, his warm eyes that offset his pale skin.

If anyone could protect her from the piper, it was Bane. And she had no doubts Denan would be back for her, as he'd promised.

CHAPTER

SMOKE AND FIRE

Mama knocked on the door to their house, which was made of fitted chunks of black stone that staggered up the cone-shaped roof. "Nesha, let us in."

The bar over the door scraped as it dropped away. Nesha's bare feet—one of them twisted and deformed—appeared. "Larkin?" she asked, her voice pitched high with panic.

Bane shouldered his way past her. Immediately, the smoke from the baking fire stung Larkin's eyes.

Mama dropped the bar back over the door. "Lay her there."

Bane set Larkin on her sleeping mat. Her head turned so she could see her mother, though she couldn't focus on her. Beyond her family, she could make out the rolled-up sleeping mats, a woven basket with their wooden plates and cups, and the coracle—a small boat made of cowhide stretched over woven willow branches. Now it held their seed rye, but during the spring, they often needed it to cross the overflowing river.

Mama knelt next to Larkin and pressed her ear to Larkin's

chest, her pregnant belly pushing against Larkin's side. "Her heart is strong." She began checking Larkin over for other injuries.

Nesha knelt on her other side. She tucked the wild mess of hair out of Larkin's face and cupped her cheeks. "Larkin?" When she didn't answer, Nesha looked to Bane. "What happened to her?"

"I don't know. I found her this way."

"The piper did it," Sela said from somewhere out of sight.

Someone banged on the door, the hinges squealing in protest. "Open the door, Pennice!"

Everyone froze. Mama let out all her breath and nodded once to Nesha, who rose to let Papa in. Out of breath, he pushed into the house. "What were you thinking, you fool girl! All you had to do was work and keep an eye on your sister. But no, you have your fool head in the sky!"

Everyone stiffened and averted their gazes. Larkin wanted to catch the breeze coming in behind her father and ride it somewhere far, far away.

Bane slipped his hand into hers—she knew because she felt it. She felt it! Her heart stuttered and started back up again. She tried to feel the mat beneath her, the mud she knew must be drying on her skin, but there was nothing besides the palm of her hand resting against Bane's. And like always, his touch grounded her, brought her back to the dark, dank hut her family lived in.

"She's suffered enough," Bane said flatly.

Papa took a menacing step toward her, then seemed to note the lord's son and think better of it. "As soon as she gets up, I want to know." He turned on his heel and left.

Mama glared at Papa's retreating form. "I need to check her over. Bane, you best go."

Bane hesitated, placed Larkin's hand on her stomach, and turned away. Her face was turned toward the door, and she had no choice but to watch him go.

Mama took a deep breath. "Nesha, you and Sela bring in pots of water. Let's wash this mud off her and see what we find."

Humiliated, Larkin lay helpless as Mama stripped her like she was a child, bathed her, and wrapped her damaged feet with boiled rags. Mama tried to dig the remaining sliver out of her palm—the pain a sharp ache Larkin was powerless to escape from—but it was too deep. Mama and Nesha went through the arduous process of washing Larkin's waist-length, curly red hair. A chill breeze snaked through the gaps around the door and window, but the cold was nothing to the horror that she would stay this way. What had the piper done to her?

Finally, Mama braided her hair, dressed her in a clean shift, wrapped her in her wool blanket, and forced some valerian tea down her. She slid Larkin's eyes closed, which eased her burning need to blink, but did nothing for her nerves. She lay blind and frozen as her family made and ate supper. Papa came home. Apparently, a watch had been set—not that it would do any good if the beast decided to come—and Papa wasn't needed yet.

The town would never need him. He was not to be trusted.

Eventually, everyone lay down to sleep. Wet sounds filled the night—the rushing river, the scattered pattering of rain, and the chorus of frogs. Larkin lay helpless and tried to pick apart the sounds for any hint of Denan coming for her.

Born on the wind, music seeped through the cracks of Larkin's hut, insinuating itself in her dreams. Her body flickered from form to smoke and back again. Rising, she turned her back on the embers of her family's dying fire. Her feet skimmed over her damp, cold blankets. Larkin soundlessly lifted the bar and slipped into a night as dark as ink on charcoal.

The music breathed into her. The cold pierced through her thin shift, threatening to pull her apart. She drew her arms around herself to keep from dissipating. She took a step away from the house, then stumbled and fell. The smoke of her body scattered and gathered back together as she sprawled over something large and fleshy. She recognized Bane's body by smell—damp soil and mists.

He didn't stir from the sleeping mat he'd spread before the door. She took form long enough to press a gentle kiss on his temple and tug his cloak over his shoulder and around the ax he clutched to his chest. The music swept around her again, her breath forming a vapor that misted against her cheeks as she walked into it. She wandered past the bridge, then between the willows and the hill bearing Bane's manor. The town beyond slumped in the shadows.

Grassy fields beckoned her up the hill. Partially frozen beads of moisture cracked against the soles of her bare feet, making her shivery with cold. She passed the last hut before the forest and slipped around a sentinel who slept in a heap next to the pigpen, his neck bent at an awkward angle.

She crested the hill and blew down the other side, carried along beside the river that gleamed onyx as a serpent's eye. At her approach, the frogs stopped singing, taking up the chorus again once she was past. She walked in this bubble of quiet until she reached the place where the river met the forest.

Before her stood a large tree covered in wicked thorns the size of her thumb—the Curse Tree. Faded bits of ribbon shifted with the breeze. On each were written curses—*Let my entire crop fail* or *May my child be born a girl and a cripple*. Some people believed they could trick the forest into cursing them with something good. Larkin thought them all fools. Nothing good came out of the Forbidden Forest.

The breeze rippled leaves and made the great boughs moan. A man stepped from the shadows, a set of panpipes at his lips. And if she was smoke, he was her fire—for one could not exist without the other. Still playing, he came to the forest's edge and stretched out his free hand.

She looked at his open palm and at him. Longing tore through her—a knowledge that if she took hold, her life would change for the better, that she would be happier than she had ever been. She knew it as surely as she knew that not taking hold would mean bitter sorrow.

And yet, she hesitated.

He reached out and ran his knuckles down her cheek. A zing of awareness bolted through her. She leaned into that touch. His hand opened, cupping her cheek. She turned her nose into his palm and inhaled the earthy, resin scent of him.

"I told you I would come back for you," he said.

He played again. His other hand slipped into hers, tugging her a single step into the forest. The pressure of his hand pushed the sliver deeper into the meat of her palm. Her hand tingled, and sudden clarity shot through her.

A small reservoir of power lay dormant inside her. That power felt right and good and *hers*. Instinctively, she reached for it. It slid up and down her skin. In an instant, the smoky haze clouding her thoughts vanished, and she was herself again.

She planted her feet and jerked her hand free of Denan's, her head shaking frantically even as the music tried to burrow past the defenses she'd built around herself. "No," she ground out.

With a look of supreme frustration, he gave up on the pipes and grasped her arm. "How are you resisting my magic? That isn't possible."

She had no answer for him, but he didn't seem to expect one as he dragged her toward the forest. She writhed and hit him with her free arm. He took both her wrists in his large hands. "Don't make me dart you again, Larkin."

She stiffened, thinking of how utterly helpless she had been in that state. It took everything she had to stop fighting him.

He relaxed a fraction. "I don't want to hurt you."

She ground her teeth. "You paralyzed me and tried to kidnap me!"

"It was for your own good. If you'd stayed with me, it wouldn't have been so painful." He dragged her forward. "Be quiet. All your screaming yesterday attracted more gilgads, and they're nearly impossible to detect in the dark."

In the silence that followed, Larkin scrambled for some way out of this. What had stopped his magic from working on her before? Even as she thought it, her palm tingled. She concentrated on it and tried to make it do something. Nothing happened. She glanced over her shoulder at the home she would never see again if she didn't find a way to free herself.

All at once, her power surged. Light flashed, and Denan went flying. Larkin didn't question what had happened. She merely turned and ran.

"Larkin!" Denan growled. "You're only making things worse for yourself!"

She didn't look back. The branches whipped her face and tore at her hair. She bounded past the Curse Tree, leaped into the pasture, and took a single step toward town before something tangled around her legs.

She fell hard and looked back. Denan was running for her. Instinctively, she lifted her hand. Light flashed again, and he slammed into some kind of barrier. Keeping her hand up, she scrambled back and tugged at the ropes wound around her ankles. Denan pressed his palm against something like curving glass, the edges of which gleamed a faint amber.

He stared at her. "It cannot be."

She pushed to her feet and backed away.

"No, Larkin!" He pounded against the solid air she'd somehow put between them. "You don't understand what you are! There hasn't been another like you born in a century!"

She shook her head. "Leave me alone, Denan."

He lifted his hands helplessly. "I will come for you, Larkin.

We have the same heartsong." She didn't know what that meant —didn't want to know.

Standing, he pulled something from around his neck. He broke a branch from the Curse Tree. "In the morning, come back for this amulet. I'll leave it hidden in the grass beneath this branch."

"I won't."

He growled in frustration. "The amulet offers you protection."

"Protection," she scoffed. "The only thing I need protection from is you."

"The Black Druids are coming."

A shiver of dread ran down the length of her body. The Black Druids answered to no one, except perhaps the Forbidden Forest. She turned and strode away, her head spinning with what she had done.

"The boy, the one with the dark hair," Denan called after her. "Do you love him?"

She whirled to face him. "Leave Bane alone!"

He lifted his head, as if she'd confirmed his question. "He's not for you, Larkin."

"And I suppose you are?"

"Yes," he said, yet he didn't seem happy about it.

"I'll die first." She turned and ran.

CHAPTER

SACRIFICE

L arkin gasped awake and shot upright. Pain blasted through her, as though her muscles had been encased in glass that shattered into shards, stabbing her a thousand times over. Her vision swam, and she fought to stay alert.

"Larkin?"

Larkin's vision slowly cleared. The familiar stone walls of her hut were illuminated by the soft glow of their cooking fire. Nesha knelt before her, concern in her vivid violet eyes, her dark auburn hair swept back in a braid. Everything appeared so normal that for a moment Larkin wondered if her foray into the Forbidden Forest was some horrible nightmare.

Breathing hard, Larkin jerked the bandage off her hand, revealing the dark sliver embedded in her palm. Terrified, she probed for the buzzing. There was only pain. Wincing, she shifted out of her blankets. Her gaze traveled slowly, reluctantly, down the length of her body. Her rough-spun skirt, once a dull blue, had faded and stained to the color of a smoky sky. It grew darker and more ragged around the hem, which brushed her ankles, where dried mud caked to her skin.

Not a dream, then. *His music called to me, and I went.* But she'd fought him off with a power she didn't understand.

"But"—Nesha stared at Larkin's feet—"we bathed you. Why are your feet dirty?"

Larkin couldn't tell Nesha the truth; it was too raw and humiliating. "Where are Mama and Sela?"

"They went into town."

It hurt that her mother wasn't worried enough to be here when Larkin woke up. "Papa?"

"He said he was asked to patrol the forest's edge."

Which meant he was at the tavern drinking himself simple. Larkin reached for Nesha. "Help me up. I have to speak with the lord."

"The lord? Larkin, you've been asleep almost a full day. You need to eat something and recover."

Larkin sagged back. *A full day?*

Nesha filled a bowl with liquid from the cookpot. She brought it to Larkin, along with a cup of water. Suddenly ravenous, Larkin downed the water and the thin soup—fresh greens and some grains.

"Where did you get the grains?"

"It's our seed wheat," Nesha said, eyes downcast.

"We need that for the planting!"

Nesha shrugged. "Papa found Mama's coins. It was the wheat seed or nothing."

Things hadn't always been this desperate, but a few years ago, wheat rot had taken more than half the town's crop. And last winter had been a bad one, sickness running rampant. Larkin scraped the remaining grains into her mouth.

"Larkin, what happened in the forest?" Nesha said. "Did you see the beast? Does it have a horrible black mouth that stinks of rot?"

35

Curved teeth lunging for her. Larkin winced, trying to get the image out of her head. "Who told you that?"

"Maisy," Nesha said softly.

"Crazy Maisy." Larkin snorted. "She watched Sela go into the forest and did nothing to stop her." Unlike Nesha, Larkin had never liked Maisy, even before she'd gone mad. Larkin had been relieved when the girl had gone to serve the druids in Landra three years ago. Maisy had returned last fall—or at least her body had. She'd left her mind behind.

Her father, Druid Rimoth, claimed she'd been blessed with the sight from the forest. Since her return, Crazy Maisy had predicted which girls would go missing next, so no one dared interfere as she wandered the fields, muttering darkly or singing and dancing.

"She went for her father," Nesha said.

"For all the good it did." Gritting her teeth, Larkin hauled herself up, braced her hip against the wall, and tugged on her wool cloak and clogs. "Sela went into the forest. I went after her. I did see a beast. It nearly killed Sela and me."

Larkin stepped into the twilight and the rain, heading toward the bridge leading to the town. The breeze came down from the forest and tugged at Larkin's cloak. She stared at the dark smudge of trees, unable to look away.

Nesha followed, her limp more pronounced in her hurry. "How did you escape?"

Larkin slowed her steps so Nesha could keep up. "There was a man," she admitted. "He saved us."

"A man!" Nesha exclaimed. "But no one can survive the forest."

This one can.

"So he saved you?" Nesha clapped her hands in excitement. "But where is he? Why didn't he bring you back?"

"Because after he saved us, he tried to lure us in deeper. I had to fend him off."

Nesha stumbled to a halt. "Why would he do that?"

Larkin went over her interactions with Denan. Something had happened. Power had rushed through her. The tingle as she'd made it ... What exactly had she done? She rubbed her palm uncertainly, trying to force the sliver out. A fierce ache spread up her arm. His words echoed through her: *I will come for you.*

Denan wanted her.

"He won't have me," she muttered under her breath.

"What?" Nesha asked.

"Nothing." No point in frightening Nesha with talk of kidnappers as well as beasts. She squinted at a glint of orange that flickered beyond the lord's mansion. *Fire.* "Have they set fire to the forest again?" Gathering her skirt, she hurried ahead.

When Larkin was ten, the villagers had set the forest on fire. In a rage over his missing daughter, Lord Daydon had ordered the men to torch the forest, down to the last tree. The flames had risen high enough to burn the sky.

But the fires had snuffed out, as if they'd come up against an unassailable barrier. That night, the five men who had thrown the torches were found dead without a mark on them, and over two dozen girls went missing—half a generation gone overnight. Over the years, the trees had regrown preternaturally fast over the corpses of the fallen trees until they were gnarled, creaking behemoths again.

It had been the first time Larkin really understood the beast wasn't a nightmare, but a creature of flesh and blood who could take her or her sisters at any time, and no one could stop him.

And now they were lighting fires again.

"It's just a bonfire," Nesha called after her.

Larkin's attention slid toward the Forbidden Forest behind the bonfire. Despite her fear and aversion, it called to her, beckoning her like the sun beckoned seedlings from the ground.

"The beast take you," she said quietly. "I will never answer that call ever again."

Nesha shifted uncomfortably beside her. "Larkin?"

The wind picked up, bringing with it the smell of ashes. "What are they doing?"

"Making a sacrifice to appease the forest."

A light rain pattered against Larkin's back. She and Nesha tromped across the bridge and down the embankment. Bane's manor house lorded over the rise before them. His home was built of the same rocks as Larkin's, but that was where the similarities ended. Two stories high, it had a thatched roof and windows for every room. The back faced the river, his family's pastures full of woolly cattle spreading out to the northeast.

Larkin skirted the hill and took the meandering path between the hill and the eerily empty town. The houses to her right were smaller, shabbier versions of Bane's. Beyond the town, the bonfire blazed in the druid's hay field, as close to the forest as the druid dared go.

Judging by the crowd's size around the fire, Larkin guessed about a third of the town were there, around five hundred people. Less than usual, as so many were sick. Still, representatives from most families huddled against the wind. They formed a long line to toss in small bundles of dried lavender smeared with menstrual blood to appease the forest's anger.

Over bowed heads and hands, the townspeople recited prayers, asking their ancestors for protection. Some of them slipped Rimoth coins and received his blessing in return. Others sang to the beat of the drums. The rain picked up. Those who'd finished started to leave.

Larkin and Nesha were halfway across the field when Nesha said, "You should put up your hood."

"It's not raining that hard."

But as they approached the townspeople, some made wide berths around Larkin, their gazes averted. Others stared, their faces set in grim lines. One old woman spat at Larkin's feet and made a sign to ward off the beast.

Larkin's steps slowed. "Nesha, why is everyone acting as though I have the plague?"

"You may as well have."

Larkin cringed as Alorica, a girl her own age, stalked toward them with the grace of a cat. The firelight cast her pretty face, dark skin, and tightly curled hair in shadow.

Nesha took hold of Larkin's arm and tugged her forward. "Come on."

Alorica sighed and fussed with the hood of her rich burgundy cloak trimmed with blue thistle embroidery. She was always drawing attention to her fine clothes and jewelry. "Eloquent as always, cripple." She scrutinized Larkin. "Crazy Maisy is telling everyone that the forest stole your soul, that it forced its magic into you. She says eventually you'll side with the trees and bring about our destruction."

"What?" Larkin choked out. How could Maisy have possibly known about the magic?

"Come on, Larkin," Nesha said.

Alorica gave a nasty grin. "Bride of the beast, Crazy Maisy called you."

"Like your sister was the bride of the beast when the forest took her?" Larkin shot back.

Hatred flashed over Alorica's face. "Keep Atara out of it, you worthless slut."

Larkin stepped forward, hands balled into fists. Nesha pulled harder on her arm. Larkin planted her feet and whirled on her sister. "She deserves it."

"People are watching you," Nesha hissed. "Hitting her will make the rumors worse."

Alorica trilled a laugh. "When you two have the time, you should really stop at the tavern. See what your father is up to." Alorica waved her fingers as she strutted away.

"Why didn't you tell me about the rumors?" Larkin growled.

"What good would it have done? Now hide your hair." Nesha jerked Larkin's hood up, tucking wayward locks out of sight.

Larkin's eyes narrowed. If Nesha had heard the rumors, then so had their parents. "Mama came to the sacrifice, didn't she?" It was required for one of them to make an appearance.

Giving up on Larkin's hair, Nesha scanned the crowd. "Yes. And she brought Sela."

"What Maisy has been saying, you have to know I would never—"

"I know, but ... the town is so afraid. Girls go missing, but not like this, not in the middle of the day. It's got them thinking ... worrying that it might be like last time. Or worse."

Larkin's insides tightened. Without any more prompting from Nesha, Larkin tied her hair back with a bit of string from her pocket and straightened her hood.

The drummers started, the rhythm pounding against her skin like a frantic heartbeat. She kept her head down as she cautiously approached the press of bodies. The faces around her were bathed in crimson light. A goat fought the tether that kept it next to the fire.

She caught sight of Lord Daydon's ankle-length purple coat. He stood with his back to her, apart from the crowd under a lone tree that separated his property from the druid's.

Larkin breathed a sigh of relief at finding him so quickly. She tugged on Nesha's arm, and the two of them made their way over to him. Someone beyond the lord spoke to him, gesturing angrily. She recognized Rimoth's voice a second later. A shiver of revulsion worked up and down her spine. She slipped to the side, keeping the tree between herself and the men so they wouldn't see her. Nesha followed reluctantly behind.

Larkin positioned herself behind the tree and peeked around so she could see Daydon's back and Rimoth's profile.

Rimoth spoke in his falsely mild way. "If you're not going

to listen to my counsel—"

"A crucible hasn't been performed in over fifty years!" Daydon broke into a fit of coughing.

Larkin's breath caught in her throat. *A crucible?* For her? Rimoth wanted to chain her up inside the forest to prove the forest didn't want her. Waiting for the beasts or Denan or ... Larkin shook her head. Bane wouldn't let them.

"Circumstances demand it," Rimoth said.

"This is different!" Daydon spat phlegm onto the ground. "She wasn't called into the forest. She went on her own."

"She's not your daughter, Daydon. I know your son—"

"I said no."

Rimoth stepped closer. "And what will you do when we awake one morning and an entire generation of girls is gone? The townspeople will be screaming for your blood!"

Nesha pulled Larkin back. "You need to get out of here," she said under her breath. "Hide by the river. I'll come for you if it's safe."

Larkin shook her head. If she was going to be trussed up like a sack of meat and thrown to the beast, she wanted to hear it from Daydon's lips. But the lord shook his head.

"There will be no crucible." He grabbed the back of Rimoth's robes and hauled him toward the fire. "You will make the sacrifice, and we will be done with this!"

Daydon released him as they approached the fire, and Rimoth straightened his robes indignantly. The druid strode toward the bleating goat, a gleaming knife in his hands. The drums and murmurs of the crowd stilled as Rimoth straddled the animal, wrenched its head back, and slashed the knife across its throat. Blood sprayed into the fire as the animal kicked and thrashed. Larkin's hand went to her own throat, and she swallowed hard. Nesha buried her forehead between Larkin's shoulder blades.

"We offer sacrifice!" Rimoth's eyes had taken on a maniacal gleam. "Blood that the beast might drink, meat that the beast might eat and be satiated. That he not hunger for the bones of our daughters. We honor the forest, knowing our own worthlessness, our own impotence, before its mighty vastness."

He looped a cord around the goat's still twitching leg, took a dozen steps to the forest, and tied the goat by a hoof from a low branch of a massive tree, where it swung in ever-shrinking arcs. He returned to the fire and washed the blood from his hands in a basin of water held by Maisy, who stared unflinchingly at Daydon.

When Rimoth was done, he flicked his hands toward the approaching lord. "My part is done. Whatever happens next be on your head, Daydon."

Rimoth stormed past the lord toward the tree Larkin hid behind. She wanted to run, but there was nowhere to go. She kept her head down, hoping he wouldn't see her face. But his steps slowed, and he came to a stop beside her. "The forest gets what the forest wants, little girl. Your resistance will bring a curse on the entire town."

Larkin glared up at him, but he was already leering at Nesha, who was by far the most beautiful girl in the town—probably in the entire United Cities of Idelmarch. If not for her clubfoot, she would have been the most sought-after girl in the town. But cripples were not allowed to marry, lest their deformity contaminate their children.

Larkin stepped in front of her sister to block Rimoth's view. Rimoth gave her a slimy smile and slithered through the crowd. Larkin turned back to the fire to find Crazy Maisy standing at the crowd's edge, staring at her.

"Larkin is lost to you." Maisy's voice carried across the field. She tossed a green pine bough into the fire behind her; sparks outlined her silhouette. As usual, she was filthy, twigs and leaves in her matted hair, her dress torn and ratty. The crowd fell silent and stepped back from her. "She will betray you all in the end."

All at once, Larkin went from terrified to furious. "The forest take you. I'm the same girl from two days ago!"

"Rimoth!" Daydon called. "Come fetch your mad daughter!"

Ignoring the lord, Maisy shambled toward Larkin. People fell over themselves to get out of her way. "Except for the magic that now runs in your veins."

How could Maisy know?

"I saw you last night." Maisy came closer. "Saw you at the woods. Saw you fend off that man with nothing more than a bit of air."

The crowd grumbled uneasily. A child started wailing. His mother gathered her brood and ushered them away, more mothers with little ones hurrying to follow.

Larkin knew better than to take her eyes from Crazy Maisy, who was likely to start throwing mud or rocks. Over the last year, Larkin had borne the marks to prove it. "You're a liar."

"Larkin's soul has been taken by the forest. The changes have already begun. Soon enough, she'll betray you all. It will be the end of us—the end of everything."

A few people made signs to ward off the beast. Lord Daydon shouted for someone to take Maisy away and then fell into a fit of coughing, but no one dared interfere when Crazy Maisy was making her predictions—predictions that had a tendency of coming true.

Was Maisy right? Denan had called Larkin out of her bed the night before. She'd been powerless to resist the siren song. Her chest heaved hard for breath that wouldn't come. Was her soul really gone? Was the piper twisting it even now?

Maisy snatched Larkin's hand, her fingertips grazing the swollen knot where the sliver was still lodged deep inside. "You know it's true, don't you, Larkin?"

Larkin jerked back, feeling the eyes of the crowd on her.

"No." Larkin's voice shook, betraying her. "It's a lie."

"There's a sure way to know," came an old man's voice. "The crucible."

Larkin reached out to the tree to steady herself. "No."

The crowd murmured in agreement. A few men started toward her.

"Larkin isn't going to betray anybody," Bane called from behind her. He leaped over the rock fence and came to stand beside her. He panted for breath, and his brow shone with sweat. Where had he been?

"You all know Larkin," he said. "She's one of us."

"And we've all seen how often you fawn after Harben's daughters," Maisy said suggestively.

"Th-that's—" Bane stuttered. Larkin had never heard Bane tongue-tied before.

Crazy Maisy laughed again—a beautiful sound, even if it was tinged with madness.

"Stop trying to cause problems, girl." Daydon reached the front of the crowd. "Or I'll send you to the druids in Cordova."

Maisy picked up a generous hunk of mud and crept closer to Larkin, who glared at her, daring her to throw it. Instead, Crazy Maisy smeared it across her own face until only her bright blue eyes stood out against the brown.

"Maisy! That is enough." The lord motioned to Bane, who stepped forward and gripped Maisy's shoulders. Twisting out of his grasp, she snapped at his hands, her teeth flashing white. With a yelp, he jumped back.

Maisy whirled to Larkin, her eyes bright with madness. "She's been touched by the forest. She'll betray you."

"Don't listen to her," Bane said.

"She's touched in the head," Nesha added, voice shaking. "You all know it."

"And what would a cripple know about it?" Maisy snarled, genuine hurt filling her eyes. "There are two kinds of women safe from the forest: married women and cripples." She laughed at her own joke.

Nesha flinched. The crowd burst into conversation, people arguing both sides.

Instinctively, Larkin stepped between her sister and Maisy. "You forgot to mention crazies."

Maisy clenched her fists, mud oozing between her fingers. "They've touched you. You'll betray—"

"If the forest's touch turns a girl into a traitor," Larkin shouted to be heard, "what about all the other Taken? Were they traitors too?" She knew she'd touched a sensitive spot with that one. Everyone loved someone who had been Taken. Larkin glanced around the crowd. Had she managed to sway any of them?

A few still argued to throw her in the crucible just to be safe.

She had to discredit Maisy before she took Larkin's whole family down. The fastest way to do that was to bring out her wild side.

"Crazy Maisy's mud and mites," Larkin said in a mocking tone, the way children sang at Maisy under their breaths. "Ran from the forest in the daylight. While the other girls were stolen away, Crazy Maisy rolled in the hay." It was a cruel song—the end referencing the way some girls slept with men in hopes the forest would spare them. As the town midwife, Mama told Larkin such things didn't work, and if she were caught, her reputation would be ruined.

Maisy shuddered, her countenance changing.

Larkin felt a twinge of guilt, which she quickly shoved down.

With a screech, Maisy lifted her fist and ran at Larkin, who took a startled step back and bumped into Nesha. Bane stepped between them, but before he could intercept Maisy, her face went slack. She dropped bonelessly into the mud.

Sling in hand, a man rode from the shadows on an enormous horse—an ax, shield, and crossbow strapped to his saddle. His hair was wild and dark beneath his felt hat, his whiskers long and unkempt. He wore the black robe, open to the front, and tooled belt of a druid. His eyes were the pale blue of ice, his gaze even colder as it landed on Larkin.

"Maisy!" a voice screamed from the crowd. Rimoth pushed his way forward and collapsed dramatically beside his daughter. He turned wild eyes toward the newcomer. "You will pay dearly for that."

The man kicked his horse closer, looking down at them from above. "It was only a knot of wood. She should live— might have a headache, though." He contemplated Larkin. "You are the witness?"

Larkin's mouth was too dry to answer.

Bane stepped in front of her. "And who are you?"

The man reached into a pouch at his waist and took a fingerful of snuff, stuffing it into his bottom lip. "My name is Garrot of the Black Druids."

CHAPTER 5

BLACK DRUIDS

L arkin was trapped in Garrot's dark gaze—the gaze of a Black Druid. Finally, Garrot released her, and she sagged, all the breath whooshing out of her. She and Nesha shared a loaded glance.

The crowd had gone utterly silent. Rimoth clambered to his feet, bowing to the Black Druids with his arms outspread. "Deepest apologies, brethren. Had I known who you were, I never would have spoken so egregiously."

"Aren't you the one who called us?" Garrot asked.

"Yes, but …" Rimoth hadn't expected them to come. To cover his embarrassment, the slimy druid bowed again, deeper this time. "I did not expect you so soon."

Ignoring the man, Garrot twisted in his saddle. The leather creaked as he studied the manor house on its hill. With his attention off them, some in the crowd edged toward town. He turned back to Daydon, and they froze again. "My fellow druid, Hunter, and I would sup with you, Lord. It has been a long journey."

Larkin noticed the man behind Garrot. With charcoal skin and broader features, Hunter was similarly equipped with ax, bow, and shield.

Garrot surveyed Rimoth and then leaned over to spit into the mud. "Bring the girl," he said without looking back. He kicked his horse to jump the fence, leaving deep gouges in the earth. "And this crowd will disperse!" he shouted over his shoulder.

He didn't need to say it. Everyone scrambled toward their homes. Daydon immediately hurried after him.

Rimoth's maid, Gilla, lifted Maisy's matted head out of the mud, her fingers coming away brown and red. "I'll need someone to carry her to the rectory," the young woman said.

"After you've seen to her, clean out the guest rooms," Rimoth said, rubbing his hands together in excitement.

"It will take hours—"

"Then hire more girls!" Rimoth spat. "There's a famine going on—someone will want the work. I want the rectory gleaming by the time I return."

Head down, Gilla nodded.

Rimoth motioned to Horace and Horgen, pointing at Maisy. "Carry her home. And be quick about it!" Frowning, they reached for Maisy's wrists and ankles.

Bane leaned into Horgen and said under his breath, "Best stay until you know she isn't going to go rabid on anyone else."

The men bore her down the hill, Gilla trailing after them.

Eyes gleaming with cruel excitement, Rimoth reached for Larkin. Bane pushed him back. "You will keep your distance, Druid."

"Garrot told me to bring her—"

"I'll bring myself," Larkin said. If she could hide somewhere they'd never find her, she'd gladly take it. Such a place did not exist.

Larkin's skin itched with Rimoth's stare. Nesha took a step

closer, which caught Rimoth's eye. "You can go home to your mama."

"I'm staying with Larkin," Nesha said.

Rimoth smiled, revealing a rotten mouth. "The Black Druids have come. They will force your tiny minds to show me the honor I deserve."

Taking each sister by the elbow, Bane pushed past Rimoth. "I don't fear your Black Druids."

"You should." Rimoth followed, so close Larkin could feel his breath on the back of her neck. "They are an army unto themselves, trained in the arts of torture and war."

Larkin picked up her pace, retracing her steps from earlier. She leaned closer to Nesha and said, "Where's Mama?"

Nesha looked out over the river. "I don't see any light from the house. Maybe she went to the tavern to find Papa."

Larkin leaned into Bane on the other side of her. "Where were you?" she asked, low enough only he could hear.

"Papa put me on watch," Bane said. "I came when I heard Maisy call your name. When did you wake up?"

"An hour ago."

Bane reached out, his hand briefly squeezing hers. "Are you all right?"

A thrill leaped through Larkin at the contact. "Mostly just sore. I have so much to tell you."

Bane glanced back at Rimoth. "Later. I need to hurry back to the house and help Venna prepare for company." Venna was his family's maid. "You'll be all right?"

"Nesha and I can handle Rimoth."

He took off at a jog. Shoulders hunched against the rain, Larkin and Nesha skirted the town and turned up the hill toward the manor, firelight glinting off the windows that watched her like hollow eyes. To the right of the farthest window stood the stocks, the town beggar currently locked in by wrist and neck, his clothes sticking to his drenched body.

Pulling his reins slowly through his hands, Garrot stood beside his horse and watched her climb the hill. She stiffened under his scrutiny. Just up the hill ahead of her, the lord called for two boys to care for the men's horses. With wide eyes and eager hands, the boys led the horses behind the manor to the barn.

Larkin hesitated to climb the steps, wondering if she could still run. Nesha breathed hard from exertion, her face tight with pain.

"Are you sure you want to come with me?" Larkin asked.

"You wouldn't leave me." It was true.

"It will be all right," Larkin said. The words gave her the strength to face the house. With her sister beside her, she entered the manor and took a single step into the large dining room.

Inside, Bane waited for them beside the long table set before a fire. Venna spent hours every day polishing the wood until it shone. Garrot threw his sopping hat onto its gleaming surface, dragged a chair over to the glowing embers, and tossed in a few precious logs. Hunter shut the door behind Larkin and Nesha, causing them both to jump, then sat beside the other druid, tugged off his muddy boots, and held his wrinkled feet toward the embers. Rimoth stood like a dark shadow beside the hearth.

Venna came in from the kitchen. Larkin had spent enough time at Bane's house to know Venna fairly well. She was around Larkin's age, a quiet girl who made the softest bread Larkin had ever tasted. She had cool-brown skin and tightly curled hair, her body soft and feminine.

She didn't hide the worry in her expression. "What's going on?" she whispered.

Larkin could only shake her head.

Garrot waved in Venna's general direction. "Woman, some hot spiced mead would be certain to restore our constitutions."

Glaring at their muddy boots, Venna pushed through the door back into the kitchen.

Daydon collapsed in a chair beside Garrot and tugged a

blanket around his shoulders. He sneezed three times and then groaned. "Bane, get me a bucket of hot water for my feet."

Bane worked his jaw, clearly unhappy at leaving them but unable to deny his shivering father. He nodded and slipped into the kitchen.

"Are you sick, man?" Garrot asked.

"Half the town is. It will pass." Daydon sniffed noisily. "Where have you come from?"

"Landra, originally. We were in Hothsfelt when the druid house received your pigeon." Hothsfelt was even smaller than Hamel, about a day's ride north.

"And why have you come?" Daydon asked.

"We heard a girl escaped the forest." Garrot's gaze swept over the rest of them, catching on Nesha. With her dark auburn hair, glowing skin, and luminous violet eyes, she was easy to look at. "No point in lingering by the doorway." Garrot's voice was rough. "Come in by the fire."

Larkin cut a sympathetic glance at her sister. Nesha hated this moment—when men's admiration slipped to pity and disgust. Nothing else for it. Larkin stepped forward, Nesha limping a step behind.

Garrot's head came up with something like surprise, and his eyes slid to her deformed foot. "What's your name, girl?"

Larkin stepped up to the table to block his view of Nesha, taking hold of the back of a chair to steady herself. "I'm Larkin. Your witness."

Garrot studied Larkin, with her frizzy red hair, layers of freckles, and plain brown eyes. "You went into the forest?"

His words sharpened the longing inside her. She couldn't help but glance in the direction of the trees, though there was only darkness visible through the wavering glass. Her wet clothes leached the warmth from her body, and she shivered.

"Rimoth," Garrot ordered. "Take her cloak and hang it by the fire."

Rimoth stiffened, clearly affronted to be asked to perform such a menial task, and took a grudging step toward her. Normally, Larkin would have been thrilled at anyone putting Rimoth in his place, but not when it brought him closer to her. Making a mental note to wash her cloak tomorrow, she shucked it off and held it over the table.

Rimoth shook out her tattered cloak and settled it on a peg by the fire, where it dripped onto the wood floor, mixing with muck from the men's boots into muddy puddles. Venna would be furious, though she'd never say a word.

"Larkin, is it?" Garrot had ducked down to catch her gaze. She nodded. He leaned forward, his wide belt squeaking. "Why did you go into the forest?"

"For my baby sister."

His brow furrowed in confusion.

"She got away from me, you see."

Nesha shifted her weight nervously. Garrot's attention strayed to her again. Larkin angled herself between them.

"And your little sister came out too?" he asked.

She nodded again.

He turned toward Hunter. "That's two of them."

The other man studied her, his brows drawn. Garrot got up and turned another chair toward the fire, gesturing for Larkin to join them. Not wanting to leave the comfort of Nesha's closeness, Larkin hesitated before moving around the table to sit, her shoulders hunched.

Bane returned. "Water's heating." He came to stand behind Larkin, arms crossed over his chest, expression sullen.

Venna came in with mugs of steaming mead and passed them out.

Garrot accepted his, breathing in the steam and making a sound of approval. "I've heard of your cooking all the way in Cordova, Venna. My companion and I have been riding since early this morning. We're looking forward to it."

Venna bowed and disappeared back in the kitchen without a word.

"Would you help her in the kitchen?" Garrot directed the question at Nesha.

Nesha blushed beautifully. Larkin knew her sister well enough to know she was humiliated at having the men see her limp. Still, she squared her shoulders and followed Venna into the kitchen. Garrot's eyes trailed after her, his expression considering. Without looking, he handed Larkin a cup. She took it, the warmth bleeding into her chilled fingers. Her cloak steamed on its peg.

"Tell us everything," Garrot said.

Larkin wished Bane wasn't present to hear all of this. She tipped the cup to her lips. Her stomach curdled at the smell—the same smell her father often reeked of when he came home late at night. She forced herself to take a swallow. The spiced honey mead was rich, sweet, and heady at once. She cradled the cup in her lap, staring into the dark gold liquid inside. She considered lying—it would go down easier than the truth—but they needed to know. Everyone needed to know.

She took a deep breath and let it out. "There was a beast—like a giant lizard. It attacked my sister and me, but a man saved us. After, he played a tune on his pipes and … The music did something to me, made me willing to follow him anywhere. It's magic, I think." Larkin had felt like her tether had been cut, and she was floating, helpless to the wind.

Garrot sat back, his expression revealing nothing. "Perhaps you should start from the beginning."

In a low voice, she told the men what had happened straight through. She even told them about last night—about sleepwalking to the forest and waking before it was too late.

Garrot turned to Lord Daydon. "You didn't set up a watch the night she came back?"

"Of course we did," Daydon blustered.

"I slept outside her door," Bane admitted tonelessly.

Larkin tried to soothe him with a look. "Everyone was asleep. It was part of the spell the piper wove."

"And how did you escape his thrall?"

She opened her mouth to tell them, but they all looked at her as if she were as crazy as Maisy. "I hit him." With magic. "And managed to run away."

The Black Druids exchanged a loaded glance. It was clear none of them—not even Bane, believed her. Larkin's cheeks heated. "I'm not making it up." Leaving things out, yes, but not making it up.

"I'm not saying you are," Garrot said. "But you *are* a woman." And a woman's word didn't carry much weight, never had. Her hands tightened into fists, knuckles turning white. "Perhaps you were simply dreaming."

"I can vouch for her," Bane said.

Bane shouldn't need to vouch for me! I know what I saw— as much as any man.

"You weren't there," Garrot said to Bane. "Women are weaker, more susceptible to the forest's magic. You don't know how the forest has meddled with her mind."

Larkin imagined all the ways she could hurt Garrot without getting caught. "I can prove it." Garrot finally deigned to look at her. "He tried to give me an amulet, asked me to wear it. He said it would protect me."

Hunter rose to his feet. "Where is this amulet?"

"At the forest's edge, where the river goes in." She closed her eyes, trying to remember, but her memories were fuzzy, dreamlike. "I think I could find it again."

Garrot handed over her steaming cloak. "Lead the way."

CHAPTER

AMULET

arkin stood before the forest, mesmerized by the way the torches threw shadows across the rustling trees. This close, the melodious undercurrent hummed beneath her skin. She'd sensed it ever since she left the forest—an awareness that grew stronger the closer she came to the forest until it demanded her full attention.

"Well?" Rimoth asked from behind her.

She started, whirling back to the four men behind her—Bane, Rimoth, Hunter, and Garrot in their fine leather cloaks. She'd forgotten they were there, forgotten everything except the forest, her gaze lost in the swirling motions.

"I—" She remembered the sound of her bare feet on the bridge, the feel of the damp grass on her legs, the songs of the frogs that had gone silent as she'd passed, and the Curse Tree, one of the branches broken.

"It's here somewhere." Bending down, she pushed through the dead grass, shot through with gray rot.

"Spread out to look," Garrot said, holding the torch over the grass she was searching. She could feel his attention trained on her as last year's rotting dead grass clung to her hands.

"There's something you aren't telling us," he said softly.

She winced. "I told you everything."

Garrot slowly shook his head. "No, you didn't. You know how I can tell?" Without waiting for her to answer, he leaned forward. "You're not nearly as afraid as you should be."

How could she explain that, in the stillness, she could sense the forest's melody and a longing flashed through her like flames through dry tinder? "There's nothing," she said a little too breathlessly.

"See here," Bane said sharply from behind Garrot. "Just because she's not a sniveling mess doesn't mean she's lying."

"We'll see." Garrot pivoted and cut away swaths of grass with his wicked-looking ax. Larkin sniffed and wiped away the drops of water that had leaked though her tattered wool hood, seeped through her hair, and dripped down the sides of her face. She kept glancing toward the forest, swearing she could feel the trees watching her.

She didn't find anything. None of them did.

"Just a hallucination brought on by the forest." Rimoth kicked the grass. "I told you women are unreliable witnesses."

Garrot rolled his neck as if he had a crick. "All right. Let's get back to the manor."

"Wait." Hunter pushed aside a clump of grass and lifted his hand, revealing a simple cord. From it dangled an amulet in the likeness of a bare-branched tree with interlocking roots. It spun lazily, a shimmer of color sparking across its surface like frost in the morning light.

Larkin's traitorous hands ached with the need to hold it. It reeled her in like a fish on a line. She stood before it, clenching her hands at her side to keep them still.

Garrot took the amulet, turning it this way and that. "This

was not made by any tradesman I have ever seen."

"Is it wood or stone?" Rimoth asked as he reached out to take the amulet.

Garrot jerked it out of his reach. "It's a piece of opal." He stretched the amulet toward her. "Larkin?"

She stared openmouthed as the amulet swayed hypnotically, the water dripping from the branching roots. Shaking with fear and maybe a little eagerness, she stretched out her uninjured hand. Garrot dropped it into her cupped palm. Her thumb ran along the surface—smooth like wood but far heavier. Her hand closed around it, and a branch on the amulet pricked her. Heat and light blasted against her, tearing a gasp from her throat, and a vision sucked her in.

She walked on a white bridge that stretched out before her, turquoise water below. As she walked, she shed her clothing, letting the pieces drop one by one. Then she pointed her hands above her head and dove. Falling. Falling. Falling.

She woke with a start, her cheek stinging. Someone was calling her name. Larkin lifted her heavy head to find Nesha grasping her head in her hands, her expression worried. Larkin was back inside the manor, slouched in a chair. At the sound of shouting and a struggle, she turned her head to find Hunter and Rimoth holding back a red-faced Bane, who lobbed threats and insults at Garrot. Standing in a bucket of steaming water, Lord Daydon shouted at everyone indiscriminately.

Larkin shook her head and rubbed her sore cheek. "What …"

"You went blank," Garrot said evenly. "Like you weren't there anymore." He pried at her hand before giving a frustrated growl. "Give me the amulet, Larkin."

Bane struggled to break free. "Get away from her!"

Brow furrowed, Larkin glanced at her fingers clenched around the amulet. She didn't want to let go. Power coursed up and down her arm—power rooted deep inside her breast. She was breathing hard, and she was afraid and euphoric and angry.

Nesha pushed him aside, her violet eyes piercing. "Larkin, you have to let go. It will be all right, I promise. Trust me, Larkin." Her hands gently embraced Larkin's, tugging at her smallest finger. Larkin released her stranglehold one finger at a time. Nesha snatched the amulet as if it would burn her and shoved it into Garrot's hand.

Again, Garrot's eyes were pinned on Nesha as he wrapped the amulet in a bit of leather before tucking it in his cloak pocket. Larkin stared at the pocket, angry he'd taken something that belonged to her. Because it did belong to her—of that much she was certain.

Bane muttered something insulting to Garrot.

"Calm down, son," Lord Daydon snapped. "He was trying to help her."

"I woke her up, didn't I?" Garrot responded.

"You still shouldn't have done it," Hunter said under his breath. "We got into this to protect women, not abuse them."

The display of sympathy from Hunter shocked Larkin, though she still wasn't sure what the sympathy was for.

Garrot sighed and clapped the other man's shoulder. "All right, my friend. No harm done. Larkin, I'm sorry I slapped you."

So that's why her cheek hurt. "It's all right, Bane," she soothed. She'd been hit plenty of times.

"I want Bane and the other two women out," Garrot said.

Bane tried, and failed, to wrench free. "I'm not going anywhere!"

"Upstairs," Daydon said. "Now!"

Bane grudgingly relaxed, and the men released him. "Let's get you back home, Larkin. You need to rest."

"She stays." Garrot took a deep pull from his mug of mead. "Until I say she can go."

Bane's fists tightened. Nesha raised a brow in question.

Larkin nodded for her to go. Casting one more look around the room, Nesha headed for the door, Venna a step behind.

Everyone held their breath as Bane stepped nose to nose with Garrot. "Don't you ever touch her again." Throwing one last glance at Larkin, Bane reluctantly went up the stairs.

As soon as Bane's door shut, Garrot and Hunter sat before plates of food that had been set out at some point—mashed turnips, a chunk of rare meat, bread, and cheese.

"What did this man look like?" Garrot asked. His tone had changed. He believed her. Judging by the way the others watched her, they all did.

"He was not from the United Cities of the Idelmarch." Memories overwhelmed Larkin. She stared into the fire as she described Denan's fine but worn clothing, the mottled pattern. "He played a flute and a panpipe—such beautiful music—music that sings to your soul of warmth and safety and comfort." Her words lay unspooled, her tears blurring the licking flames.

"Or perhaps the forest's curse is taking effect, as my daughter said it would," Rimoth said—no matter he hadn't inquired after her even once.

Larkin blinked hard, twin tears plunging down her cheeks. She reeled herself in, back from whatever had entranced her. She took a deep breath and blew it out. She had already revealed too much, had let these strange, powerful men see how affected she was.

Hunter set her now-cold drink in front of her. "Drink it. You'll feel better."

She took it, surprised again by Hunter's behavior, and drank.

"This beast—what did it look like?" Garrot asked.

Larkin described it as best she could. Garrot stabbed his knife into the lord's fine table and nodded to Hunter, who took his cloak and headed back outside. Garrot leaned back in his chair, his expression distant, haunted. "When I was sixteen years old, a group of us went into the forest. The beast found us. I saw grown men shredded, limbs ripped off. Their venom paralyzes you—much as you were paralyzed. Only a handful of us got away." He took a deep drink from his mug. "But that night, something else came. I never saw it; I only heard the screams. But the next morning, I found a man who'd been attacked. Through his ravings, we made out his description of the beast before we had to kill him."

"Kill him?" Larkin gasped.

"He turned on us," Garrot said, his voice dead.

She gulped the dregs of her too-sweet mead, wiping her mouth with the back of her hand.

The door pushed open. Dripping, Hunter came inside and tossed a large bag on the table. He untied the drawstrings and reached inside. He turned to her, a grinning skull in the palm of his hand. Larkin jumped to her feet and stumbled away from the gleaming, polished bone of a giant lizard.

"The beast." Staggering forward, Rimoth rested trembling hands on the skull and stroked its brow like a lover. "Guardian of the Forbidden Forest, taker of the sacrifice."

Hunter jerked it back. "They are the guardians of nothing!"

Larkin couldn't look away from the barbed teeth. How many of her friends had those teeth ripped apart?

"How many of these bones have you found?" Rimoth asked, eyeing it lovingly.

"Enough to know there are more," Hunter replied.

"Get that out of my house," Daydon said, voice quavering. His daughter had been taken six years ago this spring. She'd had pale blue eyes from her mother and raven hair from her father. A stubborn, wild girl who loved dancing and boys. Larkin wondered if her bones lay somewhere in the forest, bleached by sun and scored by teeth.

Garrot nodded to Hunter, who shoved the skull into the bag and tightened the drawstrings. He hauled it over his shoulder and took it outside. Garrot pulled his chair over so he was across the fire from Larkin. "I only show this so you know the truth: there is indeed a beast. You will say nothing more of the man you think you saw in the forest—or any of the rest of it, for that matter."

Her jaw hardened. They both knew Denan was real. "Why?"

"Because a Black Druid tells you to."

Larkin folded her arms. She'd never been very good at doing what she was told.

Garrot stared into the fire, pulled something from inside his tunic, and caressed it. At first, Larkin didn't understand what she was looking at. Some kind of ivory.

It was a tooth—a human tooth. She recoiled.

"We men will speak alone," Garrot said.

Because men have handled the forest so well in the past? Knowing better than to say it, she retrieved her steaming cloak, threw it about her shoulders, and reached the door in a dozen steps. As her hand tightened on the latch, Garrot said, "Stay away from the Forbidden Forest, Larkin."

She froze. Not because of his words so much as the desire that leaped into her heart. She wanted to go back, wanted it desperately. But how could she want something so wicked? Going back to the forest meant death or capture—she wasn't sure which was worse. Either way, Denan would be waiting for her. She yanked open the door and stomped outside, into the pounding rain and gusting wind that stripped the little warmth she'd soaked in from the hearth fire.

She wasn't surprised to find the way deserted—it had to have been after midnight. Holding her cloak tight against the steady patter of rain, Larkin ducked her head into the wind and headed down the hill toward the bridge.

She was nearly there when she caught sight of a couple within the willow's shadows. They were so wrapped up in each other's embrace she wasn't sure where one began and the other ended. Blushing, she halted, embarrassed to interrupt, but the bridge was the only way across. She cleared her throat noisily, and the couple broke apart. Her sister looked back at her with a caught expression.

"Nesha?" Larkin gasped. The man pulled down his cowl, hiding his features as he pushed past her. She watched his retreating back, her mouth agape. Everything she thought she knew about her sister flitted away. "Who was that?"

Nesha gripped Larkin's arm, her fingernails digging in. "You can't tell anyone."

"Who was that?" Larkin demanded again.

"We want to marry, Larkin. If he can convince his father."

A wave of pity swamped Larkin, extinguishing her anger. "Nesha," she began gently. "The druids won't allow it."

"The druids can't control everything! If we have to, we'll move in together!"

Rain pelted Larkin's shoulders through her cloak. She shivered. "You would be branded a loose woman." Twenty years ago, the druids would have staked her in the forest to face the crucible. Now, the couple and any children would be shunned, taunted, hated.

Nesha's shoulders shook with sobs. "Why should I have to spend the rest of my life alone because of a twisted foot? I love him, Larkin. More than I've ever loved anything." Larkin gathered her sister in her arms. It wasn't fair, this stupid law. "He's going to talk to his father tonight. Things aren't like they were. Others with ... defects have been allowed to marry."

Yes, daughters of wealthy, powerful men who could throw around their influence. "Mama has been training you to be a midwife. You won't need a husband to provide for you."

"I hate midwifery," Nesha said.

Larkin stiffened, surprised by the bitterness in her sister's voice. "I didn't know."

"I want to be a mother and wife—his wife."

Larkin rubbed her sister's soggy back. "Let's go home. Mama will be worried."

"You won't tell her?"

Larkin tugged her toward the bridge. "I'll keep your secret as long as I can."

"What did the druids say?"

"They told me to keep away from the forest."

Nesha chuckled. "That won't be hard."

Larkin forced herself to laugh along with her sister. They stepped over the bridge, the river roaring beneath their feet. Larkin stared toward the forest, glad for the rain and distance to drown out its song, but she could still hear it, still crave it.

"Larkin." Nesha hesitated. "I've seen the way you watch the trees."

Larkin dropped her guilty eyes. "What do you mean?"

"It's not fear in your gaze. It's longing. What if Maisy is right and he's stolen your soul?" He could convince you to betray us. Are you sure you can trust yourself against his magic?"

Larkin turned away. The truth was, she didn't know what Denan could do—or if she could resist it.

CHAPTER

FISHING

Larkin had barely crossed the bridge when she heard shouting so loud even the swollen river couldn't hide it. Larkin and Nesha shared a look of dread. Larkin took off at a run that staggered to a slog when she reached the muddy plowed field before the house. The mud sucked at her, clogs popping off, one and then the other. She left them where they lay.

"Where have I been?" Papa's words became clear. "Where were you all day? I'll tell you where. Taking supper with the lord. Probably tweaking his—"

"You shut your foul mouth," Mama shouted back.

The storm picked up, rain sheeting down, obscuring Larkin's view, but she saw enough. Mama wore her shift, and she was barefoot. Papa held her arm. He had dragged her out of the house into the field. Larkin didn't see Sela anywhere. She could only hope her sister was asleep.

Papa loomed over Mama, fist raised. "Tell me the truth."

A half dozen more steps and Larkin could get between

them—just a half dozen steps.

Mama lifted her face, defiant in the light from their single window. "I'll tell you where I went—soon as you tell me where *you* were. You weren't on guard duty."

Papa backhanded her. Mama staggered and nearly fell.

"Papa!" Larkin screamed, diving between them. "Leave her be!"

"Where?" Papa screamed at Mama, his breath reeking of alcohol.

Larkin shoved her father back. She had to make him angry with her instead. "You lazy lout! If you weren't at the tavern half the day, the fields would already be done!"

Larkin saw the punch coming. She didn't try to avoid it. She tensed as his fist connected with her stomach, doubling over as all the air rushed from her lungs. Her legs lost their strength, and she dropped to her knees. She gripped her middle, one hand braced against the mud oozing between her fingers. The pain hit her—a sharp curving blade that dug from her navel upward.

She tried to breathe, but her lungs had seized. A wave of nausea swamped her, and it was all she could to do ride it out. Finally, she choked down half a breath. She subtly shifted her head to look behind them, grateful to see Nesha slipping inside the hut to check on Sela.

"Worthless ingrates, the lot of you." Her father kicked mud into Larkin's face. She blinked away grit, her vision blurred and her eyes scratched. Her father stomped off, as he always did after he hit one of them. He'd spend the next few days drowning himself in beer or ale.

Mama knelt before Larkin and wiped the mud from her face. "Oh, Larkin, this is not the life I want for you. For any of us."

Larkin pushed herself upright, the ache sharpening so she doubled over again. "Are you all right?"

Mama nodded.

"And the baby?"

"We're fine." Her mother sat back and stared after her retreating husband, but her expression wasn't angry or hurt or lost. She looked resigned.

"You weren't there when I woke up." Larkin tried to stymie the hurt.

Her mother looked toward Hamel. "I went to try to save you."

Moving carefully, Larkin shifted to sit on her haunches and winced as pain flared in her middle again. "Save me?"

Mama finally met her gaze. "From the forest and the crucible."

"You convinced Lord Daydon to sacrifice the goat?"

"And to help me find you a husband."

Larkin glanced toward the darkness that had swallowed up her father, twisting fear rising inside her. "Mama, I can't."

Mama leaned forward and rested her calloused palm against Larkin's cheek. "You don't have to have my marriage. I will find you a good husband."

Larkin looked into the depths of her mother's soft brown eyes—she may have gotten her father's copper hair, but her eyes were all her mother's. "All I've ever wanted was to be free."

"None of us are ever free, Larkin, but we can choose the chains that bind us."

Larkin's protest died before reaching her lips. Freedom was an illusion of the naive. Larkin was many things, but not that. "Who would even have me after what Maisy has been saying?"

Mama looked away. "If everything works out, we'll know in the morning."

"Who is he?"

Mama's expression clouded. "If he doesn't work out, I'll find someone else."

The forest, the beast, Denan, the druids, and now marriage. Larkin let out a shaky breath to keep in the tears she refused to shed. "Mama, I'm scared."

"Fear is the lot of women." Her mother pushed to her feet. "Can you stand?"

Exhausted and chilled to the bone, Larkin let Mama help her up. She hunched over, one arm wrapped protectively over her stomach, as the two of them made their way slowly toward the house, fetching her clogs along the way.

Mama huffed. "There will be no more plowing until the rain lets up—the seeds will rot in the ground. Tomorrow, we'll gather greens and catch some fish for supper."

Larkin sagged in relief. She didn't think she could stand another day hacking at the mud. "Father found all our money?" They'd buried it in the orchard this time.

"He always does."

Before Larkin went into the house, she glanced toward the manor house. The candle in Bane's window was lit. He would meet her in their usual place at first light.

Before dawn the next morning, Larkin slipped outside, thankful for the clear sky. She slipped across the bridge. The swollen river licked at the boards beneath her feet. Farther to the west, the embankment had been built up. Alorica's father, Kenjin, had the money to pay for the extra labor. Larkin hurried east, skirting the clearing where the women did their washing and past the thick willows that lined the river.

Directly across from Bane's manor, Larkin parted the willows, her feet sliding between tightly woven branches as she made her way inside. She stopped twice, once to untangle her hair and once more for her skirt, which tore, blast it all.

Finally, the willows thinned, and she came out on the other side. Here, the swollen river split into a stream that cut around a little island filled with more willows. It was secluded, blocked from all sides by the tangle of branches. Only Bane could see it, and then only because of his two-story house built on a hill. It was their special spot—the place where Bane had spent her twelfth summer teaching her to swim.

He hadn't arrived yet, so Larkin knelt on the rocky bank, which was much higher than usual, and scooped cold water to scrub her cheeks. She checked the sliver in her palm. It was swollen and red—infected. Before, she'd felt a power pulse from it, but now there was only throbbing pain. Perhaps this sliver was the reason she could hear the forest's music—perhaps having a piece of the forest inside her tied her to the trees.

Using the opposite thumbnail, she pushed at the sliver's base and slid it toward the entry. The pain sharpened until the sliver shot out of her in a burst of pus and fluids. Relieved and oddly satisfied, Larkin washed the wound in the river, the cold alleviating the throbbing heat.

As it soaked, she stilled and listened for the forest's song. Music and longing whispered for her to visit the forest. It was supposed to go away after the sliver was gone. Angry, she wrapped the wound to keep it clean.

The sun peeked over the horizon, lighting the trace of smoky clouds on fire. Larkin hung her cloak on a branch, pulled the back of her skirt up between her legs, and tucked it into her belt. Naked up to her knees, she stepped in the shallows. Bending over, she let her hands trail in the water. By the time her feet started to cramp from the cold, the first slick scaled fish nibbled her fingers.

Quick as a sinking stone, she scooped it up and threw it on the bank, where it writhed, its firm lips gasping for water. Her family would have fresh meat for the first time in days. Bending back down, she waited again.

By the time one fish had grown to a small pile, Larkin's legs were bright red and numb to her thighs. She staggered out of the water, surprised to find Bane watching her from the willows.

His gaze traveled from the top of her head to her bare legs, lingering on her curves.

She sucked in a breath. Bane had never looked at her like that, and she had most definitely never noticed the way his fine shirt hung from the muscles of his chest or the way his lips pursed in thought.

"Did you hear anything after I left?" she asked breathlessly.

His expression closed off. "No, but I think they believed you—about the man you saw in the forest."

Self-conscious, she collapsed on the huge slab of rock that dipped into the river. Hunched over, she rubbed the feeling back into her feet. "Only because I had proof."

Bane squatted beside her and held out his cupped hands. "Guess." When they were younger, he was always playing a game where he made her guess what he was holding.

"Please let it be something to eat."

He opened his hands to reveal one of Venna's soft rolls lathered with butter and jam. An involuntary moan left Larkin's lips. "Tell me you brought more."

"We can stop by the house for some on our way back."

While Larkin savored every single bite, Bane rolled up his shirtsleeves and started gutting the fish—he knew how much she hated it.

He finished the last fish, chucked the guts into the river, and leaned forward to scour his hands with gravel. "The Black Druids are going to make a foray inside the forest."

Larkin washed the stickiness from her hands. "The druids are the ones always telling us to stay out of the forest."

He stripped a branch from the willow and strung the fish through it. "Rimoth nearly had an apoplectic fit, but Garrot and Hunter outrank him—by a lot."

Larkin glanced upriver. She couldn't see the forest, but in the morning stillness, she could feel it—a steady hum beneath her skin. "What does your father say?"

"Of course he's against it. You know what happened when he tried to go after Caelia, but ..." He trailed off.

"Well?"

Finished with the fish, he set them on the grassy bank and came back to sit beside her. "Larkin, I think the druids already knew there are men in the forest. I think they've known for a long time."

Her mouth came open. "What?"

"My father was so adamant they leave the forest alone that he threatened to force them from the town. Garrot waited until my father was done threatening before he said, 'What if we can get your daughter back?'"

Larkin's eyes fluttered shut. Daydon would let the whole town burn for Caelia. Though Bane had only been thirteen when his sister was taken, he hated himself for not going after her. He turned overly bright eyes to her. "What if she's still alive, Lark? What if the man you saw took her like he tried to take you?"

Larkin opened her mouth, closed it again, then she quit trying to find the perfect words and instead laid her head on the point of his shoulder, like she used to when they were younger. They sat in silence for a long time—long enough that the sky completely cleared and warm sunshine brushed the right side of Larkin's face. It had been months since she'd truly felt warm, but Bane always made her feel safe.

"Larkin, there's something else." He rubbed the back of his neck. "Well, I—You see ..." Bane was rarely flustered, and never around her. "Do you have freckles everywhere?" he blurted.

She cocked her head. "What kind of question is that?"

He looked away. "I just ... I never thought about it before."

She wrinkled her nose. "Not everywhere."

His brow was drawn in thought.

"What?" she prodded.

He looked at her, really looked at her, as if seeing her for the first time. "Your hair changes color when the sunlight hits it—it gleams like burnished copper."

Her chest felt lighter. "I thought it was 'tabby-cat orange.'"

He tugged on a lock of her hair. "It's been years since I teased you about that." More like weeks.

She dared look into Bane's eyes—dark and full of depth. The forest take her, she wanted to look at him like this forever. "Circles within circles," she whispered.

His brow creased. "What?"

She reached out, smoothing his brow with her thumb, wishing she could rub away his sorrows and worries as easily. "Your eyes. Dark brown on the outside, yellow-brown on the inside."

He didn't look away. "You noticed?"

"Yes," she said breathily.

"How long have you noticed?"

"How long have you noticed my hair?"

Her breath caught as his hand slid across her cheek, his gaze trained on her lips. He was going to kiss her. The realization cut through her like lightning. Her heart beat faster. She'd been aching for this kiss for months. She leaned toward him, silently willing him not to look away, thrilled when he didn't. His lips pressed against hers, gently, and then he drew back.

She gave a low growl in frustration. All she got was a peck? She grabbed the front of his shirt, pulled his mouth down to hers, and kissed him with all the pent-up need she'd been storing for months. Still he held back. Her frustration rising, she deepened the kiss, and her tongue brushed against his. Her arms went around him, coaxing him closer. The heat and solidity of him made her head swim. He finally responded, pulling her onto his lap, his arms wrapping around her waist.

"Sela?" came a faint call from somewhere across the river —Mama's voice. Larkin gasped and pushed back, her lips swollen and her chin raw. Bane looked at her with surprise.

Again, her traitorous gaze slid toward the unseen forest. She pinched her eyes shut and tried to calm her breathing. She rolled off him and tugged on her clogs. "I need to get home."

Bane swallowed. "Larkin, that was …" She quirked an eye-brow in warning—if he started teasing her now, she'd throttle him. He cleared his throat. "That was pretty amazing for your first kiss."

She picked up the line of fish, taking care to whack him in the back of the head with a tail in a way she could claim was an accident, and headed out of the willows. "It wasn't my first." She'd had a lot of kisses—but none like that one.

Bane howled like she'd actually hurt him and hurried to catch up with her. "It was. I know pretty much everything about you." She threatened him with another fish. He held up his hands in mock surrender, but there was a darkness in his eyes. "Who? Does he have prettier eyes than me?"

She pivoted and walked away from him. "I'll never tell." She and Horgen had always met in secret—before he became an idiot. "And yes." But even blue-and-gold eyes weren't nearly as appealing when the owner of them told his friends she'd rolled around in the hay with him. She'd thought she loved Horgen once, but really, she just loved being touched in a way that didn't hurt. But she never slept with him. She'd attended enough births to know that was not something she wanted to deal with anytime soon.

"I'm scandalized!" Bane caught up to her and playfully poked her bruised stomach.

She gasped in pain, doubling over.

A myriad of emotions played across Bane's face—surprise, confusion, and finally, understanding. "He hit you." His jaw tightened, and he started past her. "I'll have him in the stocks."

No, Bane didn't know everything about her. He didn't know how often her father hit her or how often she went hungry be-cause he drank away every penny her mother earned or this overpowering, wicked longing she had for the forest.

Larkin caught up and snatched his hand. "The stocks only

makes it worse."

Bane spun to face her. "Worse? I thought it stopped years ago."

She folded her arms, refusing to answer.

"Larkin, so help me—"

"It never stopped."

"Does he beat your mother? What about Nesha or Sela?"

Larkin shuffled her feet. "Not if I can help it."

"How bad is your stomach?"

She'd never been able to stand having Bane angry with her. "I've had worse."

Bane closed his eyes, and when he opened them again, whatever indecision had been lingering around him was gone, replaced by surety. "You're to be married."

The thought of marriage made her tense, dreading a heavy weight on her back. Her mother said she'd talked to Daydon about marrying her off. Bane must have overheard. Is that why he'd kissed her—because after this she'd belong to someone else? "To whom?"

He grinned. "Me, of course."

Her mouth came open. "You?"

"My pretty eyes are starting to feel insulted."

"What about Alorica?" The girl had been set on Bane since they were ten years old—around the same time she decided to hate Larkin.

Bane reached out and tapped her nose. "Now, don't get jealous." She gave him a flat look, and he laughed, holding out his hands in disbelief. "Alorica wants my money and my title, not me."

"But your father would approve of Alorica." Not Larkin—the poor girl with a papa who had a reputation for hitting his women.

"He's the one who suggested it, last night after you left."

Larkin was truly stunned. That explained the way Bane had

been watching her, the strange questions he'd asked. "Is that what *you* want, Bane?"

He turned serious. "I'll always take care of you, Larkin."

"That's not the same as wanting to marry me."

In answer, his hands cradled her face. Their mouths met, his lips working gently over hers. Her arms came around his strong back. She could get used to this, touching and being touched by him.

A strangled sound broke them apart. Nesha stood on the path a half dozen paces down. Tears streamed down her cheeks. Silent, gasping sobs shook her shoulders.

"Nesha?" Larkin pushed away from Bane. "What's wrong?"

"Sela's missing," Nesha shouted.

"Sela's missing?" Larkin echoed.

Arms wrapped tight around herself, Nesha backed away. "It's your fault. If you'd watched her closer the other day, she wouldn't have tried anything today." Her sister dashed tears off her cheek, pivoted on her good heel, and hustled back the way she'd come.

Bane scrambled after her. "Nesha, wait, please."

She jerked away from of his touch. "Go look for my sister." When he hesitated, she shoved him. "Go!"

He hesitated a moment more, then ran ahead, quickly reaching the bridge.

Larkin easily overtook Nesha. "Where did you last see her?"

Nesha wiped her face. "By the river, where we do the washing."

Larkin's eyes shifted again to the dark line of green. If the forest was calling for her, why not her little sister?

CHAPTER 8

RINGS ARE PRETTY THINGS

Larkin pounded over the bridge to her family's land. She heard Mama, somewhere down by the river, frantically calling Sela's name. Larkin's stride faltered. What if her sister had fallen in the engorged river and been swept downstream? She pushed the thought aside. She knew, deep in her gut, her sister had gone to the forest.

Larkin stuck to the troughs of the fields, her hair flying behind her. She crested the rise. Her sister stood before the same tree where she and Larkin had gone in before. Sela leaned forward, shifting her weight to take that last step.

Just out of reach and partially hidden in the shadows, Denan lounged against a tree.

"Sela, no!" Larkin cried. Her sister whipped around. The trees shifted behind her as if to snatch her. Larkin reached her sister a dozen steps later, grabbing her up in her shaking arms, eyes pinned on Denan. She focused like she had before and tried to call up the magic around them. Nothing happened. She tried again. Still nothing.

She glared at Denan to make up for her helplessness. "You leave her alone!"

"We never take one so young," he said. "I told her to stay."

"Liar!"

"I'm not lying to you," he said.

She backed up. Her heart hammered in her chest. Sweat rolled down her temples. She wished she had a weapon, something to hurt him so he couldn't threaten her or her sister ever again. "Touch her, and I'll gut you."

He held steady. "Take her home to your family. Say your goodbyes. Tonight, you will come with me."

"Never!"

He watched her with a burning intensity. "How did you stop me last night?"

Magic. The word whispered through her. She squeezed her hand, waiting for the power to buzz up her arm. Nothing happened. Maybe she shouldn't have been so eager to push the sliver out. "It's gone. Whatever it was, it's gone now."

His gaze turned predatory. "So, you do realize."

What does that mean? Larkin wondered.

He pulled his hood up, masking his face with shadow, and backed into the forest. Almost immediately, the dappled material made him hard to see.

"Don't threaten me," Larkin said, voice hoarse.

"I'm trying to help you. I cannot say the same for the company you keep."

Then he was gone.

Larkin's legs gave out from under her, and she collapsed in a trembling heap, holding her sister tight. Sela curled up, her face hidden in the crook of Larkin's neck. "The trees sing, Larkin."

If Larkin hadn't been so wrapped up in herself, she would have known her sister was struggling with the call of the forest too. She smoothed Sela's wild hair. "I know. They sing to me too. But we can resist, you and me. We're stronger than the other girls."

Sela lifted her wide green eyes, tears of longing lining the bottom lids. "I want to go."

Larkin felt a trembling inside her, as if something had been wound to the point of breaking. "If you go into the forest, Sela, you'll never see me or Mama or Nesha again. You'll be lost to the beast."

Sela started crying. Larkin was sorry for scaring her, but her little sister had to understand the risk, had to understand what she would lose.

"I won't go," she sobbed. "I stay with Mama."

Footsteps pounded behind them. Bane had his bow in hand, arrow nocked, ax at his belt. His attention was fixed on the trees. "Was he here?"

Larkin nodded.

His lips thinned. "Get behind me. Head for the bridge."

If Denan had wanted to take her—take them both—he could have already. The danger was past. But Larkin didn't argue. She held her sister tight and hurried toward the bridge, calling for her mother and Nesha as she went.

Looking like a wild thing, Mama ran out of the willows, Nesha a dozen steps behind. "Sela, you know you're supposed to stay by me!" She hauled Sela out of Larkin's arms and squeezed her tight. Then she noticed Bane's bow and ax and stuttered to a halt. "What—"

"It was the piper, Mama," Larkin said.

Mama's face went white, and she swayed on her feet. Nesha caught up and reached out to steady her. Tight-lipped, the five of them hurried across the bridge, Bane throwing concerned glances behind them every few steps. When they finally stepped inside the manor house, Larkin glanced around for any sign of the druids, relieved to find nothing.

"They're staying with Rimoth," Bane said, as if guessing

her thoughts. He shut the door behind them and threw the bolt into place. "You're moving into town for the time being."

Mama slumped down on a chair. Sela sat sideways around her large belly. "And who would take us in?"

"You could stay here," he said. "There are three spare rooms upstairs."

Mama's brows rose. "I've two daughters of marriageable age. It wouldn't be proper."

Bane's gaze flicked to Nesha before he crouched down to Sela's level. "Want to see if Red had her puppies yet?"

Sela stared at him woefully, her usual exuberance tamped down to embers.

"Nesha, take her out back," Mama said. Nesha's head was bowed, and she didn't seem to hear them. "Nesha," Mama said again. "Take Sela to the barn."

Nesha dragged herself up from somewhere far away. She took Sela by the hand and limped toward the kitchen door. Her leg must have really pained her, for her face was screwed up as if she were about to cry.

When the back door closed, Bane faced Mama. "It would be proper if I were married to Larkin."

Mama sagged in relief. "You've agreed to it, then."

His studied Larkin. "If she consents."

Larkin was stunned by an overwhelming rush of joy that terrified her. She loved Bane—she'd always loved him—but joy never lasted, and the only marriage she'd known was not one she wanted.

Bane came to her and enveloped her hands in his. "The forest would no longer be a threat. You would have a lovely home and all the food you could ever want. No more working yourself to the bone. No more cold winters shivering by a too-small fire. Your father could never hurt you again."

"What about my family?" Larkin asked.

"I'll make sure your father never lays another finger on

them."

Larkin looked to her mother, who gave a slight nod, and she heard Mama's advice from the night before in her head, *None of us are ever free, Larkin, but we can choose the chains that bind us.*

Larkin took a deep breath, and on the exhalation, she said, "I will bind myself to you."

Bane's mouth quirked up on one side. "Well, don't act quite so pleased about it. I am the most eligible bachelor in town, after all."

She knew he was trying to tease a smile out of her, so she smiled. For him, she always smiled.

He reached down, held her tight, and whispered in her ear, "You know, if I asked Alorica to marry me, she'd have called for the druid already."

Larkin snorted.

"That's better," he gloated. "Now, wait here. I'll be right back." He opened the door to the right of the hearth and stepped inside his father's room. Larkin heard a low murmur of voices, one of them weak and faint. Daydon must have grown sicker in the night.

Larkin turned to her mother. "How did you get Daydon to agree?"

Mama leaned back in her chair, exhaustion plain on her features. She'd aged with this pregnancy, looking far older than her thirty-eight years. "I called in a favor—something that happened years ago. It wasn't as hard as you might think. Daydon is a good man, deep beneath the politician."

"What favor?"

"I promised never to tell." Mama was better than anyone at keeping secrets. She pushed heavily to her feet. "I'll be outside with the girls."

Larkin tried to guess what favor Daydon owed that would be so powerful, when Bane slipped out of his father's room, bringing with him the scent of cloves and cinnamon. He held something in his hand, his expression playful. "Guess."

Trying not to smile, she rolled her eyes. "A sword?"

"You're not even trying."

"A sparrow's egg?"

"Why would I have a sparrow's egg in my father's room?"

"It wouldn't be the first time."

He chuckled, obviously remembering the time he'd revealed the spotted brown egg by smashing it in her face. "That was years ago." He prodded her with his arm. "Come on, guess."

She groaned. "More rolls? I'm still hungry."

He smiled and opened his hand, revealing a ring of gold vines entwined around a large ruby. Bane pushed it onto her ring finger. It fit as if made for her, though she knew it wasn't.

She watched as it caught the light like a drop of blood. When she was a child, she had watched it flash on Bane's mother's hand in the light of a bonfire. And now his mother was dead. This was a dead woman's ring, a dead woman's life she was taking over. Larkin's finger itched, and she fought the urge to rip the ring off.

Bane stared at her, his smile slowly slipping. "I've finally rendered her speechless."

"Bane, I can't wear this. It's too fine. What if I break it? What if I lose it?" It was more than the ring she was worried about breaking. She'd never live up to being a lord's wife.

He pulled her into his arms and tucked her head beneath his chin. "Larkin, everything is going to be all right. I won't let anything happen to you—I swear it."

Even now, Denan lurked out there in the trees, waiting for her. If she closed her eyes, she could feel the forest's pull. For a moment, she almost considered telling Bane how strong that pull was. But soon, it wouldn't matter. She'd be married, and the forest never took married girls.

Bane pulled back to look at her. "You don't seem to realize

how fun this is going to be. Let me show you."

Before she could protest, his lips found hers, and something stretched awake inside her. She found herself rising to meet him. She relaxed and let the fear seep out of her. She explored the planes of his face—the high cheekbones and the stubble on his jaw, the high prominent brow bones and straight black hair. Bane stroked her neck and arms, his fingers leaving trails of warmth.

"Well, I suppose you should find the druid to marry you," Mama said.

Larkin startled and tried to jump back, but Bane held her fast. "Won't you be staying, Pennice?"

Her mother stood in the entrance to the kitchen, Sela's little hand in hers. She shook her head. "Nesha took off. I need to find her."

Larkin desperately wished her mother would stay with them. None of the rituals leading up to the wedding were pleasant. Her mother turned to go.

"Mama, what's wrong with Nesha?" Larkin asked. "She's not acting like herself."

Her mother paused. "It's been a long day for all of us, Larkin." Her gaze caught on the ring. "It would be better to leave that safely here until the wedding day." Mama and Sela walked out the front door.

Larkin's jaw tightened. If Papa saw the ring, he would try to sell it. Without a word, she slipped it off and pressed it into Bane's hand. "Keep it safe for me."

He looked at the ring. "Can't you wear it, just for today?"

Bane didn't know how bad her father was, didn't know how often he stole Mama's earnings. He didn't know how broken Larkin was, how bad her family life was. She wanted him to keep that image of her—the one who made him laugh, the one he protected.

"It's only for a few days," she reassured him.

Larkin kissed him to make him forget his reluctance. The

kitchen door opening made them break apart. Venna studied them with wide eyes.

"Venna, have you met my future wife?" Bane wrapped his arm around Larkin's shoulders.

Venna smiled. "Oh, how wonderful. I'll make a cake to celebrate!" She hurried back into the kitchen. Larkin would see a lot more of Venna after the wedding, which meant more rolls and jam. Her mouth watered at the thought.

Bane kissed Larkin's temple and then stepped back into his father's room. When he came out again, the ring was nowhere to be seen. "Come on. I spotted Rimoth while I was looking for Sela. Let's get him to settle this."

They found the druid at the Curse Tree, tying curses the townspeople had paid him to put up. Larkin's gaze skittered from the forest to Rimoth, not sure which she should be warier of.

"Druid Rimoth," Bane said as they approached. "We have come to request you marry us. Tonight."

Rimoth looked down his nose at them. "Marry you? I will do no such thing!"

"It is your duty to the people of this town," Bane growled.

"My duty is to know the forest's will," Rimoth shouted, spit flying. "The same forest that she"—he pointed an accusing finger at Larkin—"blasphemed when she escaped!"

Bane advanced, his hands balled into fists. "Are you threatening her?"

Rimoth looked Bane up and down in disgust. "You privileged boy, thinking you can dictate to a druid."

"I can—"

"What is the meaning of this?" Garrot emerged from the forest. Trailing behind him, Hunter looked at Larkin with pity.

She gaped at them. They'd been inside the forest and come out again as if it were nothing, as if it were something they did every day.

Rimoth looked like he was choking. "This foolish boy wishes to marry the girl. But as I have said before, the child is a blasphemer."

Larkin dared him to deny her.

"You wish to marry him?" Garrot asked.

Larkin nodded.

Garrot and Hunter exchanged a look.

"Then prove you are worthy to remain in Hamel," Garrot said. "Face the crucible."

"That hasn't been done in decades!" Bane cried.

All the warmth drained out of Larkin, leaving her sick and cold. "Are you mad? No girl ever comes back from that."

Rimoth's dead eyes latched onto her. A smile crept up the corners of his mouth. "Ah, yes. Then we shall know once and for all if the forest claims her as its own."

"You can't do this!" Bane protested.

Hunter frowned. "It's already done."

Garrot smacked his gloves on his hand and tipped back the brim of his hat. "If you want to marry the girl, she faces the crucible."

Bane shook his head. "There's a simple solution that will save her from the forest forever—let her marry me tonight. You can't deny us that."

"I can to save ourselves the forest's retribution." Garrot motioned to Hunter, who came toward Larkin.

Larkin's hands rose, wrapping protectively over her stomach as she backed away. "No. No, no, no, no."

"It'll go easier if you don't fight," Hunter said gently.

Bane stepped in front of her. "You won't touch her."

"This backward town has no sense of the druids' power," Garrot said. "You would be wise not to resist us, boy."

Bane lunged for Hunter, arm cocked back. Hunter ducked the blow and punched Bane in the stomach. When Bane doubled over, Garrot's fist came down on his temple. Bane crumbled in a motionless heap.

"Bane!" Larkin knelt beside him and turned him over. His eyes were closed. She held her fingers under his nose, relieved at the reassuring puff. She looked up to find Garrot standing over her, his damp hair sticking to his mouth. "Why are you doing this?" she cried.

His gaze bored into hers. "The forest makes beasts of us all," he whispered. "Hunter, take her home and make sure she stays there. We'll come for her tonight."

"And do not think to run," Rimoth added gleefully. "There's nowhere you can go we cannot find you."

Hunter bent down, taking hold of her arm. When she tried to jerk free, he hauled her up. "This is a kindness," Hunter said. "A chance to spend some time with your family before the forest takes you. Most girls don't get that."

She kicked at his crotch. He twisted to deflect the blow, and his hand latched around her throat, squeezing. Darkness circled from the outside of her vision, and her knees went weak.

Hunter forced her hands behind her back and tied them. "Ready to come quietly?"

Larkin coughed and gasped, eyes watering. As Hunter led her away, she heard Garrot's voice behind her. "Rimoth, take the boy back to the house and see he's tied up. I will not have him interfering."

CHAPTER 9

CRUCIBLE

They came for Larkin at twilight, when the line between day and night blurred into something foreign and fleeting. The hut door swung open. A dozen men stood cloaked against the rain and their dark purpose. In the light of their torches, she could make out Garrot, Rimoth, Hunter, Horace, Horgen, and Kenjin, Alorica's father.

Larkin didn't understand Horgen and his smug expression. "What have I ever done to you?" she murmured to all of them, but especially him.

"What's the meaning of this?" Papa said, his words slurred. He'd slept through Larkin trying to escape through their window and Hunter forcing her back inside.

Mama shoved Sela into Nesha's arms, who went as far from the door as she could get and crouched down to make them a smaller target. Mama stood before Larkin, one hand holding Larkin's wrist so tight the bones threatened to break. "You're not taking my daughter."

Garrot ducked as he stepped into their hut. He took in the bedding on the floor around the fire, their one cook pot, the tools they used to till the land propped up beside the door. "I'm afraid you have no choice in the matter."

Larkin looked at the men's faces—all of whom she knew. She wasn't surprised Alorica's father was among them, his fine clothing flashing with color in the torchlight. Word must have reached him that Bane asked to marry her.

Papa pointed sloppily in Kenjin's direction. "My daughter's no more a traitor than yours was, Kenjin."

"Atara made her sacrifice," Kenjin replied. "Now it's your daughter's turn."

"You can't do this! It's wrong," Mama cried.

Hunter stepped around Garrot. "Step aside, woman. We don't want to risk harming the unborn."

"Harben, do something," Mama pleaded.

Papa pushed himself unsteadily to his feet. "You can't have the one who plows my fields. Take the cripple."

"The Forbidden Forest does not take the maimed," Rimoth sneered as he too stepped inside.

Larkin met her sister's eyes. This was how it had always been, Larkin and Nesha protecting their family from their father and starvation. All those years of counting on each other, of being each other's strength—it stretched between them like a rope that could never be broken. And then Nesha's gaze shuttered, and she turned away.

How could she turn away?

"Take her," Garrot said.

Larkin whipped back around. Men surged into the hut, filling it so Larkin had nowhere to go. Sela sobbed. Mama shouted. Papa threw wide punches. Rimoth and Garrot wrenched Larkin away, gripping her arms while Hunter firmly tied them. They hauled her into the pounding rain without her cloak or shoes.

She looked back at the house—the image ingrained in her

memory: her mother sobbing and reaching for her, Sela curled in Nesha's arms, Nesha doing her best to shield her sister, her expression blank, as if she'd been broken. Her father lay sprawled out on the ground, dangerously close to the fire.

"I love you!" Larkin screamed. Their last memory of her should be of defiance and devotion. She'd never see them again. The door slammed shut.

The ground was freezing. Her feet grew numb and clumsy. When she stumbled, Hunter pulled her up and marched her across the bridge, water pouring over their feet.

She was surprised how many people waited for them on the other side—nearly half the town turned out. They bore torches, their faces frightened or angry or pitying. The baker sold salted bread and dried apples to the gathered crowd. "Hot bread, fresh from the oven. Dried apples from last harvest!"

"Our seeds are rotting in the ground," one man cried, and others fell in with the same complaint.

The cobbler's wife spat on Larkin's skirts. "All my little ones are sick."

"The forest is angry!" her sister cried. "She demands sacrifice."

The cobbler's wife had lost her own daughter to the forest last year. How could she wish the same fate on another daughter, another family? A group of boys lobbed fistfuls of mud at her. Larkin ducked, wincing as one hit her chest, cold mud oozing down the inside of her shirt.

Hunter drew his ax and faced the boys down, his expression frighteningly fierce. "That will not happen again."

The crowd stilled. The boys brushed muddy hands on trousers. Hunter glared at them before leading her on again. Garrot hung back so he walked beside Rimoth, directly before Larkin.

"Did you have to get them quite so riled up?" Garrot asked in disgust.

"Righteous indignation," Rimoth said fervently. "Why

should they suffer because of this willful girl?"

"Willful? This was not my doing!" Luckily, she had a lot of experience holding back her tears. She refused to let them see her cry. Instead, she spat at Rimoth, hitting him in the back of the head. "The forest take the lot of you, and may the beast suck the marrow from your bones!" It was the strongest curse she knew.

"Silence her," Rimoth hissed.

Kenjin tugged out a handkerchief and made to tie it across her mouth. She bit him. He yelped and cuffed her head. She glared at him through the ringing in her ears. Lightning fast, Hunter punched the other man in the stomach. Kenjin doubled over, all the breath leaving his body and coming back in a strangled wheeze.

"She will not suffer more than is needful," Hunter ground out. "She will hold her tongue now." His black gaze met hers, demanding obedience. "Courage, girl. Don't let them see your pain."

How could he show compassion while leading her to the crucible? Still, he was right. Larkin squared her shoulders. She knew how to deal with pain, how to hold her tears until no one was looking. She lifted her chin and gave a curt nod. Hunter hauled her past the town, coming toward Venna's hut—nearer the forest than anyone's, save Rimoth's.

Venna's grandfather, Vyder, peered out of his house, Venna peeking out from behind him. "What's the meaning of this?" he called to the people streaming past.

"Larkin faces the crucible," Kenjin said as he mopped the wet from his forehead.

For half a moment, Venna's pitying eyes met Larkin's before her grandfather slammed the door shut and latched it. The women and children hung back around his hut—fear of the forest ran too deep.

When they'd finally reached the forest's outskirts, the

crowd thinned to only three dozen people—a good number of grown men wouldn't willingly come this close to the trees. Garrot held out his hand for those remaining to hang back as he strode toward the forest. "Bring her to me."

Hunter guided her forward. She studied the Forbidden Forest. The Curse Tree stood like a dark tower in the night. Beneath it, stakes taller than her had been pounded into the ground. Chains and manacles gleamed in the torchlight. The shadows of the boughs shifted as they sang their enchantment. She would not pass this night alone, of that she was certain. But whether Denan would come for her or the beast, she wasn't sure.

Shivering and wet, she held her head high as she strode to the center of the stakes, faced the forest, and held out her hands. Hunter stood before her and tugged at the knot binding her hands, which gave with surprising ease. The chains clinked as he shifted them. He locked her wrists in the manacles, the key shrieking in the rusted lock. The cold metal bit unforgivingly into her. He stepped back as she stood with her arms splayed, unable to take a step in either direction.

"Sometimes the innocent must pay for the sins of the guilty," Hunter whispered.

"What does that mean?" Larkin asked, disgusted at his self-righteousness.

Hunter stepped back as Garrot approached to drop a key on a leather cord around her neck. He adjusted it so it was visible in the center of her chest.

Larkin stared at the dangling key, water dripping down its length. "What need has a beast of a key?" She dared him to deny Denan was coming for her.

"Perhaps not all beasts have claws," Garrot said. "Survive the night, and I'll marry you to the lord's boy." Garrot looked over the crowd. "Go home, lest the beast take you by mistake."

The crowd grumbled and grudgingly dispersed. Larkin stood straight and tall long after the sounds of their leaving had been lost to the rain and the forest's call.

Sometime in the darkest part of night, the rain stopped. A vapor rose from the ground. She could feel the press of it against her bare skin. It muffled sounds and left Larkin completely blind. She shivered violently. The manacles leached what little warmth her body dredged up. She knew when the numbness and cold wore off, her arms would ache something fierce. Still, she marched in place, knowing she could freeze to death before morning came.

Exhausted as she was, sleep wasn't a temptation. Denan would be coming for her soon. She was honestly surprised it had taken him this long.

At the rustle of grass and the snap of a twig, she stiffened and strained to hear anything in the gloom. Then she heard it—the slog of a foot releasing from the mud—but it wasn't coming from the forest. Heart pounding, she tried to look over her shoulder, but she couldn't make out anything. "Who's there?"

"Larkin?"

She blinked in surprise. The voice was soft and feminine, familiar. "Who's out there?"

The steps came closer. "Larkin?" the voice said again, and this time, she recognized the speaker.

"Venna?"

Someone brushed her back in the darkness. Larkin shied away from the touch; touch always meant pain.

"I would have come earlier," Venna said breathlessly, "but it took forever for Rimoth to fall asleep. Here, step on this." She came around to stand before Larkin, resting something hot and heavy before Larkin's numb toes—a fire-baked rock, generously wrapped in rags.

Larkin obeyed, a moan slipping from her mouth at the heat.

Her feet tensed and cramped, simultaneously curling around and repulsed by the unfamiliar warmth. "What's Rimoth doing at your house?"

Venna tugged off her cloak and wrapped it around Larkin's shivering shoulders. "Standing watch. Some of the men are even sleeping on our floor in case you try to escape."

Larkin laughed bitterly. How could she possibly escape?

Venna's trembling finger searched out Larkin's lips. "I brought soup. It's not much, but it's hot."

Larkin opened her mouth, swallowing the trickle of soup. It was thin, but it warmed her from the inside out. She finished it in a dozen swallows. "Thank you."

"I wish I could do more." Venna's voice shook—no girl willingly came this close to the forest, especially at night. "Throw the rock away when they come to unchain you so they don't know I came."

Larkin felt her presence moving away. "Why are you helping me?" she whispered, desperate not to be left alone again.

Venna hesitated. "Because it could easily be me in your place, could have been any of us, except maybe Alorica. I imagine her father would buy his way out of it."

Despite everything, Larkin laughed. "Venna, you don't know what this means. I—Thank you."

"I should—" Venna's voice cut off at the sound of a loud cry and a struggle from the Forbidden Forest.

"Go," Larkin hissed. Venna vanished, followed by the fading sounds of her slogging steps. Trapped, Larkin huddled under the cloak still warm from the other girl's body heat.

Larkin heard movement to her right, along with ragged breathing and staggering steps, and then a thump. If only she could see something! Still, she would not be found like this, helpless as a baby bird fallen out of its nest. She might not be able to run, but she would still fight, when the time came.

Agonizing minutes passed. She froze as she felt a presence

before her face, close enough to raise the hairs on the back of her neck.

"They're giving you to me?" Denan said softly. "One of their most prized possessions, presented like a bird in a cage."

She was certainly not anyone's prized possession. She squeezed her sore palm and tried to get the magic to rise inside her again, but there was no reassuring buzz. "I'm not going anywhere with you."

She tensed, let her arms take her weight, and kicked out with her right leg. Her shin connected with his side. He grabbed her firmly behind the knee and held her tight. She balanced precariously on the rock. The manacles dug painfully into her wrists. Her one chance, and she'd blown it.

Denan drew her closer, so she was practically straddling him, the warmth from his body invading hers. His fingers brushed against her neck. "No magic this time? Why?"

"Let me go."

He grabbed the cord around her neck and tugged the key over her head. His hands slid along her arm, the key fumbling for the lock before it opened with an unholy shriek.

Suddenly free, Larkin pitched back and wrenched herself from his grasp. The remaining manacle swung her to the left. The edges dug in deep. She tried to jerk her hand through the opening. Warm blood ran down her chilled skin.

"Will you force me to dart you again, Larkin?"

Then she truly would be at his mercy. She looked for him, wishing she could see through the impenetrable darkness. "I'm supposed to let you take me?"

He sighed. "Even if you wanted to, you can't go back, Larkin."

Trembles overtook her—bone-deep, teeth-rattling trembles. She clenched her teeth to keep them from giving her away and jutted out her chin. "Don't tell me what I can and can't do."

He stepped closer, gently took hold of her hand, and removed the last manacle, but he didn't let go. She could feel him, coiled tight in case she struck out or tried to run. Still, she couldn't help it. She jerked her hand back even as she whirled and took a single running step. Fast as a lightning strike, he had both arms around her chest, his grip firm. She struggled, trying to break free.

"Last chance, Larkin."

Lying helpless for the next full day ... She forced herself to relax. She'd known this was coming, and she couldn't see any way out of it. "Why are you doing this?"

He didn't ease his grip. "Why are you fighting so hard? I saw you with the amulet. It showed you what you needed to see."

She cringed away from his breath against the back of her neck. "I didn't see anything!" A lie. It had shown her something —diving into turquoise water. But what did that mean?

"Maybe you should try again," he said.

"I gave it to the druids."

He gasped in disbelief. "No, you had to have recognized it. You connected with it. I saw you!"

Anger rolled off him. She tensed, waiting to feel his fists. "What did you expect me to do with it?"

"The amulet will tell you."

Larkin could still feel the turquoise water's kiss against her skin. "You're as crazy as Maisy."

He turned her around to face him, which was pointless. She couldn't see anything in the dark. "If you knew the value of that amulet, you would not have given it up. There is only one like it in all the world. You have to get it back."

"Why would I do *anything* for you?"

He hesitated. "I'll let you go."

Everything within Larkin stilled—her body, her lungs, even her very heartbeat waited breathlessly. "Only to try to take me again."

He released her and took a step back. "I will make a vow, Larkin, to never force you into the Forbidden Forest."

Her knees buckled at the mere chance at freedom. "Why would I trust you to keep this vow?"

"It's either that or come with me now."

She didn't trust him. "After all this to get me into the forest, you're going to let me go over an amulet? Why?"

"Who said I'm letting you go?"

"You just said—"

"You might not come with me tonight, Larkin, but you will come. We have the same heartsong, and you have a destiny. I am willing to wait a bit longer."

Her destiny was her own making. "I will never willingly come to you, piper, but I will accept your vow. It might take me a few days to retrieve the amulet—Garrot has it." The thought of taking something from that particular druid made her shiver with dread.

"Bring me the amulet, Larkin. Should you find yourself in need, squeeze it in your hand so it pierces the skin and think of me. Help will come, I swear it." There was genuine worry in his voice, as if he was concerned for her welfare.

"You mean *you* will come?"

He didn't deny it.

She scoffed. "I would *never* call for you."

"I already saved your life once tonight. Why not again?"

She took a step back. "What?"

"Did you not hear the beast fall?"

"The thumps I heard earlier?"

"The forest is swarming with gilgad coming out of hibernation. The druid … Well, I'll leave it up to you whether you want to let him spend the night helpless to the elements and the forest. After all, it's what he did to you."

One of the druids had watched her this whole time? Had he seen Venna? A full-body shudder took her. "Who is it and what did you do to him?"

"Get the amulet, little bird." She sensed Denan backing away from her, easing into the shadows from whence he'd come.

Larkin stood for a beat. She wanted so badly to run, but there was nowhere the druids wouldn't find her. And if she left one of them to die, what would happen to Bane and her family?

She turned and stumbled through the dark toward Venna's house.

CHAPTER

A MAD SORT OF BRILLIANCE

H and out to keep her from plowing into anything, Larkin staggered in the pitch black. Eventually, she heard
the soft grunt of pigs—Venna's house. Rimoth was
supposed to be on sentinel duty. Larkin changed course, moving
toward the manure smell and animal sounds.

When she heard the animal's faint breathing, she stumbled
into a fence and used it to orient herself toward the house. She
hadn't taken two more steps when she tripped over something in
the dark and landed in a sprawl across legs and mud.

"By the beast," someone burst. "What is going on?"

"Rimoth?" Larkin recoiled off him, scrubbing where her
outer thigh had touched him.

"What are you doing free of the crucible?"

Larkin hesitated. If she told the druids Denan had let her go,
they would want to know why. She couldn't tell them it was so
she could steal the amulet back. She jumped to her feet. "Hunter
is hurt. He needs help."

Rimoth grabbed her arm in a bruising grip. "Ho the house!"
Sounds came from their right, and a door was thrown open,
revealing a faint glow of ember light. A beat later, a handful of
men spilled out, bleary-eyed and carrying weapons.

"What is it?" Horace asked, what remained of his hair
standing on end.

Rimoth jerked his thumb back at her. "The girl says Hunter
is hurt."

"Start some torches," Horace said to his son. Torches were
shoved into the fire's embers. They flared to life, making Larkin
squint. Horace started toward them. His eyes widened at the
sight of her bloody hands. "Who let her free?"

"That's what I want to know." Rimoth's eyes narrowed on
her.

"Hurry," Larkin said. "There are beasts in the forest." Just
then, Venna peered out at Larkin from behind her father. Larkin
still wore Venna's cloak. She could only hope the men wouldn't
notice. "Come on."

Rimoth jerked her back to him. "Is this some kind of trick,
girl?"

"Trick?" She wanted to punch him, but that would involve
touching him more than she already was. She settled for glaring.
"What kind of trick involves me coming to you?"

He shoved her away. "Fine, but if it *is* some kind of trick
…"

Larkin didn't wait to hear his threat. She turned on her heel
and ran toward the forest. The men fell in behind her and quickly
surpassed her. They entered the Forbidden Forest without hesitation, as if they knew exactly where Hunter was. Larkin faltered
on the outskirts, unwilling to go inside, even with the druids
ahead of her.

They found him a half-dozen steps inside and gently turned
him. Horgen took off his cloak to settle over him. Had Denan
darted him? Killed him? Rimoth sent three more men to fetch a

team and wagon, then turned to Larkin.

In three strides, he'd shoved her into the Curse Tree, his forearm pinning her collarbone. "What did you do to him?"

She pushed against his arm. "Nothing!"

"Liar! How did you get free? Who helped you?"

Larkin shoved him away, snatched a stick, and held it out like a sword. He eyed her warily. She almost wished he would charge her so she could use it.

"What is the meaning of this?" Garrot galloped bareback across the fields. He slid from the animal's back and crouched beside Hunter. He searched him for some kind of wound, finding a bloody mess of flesh on his right calf. "I've seen this before. He's been bitten by a beast." He bent down and sniffed Hunter's breath. His eyes closed in relief. "Get him back to the house."

Hunter must have doubled back to watch her from the forest, and a gilgad had attacked him. But that meant he knew Venna had helped Larkin. When he woke, he'd tell Garrot. No doubt the druids would conclude that Venna had freed her. Larkin couldn't let the other girl suffer for helping her.

Garrot's gaze turned deadly as he marched toward Larkin. "Why are you still here?" Larkin held up the stick in warning. He shoved it to the side and gripped her shirt in his fist, pulling her nose to nose with him. "Answer me."

Hands up in surrender, Larkin tried not to stare at the blood on his hands. "I don't know!" she lied.

The wagon jostled toward them. Garrot dropped his voice so only she could hear him. "Why did he give Hunter the antidote?"

"What antidote? Oh ..." Garrot had sniffed Hunter's breath moments before—breath that probably smelled like pepper, like the liquid Denan had given her after darting her—the darts that used gilgad venom. Denan hadn't hurt the druid; he'd saved his life.

Teeth clenched, Garrot stepped back and called to Rimoth.

"Put the manacles back on and take her to the druid house. I'll question her later."

The wagon maneuvered as close to the trees as the driver could get it. Garrot stepped away from her to attend Hunter. Rimoth's clammy hands pawed her arm, clamping the manacles back around her torn wrists. He led her along the forest's periphery toward his house. She glanced back once to see Venna watching her from the rise her house was built on. Larkin gave her a nod. Though she hadn't had time to grab the heated stone, no one had noticed it. If they did, Larkin would never reveal Venna had given it to her.

The other girl disappeared back inside her hut. Larkin stumbled on an exposed root, stubbing her toe. Concentrating on the path before her, she focused on putting one foot in front of the other. It was almost a relief when she stepped into Rimoth's warm home. The druid tossed the keys to the manacles on the dining room table. Larkin edged closer to the fire's warmth.

But Rimoth took her by the elbow, dragged her into the kitchen, and threw open the cellar door. "Go or I'll shove you down."

"But—"

He planted his hand on her back and pushed. She fell down the stairs, knocking her thigh and head. The door slammed above her, and she lay in the dark, stunned and exhausted. At least it was dry and warmer than outside. After a moment, she pushed herself off the stairs and felt around. She found some shelves. It took her a while to figure out what was on them: sprouting potatoes, limp carrots, something fuzzy—beets, maybe. Lumpy garlic and papery onions hung in loosely woven bags.

Larkin helped herself to some carrots and potatoes, brushing away as much dirt as she could on her soggy, borrowed cloak before crunching through them. When she'd had her fill, she wrung out Venna's cloak, curled up, and fell asleep.

Larkin woke sometime later to a sliver of daylight shining in her eyes. Her clothes were still damp under her arms, between her legs, and where she'd slept against the packed dirt floor. She shifted, her muscles screaming in protest. She held her manacled hands up to block the too-bright light. Crazy Maisy peered at her from the other side of the trapdoor.

"You're beginning to look like me," the other girl mused.

Larkin looked down at herself. She was filthy, her clothing ragged and torn. One of her toenails had been nearly torn off—it hung at an angle. Knowing it would only hurt more every time it snagged, she braced herself and ripped it the rest of the way off. She tensed at the sting, bruises aching anew.

Maisy opened the trapdoor fully and held out her hand, a key dangling from her fingers.

"What are you doing?" Larkin asked breathlessly.

Maisy swung the key, seemingly mesmerized by its motion. "You won't get a better chance to search for that amulet of yours."

Larkin's mouth fell open. She started toward the other girl, but then stopped. One thing she knew for certain: she couldn't trust Crazy Maisy. Her father probably stood just out of sight, waiting to confirm something he shouldn't even know about.

"I don't know what you're talking about."

Maisy tossed the key up, caught it, and held it to her chest. "You resisted the pipers. No girl has ever resisted them before."

"How do you know that?"

Maisy sashayed down the stairs. "You are not the only one to hear the pipers' songs—the forest's songs."

Larkin backed away from Maisy. "You've seen them before—the pipers?"

Maisy laughed bitterly. "Dead ones, yes. And the ones without souls." What did that mean? The other girl gently took

Larkin's bruised hand and unlocked the manacles. Larkin's eyes watered at the sight of her torn and bloody wrists.

"You'd be better off with the dead ones than to stay here, but I can't know for certain. I never saw them alive." Maisy dropped the key around Larkin's neck and disappeared up the steps. Larkin gaped after her. Even when she wasn't acting crazy, she was still crazy.

Larkin couldn't decide if she was more afraid of Garrot and his druids or Denan. Either way, she had to get that amulet. If anyone saw her, she would claim she needed to relieve her bladder, which was true. She edged to the top of the stairs and peeked out. No one waited to kick her back down the stairs. She climbed the last few steps. Fresh bandages and salve waited on the kitchen table. Silently thanking Maisy, Larkin hissed in pain as she daubed her bleeding, cracked wrists with ointment and wrapped them. After the initial flare of pain from being handled, they felt better. She did the same for her bleeding toe.

She peered into the dining room, bedroom, and even out the windows. All she saw was Maisy pacing on a rise, facing the town as if she were standing watch.

Larkin slipped up the narrow stairs, only to find Maisy hadn't been lying. She was truly alone. Larkin searched the four rooms upstairs, checking under every rug, mattress, and blanket, inside every pocket, drawer, and trunk. Her wounds opened as she moved her hands, which made her even more grateful for the bandages. When she came to the fourth room, she instantly recognized Rimoth's perfectly pressed, greasy clothing.

If Rimoth slept up here, that meant Garrot had taken over the larger, fancier bedroom downstairs. Larkin peered out the window to find Maisy gone. Two men strode toward the house. They were too far away to make out their features, but she recognized their clothes—Garrot and Rimoth.

Larkin flew down the stairs and jerked open the door to the bedroom. Inside was a large bed, an armoire, and a washbowl on a stand. She looked around the room, knowing she didn't have time to search everywhere. Where would Garrot keep the amulet—in the bed or his clothing? Or worse still, somewhere on his person?

Larkin went to the armoire first and opened the double doors. Inside was a coat, a change of clothes, and a bag. Larkin checked the bag, wincing when she left a dirty smudge on the pristine handkerchief. Nothing. She turned to the coat and shoved her fingers into one pocket and then the other. Still nothing. Tears of frustration and defeat welled in her eyes, but as the coat settled, she noticed an unnatural lump at the breast. Stretching onto her tiptoes, she squeezed and felt something hard beneath the cloth. Her scrambling fingers found a hidden pocket and dove in. She took hold of her freedom, gripping the amulet to her chest in pure joy.

She glanced out the window to see Garrot and Rimoth coming in through the front gate, the latter dragging a mulish Maisy. Larkin donned the cord and tucked the amulet under her bodice. She panicked when it bumped against the key. No time to put it back on the dining table. She set it on the kitchen table instead and opened the cellar door enough to slide inside. She'd just closed it when the kitchen door swung open.

Rimoth cursed. "She moved the table too."

"Were she my daughter, I'd beat some sense into her," Garrot said.

"Is she still there?" Rimoth hauled open the cellar. Larkin had settled herself in the corner, arms wrapped around her legs. She looked up at Garrot, remembering to squint as if the light hurt her eyes.

"Get up here," Garrot said. "We already know Maisy let you out."

Larkin climbed the stairs where the druids and Maisy were waiting.

"Why did you let her out?" Garrot asked the other girl.

Maisy's eyes glittered with barely suppressed rage. "You're going to pay for your sins, Garrot."

Garrot raised his hand to slap her, and then lowered it slowly. "Someday. But that day isn't today." He turned his back on her and faced Larkin. "How did you escape the crucible?"

Mimicking Maisy, Larkin met his gaze. "Denan let me go."

"Why?"

She shrugged. The lump of the amulet felt conspicuous and heavy under her dress.

Rimoth stepped closer. "Hunter could have died. Tell Garrot the truth."

Larkin resisted the urge to touch the amulet. "What truth?"

Maisy rolled her eyes at her father and Garrot. "It's painfully obvious, isn't it?"

Her father leaned forward, his eyes narrowed suspiciously. Garrot threw his hands in the air. "Out with it!"

Maisy whirled back to Larkin. "She's not a virgin."

Larkin's mouth fell open. "What?"

Maisy stalked forward, and Larkin was sure she was going to tug out the amulet from her dress. Instead, she patted Larkin's stomach. "There have been rumors all over town—Alorica has been at the heart of most of them—but there's usually a smidgen of truth in the lies." She looked expectantly at Larkin, who gaped back.

Garrot rubbed his eyes. "The forest doesn't care if the girls are virgins or not."

Maisy stared at him. "Even if those girls are pregnant?" Garrot's head came up, and Rimoth stiffened. Maisy opened a box on the table and took out a lump of bread. She handed half to Larkin and gnawed on the other half. "Take your stripes, girl. Better that than waste the druids' time with any more of this nonsense."

Why was Maisy helping her? Larkin shivered with dread. "Bane and I ..." She couldn't finish the lie.

"This confirms nothing!" Rimoth cried. "For all we know, she's lying to protect herself."

"Bring the boy," Garrot said to Rimoth.

What seemed an eternity later, Rimoth ushered Bane into the room. Larkin's gaze locked on his, unspoken questions asked and answered.

Was she all right?

Yes.

She didn't look all right.

She was.

Bane was going to kill the druids.

He'd better not.

He was sorry he hadn't been able to stop this.

So was she.

"Bane, is Larkin pregnant?" Garrot sprang the question on him.

Bane's head came up in surprise. "What?"

"Don't look at her, boy!" Garrot grabbed Bane's face. "Just answer the question yes or no. Is she pregnant?"

Bane hesitated, clearly not knowing the right answer.

"Is she?" the druid roared.

"Yes!" Bane shouted. Deafening silence resounded in the room. Bane lifted his chin. "I'm going to marry her."

Garrot searched Bane as if he could ferret out the lie in his face, but then he turned away. "Give them their stripes and let them go."

"But, sir—" Rimoth began, arms stretched out imploringly.

"I'll give her two days. If the forest hasn't taken her in two days, she can marry him." Garrot slammed the door behind him.

Rimoth stared after him, jaw working. He glared at Bane. "Strip to your waist."

When it was Larkin's turn, she unlaced her bodice, aware of the hungry way Rimoth stared at her bare back, but she was already out of her body. Her twenty stripes didn't even hurt.

When it was over, Larkin simply stepped back into herself, flinching at the pain that waited for her. She and Bane walked out together. Larkin didn't realize Maisy had followed them until she whispered Larkin's name. She turned to find the other girl standing in the doorway. "Make it true, quickly." Maisy waved them away and shut the door without another word.

"Why would she help us?" Bane asked.

"I don't know," Larkin replied.

CHAPTER 11

NEVER AGAIN

That evening, Larkin lay naked from the waist up, a blanket over her backside as her mother spread witch-hazel-infused rags across the welts on her back. The fire sputtered pitifully. They were running out of firewood, and it was impossible to keep any dry in this deluge.

She picked at the scab on her palm. Now that the sliver was out, it didn't seem to be infected. Mama hummed as she worked—a lullaby she'd never known the words to—while Sela played with little animals Papa had carved for Nesha when she was a baby. The ox had three legs, the horse was missing its ear and tail, and the sheep had been broken in two, but Sela didn't seem to mind.

Nesha pushed open the door and stood dripping on the threshold. "Is it true?"

Larkin stiffened from the cold and shifted to look at her sister. "Is what true?"

"That you're marrying Bane in two days. And that"—her

voice shook—"you're pregnant with his child."

Larkin stifled the need to roll her eyes. "We had to tell the druids that so they'd let me go."

"Nesha," Mama said gently. "Come inside. You're letting all the cold in."

Nesha's glare shifted to Mama. "You did this."

Mama rose, arms stretching toward Nesha. "I did what I had to. Surely you can see that."

Nesha shook her head as she backed away. "No, Mother. I don't see. I will never see. And I'll never forgive you—either of you."

She slammed the door behind her. Larkin stared after her sister in bewilderment. "What was that about?"

Mama put some valerian tea on the fire. "I broke off her relationship with the boy she was involved with."

Larkin felt a rush of sympathy for Nesha, along with a flash of anger. "Who was he? I'll kill him for leading her on."

"It's not his fault any more than it was hers. He would have married her, had his father agreed. Better to end things now—before she's even more involved."

Larkin rested her forehead on her cupped palms. "Then why did she do it in the first place?"

Mama rubbed her forehead as if she had a headache. "Hope is a powerful emotion—and sometimes a cruel one."

An uneasy feeling crowded Larkin's chest. "And now she has to watch me get what she's always wanted. Again."

Mama poured her some tea. "Get some sleep, Larkin. You've had a trying week."

When Larkin started awake later, the fire had turned to embers. Judging by the pounding on the stone roof, it was raining harder than ever, as if the skies were determined to wash away everything. But that wasn't what had woken her.

Denan played for her, calling her with his heartsong. It surprised her that she knew this, but the song of the forest was different from the song he played for her now. This song made her think of his arms around her, his lips on hers. She pushed the image away and sat up, looking around the room. She was relieved to see Nesha had come home sometime in the night; Sela cuddled in her arms. Mama slept alone. Wherever Papa was, Larkin hoped he stayed there.

She sat up carefully and pulled on her freshly washed dress. She tugged on her cloak—Bane had promised to return Venna's when they'd parted—and clogs and slipped into the night. At their orchard, she glanced around to make sure no one was watching, then stretched to reach the second bough, her fingers closing around a leather-wrapped parcel. She took it out and tucked it into her palm.

She slipped down the hill and crossed the fields toward the forest. She paused a stone's throw from the trees. She didn't trust Denan to keep his word, and she wanted a head start if she had to make a run for it. The music stopped, and his shadowed form came to the trees' edge.

"You have it?"

She threw the package toward him. He scooped it up and unwrapped it. For a moment, the amulet glowed in the moonlight. She had difficulty dragging her gaze away. "You will keep your word? You will leave me and my family alone?"

"I will not force you into the forest." He turned the amulet in his hand and then tossed it back to her. Without meaning to, she caught it. Another vision swept over her.

She stood high up, a breeze tugging at her long, curly hair. She dropped the robe from her shoulders. It puddled at her feet. She stepped out in the moonlight.

Larkin struggled to pull herself back from the vision, to stop the tide of images pushing into her head.

"Larkin, within the forest is safety. Remember that." He disappeared back into the shadows.

"Wait! You have to take this!" She held out the amulet for

him.

"Now you understand how important the amulet is; you will not lose it again."

After all he'd put her through to get the cursed thing, now he didn't want it? "I'll throw it in the river! I swear I will!"

"You will do no such thing," Maisy said. Jumping, Larkin turned to find Maisy watching her from the hilltop a dozen paces behind her. Her voice was deeper now, stronger. "You can't throw off the truth, even if you wanted to."

Larkin wasn't surprised to see the other girl. Maisy had been shadowing her since all this began. Larkin tightened her jaw. She would show them. She would show them both. Maisy following her, Larkin marched through the fields, coming to an overlook of the river. She gripped the amulet in her hand, cocked back her arm, and—

She couldn't do it. She tried again, but her hand fell to her side.

Maisy chuckled. "Once found, power is not so easily put aside." The other girl slipped away, back into the darkness.

Feeling betrayed by her own body, Larkin looked down at the amulet. She couldn't deny the awareness that tingled through her hand. It felt like power—something she'd never known before going into the forest. Hating herself even as she did it, she hid in the willows, hiked up her shift, and tied the amulet around her waist.

She returned home and slipped back inside, shivering as the warmth hit her. She hung up her cloak, slipped off her clogs, and eased onto her mat. As her eyes adjusted to the dark, she saw Nesha watching her. Larkin froze, her mind racing with excuses.

"I saw you," Nesha whispered. "I heard you talking with that man from the forest. Is he one of them, one of the beasts?"

Larkin's breath caught in her throat. "You don't understand."

"Explain it to me."

Larkin closed her eyes. "I made a deal with him in exchange for him to leave me—to leave our family—alone."

Nesha watched her, eyes glittering in the firelight. "What could we possibly have that the piper would want?"

Larkin felt a flush of relief. Nesha didn't know about the amulet resting against her stomach. She ached to tell her sister, but Nesha's earlier cruelty made her hesitate.

"You're not going to tell me."

Larkin clenched her teeth to keep the words behind them. With a huff, Nesha rolled over. Judging by her sister's too-quick breathing, she didn't sleep that night. Larkin could tell because she didn't either.

The next afternoon, Larkin cupped her hands and scooped kernels of their seed wheat from the coracle into their grinding stone and twisted the handle. After several minutes, flour fell like snow into a shallow stone dish. Nesha had already gathered the flour from this morning's grinding, mixed it with their sourdough starter, and set it in a pan over the fire. Mama lay on her mat, piled under nearly every blanket they had. Sela played with her rag dolls by the fire.

A rowdy, bellowing song started up from somewhere far away. A few beats later, she recognized her father's voice. He sounded drunk, though not as much as usual. The voice drew steadily closer until the door shoved open. Papa finished the song, arms upraised as if he expected applause.

They all stared at him. His bloodshot eyes landed on Larkin, and he pointed a wagging finger. "I always knew you were the clever one—getting pregnant by the lord's son is the fastest way to rise to the top of the world. Risky, but worth it if he's an honest sort. And we all know Bane is the honest sort." The last was said with a touch of bitterness. It *was* Bane who'd put Papa in the stocks for beating them.

He must have heard of Larkin's engagement at the tavern and proceeded to celebrate. He sat down beside her, smelling of sour beer and piss, and hooked an arm around her shoulder. "Now, what has he agreed to pay for your dowry?"

This was why Larkin had left the ring at Bane's house. If her father got his hands on it, she'd never see it again. "Nothing."

"Nothing?" He pushed back to his feet and wobbled toward the door. "Well then, we shall renegotiate!"

Larkin watched her father with her mouth drawn in a tight line. She'd never hated him more than this moment.

"She'll be safe from the forest—that's what matters." Mama stirred the pot, which contained the fish Larkin had caught. "Sela, go fetch us all some water, eh?"

Sela took the wooden cups, slipped on her too-big clogs, and stepped to the rain barrel out of sight of the doorway.

"There's opportunity in this." Papa mashed on his damp hat. "Daydon has plenty to spare. I'll go talk to him now and work something out."

Larkin scrambled after her father. "Papa, no."

He looked at her, aghast. "It's proper a man give a worthy dowry to his girl. I'm only asking for what's mine."

It wasn't his; it was Larkin's. A dowry was meant to support a wife and children if their provider died. "He gave me a ring," she admitted to keep him from humiliating her.

Sela returned and handed Papa his cup. He looked at it like he wasn't sure what to do with it. Larkin accepted her cup quietly.

"This ring," Papa said. "What did it look like?" When Larkin didn't answer, he wrapped his arm around her shoulder and whispered loudly, "Is it the ruby his mother used to wear?" He took her silence as a yes. A hard gleam came over his eyes. "Better than I could have hoped for. A couple months after the marriage, you will lose it." By lose, he meant give it to him. "Give me a year, and I'll have the ring back plus a nice little sack of coins for our investment." And by investment, he meant gambling.

She tried not to gag at the smell of his breath.

"I always knew you'd be the one to come through for our family. Just like your old man, always up to something with a big reward at the end."

Nesha snorted derisively. "That's not all she's been up to."

Larkin glared at her sister, who refused to meet her gaze as she checked the baking bread. Sela set Nesha's cup beside her and retreated to Mama's arms.

"What's that supposed to mean?" her father asked.

"Why don't you ask Larkin where she was last night?"

Papa chuckled and shook Larkin's shoulders like they were old friends. "Probably meeting her fiancé. Gotta keep him coming back for more, eh?"

Nesha folded her arms. "You tell him, Larkin, or I will."

Larkin silently pleaded with Nesha not to say anything more. "I was with Bane."

Papa chortled as he ladled fish stew from the cook pot. He sat down beside the fire.

Nesha took the bread off the fire and slammed the pan down on the bare floor. "The beast is twisting you, and you can't even see it."

Papa drank, ignoring the broth spilling down his beard. He wiped it with the back of his hand. His expression darkened. "Beast? What about the beast?"

Larkin let out a long breath and reined in her temper and her pride. *Nesha, please*, she mouthed.

Nesha threw down the rag she'd used to protect her hand from the handle, cut the circular bread, and tossed Larkin a piece. "You promised the druids to stay away from the forest. You broke that promise."

Papa's face went red as he looked down at Larkin. "What were you doing at the forest?"

The steaming bread burned Larkin's hand, but her pride wouldn't let her set it aside any more than she could tell them about the amulet or Denan. "Nesha's confused. It's where I was meeting Bane."

Nesha laughed bitterly. "She was meeting the piper. I saw them. So did Maisy. It's probably all over the town by now. Everyone's calling our family tainted. I wouldn't be surprised if Bane called off the wedding because of it."

Larkin's fist closed around the bread and smashed it into a lumpy mass that burned deep.

Papa's furious gaze settled on Larkin. "What have we always said about the forest, girl?"

Breathing hard, Larkin dumped the bread into her empty bowl. Her palm was red, but not blistered. "I was meeting—"

"The one person who would know the truth of that is Bane himself," Nesha said. "Shall I go ask him? Maybe I'll tell Garrot, see what he thinks."

Papa backhanded Nesha so hard she careened into the wall and slumped into a heap at its base. "You will keep your worthless little mouth shut." Papa kicked her middle. "You ruin this for us, and I'll break your good foot."

Larkin darted to her feet and hauled on his shoulder to try to pull him off. A beat later, Mama pulled on his other side. He threw them off and stood over Nesha. "You hear me?"

"Yes," Nesha choked out.

"Harben! Leave her alone!" Mama cried. Sela huddled under the blankets, keeping perfectly still like they'd taught her to when Papa was dangerous.

Papa wiped his nose as he backed away. Larkin positioned herself between her sister and her father. His glare transferred to her, and his arm cocked to the side. Seeing the hit coming, Larkin clenched her jaw so he wouldn't knock out any of her teeth.

The back of his hand flashed across her cheek, and her head jerked to the side. Her vision went black, then red. Blind, she blinked until she could see again. Her head swam, but the pain didn't come—not yet.

"You stay away from the forest, Larkin." Her father's voice was deathly quiet. "Or you won't live to see your wedding."

Mama snatched the pan and held it before her like a sword. The steaming bread fell to the dirt floor and broke apart. "Get out, Harben, and don't ever come back."

Papa eyed the hot pan, trying to see a way around it. "You've tried to divorce me before, Pennice. But the druids never granted it, because they know there's nothing wrong with smacking some sense into your womenfolk."

"Which is why they put you in the stocks when you tried to kill me?" Larkin's eyes locked with Papa's, the memory ripe between them, shame beneath the defiance. When she was twelve, Papa had gone into a rage and thrown her into the river —only, she couldn't swim. She struggled, just under the surface, her lungs aching for air. When the world started to go soft, a hand reached for her and pulled her to safety—Bane's hand.

Larkin balled her fists. "I'll never give you that ring, nor speak to you again. I swear it, *Harben*." She would never call him Papa again.

Harben ground his teeth, and she knew he'd hit her again if Mama wasn't between them with a hot pan.

"Larkin is marrying into the most powerful family in Hamel," Mama said. "How do you think her fiancé will feel about her bruised face on their wedding day?"

At this, Harben hesitated. "She's pregnant. I had to discipline her."

The pan in Mama's hand faltered, and she breathed out, "Just go."

Harben considered her for a moment before he stalked out into the rain, slamming the door behind him. Sela cried softly.

Larkin spat blood onto the fire.

As the smell of burning blood filled the hut, Mama knelt beside Nesha, hands fluttering over the bruises already forming on her face and arms. "Is anything broken?"

Panting, Nesha pushed herself up to a sitting position, one hand wrapped around her ribs.

Larkin glared down at the sister who'd just betrayed her. "Why?" she asked, venom in her voice.

Nesha pushed to her feet, kicking the bread on the floor. "Because someone has to beat some sense into you!"

And instead, Harben had beaten Nesha. "I told you," Larkin said. "I had to go."

"Stop it, both of you!" Mama said, one hand on her back, her eyes screwed shut.

Nesha made an exasperated sound and took down her cloak. Larkin stalked after her. "Where are you going?"

"Out," Nesha said.

"Nesha, please. I need you," Mama said.

Without a backward glance, Nesha left. Larkin snatched her shoes, determined to go after her sister.

"Larkin," Mama said, and Larkin didn't miss the betrayal in her voice. "Why?"

Larkin faltered. "He would have taken me during the crucible, but I'd given his amulet away. He promised if I got it back, he would leave us alone."

Mama went to Sela, gathering her into her arms and shushing her. Her brow furrowed in thought. "Stick with the story you gave me—you were meeting with Bane. Do you think he'll agree to it?"

Larkin nodded.

"Good. Find him and tell him the truth, and what he must say if asked, then find Nesha and bring her back here. Take Sela with you."

"Because Nesha listens to me so well?"

"My water broke this morning. My pains have been growing stronger all day. I need Nesha to help me deliver the baby."

Larkin stiffened. "But ... Now?"

Mama grunted in pain. "Children are experts at bad timing."

"Why didn't you say anything?"

"Because I didn't!" Mama snapped.

Sela clung to Mama as if she sensed something was wrong. "I stay."

Larkin swung on her damp cloak, noticing how musty it smelled. She forced a smile for Sela. "Want to see Red's puppies again?"

Sela's gaze turned wary. "I named one Socks."

Larkin held out the girl's cloak for her. "I bet Bane would let you name all of them."

Sela scrambled for her clogs. Properly dressed, Sela headed toward the door but faltered and turned back. "Mama?"

Mama gave a strained smile. "When you come back, you'll have a little sister to hold."

That seemed to do it for Sela. She opened the door and marched out into the rain. Larkin paused at the threshold. "You'll be all right until I get back?"

Mama breathed out, her hands kneading her back. "Hurry."

CHAPTER 12

BIRTH

Larkin pounded on Bane's door, listened for steps, and pounded again.

Finally, Venna answered, wiping a flour-whitened hand on her apron. "Larkin?"

"Bane. Where is he?"

"Puppies," Sela said.

Venna backed into the house. "He's not here. What's wrong?"

"Mama's gone into labor. I have to find Bane and Nesha. Can you watch Sela?"

Venna's eyes widened. "Of course."

"What's the meaning of this?"

Larkin looked up to see Lord Daydon leaning against the doorframe of his bedroom, panting.

"Oh!" Venna cried. "Master, you aren't ready to be out of bed. Let me—"

He waved her off and sat at the table. Daydon eyed Larkin's

cheek, which was no doubt swollen and bruised. To her relief, he didn't ask questions. Instead, he turned to Venna. "Weren't you making an apple pie? Little girls should have apple pie." He winked at Sela.

Venna shot Larkin a questioning look, but she knew when she'd been dismissed. She scooped up Sela and took her into the kitchen.

Daydon studied Larkin as she shifted uneasily. The whole town had turned against her. Why hadn't Daydon? "Why are you helping me?" *Why are you letting me marry your son?*

Daydon laced his hands over his belly. "Your mother did a great service to me once. She's a good woman—the best kind of woman. She doesn't deserve the hand that's been dealt her, and neither does her daughter." Larkin didn't understand how much she'd needed a little kindness from someone until then. Daydon's voice softened. "He went to the apothecary to fetch more medicine."

Nodding, Larkin turned to hide the tears brimming in her eyes and hurried outside. She tucked her hair out of sight in her hood and hustled through the town, head down. For once grateful for the rain that drove everyone inside, Larkin stepped into the apothecary and searched the small shop for any sign of Bane. He wasn't there.

She stepped up to the counter. "Have you seen Bane?"

Standing at the back shelves, the apothecary froze at the sight of her, then moved toward the counter. "I don't care if you are marrying the lord's son, you're forest cursed. Stay out of my shop." He leaned over the counter. "And if you know what's good for you, you'll stay out of the town too."

Larkin stumbled back as if she'd been slapped. "I passed the crucible."

"Passed or was released?"

"May the forest take you," she hissed at him. She stomped outside and glanced up and down the mud-churned streets. Normally, she would ask someone for help. Under the circumstances, that was clearly out of the question. She needed to find Bane so they could get their stories straight, and she still needed to find Nesha to help with the birth. What if Larkin couldn't find either in time? What if Mama was in trouble?

At the sounds of chatter and laughter from within the tavern across the street, she hesitated. Surely, Harben would help. After all, Mama was having his child. Crossing the street, she glanced within. Apparently, the streets were empty because everyone had escaped the miserable weather to come here. She searched the patrons' faces through the wavering glass, stilling at the sight of Harben.

He looked so carefree and happy that at first she didn't recognize him. He laughed with a group of men, slapping one of them on the back. The widow Raeneth rounded the table, refilling drinks as she went. Larkin watched as she and Harben latched gazes, her hand resting protectively on her rounded stomach—though her husband had been dead some three years. Something intimate and forbidden passed between them.

Larkin stepped back, her fists balled at her sides, anger turning her blood to steam. Before she could think better of it, she shoved through the door, words burning upon her tongue. But before she could voice them, a voice shouted, "The forest take you, Harben."

Bane burst into the room through the kitchen. The constable trailed behind him. Bane was soaked through, his expression murderous. He crossed the room in two strides and slammed his fist into Harben's face. Her father toppled backward over his chair, Bane on top of him, fists slamming down. Larkin surged forward—to help him or stop him, she wasn't sure—but the men at her father's table were faster. It took the constable and three others to pull Bane off, and he was still lunging and cursing.

Larkin shoved through until she stood before Bane. His eyes locked on her swollen cheek. "I'll kill him. I swear I will."

The chaos settled like the silence after a thunder strike.

"Seems all Harben's girls want to be filled with a baby, eh?" someone said. A familiar voice, though she wasn't sure who said it.

Another laughed. "Too bad they're all cursed."

Fuming, Larkin whirled to see who spoke. No one would meet her gaze.

Harben wobbled to his feet and spat out a tooth. He looked at Bane. His mouth twisted with hate. "I don't care how much you're worth, boy. You'll not bed a daughter of mine."

Bane huffed in disgust. "The wedding's going to be hard to protest from the stocks." He nodded to the constable who'd followed him across the room. "Lock him up for excessively beating his daughters."

Larkin stiffened. How had Bane known ... unless Nesha had gone to him?

"It's my right to discipline my girl for her wanton ways," Harben protested as the constable rounded on him.

Larkin cringed and forced herself not to drop her head in shame. There were more important things than her reputation right now. "Mama's having the baby. I have to find Nesha."

Bane ignored her. "It's forbidden to hit a woman with child."

The constable dragged Harben away—the word of the lord's son standing as judge and jury. She watched. Perhaps it was worth telling the whole town she was pregnant if it meant her father was punished for what he'd done to Nesha. But Larkin mentally stumbled at the thought of her sister—how she'd betrayed Larkin's trust.

"Leave him alone!" Raeneth cried, trying to pry the constable off.

He glanced down at her rounded belly. "Fornication is punishable too." He motioned for her to precede him. All the fight drained out of her.

Larkin turned her back on them and pushed outside, dragging Bane with her. Once they were out of earshot, she whispered, "I was with you last night in the woods, if anyone asks."

"Where were you, really?"

"Returning that blasted amulet." She quashed her guilt at the fact that it now hung over her navel. Bane nodded. *More important things to worry about.* "Find Nesha. Make sure she gets back to the house. If she won't go, tell her Mama is having the baby."

"I know where she is," he said. Nesha *had* gone to him for help. Good. At least she had some sense in her.

Larkin pulled up her muddy skirts and sprinted through the town and over the bridge, water bubbling around her ankles. Over the sound of the river, she could already hear her mother's pained cries.

CHAPTER

FLOOD AND BLOOD

Sometime after twilight, Larkin wiped the gore from the baby and laid her gently in her mother's arms. "What will you call her?"

Mama's face lit up with joy. "Brenna, after my great-great-grandmother."

"That's a pretty name."

Her mother suckled the child. "She was a determined woman—like this girl must be if she is to survive."

"Don't say such things," Larkin said. "She's a perfectly healthy baby. Everything will be fine."

"Papa won't like it," Nesha said.

Remembering what she'd seen at the tavern—the secret look her father had exchanged with a very pregnant Raeneth—Larkin bristled. "Why should we care what Harben thinks? He a lazy, no-good, lying, stealing, cheating ..." She sputtered as she ran out of insulting names. "I hate him! I hate him, and I'll never speak to him again!" She deflated, all the fight draining out of her. She'd lost something—something that should have been hers, but it wasn't. It never would be.

Mama sighed in exasperation. "Nesha, take the afterbirth and bury it beneath the Curse Tree. Tie up a ribbon asking the forest to curse your sister."

Nesha smiled smugly at the honor. "Yes, Mama." She wrote on a bit of ribbon, took the bowl with the afterbirth, and disappeared outside.

"Larkin," Mama whispered. "How long have you known?"

Larkin washed her hands. "About what?"

"Raeneth." Larkin stiffened and turned to her mother in surprise. Tears slipped down Mama's drawn cheeks. "If she delivers a son, he will grant me a divorce."

More than anything in the world, Harben wanted a son, and he would throw the rest of them away to get one. Larkin should be past the hurt, but there it was—an icy, achy feeling that spread through her muscles. "Good. We're better off without him. I hope they beat him senseless." Fifty canings for infidelity, delivered over two days, plus whatever he got for beating them.

"He will take his caning, as you have, then petition for a divorce. He will get it and the land. I've taken care of you and Nesha, but the little ones ... I was hoping you and Bane would adopt the baby as your own. Perhaps take Sela as well. At least until I've saved up enough money to rent a room in a small house."

Larkin's mouth tightened into a thin line. "No. You will all come live with me and Bane. There is more than enough room in that old manor."

"What if Daydon doesn't agree?" Her mother's voice was very small.

Larkin took her mother's hands. "He's a good man, Mama. They both are."

Hope entered her mother's eyes for the first time in a long time. Larkin went about cleaning up. Nesha stomped back inside, soaked through. Larkin glanced at the sky behind her; dark wasn't fully upon them yet. She had time to stop in at the lord's house.

"That was fast," Mama said.

Larkin reached for her cloak. "I'll go talk to Daydon and pick up Sela."

"You won't be going anywhere tonight," Nesha said as she wrung out her own cloak. "The bridge has washed away. I buried the afterbirth on this side of the river. The curse will have to wait."

Larkin jerked open the door to see for herself. In the dying light, she could make out the churning river with no line of old, creaky wood dividing it in two.

Mama groaned. "Blast. Now we'll have to use the coracle every time we need to go into town. We'll worry about that in the morning. For now, let's get some sleep."

Mama gave Larkin a look that said she'd better not tell Nesha what they'd talked about.

From her place beside the door, Larkin woke to a cold, wet shock to her right side. Gasping, she bolted upright. In the ember light, she saw black water rushing in from under the door. Nesha yelped from beside her and sat up, water dripping from her hair. The fire hissed steam before gutting out, leaving them in total darkness.

"Girls, pack up everything in the coracle. We need to get to higher ground," Mama said.

What remained of the wheat seed was already inside. Working blindly, Larkin and Nesha scooped up the remainder of their food and some of their bedding and piled it in the little boat as the water rose above their ankles. Thank the ancestors that Sela was safely with Bane and Venna.

Larkin took hold of the mooring line, felt for her cloak, and tried to push the door open. Water pushed back. "Nesha, help me."

Working together, they shoved the door open. More water rushed inside and settled around their shins. Something hot touched Larkin's calf, and she yelped and jumped back. The remnants of their fire floated about her legs, the bigger pieces still hot enough to burn. Larkin kicked them away.

She plunged outside and was soaked in seconds. She looked toward Hamel but saw no light to mark the town. No one would come for them. No one would even know they were in trouble until morning. "Wait inside, Mama. Nesha and I will find a way out."

They held the boat's rope and started toward the next highest hill. As they moved downhill, the water grew deeper and the current stronger. From behind Larkin came a splash, and Nesha sputtered and gasped. The rope went taut, and Larkin braced herself to keep the boat from being swept away. Nesha couldn't swim. She must have gone under and grabbed the boat to keep afloat.

Larkin towed them both back to the hut. "Go back to Mama. Take the boat with you." Their hands brushed in the dark as they exchanged the rope. Larkin circled the entire house, but the water was above her chest everywhere. She knew from experience the coracle wouldn't hold two people. They were trapped on a rapidly shrinking island. It might be hours before anyone noticed their plight, and perhaps longer still before anyone came for them.

Moving up the slope, Larkin splashed through water up to her knees back to the house. "Stay here until the water's too deep, then climb on the roof."

"What are you doing?" Nesha asked in surprise.

"I'm going for help."

Mama gripped her arm. "No."

"Mama," Larkin said soothingly. "Only one of us can fit in the boat at a time, and the rain hasn't let up."

Mama gripped Larkin's hands, her voice shaking with tears. "The water's moving too fast. You won't know where you're going."

"The current will move me downriver. I just have to cross the channel." Larkin gently untangled her mother's fingers. Undoing her cloak, she wrapped it around Mama's shoulders. Even when wet, the wool was warm, and she shuddered without it. "I'm the only one who can swim." To her sister, she said, "Hold it steady while I climb in." Nesha gripped the sides while Larkin slid in one foot and then the other. She took the single paddle. "Let go."

Instantly, the river caught hold of Larkin and carried her downriver, to the west. Instead of fighting the current, she paddled hard to cross the river. If she could reach the opposite shore, she could hike back to Hamel. They could launch a bigger boat to fetch her mother and sisters. But first she had to keep from being toppled over in such a lightweight craft, and then she had to make it to the opposite shore before she crashed into the Forbidden Forest.

The craft bobbed along, picking up speed the closer she came to the main channel. There, she careened down a dip and back up again. The boat launched into the air, hitting the water hard. The craft spun, old leather straining. She slammed into something. The boat came apart beneath her. Cold enveloped her and drowned out all sound. She hurtled through something that whipped at her. With no sense of up or down, she scrambled to grab hold of whatever it was. Branches? She must have already hit the Forbidden Forest. Something struck her leg. A blaze of pain stabbed her side. She was going to die. Around her waist, the amulet slapped her stomach. She grabbed it through her clothes. *Help me!*

A vision opened, superimposed over the darkness. Below

her, a small bird left the nest for the first time, shooting away from her feet. She bent in half and kicked after the bird, though the branches and debris snatched at her.

Wind wove through her fingers. Her face popped up, and she tasted sweet air. She gulped it down as she struggled to keep her head above water. Branches scratched at her. Her hands clawed at the water as she managed to catch one. It broke under her grip.

"Help!" she screamed.

The river pulled her back under. Something caught her ankle. The current was so strong she couldn't kick free. Her hands scrambled through the air above her head.

Suddenly, something fibrous was in her hand—something like a rope. She grabbed on with both hands. The rope went taut, hauling her toward her trapped foot and against the current. It was all Larkin could do to hang on. And then she was free. She took a desperate breath as the current whipped her around like a fish on the end of a line.

"Hold on," Denan cried.

Seconds later, his hand gripped hers and plucked her out of the river and against his strong chest. Completely spent, Larkin collapsed. Denan's trembling hands patted her as if searching for injuries. "Ancestors, Larkin, you have an uncanny knack for nearly getting yourself killed."

Larkin found she couldn't dredge up any more fear—it was already spent. "You said help would come. And it did." The amulet had saved her. Denan had saved her. Her hands reached out and touched the rough surface beneath their tangled bodies—a tree. She was in the forest somewhere. The water must have flooded out the trees. "How did you know where to find me?"

"Besides the screaming? The amulet drew me in."

She closed her eyes. Was that it, then? After all she'd done, she was trapped again. "You have to let me go. My mother and sisters—they're stuck on our rooftop." Even as she asked, she knew he would never release her.

"I know."

She stiffened and turned to face him. "They'll die if I don't get help."

He pushed to his feet. "Which is why you must save them."

"You're letting me go—again?"

He chuckled bitterly. "I make a very bad kidnapper. Also, I promised never to force you. Say what you will about me, Larkin, but I keep my promises."

She tried to look around but could see next to nothing in the dark. "Where are we?"

"The river flooded the forest. We're in the boughs of a tree along the bank. Keep up with me. Step where I step." His hand found hers, and he tugged her along after him.

With Denan's help, she managed to cross the branches of an enormous tree. He moved with the grace of a cat. Larkin began to make shapes out of the shadows. Dawn was coming. Finally, they reached the shallows. Denan splashed down and held his arms out to her. She dropped to him and splashed in water up to her knees. Taking her hand again, he led her out of the water and onto dry ground.

She started toward Hamel, but he didn't let go. "I don't suppose it would do any good to make you swear to come back?"

His form was a dark contrast to the forest behind him. She almost lied to him—what if he changed his mind and refused to let her go?—but then she shook her head. "No."

He sighed and released her. "Well then, fly away, little bird."

She left the forest at a jog. She would have gone faster but she still couldn't see the ground. Finally, she was able to make out the faintest square of light—a window illuminated by embers. She reached an outlying farm and banged on the door with her fist. "Please help! Please!"

She didn't stop pounding until someone yanked open the door. To her shock Kenjin, Alorica's father, stood before her. "What is the meaning of this?" he demanded.

"Our house is underwater. My mother and sisters are trapped. Please, you have to find the men with fishing boats and go fetch them."

Kenjin looked down his nose at her. He either didn't believe her or didn't care.

"The river," his wife, Patrina, said from upstairs. "It's covered all the lower fields."

Kenjin pushed past Larkin and peered at the moving river not more than two-dozen paces from his own front door. The dim light revealed the river swollen to more than five times its normal size. The water ate up fields and swaths of the trees where it entered and exited the forest. "The embankment didn't hold," he growled.

"Please," Larkin begged. "You can't leave two women and a baby to die."

His jaw hardened. "Boys, fetch my horse." Kenjin shoved his feet into his boots. "Quickly now!"

Larkin sagged in relief as Alorica's two teenage brothers rushed to the stable and brought out a heavy-boned draft horse. Kenjin swung onto the animal bareback. Without looking back, he tore down the road toward Hamel.

"You might as well come inside," Patrina said as she lit a candle. "Alorica, fetch some dry clothes."

Alorica glared at Larkin.

"Thank you," Larkin said, "but I have to make sure they're all right." Hurrying after Kenjin, Larkin glanced back toward the forest. She could feel Denan's eyes on her, watching, waiting.

CHAPTER

SECRETS

Larkin woke not knowing where she was. A wardrobe crouched in the corner and a small stand hovered by the bed. She had collapsed in Caelia's room after her mother and sisters were rescued. On the stand was a tray with some bread, a cup of water, and an enormous ruby ring. Coming fully awake, she reached out, took the ring, lay back, and held it up. She slipped it on her finger and admired the bright slash of color in the dreary gray light of a rainy morning.

But lying in the bed of one of the Taken and wearing a dead woman's ring made her uneasy. Sitting up on the straw tick mattress, she downed the water and tore into Venna's soft bread. She chewed as she stood, surprised at how much her legs hurt. She glanced down to find them covered in welts and bruises.

Wearing her ragged shift, she stepped to the window, the glass smeared with rain. Outside, the river glutted itself on her family's fields. She searched for the place her home should have been. There wasn't so much as a ripple. She studied the dark line of green forest beyond. She did not fear it as much as she once had. After all, Denan had saved her life. He had her in his grasp, and he let her go—again. Though he was certainly still a villain, he was a human one.

She turned away from the forest. Munching on the bread, she looked around for her clothes. Nothing. She opened the wardrobe, hoping to find them inside. Instead, she found Caelia's old dresses. She reached out and ran a finger down the finely woven cloth, remembering the way the girl who'd worn them had burned so bright and hot that Larkin had been afraid to touch her.

Pulling back her fingers, she wrapped herself in the blanket, poked her head out, and peered up and down the hallway. There were four rooms—Bane's was right next to hers on the left. The one across from Larkin was empty, the door open. Through the window, she could make out the frantic scurrying of townspeople.

Curious, she slipped inside and peered out. Floodwater had spilled over the trenches the townspeople had built and invaded the first row of houses. People carried goods—bedding, furniture, and baskets and pots of food—stuffing them into buildings higher up. She caught sight of Bane, his dark head rising above the others as he directed people carrying goods up to his own barn.

"I thought I heard someone." Larkin turned to find Venna standing behind her, her gaze catching on the ring. "Bane threw away your old dress—said it wasn't even any good for rags. You're to wear Caelia's clothes."

Larkin fidgeted with the ring. *Wearing Caelia's dresses will not make her fate mine*, she tried to reassure herself. "And Daydon is all right with that?"

"He keeps mentioning that his grandchild needs taking care of," Venna answered without looking up.

Larkin hated this lie more with every passing day. Moving

with a confidence she didn't feel, she went back to the room, opened the armoire, and pulled down a dress and shift. The cloth's movement released the musty smell of something shut away for too long. Venna turned her back as Larkin pulled them on, pretending that her skin wasn't crawling to have them off.

"My mama?" she asked as she tied the belt.

"Still sleeping, as is Nesha."

"How's the baby?"

"She seems fine."

Relieved, Larkin slipped on a pair of leather boots that laced up past her ankle. They were supple and well made. She hurried down the ladder, Venna following. In the kitchen, bread was rising on the table, more bread cooling beside it.

Venna cut another slice for Larkin and opened the door to the cellar. "There's a ham the lord said we could have."

Unable to resist, Larkin tore into the bread. Venna came back up with a chunk of ham the size of her fist, as well as some carrots. Larkin watched as she cubed the ham and rinsed the carrots. "Why are you helping me?"

Venna sliced the carrots into thin rings. "Because you're my friend, Larkin."

Not the kind of friends that owed each other anything. But Venna didn't really have any other friends. Maybe she needed one as much as Larkin did. "Thank you."

Venna smiled shyly. She dumped the carrots into a pot and added potatoes she'd cut earlier. "I need more water from the well. Be right back." She pulled on her cloak and slipped outside.

Larkin enjoyed the smells of baking bread and the delicious heat coming from the hearth. The quiet was soon interrupted by footsteps and a door opening and closing. Moments later, voices came from the dining room.

"Perhaps not in Hamel." Daydon sounded out of breath.

Rising, Larkin crept closer and peered out the not-quite-closed door. Bane hung his father's cloak by the fire and pulled out his chair. Daydon sat heavily. His hands rested atop a new cane.

"What do you mean?" Bane's voice was tight, like a rope about to snap.

Daydon took a moment to answer. "Landra. The lord is a friend of mine. I'm sure he can, discreetly, find her a job—just until things settle down."

Bane hung his own cloak and then braced his hands on the back of a chair. "Is that really necessary?"

"You heard the way the townspeople are talking about her. Horgen and Horace are blaming her for their family's sickness, and they're not the only ones. The town has turned against her. It's not safe for any of them in Hamel anymore. Her mother and sisters will have to go as well."

"I can protect them."

"Not from the druids, you can't." When Bane didn't answer, Daydon went on, "Bane, saving her won't bring back Caelia."

Bane sat down hard on the chair and leaned over his folded hands. "What about our baby?" Larkin was impressed by how smoothly the deception left his mouth.

"There isn't anything here for her or the child but heart-ache."

"I'm here. And I thought you wanted this baby!"

"Of course I do, but at this rate, she won't live to deliver."

Larkin flinched, then rested her forehead against the wall. She didn't want to leave Bane, not when he'd finally started looking at her the way she'd always wanted him to. The moment she left, Alorica would dig her claws into him. But her family ... she wouldn't risk their safety, not even for Bane.

Daydon's head tipped back as if he'd realized something. "You haven't told her?"

Bane stood back up. "What good would that do?"

"Secrets are dangerous things to keep."

Bane paced the length of the table, his brow drawn. What secret was he keeping from her? Her hand strayed to the amulet around her waist, her fingers pressing it against the skin below her navel.

"I'll go with them," Bane said. "They'll need someone to look after them."

"Pennice can take care of herself and her daughters. They don't need you. I do."

Bane braced himself against a chair. "When?"

"Tomorrow morning, first light. And, Bane, the ring ..." The implication was there. Daydon wanted it back.

"She's keeping the ring."

"But—"

"She's keeping it," Bane growled.

Daydon pursed his lips but nodded in agreement.

Feeling numb, Larkin backed into the kitchen and leaned against the table. They were sending them away. By the way Daydon talked ... she wasn't sure they were ever coming back. Maybe he was right. It would be safer for them away from all this. Perhaps she could even slip out of Denan's grasp. But Bane ... What would happen to their engagement?

She wasn't sure how long she'd been standing there when Venna stepped back inside, bucket in hand. The voices from the other room ceased, followed by footsteps and a door swinging shut.

Larkin pushed herself away from the table. "I better see to my mother."

"Here, bring her some bread." Venna loaded a plate with bread slathered with butter and jam.

Taking it, Larkin plastered a smile on her face and stepped out of the kitchen. Daydon looked at her, his expression sad.

"I'm glad to see you looking better," she said with forced cheer.

He nodded. "Your mother is awake."

Taking the hint, Larkin slipped into the bedroom. Sela lay on the bed, her thumb in her mouth and her eyes closed. Mama sat up next to her and nursed the baby.

"How are you feeling?" Larkin asked.

"Hungry. And Brenna needs changing."

Larkin wanted to tell her about the secret Bane was keeping from her and the fact they were going to have to leave Hamel, but at the sight of her mother's bloodshot eyes, she decided against it. She handed her the plate of bread. "Venna's fixing supper. I can wash the swaddling."

Mama nodded gratefully.

Larkin hesitated before asking her next question. "Have you seen Nesha?"

Mama wouldn't meet her gaze. "She's taken a job in town. She'll move into the servant's room tomorrow."

The silence hung heavy between them, interrupted by the soft sounds of the baby sucking. Larkin slipped outside, did the washing, and brought it back inside to dry on strings crisscrossing the kitchen. At supper, Larkin's family ate in the dining room with Daydon. Nesha was still working; she wasn't expected back until after dark. Venna served them soup and bread. Mama sat on a cushioned rocking chair, her legs stretched out before her, meal on a tray beside her.

When Venna retreated to the kitchen, Daydon faced Mama. "Larkin is no longer safe in Hamel."

Mama's face tightened. "Garrot said she had two days. She should be safe after tonight."

"It's not Garrot I'm afraid of," Daydon said gently. "The townsfolk have turned against her. I promised you I'd take care of her, and I mean to keep that promise. Right now, that means she must leave. I'm sending you and the rest of your daughters with her. There is nothing holding you here, and I'm not convinced you're much safer than Larkin is."

Brenna fussed. Mama leaned back, patting her. "I suppose

that means breaking the engagement with Bane?"

Daydon took a long breath and let it out. "She'll keep the ring as a token of their continued engagement, and when things settle down, she'll return and everything will proceed as planned."

"And if it doesn't settle down?" Mama asked.

Daydon made a helpless gesture. "What do you want me to do, Pennice? Am I to give up my position as lord? My son? What else do you want from me?"

She cleared her throat. "What of my husband?"

Daydon was silent for far too long. "It took some persuading, but Garrot granted a divorce in exchange for lenience for Harben's sentence."

Larkin felt an uneasy relief—why would Garrot help her father? Mama's eyes fluttered closed. When she opened them again, her face was resigned. "Is it safe for Larkin to travel along the forest road?" The passages between cities and towns were narrow and surrounded by the Forbidden Forest.

Daydon visibly relaxed. "Bane will accompany you to Landra. It's much larger than Hamel. You should blend in fine. Would you like me to send Venna to inform Nesha to be here first thing in the morning?"

"Nesha will be staying in Hamel," Mama said. "She'll move in with her master tomorrow."

Daydon's brow furrowed, and he leaned forward, then seemed to think better of asking and started into his soup. Larkin felt her mother's scrutiny. They ate in silence for the rest of the meal and spent the evening packing everything they owned for the trip, Larkin silently listening for the sound of Bane's arrival.

He never came.

Larkin woke as the front door opened. Sitting up from the dining room table, she rubbed her eyes and saw Bane's shadowed outline by the door.

"You should be in bed."

"You've been avoiding me."

He hesitated, then came to sit beside her. The arm that rested against hers was damp. "Making up for lost time. I won't be here tomorrow to help with the flooding."

"You're still avoiding me."

He didn't bother denying it again. "Larkin, this isn't a banishment. As soon as things settle down, you'll come back and we'll be married."

She looked at him sideways. "Is that what you want—to marry me?"

He hesitated a beat too long. "Of course it is."

"And what of our *baby*?"

He sighed. "You'll have to lose it."

Larkin wanted to ask him about the secrets his father had mentioned, but that was only fair if she told him her secrets. He leaned toward her. His fingers tipped her jaw as he leaned down for a kiss. She debated pulling away. But after tomorrow, she wasn't sure when she would see him again, if at all. So she stretched up, their lips meeting in a kiss that softened the brittleness inside her. But it wasn't long before the kiss was seasoned with the salt of her tears.

Bane pulled back. "Why are you crying?"

Because that kiss tasted like goodbye. Because she had only ever been sure of two things: the forest was evil and he was everything good in the world. Now, she was not sure of either.

But she didn't say any of that. She squeezed his hand and went upstairs. She sat on the bed's edge for a long time and stared at the ring in her hand. Then she slipped it off and left it on the bedside table, having no intention of ever picking it up again.

The music started that night, full of longing and hope and warmth. It spread through Larkin like sunshine, but it did not speak to her as the other songs had. She pushed herself up and went to the window. It had finally stopped raining, the moon bright above. Below, the town was shrouded in mist, water lapping against the buildings the only sound. She shot a glare toward the forest. Denan's song wasn't going to work this time.

She turned to go back to bed, but a figure wading through the floodwaters made her pause. Thick, curly hair and a thistle-embroidered cloak. Alorica—it had to be. But girls were never supposed to be out this late.

Larkin struggled with the rusty catch on the window before finally managing to shove it open. "Alorica? Where are you going?" The other girl didn't so much as turn around. Larkin called again, louder. Alorica faded from view. Larkin pulled the window shut and hauled her dress over her head.

She hurried to Bane's room. "Alorica's out and she wouldn't answer when I called." She tugged on her boots. "Something's definitely wrong."

She moved to shut the door so he could get up and dress, but Bane didn't stir. She hesitated, before stepping fully into the room. "Bane, get up!" When he didn't respond, she went to his bed and shook his shoulders. Still nothing. Taking his pitcher of water, she dumped the contents over his head. His deep sleep breathing continued.

Larkin dashed down the stairs, grabbed her cloak, and plunged into the mists. The vapors trailed cold fingers along her cheeks, droplets sliding down the collar of her dress. At the hill's base, she splashed in the floodwater that snaked past her thighs, but she could no longer see the other girl.

"Alorica!" she called. In answer, the mists swirled about her, impenetrable and dark. She turned this way and that, unsure what to do. But she knew where Alorica was headed. Moving as fast as she could, she left the town and started up the rise, leaving behind a bit more of the flood with each step. She emerged from the mist, though tendrils of it still snaked up the hill. Alorica was before her, a dark outline against the even darker sky.

"Alorica," she huffed as she hurried to catch up. "Where are you going?"

The girl didn't answer, didn't even acknowledge Larkin's presence.

"Are you hearing the music? The heartsong?" It was too dark to make out her expression, but Larkin could imagine the longing, the hope. "It's a lie, Alorica! You can resist it, as I have. You don't have to be lured into the forest."

When Alorica still didn't answer, Larkin reached out and took hold of her arm. No reaction. She stepped in front of the girl. Alorica simply stepped around her. Larkin looked around for help, but they were alone in the darkness. Everything was eerily silent. Even the rain had stopped its incessant pattering. A fire catching within her, Larkin stepped in front of Alorica and blocked her path. When Alorica tried to step around her, Larkin blocked her again. After the third time, Alorica shoved her and continued.

Heart pounding, chest heaving, Larkin watched as another girl emerged from the mist, gaze fixed on the Forbidden Forest—Venna. Larkin's hands flew to her mouth. "No," she said from behind her fingers. She stumbled after her. "Kenjin! Patrina! Come save your daughter!"

No one came.

"Daydon! Vyder! Rimoth! Garrot! Someone, please!" Her voice fell away, leaving only aching silence. Larkin was helpless and alone. *Ancestors help me!*

She ran to Venna, wrapping both her arms around the girl. Perhaps she could knock her out, tie her up, something. Venna whirled, delivering a blow to Larkin's head that dropped her feet out from under her. Ears ringing, she watched the two girls, not knowing how to stop them without hurting them. They were converging on one point. Though she was too far away to make out the details, she knew what it was—the Curse Tree.

Pushing to her feet, Larkin stared into the dark shadows. "Denan!" she called, her voice absorbed by the forest. The tree before her rustled, and a dark figure dropped down. Moments later, two more joined the first. She backed up a step, wondering if even now she was close enough for them to grab her. "Leave them alone." Her voice shook with anger and fear.

Denan came toward her. "The heartsong calls to them, Larkin. They're ours now."

Tears of helplessness welled in her eyes. She blinked them away. Denan's words shook her to her core. The visions she'd had. *Running along branches the size of a river. Diving into turquoise water. Following a bird to safety.* She staggered back from the tethers that bound her to him. The closer she came to the forest, the more she felt those tethers, and the less she wanted to break free. "You've put a spell on me, put these lies in my head."

He continued toward her. "What cruelty have you known that you would believe that before the truth?"

She gritted her teeth, her hands fisted at her sides. "You're taking them to punish me.

You promised to leave me alone—swore to me you always kept your word."

"And so I will." He turned his back on her, disappearing inside the forest. Alorica and Venna were already gone.

Larkin whirled and ran back the way she'd come. She reached Vyder's door first, pounding against it. It shifted open. She pushed inside and found Vyder snoring by the fire. She shook him, begged him to help her. She even slapped his face. His snores never paused. She sat back on her heels. She'd never felt so helpless, so useless.

Vyder had lost everything, and he didn't even know it yet.

Sobbing and disoriented, she stumbled back outside. She pounded on doors and screamed for the townspeople to wake up until her knuckles were bloody and her throat raw. No one heard her. No one came. She reached the manor and rushed into Bane's room. She shook him and screamed and cried, but he may as well have been dead. Perhaps it was she who was dead, and she only hovered over him like a ghost.

Shaking, she backed into a corner and slid down, waiting for the spell to release him.

CHAPTER

TRAITORS

"Larkin?" Bane rolled out of the bed, eyes drawn with worry. He wore his long shirt. He hurried to push his feet into his trousers. "What's wrong? Why are you all muddy? Why am I wet?"

Larkin was still wedged in the corner, her arms wrapped tight around her legs. "The pipers took them." Her throat ached. "No one would wake up. No one heard me scream."

His eyes took in the empty pitcher lying by his bed. His hands pulled through his damp hair, and he swore softly. "Who?"

She couldn't say their names out loud. If she did, then they were really gone. She rocked back and forth. From outside came the distant ring of shouts. Bane glanced out the window and whatever he saw sent him staggering back. He crouched before her. "We have to get out of here. Grab your things. Hurry."

Daydon appeared at the door, throwing his cloak over his shoulders. "There's nowhere for her to run."

Bane frowned. "Landra—"

"You think the townspeople wouldn't hunt you down?" He shook his head as if answering his own question. His studied Larkin. "Where were you?"

"I tried to stop them," she said, voice trembling.

"Who?" Daydon asked.

"Venna and Alorica." Their names caught in her throat, leaving an imprint she could never wash away.

Daydon grunted. "Clean yourself up and all the muddy footprints. You were here all night. You never went out." He disappeared. "Pennice! Hurry! A mob is coming!" Movement sounded from the bedroom below.

Bane hauled her up. "Larkin, why were the girls taken but not you?" She finally looked at him. He softened at whatever he saw on her face. "I ask because that's what the villagers will want to know."

"He promised to leave me be in exchange for the amulet." Which wasn't something they could ever explain to the towns-people. Larkin tried to pull herself together. "The others couldn't resist the heartsong." If a mob was coming, she wasn't the only one in danger. Something in her hardened. They would not hurt her family. She wouldn't let them.

The shouts grew louder, closer. Bane's mouth thinned, and he hurried out the door. "Clean up. Quickly!" She followed him downstairs and into the kitchen, where he shoved his feet into his boots. He tugged his coat on. "Lock the door after me and don't open it for anyone else." Bane drew up and looked behind her. Larkin turned to see Nesha staring at him. "Help her, Nesha, please."

Mama ushered Sela up the stairs and handed the baby to Nesha. "Hide them." Nesha turned away without a backward glance. Larkin watched her go. How could her sister abandon her right now, when she needed her most? Yes, they'd been fighting, but they were sisters—loyal to each other, above all else.

Throat thick with tears she refused to shed, Larkin stripped out of her soiled dress and dunked it in a barrel they used for wash water. She scrubbed the night's evidence from the fabric, wringing her screams from the folds, and set it before the kitchen fire to eliminate the last traces of her horror. She borrowed another of Caelia's dresses and came downstairs to see her mother scrubbing the floor. Larkin dropped down to work beside her. Outside, the crowd grew louder—grumbles and angry mutterings intermixed with shouts.

"What do they want?" her mother whispered.

Me. They've come for me. She couldn't retell it, not again.

Upstairs, the baby began to cry.

"The little ones—" Larkin began.

"Nesha will protect them."

Larkin had always been the strong one, the one who made things better. But now, everything she touched seemed cursed. She scrubbed harder. When the mob came, they couldn't find mud. The baby screamed louder, wails counterbalanced by the mob outside.

Someone pounded hard on the door, making Larkin jump. She froze, one foot on the bottom stair. She wanted to dash upstairs and hide, but where could she go? She tiptoed to the curtains and peered out, careful not to disturb the fabric. Garrot, Hunter, and Rimoth stood in front of what appeared to be the entire town, armed with pitchforks, scythes, and axes. They wore anger and fear like a second skin, and all the anger was directed at her.

"Larkin," Garrot called. "Open the door."

She hadn't been seen yet. She swallowed hard. Where was Bane?

Mama frantically wiped up the last of the water and took both buckets, heading into the kitchen. "Don't answer it." Through the open door, Larkin watched as Mama pulled up the trapdoor and poured the muddy water onto the dirt floor of the cellar. "Go upstairs and hide. I'll deal with them."

"You can let us in or we can break down the door," Garrot said calmly.

Larkin would not put her family at risk, especially when it would do no good. "There's nowhere to run, Mama," she said softly.

"Larkin, no." Dropping the cellar door, Mama rushed to stop her.

Larkin hesitated a moment, her hand closed over the cool metal. She felt fragile, like the smallest breeze might send her caterwauling up the chimney and into the gray sky. *Bane, where are you?* Gathering up the shattered bits of her courage, Larkin cracked open the door to reveal a sliver of Garrot's dark eyes and unkempt hair.

"Larkin," Garrot said gently. "Let me in."

Larkin shook her head.

Garrot's hand shot through the crack. He forced the door open. Larkin didn't resist as he, Hunter, and Rimoth came inside. Mama planted herself before Larkin. Baby in her arms, Nesha appeared at the top of the stairs. Rimoth took up position before the kitchen. Limping, Hunter blocked the bedroom. Both had their hands on the knives at their belts, while Garrot paced before the front door like a wolf who smelled blood.

"Why couldn't you go into the forest like all the other girls?" Garrot muttered. "Why do you have to cause so much trouble?"

Larkin didn't think he was asking—more like he was chiding her. What she didn't understand was why. "I didn't cause any trouble."

He finally looked at her. "They're calling for your life, Larkin, demanding you burn at the stake. I must give them an answer. Two girls were taken last night. Do you know anything about it?"

"No!" Larkin burst out.

"I don't believe you," he said softly.

"She doesn't know," Mama said. "Now get out."

Garrot's gaze flicked to Nesha, and then he slipped inside the kitchen. When he came back, he held Larkin's mud-stained boots. "Why are your boots muddy, Larkin? Where have you been this morning? And why is there a dripping wet dress before the fire?"

Larkin wiped her sweating hands on the front of her dress. "Just out to the privy. I washed my dress, and it's drying."

He looked through the kitchen to the back window. "The way to the privy is paved with stones. Still lying?"

"I don't know anything," she whispered.

He stalked toward her. She backpedaled around the table. Rimoth took hold of Mama's arm and pushed her into the corner. "Stay out of this, Pennice."

Mama scowled. "Get out of my way, you filthy, conniving—"

"You've got three other girls," Hunter said over her as he came at Larkin from the other side of the table. "I suggest you think of them and not just Larkin."

Splitting her gaze between Hunter and Garrot, Larkin ended up with her back against the cold bricks of the mantle. Garrot spread his legs, his hands on either side of her head. Though no part of him touched her, she was boxed in all the same. "I'm not even sure the truth matters at this point," he said softly. "There are too many people who would see you dead."

Her mouth went dry, and her throat closed. She couldn't breathe, couldn't think. "You mean to kill me?"

"If I must," Garrot answered.

"You leave my daughter alone." Mama tried to shove past Rimoth, but he pinned her against the wall.

Where were Bane and Daydon? Neither would allow this. … Of course. They weren't here because they couldn't be. Larkin's jaw hardened. "Where are Bane and Daydon?"

"Somewhere they can't interfere," Garrot said.

The color bled out of Mama's face. "Please. Just leave us be."

"Garrot," Nesha called from above, pleading in her voice.

Larkin shot her sister a confused look.

"Go upstairs with Nesha and your baby, Mother Pennice," Garrot ordered.

Larkin jerked her chin toward the stairs. "You can still help them, Mama." *But not me, not anymore.*

Tears slipped down Mama's cheeks. Like Larkin, Mama was no stranger to force. She knew when she was beaten. She slowly climbed the stairs and took the baby from Nesha. Baring her breast defiantly, she suckled Brenna, who got her first mouthful of milk and her screams settled to baby grumblings and swallows.

"What have you done with Bane and Daydon?" Larkin tried to make her voice hard as flint, though a tremor betrayed her.

Garrot leaned toward her. "Why were you at the forest last night?"

Taking a shuddering breath, Larkin forced herself to meet his gaze. "The forest take you."

"Wrong answer." Garrot grabbed her by the back of the neck and hauled her toward the door.

"Larkin," Mama cried.

The townspeople cheered when she appeared in the doorway, lifting pitchforks, scythes, axes, and even roughly hewn clubs into the air in triumph.

"Burn her!" Horace shouted.

"Drown the ashes," Horgen said.

"She's caused the floods and famine!" a voice cried. More joined in, the individual words lost to the onslaught of hatred flung at her.

Those closest spat at her feet. Garrot forced her to turn left, toward the weather-beaten wood of the four-man stockade. She reached out to the manor house wall to steady herself, searching for sympathy in the faces she'd known since childhood—friends of her parents and parents of her friends. Their crazed, hateful eyes were full of accusation, as if she'd been the cause of their lost daughters and friends, and she suddenly understood. They couldn't make the pipers pay, but they could make *her* pay—she who had the audacity to escape when none of their daughters had. Fear expanded within her until her chest threatened to burst. A rock slammed into her shoulder, driving the breath from her as the pain radiated.

Rimoth and Hunter became her protectors, as they shoved the crowd back. Larkin stumbled. Garrot's fingers dug into her neck, forcing her up. She squirmed and winced, knowing she would have bruises.

On the top step of the platform, he gave her a shove. She flew forward and landed hard on her hip. She gasped at the pain shooting down her leg. She braced herself but didn't rise. Rimoth and Hunter took positions on either end of the platform—to keep her from escaping or the crowd from thronging her, she wasn't sure. Maybe both.

Mama shoved wildly through the crowd, her breast bare, milk leaking as she struggled to reach the platform. Copper flashed beside her, and Harben grabbed her by the arms, restraining her. "Pennice, there's nothing you can do."

So, Harben had been released from the stocks, only to have Larkin take his place. The man had betrayed them, abandoned them. Why did he care what happened to them now?

Her mother threw an elbow into his middle. "Liar! Coward!"

Rimoth pointed to Horace and Horgen. "Lock Mother Pennice up in the cellar until this is over."

The men took hold of Mama, dragging her away as she screamed. Larkin didn't protest. It would be better if her mother didn't witness whatever happened next.

"Hang her," Kenjin shouted.

"You can't kill her," Vyder, Venna's grandfather, cried. "She's expecting."

Garrot held up his hand. To Larkin's surprise, the crowd stilled—all except Crazy Maisy. "Flood, blood, diberdud. Toad, foad, diberdoad. Ditch, stitch, diberditch."

"Shut her up, Rimoth," Garrot said.

Rimoth dropped from the platform and headed toward his daughter. Before he reached her, Maisy finished her song with a whimper and a rough series of twitches.

"The truth now, Larkin," Garrot said with seemingly infinite patience. "This is your final chance."

Larkin set her jaw. "The truth is a great evil has come upon Hamel, and it doesn't originate from me." Her gaze settled accusingly on Garrot.

Garrot backhanded her. She staggered, barely managing to keep her feet. She tasted iron and salt, the inside of her cheek bleeding where her teeth had cut it. She laughed. Garrot thought to intimidate her with violence, but she'd grown up with pain inflicted by the one man who should have protected her. At the bottom step, her father glared at her.

She faced Garrot, her chin high. "You don't frighten me."

"What is the meaning of this?" a voice cried. Larkin nearly staggered with relief as Bane shoved his way through the crowd toward them. His left eye was blackened and nearly swollen shut, but other than that, he seemed intact.

"You were supposed to see he was detained," Garrot growled under his breath to Rimoth.

The other man shrugged as he climbed back up the platform. "I thought I had."

Bane climbed the first two steps before Hunter blocked him. Bane's gaze raked over Larkin, before settling back on Garrot. Larkin knew Bane well enough to see the calculation in his eyes as he weighed the crowd's mood and the strength of the three men before him. She saw when the realization came over him as it had for her: this was not a fight he could win by force.

"Garrot, I don't care who you are. You will not incite violence in my town, and you will not harm my pregnant fiancée. Now, take your friends, get out, and never come back."

It would be ironic if this fake baby saved my life, Larkin thought.

"Are you sure it's *us* you want out?" Garrot said.

"I'm sure," Bane said through clenched teeth.

Garrot turned to Larkin. "Larkin was telling us she has no idea what happened to the girls last night, isn't that right, Larkin?"

Larkin glanced at Bane, who gave a minute nod. "That's right."

"So, you didn't go to the forest last night or the night before that ... or the night before that." Garrot sounded almost bored.

"Of course she hasn't," Bane spat. "Now let her go."

Garrot made a gesture of agreement. "If I find no proof of guilt and *you* promise to keep silent through my questioning, she shall go free."

Bane searched the crowd, weighing his options. He had none. Larkin knew it as well. "Fine."

Garrot circled Larkin, leaning into her from behind, his breath against the soft skin of her throat making her shudder. "I have a witness."

"Fly. Lie. Die," Crazy Maisy shouted as she twirled, head thrown back.

"Maisy?" she said incredulously. "She's your witness?"

Bane huffed, shoulders relaxing in relief. "I'm afraid you'll have to do better than that."

"You agreed to remain silent." Garrot paced from one end of the stockade to the other. "How many times have you been to the forest?"

With Maisy as their witness, Larkin might survive this, if

she stuck to her story. "I only went once! Sela wandered into the woods. I went after her."

"Have you been communicating with a man who lives in the Forbidden Forest?" Garrot went on. "A servant of the forest, same as the beast."

She had, but admitting to it would have her burning to death faster. "Absolutely not."

"This is ridiculous," Bane said.

Garrot huffed. "And did you dance naked before the river, calling up the flood that has ravaged the town?"

"What?" She had lifted her shift to put on the amulet. She'd thought herself hidden, but perhaps Maisy had seen?

Garrot spat in front of her. "Answer the question."

"I nearly died in that flood," Larkin said. "Why would I call it down on my own land?"

Garrot eyed her. "A clever ploy to win back the town's favor."

"That's not what Maisy says," Rimoth hissed. "Maisy says you were communing with the river."

"Insane, main, diberdain!" Crazy Maisy chanted.

"You aren't even carrying a baby, are you?" Garrot said, a gleam of triumph in his eyes.

Bane started toward Larkin. "I will not stand by and watch this farce continue!"

Hunter and Rimoth closed ranks and shoved him back. The baker showed up with his cart and called out his wares to the crowd.

Garrot pulled his knife and held it loosely in his right hand. "Back. Up."

Perhaps seeing the murder in the other man's eyes, Bane lifted both hands in surrender and stepped down.

"Maisy knows things," Patrina cried. "She knew the flood would threaten the town. She knew our daughters would be taken!"

"Everyone knew the town would flood if the rains didn't let up," Bane shot back. "And girls go missing all the time!"

"Silence!" Garrot shouted. He turned to Larkin, his gaze narrowing. "Are you, in fact, pregnant, Larkin?"

Garrot knew something—he wouldn't be asking all these questions if he didn't—but Larkin was in too deep now. "Yes," she whispered.

"I have given you so many chances to tell the truth." Garrot almost sounded sad. "You have turned down every one."

She wiped her sweating palms on the front of her dress. "It is the truth," she said, her voice tremulous.

Triumph in his eyes, he looked toward the house where Nesha stood at the manor's front door, her eyes glittering with fresh tears. Larkin went numb from the inside out. At a gesture from Garrot, Nesha limped through the crowd and up the stairs to stand before him. The whole crowd went utterly silent. All Larkin could hear was the blood pounding in her ears.

For the first time, Nesha met her gaze. "Larkin is lying," she said, her eyes as cold and dark as the winter solstice. "I know of three times she sneaked off to the forest. I saw her stand naked before the river the night it flooded. And she isn't pregnant with Bane's child. They made up that lie to save her from the crucible. I know she hears the piper's music day and night—she says it calls to her. She believes she is strong enough to withstand its call, but she's wrong. It has twisted her soul, twisted her into one of them."

Larkin looked at the girl who could not be her sister—not the sister who slept by her side every night, the sister she'd taken countless beatings for—because her sister would never offer her up like bait on a hook.

"Nesha ..." As if from far away, Larkin heard the crowd roar, drowning out whatever words she might have said. Her sister simply turned away, as if Larkin no longer existed.

CHAPTER 16

INTO THE FOREST

Rimoth stared at Larkin with something beyond fear and hatred. In his eyes was righteous indignation. In his eyes was her death. "You will burn," he whispered it like a prayer.

Instinctively, Larkin's hand tightened around the amulet hanging from her waist and squeezed so hard the branches pierced cloth and then skin. Surrounded by hundreds of people calling for her death, a dark calm settled around her. Whatever was coming, there was nothing she could do to stop it, but she still had her pride—that they couldn't take from her. She straightened her shoulders as the wind tugged at her unruly hair, shifting it across her back.

With a roar, Bane punched Hunter in the jaw and ducked around him. Garrot reached for her, and she thought, *No.* A sudden, achingly sweet burst of power throbbed through her. His hand stuttered to a stop, as if there were a perfectly clear barrier between them.

"It cannot be," he gasped.

Larkin's confidence wavered. What was happening? She staggered back from the hatred directed at her, tripped over her own feet, and fell onto her back. Garrot reached toward her, something like awe on his face.

Bane appeared behind Garrot, delivering a vicious kick to the man's knee. Garrot went down. The crowd roared in fury. Bane hauled her up, wrapped his arms around her middle, and boosted her toward a second-floor manor window. She tipped forward, hands scrabbling to catch herself. Bane gripped her feet and shoved her inside before he was tackled by Rimoth.

She hit the floor hard, her lungs empty and unable to draw breath. Garrot pushed himself up behind her. She slammed her heel into his nose, feeling it crunch. His head whipped back, blood spurting, but he managed to hold on. She lunged to her feet and grabbed the swinging window, slamming it into his face. With a cry, he let go.

"Larkin, run!" Bane screamed from below.

Larkin heard the front door crack against the wall as someone threw it open. Footsteps pounded below. She shot into the room across the hall. She ran to the window. The mob hadn't moved to the back of the house yet. She threw open the window and climbed out, letting herself dangle before dropping two stories to the tufts of grass below. She hit hard, feet stinging, legs buckling. The crowd's outliers rounded the house. She scrambled to her feet and flew down the hill. Her hair swept across her face as she glanced back to see the crowd streaming after her.

And though she was fast, she was not faster than Hunter, who had managed to find a horse. He rode bareback, running her down. She pumped her legs faster, harder, leaping the fence and sending the cattle bawling. Still, she was no match for his horse as it came alongside her. Her scalp prickled, and from the corner of her eye, she saw Hunter reach for her hair.

She ducked and rolled through the pasture, the horse overshooting her. Hunter slid off the back and came for her from the direction of the forest. She pivoted, angling up the next hill, away from him and the crowd. The only thing before her was the forest.

She didn't hesitate, for once giving in to the lure that had dangled before her for days. It was home. It was safety. It was where she should have gone days ago. The trees stretched toward her, urging her onward, welcoming her home.

She was so focused on them that she didn't realize how close Hunter had come—not until his fingers wound around her hair and he jerked her back. They went rolling, coming to a tangled stop. Her back to him, Larkin beat at him with her elbows and the heels of her feet.

Something solid connected with the back of her head. She saw stars, and her muscles lost their strength. The mob's outliers reached them, cheering breathlessly. Hunter flipped her over, his legs around her hips, hands pinning her wrists. The sky was an angry, throbbing mass behind his head.

Sweating and red-faced, Hunter looked down at her with pity. "Garrot wants a public execution," he said softly enough that only she could hear him. "I miss my sisters, but I don't see how this will make that right."

He slid his knife from its sheath and held it against her exposed throat. She was going to die. She was drawing her last breath and seeing her last sky. She would never again fly across the fields while her mother and sisters chattered and laughed, never know the joy of warmth after bitter cold or the taste of spring water when she was thirsty, never stand on the ridge on a windy day and imagine she could fly.

"I am sorry," he said as he pressed the blade into the delicate skin.

No! She wasn't going to die—not today! She twisted and bucked. The knife slipped across the surface of her throat, but Hunter rocked back, his gaze going wide. They both looked down at the spreading red stain on his chest. Larkin marveled at the arrow shaft buried in his ribs up to the fletching. He gave a single gasp and then coughed. Warm, wet blood splattered her face and dripped into her hair.

He fell off her, and she scrambled back. For half a moment, the crowd was shocked into silence. Everyone looked around, trying to understand what happened. A strangled sound came from her left. Horgen pointed behind them. Larkin turned as Denan shot from the trees, his mottled cloak flaring behind him.

Even as she watched, Denan drew back his bow and released in one smooth motion. Behind her came a thwack and a grunt. She whipped around to see Horace poised over her, Hunter's bloody knife clutched in his hand. The man collapsed around the arrow in his middle, his expression angry and shocked.

"It's the beast's servant!" someone screamed.

The whole mob turned and fled, cutting across the fields toward town. Larkin scrambled to her feet and sprinted toward Denan as if drawn by a lodestone. The moment he reached her, he tipped her head back, examining her throat. Wetness slid down her chest.

"It's superficial," he said. "Come on."

She hesitated, glancing back at Hamel as Bane pushed his way through the retreating mob toward her. "Larkin!" he cried. "Wait! No! Larkin!"

Behind him, Garrot and Rimoth charged toward her on horseback, axes in hand. "Stop her!" Garrot screamed.

She shook her head at Bane, trying to communicate that she was sorry—that she had no choice.

"No!" he cried again.

She turned her back on him. "Let's go," she said to Denan. Running side by side, they entered the dark forest.

CHAPTER 17

WITHIN THE SHADOW

Larkin ran flat out, dodging trees and roots and vines. She wasn't sure if she was running from the mob or from Denan, who was now behind her. Perhaps both.

"Larkin, wait. You're going to hit the barrier," Denan warned.

She didn't care. She had to get away from the people—the sister—who betrayed her. But then the branches wove toward her, hissing like snakes. Fear oozed in through her pores, infecting her with terror. She collapsed, sobbing and gripping handfuls of moldering leaves and sticks in her hands. *Please stop. Please stop. Please stop.*

"Where's the amulet?" Denan hovered over her, his fingers searching her neck.

She clawed her way through the fear to grip the amulet dangling from her belly. Denan wrapped his hand around hers and squeezed; the sharp-edged branches eased into her skin. Instantly, the snakes were simple branches again, the terror abating.

"Hold it tight until we're through." Arms scooped her up. She didn't fight as he ran with her through the Forbidden Forest. She gripped the amulet tight, blood tracing lines from her palm around to the back of her hand.

"You can let go now," he whispered. He had stopped moving. She fought her instincts and tried to relax her death grip. He set her down and crouched before her, watching something behind her. She finally released the amulet with a gasp, the branches easing from her flesh. Denan held his finger to his lips.

In the distance, Bane called her name, his voice breaking. Larkin peeked around a tree. He wandered through the forest, his hands out as he stumbled and staggered. The stirring—the barrier—had caught him. She let out the breath she hadn't known she'd been holding.

For a moment, she imagined herself standing up, calling for him, going to him. But then what? She couldn't go back to Hamel. She could never go back. *He's better off without me*, she firmly reminded herself. *He might not realize it now, but someday he will.*

Loving Bane was leaving him.

Bane fell, and when he got up, he headed away from them, still calling for her. Denan held a hand out to her, silently asking her to come with him. She studied it, calloused with dirt under the nails. She didn't take it but motioned for him to go first. He moved into a crouch and eased away from Bane. She followed, slipping away from the one person besides her own mother who had tried to fight for her.

When Bane was out of sight, Denan straightened to his full height and jogged ahead, looking back every once in a while to make sure she was still following. She paused when Bane's voice was faint, little more than an echo, and tried to memorize the way he sounded—something to hold on to in her uncertain future. The wound at her neck throbbed in time to her heart being torn in two.

Ahead, Denan grabbed a pack from beneath a rotting log and took out a wooden jar. He pulled out the cork, releasing a sharp herbal scent. He dabbed the contents with a clean white cloth and started toward her.

She backed away. "What are you doing?" she asked, her voice shaking.

He raised an eyebrow. "Treating your neck so you'll stop bleeding."

She hesitated, then tipped her chin up. She winced as he pressed the cloth to her wound. "How bad is it?"

He pulled out another long strip of fine cloth and wrapped it around her neck. "You'll live."

To her surprise, it didn't sting as much as she expected and the cloth he'd used was incredibly soft. "What do you want?"

He met her gaze, his fingers still on the bandage. "I thought I'd made that perfectly clear."

"But why me?"

He rubbed ointment onto the cuts on her palms. "Would you believe I like redheads?" She slapped him. He rubbed his cheek. "I barely know you, Larkin, but the heartsong is never wrong."

She studied the prick marks on her hand as he quickly wrapped them. "The amulet stopped the stirring," she said.

"Barrier, and yes, it did."

She looked up at him. "Is that why it doesn't affect you? Because you have an amulet too?"

He put the ointments and bandages away. "Something like that. Come on, we need to move."

She planted her feet. "I deserve some answers, piper."

He shrugged the pack onto his back. "A druid is dying or dead. The others will want us to pay for that death."

She winced at the thought of Hunter and his shocked expression as he'd realized he was hit. Denan moved at a swift walk as if her following him was a foregone conclusion. She supposed it was, especially if Garrot was after her.

Wrapping her arms around herself, she hurried after him. "What would you do to them if they found us?"

He glanced sidelong at her. "There are two rules to the Forbidden Forest. First, move swiftly and silently so as not to draw attention. Second, do as I say, when I say it. Obey these two rules, and we will most likely reach the Alamant alive."

A pulse of fear shot from her middle up to her throat. She cast an uneasy look around them and decided not to risk any more questions. They ended up in the same meadow as before— the one with the babbling brook. Up ahead, she saw four people, two of whom she immediately recognized.

"Larkin," Venna cried out and ran toward her.

Larkin sucked in a panicked breath and turned to Denan. "Don't tell them the villagers forced me into the forest." When he didn't respond, she looked up at him. "Please."

He sighed. "Fine."

Venna reached them and wrapped Larkin in an embrace, her body shaking with sobs. "Oh, Larkin, they got you too! Oh, your poor mama."

At the mention of her mother, Larkin squeezed her tighter. "Are you hurt?" she whispered.

"No, but they won't let us out of their sight." Venna pulled back and shot a dirty look at Denan.

"Talox," Denan said. "You were supposed to talk to her about keeping quiet."

A big man loped after Venna. He had dark skin and a queue of tightly curled hair behind his ear. "I did, but girls are loud— and I got the quiet one." He stepped up next to Venna. "Shh, Venna," he said gently. "The beasts will hear."

Backing away from him, Venna made a choking sound as she tried to swallow her sobs.

Sneering at Talox, Alorica gave him a wide berth. Chin up, she fixed her undaunted gaze on Larkin. "My papa and mama, are they all right?"

"And my grandfather?" Venna asked, her voice a quavering whisper.

Thinking of Alorica's father chasing her with a pitchfork, Larkin suppressed a shudder. "They were fine last I saw."

A third piper trailed behind Alorica. With eyes the bright blue of a spring morning, curling blond hair, a wiry body, and a mischievous expression, he looked more like an imp than a man.

"Talox, report," Denan said.

"All is quiet, sir. The women are in good health."

"Tam?" Denan asked.

The impish man handed Denan an ax and a shield that matched the ones the other men wore strapped to their backs. "We can head out now?" Tam's voice was high and musical, the words dancing across his tongue, though he was clearly trying to rein in his excitement.

Denan strapped his ax and shield on. "Has she given you any trouble?"

Tam's eyes crinkled like he was trying not to smile. "None beyond what's expected."

Denan shot a knowing look at Alorica. She glared back. He grunted and looked at Tam. "Don't let that one out of your sight."

Tam's grin finally broke free. It reminded Larkin of a fox. "Gladly, sir."

Alorica made a disgusted sound.

"You'll catch up?" Tam said.

"Hopefully by nightfall," Denan said, his unreadable gaze fixed on Larkin. "If not, the next day."

Larkin frowned. "You're leaving?"

Denan took a step closer, close enough to feel his breath against her ear. Despite herself, she shuddered. "I have to make sure no one can find our tracks."

"And by no one, you mean Bane?"

He wouldn't look at her. "Or the druids."

Tam's head came up, surprise on his face. "Why would the druids come after us?"

Denan's jaw tightened. "One of them threatened my charge."

Tam and Talox exchanged loaded glances.

"Swear you won't hurt Bane," Larkin said.

Stepping back, Denan met her gaze evenly. "Only to save my life. Stay with Tam and Talox. Do what they say. They'll protect you." He turned and loped across the meadow, his long legs eating up the distance.

Tam glanced at the sky and trotted across the meadow. "This way."

Talox gestured for them to precede him. Larkin exchanged uneasy looks with Venna and Alorica before following Tam. She couldn't help but glance back in the direction Denan had gone. He was far from someone she trusted, but at least he was known.

"He'll be all right," Talox said gently.

Alorica rolled her eyes. "As if Larkin could care about one of you pipers." She took Larkin's hand, pulling her and Venna ahead. Larkin stared at her hand in Alorica's—a girl who'd hated her for years. She supposed a common enemy made them friends.

"I'm coming up with a plan," Alorica whispered fiercely. "Be ready for anything."

"The villagers will turn against you," Larkin said. "Like they turned against me."

"My father would never let that happen," Alorica said.

"I wouldn't try anything," Talox said mildly from behind them. "You won't like the results."

Any illusion Larkin had that maybe she had a choice in being in the forest evaporated. She looked back at Talox, wondering how he'd heard them from so far away.

Alorica huffed and moved ahead. Larkin and Venna shared a look. "I don't believe they mean to hurt us," Larkin said gently.

Venna looked away, but not before Larkin saw the uncertainty on her face. Larkin couldn't tell the other girl that Denan had saved her life, not without facing what had happened that morning, and she wasn't ready—not yet.

"Don't be simple," Alorica hissed from in front of them. "They've already kidnapped us."

"I didn't say we should trust them," Larkin shot back. "Only that they're not going to rape us or slit our throats."

Alorica rolled her eyes. "Of all the girls in the town, you had to be taken."

"There's the Alorica I know," Larkin said.

They crossed from the meadow into the forest, and a hush fell over them. Almost immediately, the rain stopped tapping at Larkin's shoulders. Instead, great drops plunked down on her head, streaking a cold path on her scalp.

Larkin couldn't help but feel claustrophobic with hundreds of trees pressing down on her from all sides, blinding them to the danger that could be hiding a dozen steps away. Perhaps it was her experience with the stirring, but it felt like the trees knew she was here. She had the sense of stepping into something alive and connected and aware. She wondered if the other girls were feeling the same thing.

The brush was dense at first, but then cleared out. Ahead and to the right, a mother deer and her two fawns snapped their heads up at the sight of them and then bounded off into the forest. Larkin watched them go in wonder. The barrier had kept the wilds away from her town as much as it had trapped them inside.

Larkin expected the men to watch their captives closely. Instead, they watched the forest, bows in hand. A low rumble sounded through the trees—a sound Larkin had heard before.

"What was that?" Alorica gasped.

"Quiet," Talox said, voice low. His gaze locked with Tam's, and he made a series of hand gestures.

"Sorry, Princess," Tam said to Alorica. "I'm going to have

to break my promise and take my eyes off you for a little while. I'll make it up to you though."

The look she gave him could have stripped the bark off a tree. With an impish grin, Tam pulled out his pipes and trotted off to their right.

"Was that the beast?" Larkin asked quietly.

"We would die before we allowed harm to come to you," Talox said, his reassuring gaze pausing on Venna.

At least he didn't say they weren't in danger. There was some comfort in his honesty.

"Why won't you answer Larkin?" Alorica demanded.

From up ahead, flute music drifted back to them. Larkin suddenly felt skittish, like she needed to run. Venna sucked up to Larkin's side, her hand twisted in Larkin's skirt in a way that reminded her of Sela when she was scared. She wrapped a reassuring arm around the other girl's shoulder.

"Steady," Talox said evenly. "He's clearing a path for us."

Larkin could well believe any beast of the forest would clear out from that sound. A few minutes passed, the music growing more distant. As it did, her overpowering need to run faded. She let out the breath she'd been holding.

"What else can your pipes do?" Alorica said uneasily.

"We've all sworn not to use our pipes for evil," Talox said.

"What do you call kidnapping three girls from their homes?" Alorica spat back.

"We do what must be done," Talox said as if by rote. He moved past Alorica without bothering to glance her way. "Stay close and keep silent."

They started off again. Venna had her head down, her expression defeated. Alorica was too busy mouthing curses to notice. Every once in a while, distant flute music set them even more on edge.

Larkin rubbed the marks in her palm. The amulet had stopped the barrier from affecting her. Her thumb touched the raised scab from the sliver, and she froze. Had the sliver stopped the barrier when she brought Sela back through? Was it as simple as a piece of wood inside flesh?

But that didn't make any sense. Sela had defeated the barrier without any sort of sliver. And the amulet was supposed to be special—special enough for Denan to let her go to retrieve it.

"Larkin?" a voice whispered behind her.

She jumped. Talox watched her with a concerned expression. Realizing she'd stopped, she hurried to catch up. Larkin continued to rub the scar on her palm, trying to figure out how the amulet, maybe even the sliver, fit into all of this. Hours passed, and they came to a spring that gasped its way between rocks. Talox crouched beside it, filling his water gourd. He handed them each a piece of travel bread. "Rest for a moment," he said to them.

Larkin found a rock to kneel on, cupped her hands, and drank long and deep. The water tasted of minerals, and it was bitterly cold as it slid down her throat.

Venna knelt beside her and drank. She sat back and wiped her mouth. "Did Denan do that to your neck?"

Larkin stopped herself from touching her dressing. "No." She bit into the hard, dry bread and filled her mouth with water to soften it.

"Does it hurt?"

Larkin was relieved she hadn't pried. "Only if the skin pulls."

Larkin and Venna were forced apart when Alorica dropped between them. "I'm going to make a run for it. You two are coming with me."

Lowering her bread, Larkin glanced around to find Talox standing on the rocky outcropping, surveying the forest around them, one hand on his bow.

"Alorica," she whispered. "There are dangerous things in these woods. We have to stay with the pipers."

"They're trying to make us afraid," Alorica hissed.

"I was attacked the first time I came into the forest," Larkin said. "By a lizard bigger than a man."

"I'd rather face a lizard than the pipers." Alorica pointed toward Talox. "He can't chase all three of us, so at least two should escape. I've been paying attention. The river is always at our left. If we keep it to our right going back, we can make it."

Larkin shook her head. She needed to tell them what waited for them if they went back—how the villagers would turn on them too—but she couldn't get the words out.

Alorica clenched her jaw. "We won't get a better chance." She turned expectantly toward Venna, who stared at the water bleeding from the rocks.

"I think—I think Alorica's right." Larkin shot her an exasperated look. Venna licked her lips nervously. "I want to go home."

If Larkin didn't warn them, she'd never be able to live with the guilt. She touched her dressing, wincing at the ache. "The town blamed me for anything bad that happened after I escaped. They blamed me when you two disappeared, even though I tried to stop it." Larkin sniffed, her eyes aching with the tears she refused to shed. "They'll do the same to you if you go back."

"Larkin," Venna began, reaching for her as if to comfort her.

"I'm not you," Alorica growled. "And my father isn't the town drunk. We'll tell everyone the truth, and Papa will protect me." She lifted her chin. "And I'll protect you two."

Larkin winced. "Bane's protection didn't help me much, and he's more powerful than your father."

"Fine. Stay," Alorica ground out. "But Venna and I are leaving." She gripped Venna's wet, shaking hands. "If we get separated, follow the river out."

Venna nodded, her eyes too wide in her round face.

"Don't do everything Alorica says just because she's a bully," Larkin said.

Ignoring her, Alorica pushed to her feet, nodded at Venna, and then took off running, Venna a beat behind.

Larkin took a step after them, her instincts demanding she follow, but her mind insisting she was safer here. For half a breath, she wasn't sure which was louder, but then she heard a puff of breath and felt something whiz past her. Alorica jerked but kept running, a dart in her back.

"Venna, don't make me dart you too!" Talox's deep voice cut like a knife.

Venna staggered to a halt. Her body quivered with fear. She turned and started back. Alorica was still running, though one of her arms had gone limp and she dragged a leg.

Talox jumped down from his rock and rushed past them. "Both of you stay here."

Cowering, Venna slunk back to the spring. "Is that what the other piper did to you—hit you with a dart?"

Larkin nodded.

A few minutes later, Talox returned with Alorica thrown over one shoulder, her limbs swaying bonelessly. "Come on," he said gruffly as he hurried on ahead of them. "We'll have called every gilgad for miles."

He set a grueling pace, and Larkin found it harder and harder to keep up. She had no idea how he could press on with Alorica's weight slowing him down.

"You can't blame her for wanting to run," Larkin finally said in exasperation, tired of being punished for Alorica's impulsiveness.

At the sound of more rumbling, Talox stopped and stared off in the distance. "No talking." He switched Alorica to his other shoulder and started jogging.

Breathing hard, Larkin stared in the direction the rumbling had come from. The sound had to be made by gilgads. With Tam and Denan gone, Talox was the only warrior they had left.

CHAPTER 18

CURSE

Talox paused beside a tree and set Alorica down. He interlaced his fingers and held them low. "Venna, I'll boost you up."

Perhaps because of the quiet intensity radiating from him, Venna didn't question him. She stepped into his hands. He lifted her, her hands scrabbling for purchase. Talox turned for Larkin. "You next. I'll hand up Alorica."

Before Larkin could step in his hands, he suddenly whipped up his bow, an arrow drawn and aimed at something to his left. She listened hard. Something moved through the brush. She grabbed a branch and stood over Alorica. Ancestors, had Larkin survived the mob only to be devoured by beasts in this blasted forest?

Talox let out a whistle that sounded like a bird. An answering whistle called back. Talox lowered his bow, his shoulders rolling forward with relief. Moments later, Tam emerged from the forest.

Larkin let out a breath she hadn't known she'd been holding. "What did you think was after us?"

Infuriatingly, Talox glanced at her sideways and didn't answer. When Tam reached them, he crouched beside Alorica, resting his fingers against her throat.

"She and Venna tried to run for it," Talox said as he helped Venna down from the tree.

"Probably not the last time. I'll carry her." Tam swung Alorica over his shoulder.

"Any gilgad?" Talox asked.

"I cleared us a path all the way to the river." Tam started out, his steps light despite his burden. Talox ranged ahead, his long stride eating up the distance. As the two men came even with each other, Larkin couldn't help but compare the two. Talox was like a lumbering, sleepy bull—all muscle and measured thinking. With his boyish features, Tam reminded her of a fox, with a grin always itching to tug up his slim cheeks.

Larkin glanced back, wondering when Denan would catch up and why it mattered to her that he did.

By late afternoon, the vegetation grew thicker. Ferns shushed against Larkin's thighs. Fuzzy moss blanketed the tree trunks. A sound grew louder in the distance—the roar of breaking water. The damp pressed against her skin, the weight of it settling in her lungs.

They came upon a clearing surrounded by trees. Talox gathered wood for a fire. Tam settled Alorica in the hollow space between tree roots. Breathing hard, Larkin rested a hand on a tree for support. Through the boughs high above, she could make out the top of a waterfall more than four times the size of the tallest trees. Leaving the trees' shelter, she stepped around boulders toward a rocky outcropping. The waterfall came into full view.

Surrounded by green, a roar of white plummeted into a wide pool of turquoise water. Such beauty seemed out of place in the

169

world Larkin lived in. Everything should be barren and full of thorns, not filled with shades of green so bright they hurt her eyes or water so blue it looked more like a liquid jewel than the dirty river that sloshed past her town. She longed to step into that cool water, to let some of that beauty wash away the darkness staining her soul.

"Larkin," Tam said in his high tenor. "Come help me with Alorica."

She backed away slowly, not wanting to leave. She stepped into the shadows of the trees. Talox was bent over kindling. Tam approached her and held out a water gourd. "She should be coming out of it enough to swallow. Keep her head up so she doesn't choke."

Settling behind her, Larkin propped up Alorica's head while Venna gave her slow, measured doses of water. They'd just finished when Denan strode into the firelight, a small, eviscerated gilgad draped across his shoulders. He saw her and the tension around his eyes loosened.

"Talox, report."

"We were waiting for you before we crossed," Talox said. "Alorica and Venna tried to run for it. I had to dart Alorica."

"Tam?" Denan asked.

"I cleared out the ..." Tam's voice trailed off, and he shrugged.

Denan seemed to know what he meant. "We do what must be done." The same words Talox had said earlier. "I threw them off our trail. We'll cross in the morning." He dropped the gilgad.

"And no one was hurt?" Larkin asked, an edge to her voice.

"No one was hurt," Denan said.

A rush of relief coursed through Larkin. Unable to resist, she settled Alorica's head and hesitantly approached the gilgad. Its skin was mottled brown and green—like the pipers' cloaks. Its pupils were slitted, scales diamond-shaped, teeth curving and serrated. Gathering her courage, she reached out and ran her fingers down the hard spikes along its back.

"Don't touch the head." Denan crouched beside her. His knife carefully slit the skin behind the nostrils and pulled the hide back, revealing pink bladder-like sacs. "Those are the venom sacs."

Feeling queasy, Larkin went to sit beside Alorica. Denan tied up the creature out of the range of their fire and dressed it with quick, efficient movements.

"The gilgad"—Denan's voice took on a lecturing tone— "while formidable, is only a beast. There are worse things in the forest—much worse. You need us to protect you. That's harder to do if we have to lug you around."

What could be worse than the gilgad?

Tam knelt beside them and unstopped a vial. "Prop her head back up," he told Larkin.

Larkin held out a hand to block him. "What are you doing?"

"Poison," Tam said. "After luring you from the town and forcing you to traipse through the forest for a full day, now we're going to kill you the sneaky way."

Larkin blinked at him.

"What—You can't—" Venna began.

Tam tipped his head back and laughed. "It's the antidote. Talox already gave her the first dose, or she'd be dead by now. This one will bring her out of it faster and with less pain."

"You think this is funny?" Larkin asked, jaw clenched.

Tam looked around the group. "Ah, come on. It was a little bit funny."

Remembering how she had slept for a full day and woken so painfully, Larkin shot a glare at Denan. He shrugged, a hint of amusement gleaming in his dark eyes. "I told you it would have been easier if you'd stayed with me."

"Fine. And now you've won. You have me. You have all three of us. What do you intend to do with us?"

The pipers had the decency to look chastised. "We won't

hurt you," Denan said.

"Forgive me if I don't trust your definition of *hurt*."

"We have a right to know," Venna said softly.

"You will come with us to our home in the Alamant." Talox directed his words to Venna. "Someday, we hope you will chose us as your husbands."

Venna made a choking sound and shrank back.

Larkin had known this. Deep down, she'd always known. But to hear it said so plainly ... She swiveled to Denan. "I will never willingly marry you."

Denan pointedly turned away. "Talox, take first watch. I'll bring you some food later."

Taking his bow and ax, Talox lumbered off.

If Alorica's head hadn't been cradled in Larkin's lap, she would have stormed over to Denan and slapped him. "What did you expect—that I would throw myself at your feet? You're my enemy!"

"I'm your enemy?" Denan snapped as he hacked off a chunk of meat and tossed it onto the animal's hide. "And what of your own people, the ones running you down earlier? Are they your friends?"

Larkin's hand strayed to the bandages around her throat. She looked away, focusing on Tam, who strung the meat up on a stick. "And whose fault was that?" she said, voice shaking.

"Larkin." Venna's hand went to her own throat. "Who did this to you?"

Larkin glanced down at Alorica. Her eyes were closed, but Larkin would bet she was listening. "Hunter," she finally managed. "The Black Druid." Again, the vision of him being struck by the arrow, his shock and devastation. She pinched her eyes shut, but the images were leeches draining the life from her. "The townspeople, they were going to ..." She shook her head, unwilling to say it out loud. "I got away. Hunter caught up to me. He had a knife."

She held her hand protectively over her neck. Her head ached with the tears she couldn't hold back, but she never let anyone see her cry. Settling Alorica down gently, Larkin hurried from the camp.

"Let her go," Denan said softly. "She knows not to go far." One of the pipers must have made to follow her.

She was tempted to prove Denan wrong, but the gilgad were out there, tracking them. She waded into the pool and perched on a boulder, her feet dangling in the cool water. She stared down at her reflection—her wild copper hair, the dance of freckles across her face, her large dark eyes. For a moment, everything she'd ever wanted had been within her grasp—safety for her family, no more fear of her father's fists, and Bane … he had been hers. But even at its brightest, her future had been tainted, darkened at the edges by fear and hatred.

Then she couldn't see anything for the tears blurring her vision. She wrapped her arms around her drawn legs and buried her face on her knees and sobbed the only way she knew how—silently. The last of her tears spent as the day lost its sharpness. She lifted her face to the steel-blue sky, reveling in the cool mist shifting against her hot cheeks, imagining she was a bird with the wind against her face as she soared to freedom.

The savory smell of sizzling meat had Larkin's mouth watering in earnest. She ignored her hunger. She'd rather be hungry than anywhere near Denan, but he stepped out of the camp to wash the blood from his arms. Flicking his fingers, he stared up at her while she pretended not to know he was there. She wasn't sure what to do when he removed his boots and sloshed into the pool behind her. She did her best to ignore him as he sat down on her rock at a respectable distance and settled a broad leaf covered in cooked meat between them. Even if she wanted to say something, she doubted she could talk through the saliva filling her mouth.

"I'm sorry," he finally said. "I shouldn't have snapped at

you."

She swallowed. "If not for you, the townspeople never would have turned on me in the first place."

"I know."

"I've lost everything because of you!"

"I know."

"Then why?" she demanded.

He let out a long breath. "I do what I must."

She glared at him, for once not caring if someone saw that she'd been crying. "Don't force your platitudes on me. What you've done to me—you had a choice in it."

He softened, which only made her angrier. He reached for her hand. She jerked back. "You said you wanted to know why."

She wasn't sure what that had to do with touching her. Eyes narrowed in warning, she thrust her hand out. He gently unwound the bandage, his fingertips brushed across the scabs left by the sliver and amulet. Cringing at the feel of his flesh on hers, she wrenched her hand back and briefly touched the amulet at her waist, out of habit.

His eyes tracked her movement. "Clever hiding place." His irises were nearly black in the failing light. "What does the amulet do?" he asked.

"Shouldn't you be telling me that?"

He looked away from her, his sharp features traced by shadows. "I want to—you have no idea how badly—but I'm afraid you'll have to figure it out for yourself. I can't tell you."

She ground her teeth. "Can't or won't?"

He growled in frustration, rubbing his hand over his bristled scalp. "I told you—it's the only one of its kind."

"Surely you've used it." He watched her, as if waiting for something. Unless … "Unless you can't?"

"I use these." Denan pulled out a panpipe and a flute from around his neck. They appeared to be made of the same material as the amulet. She reached out, just to be sure. Their surface had the smoothness of polished stone, though they were lightweight, like wood. She'd seen the other men with similar pipes.

Denan lifted the pipes and blew ten notes. She could feel the magic tugging her back up straight, sharpening her attention. He repeated it, a little faster, then tugged the cord over his head and held the pipes out to her. "Try it."

She hesitated, not wanting her mouth on something that had been so near his. But maybe, just maybe, she could use it the same way he had. There was power in that, power in the magic, and she'd always been so powerless.

Already, the spell he'd woven was fading. Steeling herself, she brought them to her lips and found it easy to copy what he had done, but the notes held no power, no magic. She thrust them back to him in disgust. "I don't know how to play well enough."

He took them, tucking them and the flute back in his shirt. "You played fine."

The intense way he watched her—he wanted something. He was trying to tell her something, and suddenly it clicked. "I can't use the magic pipes, and you can't use the magic amulet."

He smiled, looking relieved. "There is women's magic and men's magic. One cannot use the other."

"Why?"

He sat looser now, his arms braced behind him. "That's a question for a theologian. A better question would be how to use the amulet."

"I thought you didn't know."

"We don't, not really."

We? Who is we? Larkin stared at the tiny scabs on her hand. The amulet had pierced her skin, giving her visions—and something else …

"What I do know is that you used it to get through the barrier. Do you understand how?"

She looked at him. "Why should I help you?"

175

He sighed in frustration. "We both want to know how that amulet works. We can help each other."

She considered him. She wanted so badly to refuse—to hurt him in even the smallest way—but he was right. She wanted to know how to use the amulet more. "It works when the branches pierce my skin."

He nodded. "What else has it done?"

She hooked her arms around her drawn knees. Telling him any of this felt like a betrayal, but she wasn't sure of whom or what. "I've seen visions. And when Garrot attacked me ... for a moment, there was a barrier between us and he couldn't touch me." Pride swelled within her. She'd stopped the druid, even if for a moment.

When Denan didn't respond, she stole a glance to find him smiling. "You have women's magic," he breathed, something like reverence in his eyes. She scooted a little farther from him. "Larkin, the first time you accessed the magic, before I even gave you the amulet, how did you do it?"

Something about his intensity made her uneasy. He wanted this answer, wanted it badly. Inside her fist, her thumb brushed across the sliver scar.

"Surely, you must have an idea," he said when she didn't answer. "When was the first time you felt the magic?"

She lifted her palm for him to see. "I had a sliver. When it came out, I couldn't access the magic anymore." She sniffed. "I've answered your questions, piper. Now you will answer one of mine: why me?"

In answer, Denan rested his pipes against his lips and breathed out a melody that had her soaring with freedom, with claws and a beak sharp enough to protect those she loved. And if she was a bird, he was the wind that bore her. She was free—free and powerful and in control of her own destiny.

When he finished playing, she found herself leaning toward him, yearning flowing through her like spring water. His eyes were dark—black bands around the inside and outside of his iris, with a touch of brown between—and his lashes were long and black. Unable to resist, she ran her fingertips across the dark gold of his cheek, surprised to find it as smooth as her own.

"That's why," he said softly, as if the song affected him as well.

She jerked her hand back as if burned and scooted away from him. It was cruel to trick her into feeling something that wasn't real. "I love Bane. I've always loved him. And I hate you."

Denan's expression shuttered. He slid off the boulder and into the water. "You should eat. Meat's never as good cold."

Hoping that she'd hurt him, Larkin stared at the food he'd brought her—gilgad meat. Her lip curled in distaste, but she couldn't ignore her hollow stomach anymore. She took a bite, juices flooding her mouth. It tasted a lot like chicken and a little like fish. She took another bite. She ate all of it and wished for more, despite her swollen stomach. She looked out at the sun, kissing the horizon in the distance.

"So, maybe I shouldn't have made a joke out of poisoning you." She turned to find Tam on the shore, his hands in his pockets.

She glared at him.

He sighed in frustration. "What is it with women and glaring? It's like you're trying to kill someone with your eyes."

Despite everything, she felt the corners of her mouth twitch.

Tam shrugged his stooped shoulders. "I'm supposed to bring you in. I think Denan doesn't want any more death eyes, the coward."

"Will you dart me like Talox did Alorica if I refuse?"

He rubbed the back of his neck. "It would be a nice break from the death eyes, but my shoulders still hurt from packing Alorica—she's heavier than she looks—so I'd rather not."

He made her want to laugh, and that made her angry. How

dare he be anything other than awful! She debated throwing a rock at him—one with slimy moss so it would hurt *and* make him dirty.

His gaze traveled slowly across her face. "From what Denan tells me," he said softly, "you don't have much to go back to. Why are you fighting so hard?"

She slipped into the water and found a rock big enough to do some damage, but not big enough to kill him. She chucked it at him, but he easily danced out of the way.

Tam sighed. "I'll fetch Denan."

Muttering under her breath, she sloshed after him. Back at camp, she sought out Venna, camaraderie snapping into place between them.

She's my friend, Larkin realized. *She's always been my friend.*

Tam slipped into a tree, climbing until he was out of sight, though she could still hear the rustling of the boughs.

Denan laid out a blanket and supplies next to a fire, where some water heated in a small pot. He took the pot off the fire. "Lie down, please."

"Why?" Larkin asked warily.

He glanced at the setting sun. "I need to change your bandage."

She hesitated, not wanting him to touch her. "Can't Venna do it?"

"Venna hasn't been trained in field dressings," he said with a touch of impatience.

She really didn't want him touching her again, but by the way her wound kept breaking open, it probably did need to be treated. Reluctantly, she lay down and looked off into the trees. Denan untied the strips and unwound them. He gingerly pulled back the bandage. Venna gasped and looked away.

"Is it that bad?" Larkin asked.

"No," Denan said as he dropped the strips into the boiling

water. "Though I need to stitch it."

"It's a little late for that," she huffed.

From his pack, he removed a packet wrapped in cloth, opening it to reveal black catgut threads and a hooked bone needle. "It isn't."

"I'll be fine," she insisted, wishing she could see it for herself.

"Larkin," Venna said, her voice thin and wavering. "Let him."

Denan was probably being overprotective, and Venna was probably overreacting. The truth most likely lay somewhere in the middle, which meant it was serious, but not life-threatening. She waved him off. "I've had worse."

Denan stilled. The silence grew awkward. Larkin looked away. "I shouldn't have said that." She was used to keeping Harben's abuse a secret, as much out of shame as to keep him out of the stocks—he always beat them more after he returned—but here, she had no one to protect. And she suspected Denan already knew.

"You can say whatever you want." He held out a silver flask. "One swallow. No more."

She took it from him reluctantly, watching as he threaded the needle. "You said you wouldn't hurt me. You keep breaking that promise." She knew this didn't count, but she felt like being mulish.

"Apparently, I'm a liar." Denan's eyes flicked nervously to the west. "Because to save your life, I will do whatever I have to. There isn't time to argue, Larkin."

"What's the hurry?" she muttered. She tipped the flask to her lips. Fire and bitterness streamed down her throat, making her eyes water.

"Everything is set up," Tam called from somewhere above. "It's time to be off the ground, Denan."

"Not enough time for the medicine to kick in," Denan muttered to himself. "Soothe her," he called up to Tam. Moments later, music drifted down, and Larkin's limbs grew heavy and her thoughts slow. She felt like she was falling into a tunnel, everything around her distant and echoing. Denan scrubbed his hands in steaming water, hissing at the heat. When he pulled them out, they were bright red. The needle pricked her, the thread pulling tight. The pain was there, but distant, like a dream. When he was finished, Denan wrapped it gently. "Any deeper, and he would have cut into your vocal cords."

Larkin melted into the blanket beneath her. Rainbow auras surrounded the flames. Colors circled his body. Why did he have to be so beautiful? It would be so much easier to hate him if all the horrible things he'd done had stained his outside to match his inside.

Denan pulled the old, steaming bandages from the water. He waited for them to cool before scrubbing her blood from them and dipping them again. When he was satisfied, he hung them up to dry on a bush.

"You see the colors yet?" Denan asked.

"Mmm," was all she could manage.

"That's enough, Tam," he called into the tree.

As the music faded away, she came back from the waking dream. Her body lay heavy and thick. The pain was there; she just didn't care about it. "I suppose ..." Her mouth was lazy, slow to form the words. She furrowed her brow, concentrating, and tried again. "I suppose you want me to thank you for saving my life—again."

"As you pointed out earlier, I'm the one who put it in danger in the first place." He hurried to pack everything back up. His tension stole through the colors and into her syrupy thoughts. She shifted her attention to the growing shadows of the darkening forest.

Talox reappeared to scatter the now-dying coals. "Sunset," he said simply as he scooped up Alorica.

Alarm bells ringing through her delightful haze, Larkin forced her heavy body to shift to a sitting position. "What are you doing with her?"

Talox handed Alorica up to Tam.

Larkin stood up too fast and stumbled. A second later, warm arms steadied her. Dizzy, she rested her forehead against a strong chest. "What if he drops her?" she mumbled.

"He won't." She was too dizzy to protest as Denan swung her up into his arms. "And I won't drop you either."

He passed her up to Tam, and the two of them switched passing her off to one another as they climbed higher and higher. "I'm going to fall to my death," she said. She should be terrified, but she was too busy studying the last wisp of the sun wavering on the horizon.

"We've trained for this," Tam said.

They passed what looked like a pied peapod that hung from a pair of sturdy branches. Inside, Larkin could see Venna peeking out at them.

"You trained to put unconscious women into peapods high up in the trees?" Larkin asked.

Denan chuckled. "That's even what we call them—pods."

Tam held open a pod while Denan eased Larkin inside and wrapped her in a blanket. She watched him, satisfied he didn't touch her a moment longer than needed. Finished, he pulled up the hood of his cloak so his face was hidden in shadows and tightened the toggles of his cloak. From below, he would be nearly impossible to spot.

"Denan," she asked. "What are you hiding from?"

He held his finger to his lips and bent closer, pulling the edges of the pod together. "Until sunrise, you must remain quiet and still."

She glanced past him, at the steel sky streaked with red. "Is it the gilgads?"

His mouth tightened into a thin line. The way he was looking at her—there was something else. "What's worse than gil-gads?"

"I hope you never find out."

Why was he playing all these games? Why not come out and tell her? "May the beast gobble you up and spit out your bones," she tried to say, but the words got jammed on their mad rush out of her mouth. She figured Denan would get the gist anyway.

"That's exactly what I'm afraid of," he muttered as he pulled out his pipe. Music wove with the coming darkness, pulling Larkin under, colors playing out behind her closed lids.

CHAPTER

ESCAPE

L arkin woke with a start, her neck throbbing. All around was the smell of death—stale, cloistered spaces and cloying rot. Above her, the leaves rustled a warning. From far below, she heard voices—nonsensical and wrong, like the chittering of insects. Whatever the pipers were afraid of, whatever they'd climbed this tree to escape, it was here.

"Larkin," Denan whispered, so softly she could barely hear it over the chittering and the warnings of the tree. He appeared over her, a shadow in the shadows. He pushed the flask into her hands. "One swallow. It will help with the pain ... and the fear."

"It's the beast, isn't it?"

His shadowy form shifted. "We call them wraiths."

Hands shaking, she took one swallow, eager for the colors to take her under again, away from the horror all around her.

"Sleep," he said. "I'll stand guard."

When she woke the second time, fear lingered like a bad aftertaste. She swallowed, wishing she could banish the feeling as easily. Denan's voice echoed back to her: *We call them wraiths.*

What kind of nightmare forest had she wandered into?

At that moment, the sun peeked over the horizon. She blinked at the light, shocked that dawn could return after such darkness. No matter how dark the night, dawn would always rise. And so would she.

Despite everything, she felt better rested than she had in weeks. She had Denan's music and whatever was in that flask to thank for that. Sleeping in the pod had also been surprisingly comfortable, more comfortable than her woven mat or even the straw tick mattress of Bane's house. At the thought, a pang of longing shot through her. What was Bane doing right now? Were her mother and sisters safe? Then, remembering Nesha's satisfied expression when she'd betrayed Larkin, she decided it was best not to think altogether.

Desperately needing to relieve her bladder, she peeked out of the pod. Wrapped in a pied blanket, Denan had situated himself at the intersection of trunk and bough, his head cocked at an uncomfortable-looking angle. She took a moment to study him unfettered—the way his dark lashes swept across his cheek like a raven's wings. His cheeks were angular but pitted with pockmarks. Dark hair shadowed his scalp—he probably needed to shave.

He is handsome, she admitted begrudgingly. *Doesn't mean I have to like him.*

Annoyed with Denan for that handsomeness, she pushed herself up—neck stinging and tight—and reached for a smaller branch to steady herself. She managed to plant one foot onto the bough, but when she tried to pull out her second foot, it tangled in the blankets. She tugged but couldn't manage to extricate herself. When she shifted to try to free her foot, she lost her balance, her hold on the branch the only thing keeping her from falling.

A hand reached out, catching hold of her waist and setting her up straight. Denan reached down and released her foot. Without a word, he went about untying the knots that held the pod to the tree. His eyes were bloodshot, as if he hadn't slept well.

"I still don't trust you," Larkin said.

"You're not a very trusting person."

She bristled. "I've had plenty of reason not to be."

He grunted in agreement.

"The wraiths … What are they?"

Denan wrapped up the pod and stuffed it in his pack. "They were men once—men who used their magic for evil until they'd corrupted the source, which in turn twisted them into something no longer human."

The others stirred. She followed him to the last branch. She wasn't sure she could jump out of the tree without losing control of herself. When he saw her hesitating, he held out his arms. She didn't want him to touch her, but she didn't want to wet herself either. Eventually, necessity won out over her pride, and she reached out for him. On the last branch, he lowered her easily to the ground. She immediately stepped back and headed toward the bushes.

"Larkin," he called after her. "You can wash up, but don't go far."

She eyed him. "You won't peek."

He grunted. "If I do, you can tell my mother. She'll promptly break my neck."

It was hard to imagine that Denan had a mother. Larkin hurried out of sight beyond a clump of trees. She would have liked to strip and take a proper bath, but there was no way she was taking off all her clothes, no matter what Denan promised. After relieving herself, she removed her dress and waded out in her shift.

Venna came into view, Alorica propped up at her side. The

girl moved stiffly, her face a grimace of pain and fury. Larkin considered helping Alorica into the pool, but if the girl could run for it, she could deal with the consequences.

Shuffling awkwardly, Alorica managed to strip to her shift and reach the water. She bent down to wash herself and glanced back toward camp. "We have to try again, tonight."

Larkin stiffened before scooping up water to scrub under her arms. "Didn't you sense the—" She tried to say "wraiths," but her mouth refused to form the word. She tried again and ended up standing there with her mouth gaping.

Alorica took an uneasy step back. "Are you going to be sick?"

"I can't say it." Denan hadn't been lying. He really couldn't tell her what was going on. He had only been able to tell her about the wraiths after she'd experienced them herself. "But there's something out there, something far worse than the gilgad. It came under the tree last night. We have to stay with the pipers."

"You saw it?" Venna asked in a small voice.

Larkin hesitated. "No, but I felt it."

Alorica rolled her eyes. "The pipers are the real beasts. I'll not stay with them another moment. Don't you want to be free?"

Larkin wanted nothing more. She watched the sun crest the top of the waterfall, turning its waters crimson—like the blood that had spilled from her throat the day before. The sounds of the townspeople calling for her death rang in her ears, and she swayed on her feet, feeling as if she wasn't attached to her body.

"I already told you, my father—" Alorica began.

"You think you're so much better than me," Larkin snapped. "That what happened to me can't happen to you. You're ignorant, Alorica. And that ignorance is going to get us killed."

"We'll go with or without you," Alorica said coolly.

"You need my help or you wouldn't be bothering," Larkin

said.

"Are you that much of a coward?" Alorica hissed.

Larkin turned to the two girls. Her eyes glittered with rage. "Your father, Alorica, wanted me dead by hanging. Garrot leaned toward burning me at the stake. I don't have anything to go back to."

"Didn't my grandfather help you?" Venna asked in a small voice.

"He tried," Larkin said. "But Denan saved my life."

Venna reached for Larkin's hand. Larkin pulled back; she didn't want to be touched. Venna curled her fingers against her chest. "I-I'm so sorry."

Alorica folded her arms. "Then go somewhere else! There's more to the Idelmarch than Hamel. There's Landra or Cordova or a smaller town. I'll help you—hide you and give you enough money to get started. You can take your family. No one would know you came back, so no one would look for you."

Was it possible? Could she really go back? Larkin swayed, thinking of Mama and her little sisters. They needed her. She couldn't imagine living the rest of her life never knowing what happened to them. "How would this time be any different than yesterday?"

"I don't want to be pricked with one of those poisoned darts," Venna added.

Pleased with herself, Alorica fussed with her gold bracelet. "That's just it. We'll use their weapons against them, as Larkin did when she escaped." She waded closer, voice rising with excitement. "We wait for our chance and steal three darts. We hit each man at the same time, and then we run all the way back to Hamel."

"There's a couple minutes between being darted and total collapse," Larkin pointed out. "Plenty of time for them to dart us too. And they'd be furious when they came around."

"They'd fight us off before we ever even got close," Venna

added.

A diabolical light gleamed in Alorica's eyes. "We'll let them share the pods with us. They won't be able to resist. No man would. In the morning, we dart them all at the same time. Then we run."

"What about the beast?" Larkin asked.

Alorica waved away her warning. "If there is a beast, we'll handle it."

Larkin splashed water on her face. "We don't know how."

"Hiding in a tree seemed to work last night," Alorica said. Venna nodded in agreement. "Now, how will we know when to stick the pipers?"

"You could cough for the signal," Venna said. "Once to let us know to get ready. Once to stick them."

Alorica broke into a grin. "Venna, you're brilliant."

Venna blushed. "And then we simply follow the river home?"

"We'll be home in a couple days. Less, if we hurry," Alorica said.

"Larkin," Denan called. "Stop plotting and come eat your breakfast."

She froze. Had he somehow heard them?

"Remember," Alorica whispered as she sloshed to shore.

Larkin followed, legs numb and red. She touched her amulet. Before, there had been a need to hide it. There wasn't anymore. She untied it from her waist, retied the leather cord, and dropped it over her head. She studied the way the light played off the colors gleaming deep within. If she did manage to escape, she would never learn to use her magic, never be more than a powerless girl at the mercy of druids and pipers and men.

"Larkin, hurry up," Alorica said.

If she stayed, she would give up her family. That was a price she would never willingly pay. Larkin finished dressing and cringed at the feel of her damp shift under her clothes.

Talox handed out a breakfast of leftover meat and more greens. After they finished, Tam swam across the river with a rope. Denan had them climb a tree and zip across in a thrilling, twisting ride without the need to get wet. They headed northeast, climbing upward with every step. One of the men always ranged ahead.

Larkin hurried to catch up to Denan. He looked at her in surprise. She refused to meet his gaze; she didn't want to look too eager. "You really can't tell me the truth, can you?"

He grunted. "Curse bind your tongue?" She nodded. "The others have to figure it out on their own, as you did."

I am not like you, she thought. What she said was, "Tell me about the curse." He shook his head. She growled in frustration. "I already know about the wraiths. Tell me about them." She needed to know how to handle them if they were escaping in the morning.

"In the ancient language, wraith meant 'children of the light.'"

"You said the magic corrupted them?" She shuddered at the possibility of her magic turning her into something that radiated such evil.

"They were twisted, both in form and in mind. Their bodies shifted from beautiful to terrible. Their purpose from goodness to chaos. They are evil, Larkin, and cunning and cruel and depraved. All the things we as a people fight for, they fight for the opposite."

"What do they look like?"

He held back a branch and let her through. "At first, they're mere shadows, then those shadows take shape."

What did that even mean? She wasn't sure she wanted to know. "How do you kill them?"

"You cannot kill what is already dead. A deathblow from a blade made of the White Tree will banish them for a time, and they cannot cross water." Denan stopped, his hand going out to stop her, his face hard as stone.

At the sound of distant flute music, Larkin shared a worried glance with the other girls and stepped closer to Denan. "What's going on?"

He unhooked his bow and strung it. "We are being hunted."

She worried her bottom lip. "Wraiths?"

He shook his head. "They come out after the sun sets."

She breathed a sigh of relief. "Gilgads?"

"No."

She swallowed. "There's something else?"

His jaw tightened. "There's a narrow stream not far from here."

Larkin shot a glance back at Alorica. She had to convince the other girls to reconsider their escape plans.

Denan shot her a suspicious look. "Why so many questions?"

"I need to know how to defend myself," she said a little too quickly.

"Let us worry about that."

They reached a little burbling spring not long before sunset. Such a little thing, but Larkin felt an overwhelming sense of relief when they crossed it. They hadn't taken any fresh meat during the day, so Talox handed out travel bread and they split up the nuts and greens they had all managed to gather along the way.

They were given a little time to wash up before bed. Larkin waited until the men had taken a few steps away before kneeling next to Alorica. "I'm not sure—"

Alorica rubbed water across her face and neck. "You will do your part and keep your mouth shut."

Larkin made a show of cleaning her teeth. "Are you willing to die for it?"

Alorica leaned closer. "Absolutely."

Before Larkin could reply, a cry brought her head up, heart

pounding. Venna had crumpled to the ground. Water running into her collar, Larkin shot to her feet and hurried toward her. "Venna, what happened?"

Venna's face beaded with sweat. "I fell."

Larkin shot a glare at Talox. "Did you dart her?"

"No." He knelt next to Venna. "Where does it hurt?"

She panted, eyes squeezed shut. "My ankle."

He gently reached out, untied her worn boots, and ran his fingers over her unblemished skin. Denan and Tam came over too, concerned. Venna's eyes locked with Larkin's, and her expression wasn't full of pain, but guilt.

Suspicious, Larkin sneaked a glance at Alorica, who slipped three darts wrapped in leather from Talox's dropped pack. She held her finger to her lips as she slid them in her pocket. Larkin's mouth fell open, but no words came out.

"Larkin?" Denan followed her gaze. Alorica was striding toward them. She knelt beside Venna.

"You should try walking on it. Sometimes that will loosen it up." She ducked under Venna's arm and helped her up. Venna took a limping step. Larkin folded her arms, not liking that the two had conspired without telling her.

"It's feeling better," Venna said after half a dozen steps. "I think it will be all right."

"Still, it won't hurt to wrap it." Talox went for his pack.

Tam shot Alorica a suspicious look. Her eyes went wide and innocent. "Is there really something out there, hunting us?" she asked breathlessly, and it somehow made her look alluring.

Tam gave a slow nod. She bit her lip and considered the darkening forest. "You could probably defend us better if you got a decent night's sleep." He nodded again. She sighed. "All right. You take the pod. I'll sleep on the bough."

"They're strong enough we could share," Tam offered a little too eagerly.

Alorica blushed prettily. "I don't—I mean, that wouldn't be

proper."

He bounced on the pads of his feet. "We can tie them flat. Not as much protection from the elements, but it shouldn't rain tonight anyway."

She looked at him demurely. "I suppose, but only if you promise to keep your distance."

"You're always safe with me," Tam said breathlessly.

It took everything Larkin had not to roll her eyes.

Alorica turned her wide brown eyes on Venna. "Don't you want your piper to have a good night's sleep so he can defend you?"

Venna sat on a log, eyes on the ground. "I suppose."

Alorica turned that same gaze to Larkin, who folded her arms. "No."

A glint flashed in Alorica's eyes. "If you won't do it for yourself, do it for us."

Knowing what she really meant, Larkin wavered. The forest was dangerous—more dangerous than any of them really knew—but she'd already warned them, and they still wanted to risk it. Did she really have the right to force them to stay? Maybe Alorica was right, and Larkin was a selfish coward for not facing the danger to return to her own family. "Fine. As long as he doesn't touch me."

She could feel Denan's stare, his suspicion burning her from the inside out. "I can take the bough," he said. He picked up his pack, set it next to the spring, and refused to look at her. The other pipers headed back into the forest, probably to set up the pods in the tree they'd staked out earlier.

Alorica's fingers dug into Larkin's arm, and she slipped the dart into her hand. "Fix it."

Larkin shoved the dart into her pocket. Alorica gave Venna a hug good night—if the pipers knew her at all, they would have realized how out of character that was. Larkin saw her drop the dart into Venna's pocket.

No more wavering. Larkin had decided; now she had to live with it. Gritting her teeth, she marched toward the spring where Denan knelt next to the flowing water. Shirtless, he rinsed the soap from his torso. Water slid down his honed body, dark honey skin gleaming. She stopped in her tracks, mouth falling open. He was beautiful. As she watched, he ran a blade over his scalp, shaving the prickling of dark hair.

"What is Alorica up to?" Denan asked.

Larkin started. She'd thought herself hidden from sight. Apparently not. She turned her back to him, as much to give him the privacy she should have given before as to hide her flaming cheeks. "Wh-what do you mean?"

"You know what I mean."

"Few can resist Alorica—not once she sets her sights on them." And secretly, Larkin wished she had that power over men.

"I could."

She glanced over to see him rinsing the soap from his gleaming scalp. "Just so long as you stick to your side of the pod."

"You detest me. Why would you want to share a pod?"

She couldn't look at him for fear he would see the lie on her face. "Because I felt the wraiths last night." She heard rustling clothes and more splashing. She turned to see if he was nearly dressed, only to find him perfectly naked, his buttocks as toned as the rest of him.

Blushing even harder, she whipped around. "Have you no shame?"

"You're the one hanging around while I'm trying to bathe."

She had to focus, had to figure out what other dangers they faced. "What's the other thing hunting us?"

"You know I can't tell you."

Larkin tried to block out the sounds of him washing. "Something the music holds back, but only for a little while."

"How did you know that?"

"Tam was playing his pipes, but you said we still had to cross the river. Are they as bad as the wraiths?"

He grunted. "No. The magic drives away the weaker ones for a time."

"And the stronger ones?"

"Just seems to enrage them."

"So how do you defeat them?"

"Weapons, mostly."

Larkin looked up through the branches above her. How were they supposed to cross the Forbidden Forest full of gilgads, wraiths, and something she didn't even have a name for? She had no more idea how to use a bow than a sword. Deep in thought, she prodded her bandage, wincing at the soreness.

"Let me check that."

She jumped, surprised to find him right next to her—so much skin exposed she wasn't sure where to look. "Put your shirt on!"

He grunted. "It's still drying." He pulled out the salve from his pack. She let her gaze trail down far enough to affirm he had on a clean pair of pants.

She didn't like him that close to her, but the salve did help with the pain. She tipped her head to the side, and he changed the bandage, adding more salve. "Healing nicely. In a couple days, we can take the bandage off."

He replaced the salve and shouldered his pack. She followed him to another tree. "Talox," he called up. "Your turn."

Talox dropped heavily to his feet and strode past them.

"He doesn't say much, does he?" In contrast, she could make out Tam chattering above them.

"Only when he needs to." Denan jumped up and grabbed a bough, pulling himself up and holding a hand out to her. After a moment's hesitation, she took it. This time, when he set up the pod, he tied the four corners down so it was flat. He settled down the blanket. "In you go."

Spreading his shirt and damp pants across a branch, he pulled his cloak from his pack while she climbed across the pod. Denan placed the pack between them and climbed in. Their weight pulled them together, the pack a divider of sorts, but their hips and legs still touched. Larkin rolled to her side to avoid the contact. She listened to the sounds of the coming night, trying not to think about the dart in her pocket.

"What's your favorite color?" he asked.

"Turquoise," she said immediately. "Like the tail feathers of an amala bird." She imagined herself soaring through the sky, free in a way she never had been before.

Sometime before dawn, Larkin started awake to the sound of coughing. She came face-to-face with a bare chest. She was tangled up with Denan, her head on his chest, his arms snug around her, their feet intertwined. Her breath hitched in her throat, panic shooting through her.

She froze, horror and repulsion drowning her. She couldn't seem to catch her breath. At the sound of more coughing and a muffled shout, Denan jerked up, instantly alert. A couple beats later, Larkin remembered what she was supposed to do. She wrenched the dart from her pocket, but Denan was already half out of the pod.

"Denan," she cried. He whipped around, a panicked look about his eyes. She stabbed him in the arm. He yanked out the dart and stared at the welling blood in disbelief. Blood trickled down his arm, and she cringed at the betrayal in his eyes.

"You can't want to go back."

"I can't leave my family." Why was she giving him an explanation? She owed him nothing.

"I watched you. I saw the way your father treated you, the

way the townspeople treated you. You deserve better, Larkin."

Her two little sisters. Her mother. "My family needs me. And Bane—"

"What about what you need?"

No one had ever asked that before. "I'm sorry."

His arm dangled; his left cheek sagged. He went to his pouch, removed a vial, and took a quick swallow of antidote. "You have to keep the other girls alive." He tried to do up the strap on the pack, but his fingers kept fumbling. She did it for him. "You can't go back the way we came. There are four wraiths tracking us. You'll have to cross the river."

She nodded.

"The wraith's blades are poison and the—" He swore and hit the branch with the flat of his hand. "I can't say it!" He pushed a knife into her hand. "There's more of the other ones." He half fell into the pod. His legs dangled, their weight pulling him down. Trying to push aside her crushing guilt, she lifted them into the pod. He lay back, his gaze locked on hers. "You have your amulet?" She nodded. "If it comes to it, use it like a shield, but your safest bet is to be in a tree before sunset. Promise me, Larkin. Swear it."

She nodded. "I will."

"They can't climb trees." His words were becoming slurred. "And they won't cross swiftly moving water."

"Will you—Will you be all right?"

"I won't be able to come for you until tonight, but I will come for you. I will always come for you." It didn't feel like a threat, but a promise. The tree shook. Larkin half expecting a wraith to come at her. "Protect the others, Larkin." She gripped the knife tighter to hide her shaking. He reached up and clumsily brushed her cheek with the back of his knuckle. "Stay safe, little bird." Then his hand dropped, and he went still.

Larkin stared at him for a long time, reminding herself he wasn't dead. He would come around in a few hours. So why did she feel a desperate, wailing panic cresting in her chest? Unable to resist, she held her hand under his nose, reassured by the puff against her fingers.

"Larkin?" Alorica hissed.

Sniffing, Larkin turned to see Alorica and Venna climbing toward her. Venna was pale. Alorica looked disheveled, her hair coming out of its braid. "Take his pack. Let's go." She started down the tree.

Larkin glanced back and saw Denan's foot dangling from the pod. She tucked it back inside.

"What are you doing?" Alorica hissed.

Larkin took the pack, leaving him some travel bread as well as his bow, shield, and ax—she didn't know how to use them anyway—and walked carefully along the bough. "Did you give the others the antidote?"

Venna nodded.

"Tam took his after he failed to tie me up," Alorica said as she stepped down.

Larkin wondered if she would have given it to him on her own.

"Talox didn't even seem angry," Venna said miserably. "He kept saying the beasts were coming and to stay in the trees."

"Of course he would tell you that," Alorica snapped.

Larkin dropped to the ground. "The beasts are real." Even as she said it, she searched the forest as she'd seen the men do now for two days. The forest take her, she didn't even know what to look for! "We need to cross the river."

Alorica rolled her eyes. "I can't swim!"

"You could hold on to a log and drift across," Larkin said.

"Talox told me to cross too." Venna wrung her hands. "I can't swim either."

Larkin was even more grateful that Bane had taught her after she'd almost drowned.

"They're just trying to slow us down." Alorica didn't look

back.

Larkin couldn't stop thinking about Denan's warning. "Alorica, if you don't cross the river, I'm not going."

"Then don't come," Alorica called over her shoulder.

"Alorica!" Larkin called after her, but the other girl didn't slow.

Larkin and Venna exchanged a look. "We can't let her go alone," Venna said and took off after her.

Larkin seriously considered leaving them to their fate, but then she glanced up at the shadows of the men in their pods. She'd promised Denan she'd look after them.

With a growling sigh, she hurried to catch up.

CHAPTER

20

WRAITHS

Larkin's shoulders ached with the weight of the stolen pack. She wanted to pull her hood up, but she didn't dare lose sight of the forest for even a moment. It was so still even the birds had stopped singing. A dark feeling itched under her skin, like she was being watched.

"The sun will set in minutes. We need to get up the trees," she called to the others.

"The men will be waking soon, if they haven't already," Alorica said. "We have to put as much distance between ourselves and them as possible."

Venna had always been the more reasonable of the two. Larkin appealed to her. "The pipers never went anywhere without a scout, and certainly not in the dark. We could be walking right into a pack of beasts and—"

Venna lifted her chin. "I saw the gilgad Denan brought in. It wasn't that scary. Besides, we have all the antidote."

"There's something worse than gilgads," Larkin pleaded.

"Something you don't understand."

Venna bit her lip. "What?"

"It's a—" She couldn't say it. Idiotic magic binding her tongue! "It's the beast! I promise!"

Venna gave her a pitying look and hurried after Alorica.

Larkin caught up to them. A dark shadow shifted ahead. The three of them froze. Sleek with golden eyes, a huge cat tensed as it looked back at them. Alorica staggered back. Venna let out a strangled shout. The cat tensed and darted into the brush.

They were silent a beat, and then Alorica let out a nervous laugh. "There's your beast, Larkin, and Venna frightened it off with her all-powerful voice." She strode out. Venna shot Larkin a nervous glance and kept walking.

Larkin wanted to scream in frustration. To know the wraiths were out there and not be able to warn her friends! Something shifted to Larkin's left. She whipped around, her neck wound pulling, only to find nothing there.

They came out into an open meadow. The last dredges of sunlight brushed against Larkin's face in warning. The grass all around them was tall and green, and a little pond lay to their left. Where were the deer and other animals? This meadow was perfect grazing, and yet not a strand of grass had been chewed down.

Alorica gestured. "There, open space. Do you see any beasts?"

All Larkin could see was wavering grasses. "But—"

"If you want to go back, go back!" Alorica adjusted her pack and stormed off.

"Venna," Larkin tried again.

"I want to go home," Venna said. "Alorica's right. I think you're afraid to go back—not that I blame you, but still. There's at least another hour of light left after the sun sets, and I'm not going to lose it." Venna cast an apologetic look over her shoulder.

Out of the corner of Larkin's eye, the trees' shadows wavered. When she turned to look, she saw nothing. Denan said they came from the shadows. By now, Alorica was more than halfway across the meadow, headed straight toward the forest's reaching shadows.

A dark foreboding grew in the pit of Larkin's stomach. She hesitated. Should she climb a tree now and leave the girls to their fate? She'd promised Denan she'd look after them, and she couldn't just let them walk into danger. She ran after them, the pack jostling awkwardly.

She passed Venna and caught up to Alorica, snatching her arm steps before she reached the shadows stretching toward her feet. "Alorica, stop," she said breathlessly.

"What are you doing?" Alorica jerked free.

"Please, you have to listen—" Larkin began.

Venna's cry of alarm shut them both up. Larkin followed her horrified gaze. The trees were mammoth conifers with serrated branches, and though they held perfectly still, their shadows writhed on the ground like tortured snakes. The shadows condensed and rose up into a black vapor. In the midst of that vapor appeared two sets of jagged irises the color of jaundice shot through with blood. Where white should be, there was only consuming blackness.

"Wraiths!" Larkin stumbled back, the word finally coming easily from her mouth. "We have to get in the trees."

Alorica clutched Larkin. "They're coming *from* the trees!"

"No. From the shadows." Larkin looked behind her, at the final vestiges of sunlight illuminating the trees to the east.

"Run!" Venna cried. They bolted back the way they'd come, Larkin in the lead, Venna and Alorica right behind her.

"Larkin, look out!" Venna cried.

Larkin stuttered, half turning back. The pack on her back

inexplicably tightened, pulling her sideways. She staggered, barely catching herself from falling. She whirled to face whatever was behind her, the contents of her pack spilled in an arch over the meadow as if it had been cut open. Something scuttled in the shadows of a felled tree, something like a ghost that hid its features behind a cowl of writhing shadows. It was dressed differently from the others—a square black mantle across its shoulders. It drew back a corporeal sword—a sword that emitted its own darkness, sticky and oozing—and stabbed at her. Reeling in horror, she threw herself back and landed hard.

The sword stirred the air before her face. The wraith screamed in frustration, the sound tearing her in two. Black emptiness swirled around those horrible eyes. She couldn't look away, couldn't move. It arched the sword above its head. She tried to scramble back, but her body refused to obey her desperate commands.

She was going to die.

With a war cry, Alorica lunged at the wraith, bashing it with her pack. It shattered like torn shadows and whipped back to form in the space of a blink. Alorica danced out of reach as the creature fixed its malevolent gaze on her. Venna linked her arms under Larkin's and hauled her back as the wraith spun, sword slamming into the ground where they had been. The grasses turned a brittle, crumbling black. A mailed hand reached for them, sizzling and smoking when it crossed into the sunlight. Hissing, the wraith jerked back into the shadows.

"Idiot!" Alorica's eyes were wild and furious. "Why didn't you run?"

"Don't look into its eyes," Larkin warned.

"We have to get in the trees!" Venna dragged Larkin to her feet and pushed her in the right direction.

Becoming more corporeal by the second, the wraith gnashed and shrieked, pacing on the shadow's edge like a predator at the bars of its cage.

"They can't leave the shadows," Larkin said. "As long as we have the light, we're all right." She hoped.

Avoiding anything with a large shadow, they fled to the other side of the meadow. The sun disappeared, plunging them into twilight. Three wraiths surged forward with inhuman screams of triumph, their forms becoming more fixed with each stride.

Denan had said there were four of them. Where was the fourth?

Alorica jumped for the nearest bough, Venna a handful of steps behind. They couldn't see what Larkin could. The fourth wraith lurked in the shadows on the opposite side of the tree. This wraith also wore a mantle, but a corroded crown encircled his cowl. He rose up, his body taking shape even as Venna jumped for the branch, her pack weighing her down.

Larkin surged forward. "Venna! Watch out!"

Venna fell onto her back. Her body went unnaturally still in the wraith's thrall. It pulled out a smoldering sword.

Her amulet! Larkin yanked it over her head, squeezing so the branches slipped inside her skin. The wraith lifted its poisonous sword. Larkin jumped in front of Venna and held up the amulet, hoping against hope it formed a barrier between them. The wraith's sword arched toward her with enough force to cleave her in two.

Shadow and smoke slammed into fire and light. Larkin's arm went numb—whether from the force of the blow or some magic, she didn't know. The wraith shrieked, the sound driving all hope and warmth from Larkin, nearly sending her to her knees.

She gripped the amulet hard. The pointed branches dug in deep. "No!" she screamed as she swung the shield at the unnatural creature. A convex pulse of golden light slammed into the wraith, its shadows writhing their death throes before disappearing altogether.

"Behind you!" Alorica cried.

Larkin whirled as another wraith came at her. She recognized the square mantle—the wraith from the middle of the meadow. She ducked and brought the amulet up, the shield forming even as she swung it at the creature, connecting with its body. It flew backward, slamming into the tree, where it thrashed as if it had touched acid, its body burning away to shadow again. From the tree's base, its sickly eyes glared up at her. It was injured, but not dead. And now it was between her and the tree.

"The other two are coming!" Alorica warned from above.

A glance to the west showed the other wraiths nearly across the meadow. Larkin dragged Venna up. "Come on!"

Larkin took a dozen running strides deeper into the forest and looked for a tree with a low enough bough that she could reach it with a running jump. There. Dropping the amulet back around her neck, she changed course, timed her steps, and leaped. She reached the branch and swung, hooking her foot around it and pulling herself up. She turned in time to see Venna leap, but she missed and fell.

"Drop your pack!" Larkin screamed as the wraiths reached the tree's edge. Venna shrugged out of the pack. Hugging the branch, Larkin stretched for her as she jumped, grabbing hold. Larkin pulled while Venna's feet scrabbled for purchase along the trunk. She had managed to hook one leg around the bough when the mantled wraith swung its blade. Larkin screamed a warning as the blade whistled past.

It missed. He drew his arm back, stabbing toward them. Larkin grabbed the amulet dangling in front of her, squeezing hard. Golden light danced as the wraith's blade connected with her shield. The wraith screamed in frustration, then prowled around the tree's base with the others, their steps eerily silent.

Still holding the amulet, Larkin whispered, "We need to get higher."

Venna groaned. Moving carefully, they made their way to a

sturdy branch beyond the wraiths' reach. Venna sat with her back against the trunk, her legs dangling on either side of the bough. In the twilight, Larkin could make out the differences between the three. Their unnatural cloaks were all a little different. One was bigger and brawnier than the others; one was small, almost petite. The mantled one seemed to be in charge, for the others followed when it pointed back toward Alorica's tree.

"They should be gone by morning," Larkin whispered as she dropped to straddle the branch. Her hands came away damp, and she wiped them on her skirt. "I think we're going to be all right."

"Larkin." Venna's voice sounded strained.

There was a steady drizzling sound. Larkin scooted closer, her hands almost slipping on the wet bough—except it wasn't raining. She lifted her hands to her face. There was just enough light to make out the smears of blood on her palms.

The wraith hadn't missed. Its blade had sliced Venna's foot.

CHAPTER 21

LINES OF BLACK

L arkin stared at the blood, Denan's warnings pounding through her head, especially the warning about poisoned blades. She scooted close enough that her knees touched Venna's. "How bad is it?"

Venna tucked her bloody foot between them. "It burns like fire." Blood bubbled up through the slice in her boot. Larkin moved with steady slowness as she removed the boot and sock, revealing shredded muscle and ligaments from the pad of the foot all the way to the heel. The wound itself appeared scorched, and the blood was tainted black.

"Venna? Larkin?" a faint, tremulous voice called—Alorica.

"Don't go down!" Larkin called out a warning. "The wraiths are still here."

The mantled wraith whipped toward the sound and called out something in a shrieking voice. The other wraith answered in kind. Larkin and Venna cringed at the sound.

"They can communicate," Venna whispered.

"Denan says they were men once." She could feel the baleful glare of one of them, like rot moldering in her veins.

Alorica made a panicked sound. "What are we going to do?"

Now she wanted Larkin's advice? Anger flooded through her. "Stay put until morning. The pipers will come for us."

Larkin turned back to Venna's injury.

Venna panted. "How deep is it?"

Mama and Nesha were the ones trained to deal with this sort of thing, not Larkin. "It's too dark to really tell." Afraid Venna would hear the lie in her voice, she added quickly, "We need to stop the bleeding." She tore off the sleeve of her dress and turned it inside out—it was cleaner on the inside. "Try to hold still."

Larkin straightened Venna's leg so her foot rested on Larkin's thigh. She braced herself and wrapped the sleeve tight. Venna screamed, the sound like a knife to the unnatural stillness of the night. Alorica called out to them, but Larkin ignored her, continuing even as Venna succumbed to sobs. When she was done, Larkin tore half the sleeve back and tied it off.

"I'm done." She was shaking, hands sticky with blood.

"What's going on?" Alorica sobbed. "Larkin, please, answer me!"

"Venna's hurt," Larkin managed. "I had to stop the bleeding."

"How is she hurt? Where?"

As if in answer, Venna pitched forward. Bracing herself, Larkin barely managed to catch her. Venna's whole body convulsed. "Venna!" she cried as she tried to hold the other girl up, but she was slipping. The shaking stopped, leaving Larkin with nothing but dead weight. They started sliding to the left. If Larkin didn't let go, they were both going to fall.

"Talk to me!" Alorica demanded.

If Larkin lived through this, she was going to strangle Alorica. Digging in her right heel, Larkin cried, "Venna!"

Venna gasped as if coming awake and curled forward, grabbing the branch. When Larkin was sure the other girl wasn't going to fall, she leaned back to center herself. She stood carefully and maneuvered behind Venna. If she had another fit, it would be easier to hold her from behind. She wrapped her arms around Venna and pulled her close.

"Larkin," Alorica wailed.

"Shut it!" Larkin screamed back.

Alorica finally went silent.

"Why didn't you tell us of the wraiths?" Venna asked.

"I tried, but the magic stopped me." For the first time, she had a little empathy for Denan.

Venna accepted this without question. "The blade—it was poisoned."

"How do you know?" Larkin asked in surprise.

"I can feel it," Venna said through clenched teeth. "It's like clawed spiders scrambling up my veins."

"You're going to be fine." Larkin wasn't sure if she was comforting herself or Venna. "We just have to make it till morning."

"Do you have a knife?"

"A knife?" Larkin was still trying to catch her breath. "No. We lost it when we dropped the packs."

"I need you to cut it off," Venna said between gritted teeth, "before it's too late."

"Cut what off?"

"My foot!"

Horrified, Larkin shook her head. "The pain is addling your brain."

Venna whimpered. "Please, you don't understand. It's killing me."

"You'd only bleed to death! There has to be an antidote. Denan said he would come for us at nightfall. They should reach us before morning."

Venna slumped in Larkin's arms, the back of her head resting on Larkin's shoulder, her skin damp and hot.

"You're going to be all right," Larkin whispered. "Denan swore he'd be here by morning. He'll help you."

"Promise?"

"I promise."

For a time, there was only Venna's ragged breathing and the distant sound of Alorica sobbing. Larkin sat in vigil, watching the last light of day die, falling to total darkness. Though she couldn't hear or see them, she could feel the wraiths stalking them like death. Horrible as they were, not seeing them was worse.

"You want to know why I helped you, back in Hamel?" Venna sounded parched, her voice heavy. "You never needed friends—you had Bane and Nesha—but I did, and you were the closest thing I ever had."

Larkin felt a surge of guilt. Until recently, she'd never been close with Venna. "I'm sorry I wasn't a better friend."

"Talk to me." Venna wiped her cheeks. "I can't stand the silence."

The only thing Larkin could think to do was sing, like her mother used to when they were hiding from her father. Larkin sang all Sela's favorite lullabies, her tears wetting Venna's hair. She even hummed Mama's special melody, the one that had no words.

Venna's body went limp. Larkin's back and arms cramped from holding her, but she didn't dare shift her position for fear of sending them both toppling. Venna grew hotter and hotter, her breathing labored.

The world finally shifted from black to gray, allowing Larkin to once again make out the wraiths below, with their cloaks of torn, writhing shadows. Once, she caught sight of a torso covered in mail. Larkin couldn't see their faces because of their cowls, but occasionally she could make out the gleam of sickly yellow eyes, and there was the ever-present smell of the grave.

With the added light, Larkin was forced to watch as thick black lines crawled up Venna's dark skin all the way to her thigh. Larkin had never felt so utterly alone or helpless before.

"Are you two still alive?" Alorica called, her voice hollow.

"Yes," Larkin called back.

"Venna?" Alorica asked.

"She's alive," Larkin rasped.

Venna suddenly shifted and groaned in pain. "Larkin, it hurts. It hurts so much."

Tears welled in Larkin's eyes and she said the words she'd been wanting to say for hours now, "Thank you for saving my life."

"Hurts," Venna managed.

Larkin forced her exhausted arms to hold her friend tighter. "I'm sorry."

Venna's head slumped, and she convulsed again. When she finally stopped, her skin was so hot Larkin began sweating despite the chill. Her arms shook, and she could barely link her hands together. Larkin didn't think she could hold her if she convulsed again.

The wraiths had grown increasingly agitated as the sky continued to lighten. Now, the three of them grouped together, a rasping, shrieking whisper that made Larkin ache to cover her ears. They came toward the tree three abreast, the mantled one in the center slightly ahead of the others. In their fists, their swords gleamed like corrupted smoke. The wraith ran forward, cocking back its arm to launch the sword.

Larkin scrambled to free the amulet from where it was trapped between her and Venna. The wraith screamed—the sound like a death keel, the sword dropping from its fingers. It flickered to shadow and then back to solid form, a white arrow sticking out of its arm. It hissed something, and the other two came at Larkin, their sword arms cocked.

"Wraith!" a voice shouted a challenge.

Larkin knew that voice. Denan sprinted through the trees. Ahead of him, Tam drew back his bow, released another arrow, and struck a wraith as it launched its sword. The arrow struck its neck, and it imploded. Writhing shadows sucked in until there was nothing left.

But the third, smallest wraith released its sword, trailing tendrils of black swirling smoke. Larkin shoved the amulet before Venna and imagined the barrier rising.

The sword struck the barrier with a clang, then fell apart like charcoal. Larkin felt a single moment of triumph before Venna's whole body seized, going rigid. Larkin tried to hold her, but her strength deserted her. She cried out as Venna fell.

"No!" From the opposite direction of Denan, Talox burst into view from behind a nearby tree. He dropped his bow as he lunged, managing to break Venna's fall. Rolling her off him, he knelt on the ground. He took in her wound with a sorrow that broke him. He cradled the girl in his arms, his lips against her forehead as he murmured something that almost sounded like a spell.

Beyond him, Tam and Denan fought back-to-back against the two remaining wraiths. The pipers moved like lightning amid boiling clouds in a dance that was both beautiful and deadly, their weapons catching the morning light.

Denan finally managed to strike, his ax sinking into the mantled wraith. Its gaze locked on Larkin as it imploded. The third was harder to kill. It slunk with the shadows. A blow from its sword didn't even ring against Tam's shield. Daylight threaded through the trees, striking the shadow. It hissed as smoke rose from it. It backed toward the deeper shadows, sword held defensively before it.

Denan and Tam boxed it in, axes held in the ready position.

"You found her," the wraith said in an inhuman voice. "My king will be so pleased."

Larkin stiffened. *Her? Her who?*

Denan slid closer. "I don't know what you mean."

The wraith laughed—a horrible sound. "How many times have we danced this dance, Denan of the White Tree? You cannot kill us. You cannot defeat us. The only remaining option is to join us or die."

"Go back to your grave where you belong, Hagath," Tam said in a hard voice.

The wraith's attention shifted to him. "I will make you one of my playthings, and I will enjoy seeing you beg."

Playthings? Larkin noticed the curves hidden beneath the wraith's cloak. The wraith—Hagath—was smaller than the others because she was a woman. Larkin's mouth fell open in shock. Hagath rushed Denan, her form disintegrating to something ghostlike as she left the shadow's shelter. Denan caught her blade with his shield, shoved it up and out while stabbing with the pointed tip of his ax. Before his ax connected, the sun crested the horizon, golden light stabbing the wraith. She tipped back her head and screamed as her body burned away to ashes.

Denan whipped around. "Where's the fourth?" he called up to Larkin.

"Gone," she answered.

As soon as the words left her lips, Tam ran toward the tree Alorica was in.

Denan's gaze locked with Larkin's. She expected anger or disgust. Instead, fear dominated. His shoulders slumped in exhaustion. "You banished one of them?"

"If banishing means it imploded, yes."

His eyes slipped closed. "The amulet is safe?"

"Yes." The forest take her, he'd saved her life again. Counting the warning he'd given when she'd escaped, that was the third time.

"Can you come down on your own?"

In answer, she swung her leg over the branch. She tried to

dangle from her fingertips to drop to the next one, but her hands gave out. She landed off-balance on the bough and tipped backward, then she was falling. She closed her eyes, too exhausted to flail.

She landed in a pair of arms, knocking the wind from Denan. He managed to keep upright and set her on her feet, where she swayed unsteadily. His hands settled around her waist. Wincing, she backed away from his touch and staggered to Venna's side. Her friend was unconscious—her skin ashen and her breathing too fast. Talox chanted over her.

Larkin started to push him back—he had no right to touch Venna—but at the tears slipping down his cheeks, Larkin froze. How could he be so upset? He'd only met Venna three days ago.

Denan crouched on the other side of Venna. He pulled down the collar of her dress, revealing angry black lines climbing up her collarbone in jagged, rectangular patterns.

"Oh, Venna," Denan said, voice heavy with grief.

"You have to help her." Larkin wiped her nose, throat aching. "There has to be something you can do."

Denan closed his eyes. "There isn't."

That knocked the breath from Larkin. "No! Please, I promised her."

"I should have left her in that town," Talox's voice wavered. "At least she was safe there."

Larkin shook her head. "Sicknesses can be treated. Even plagues are survivable, and Venna is strong." Even as she said it, she didn't quite believe—not with those black lines inching up Venna's chest.

"Talox," Denan said gently. "We have to go."

Talox bowed his head. "I just found her, Denan."

Denan reached out, resting his forehead against Talox's. For a moment, they sat that way, bowed together, sharing grief as if they'd done it a hundred times before. Denan pulled back—reluctantly, inexorably, but he did it. One vertebra at a time, he straightened, his expression hardening. When he looked at Larkin, his compassion was gone. "It will take us all day to reach the river. We have to go."

Tam returned with the three packs, one he'd hastily stitched together with cords of leather. Alorica trailed behind him, arms wrapped around her tiny waist. She looked haggard, her hair a tangled mess, her cheeks blotchy from crying.

Her eyes widened when she saw Venna, a cry of relief turning to a wail. She ran to the other girl and rested a hand on her forehead, but quickly jerked back. "What's that on her skin?"

Tam handed the damaged pack to Denan, who strapped it on. "The poison. Once it reaches her eyes …" Tam trailed off at a sharp look from Denan.

"Tell me," Alorica demanded.

Denan held Talox's pack out to him. "Leave with the others. I'll catch up."

Talox's expression hardened. "No."

"It's a kindness," Denan said.

Talox glared up at Denan. "No!"

Larkin jumped to her feet. "You mean to kill her?"

Denan turned to Tam. "Get the women to the river—now."

Tam gripped Alorica's upper arm and then reached for Larkin. She jerked away and stood over Venna. "I'm not going anywhere!"

Denan glared at Tam. "Go now."

Alorica fought against him. "No! Venna!"

"Talox," Denan said, voice low. "Tam can't handle them both by himself. Go."

When Talox didn't move, Denan grabbed him by the shoulders and slammed him against the tree trunk. He held his forearm against the bigger man's throat. "I won't risk Larkin and Alorica's lives. You will obey orders, or I'll see to it you're banished."

Larkin removed her amulet and bore down. The shield came

easily this time, a convex of golden light emanating from her arm. "If you kill her, I will fight you every minute of every day for the rest of my life."

All three men turned to face Larkin.

"Women's magic," Tam whispered, his hands falling slack at his sides. Alorica shrunk back, as if the sight of Larkin frightened her. Talox made a small sound in his throat.

Denan rounded on Larkin, assessing her barrier for weakness. For the first time since she'd been taken, she was afraid of Denan. She lifted the barrier high and bent into a crouch, ready for him to strike.

Talox fell to his knees. "I'll carry Venna."

"It's thirty miles!" Denan said.

From a distance, Larkin heard a roar, the leaves around her shaking. Gilgads. Denan's head whipped toward the sound, and he went for his bow, nocking an arrow.

"Talox," Tam said. "You've been running all night after being pricked with gilgad venom. The wraiths know our location. They'll send their …" He choked, unable to finish. "You won't make it."

"Send their what?" Larkin asked.

The men ignored her. Talox rose to his feet. "Then I don't make it."

"Do this, and you'll face court martial," Denan said.

"I know." Talox stood before Larkin, his hands spread palm out. "Let me take her, Larkin. I will see she reaches the river safely."

Larkin looked into his eyes and saw earnestness and an immense sadness. "You won't let Denan hurt her?"

"No," he replied simply.

The fight drained out of Larkin, the amulet slipping to her side and the barrier winking out. She stepped back as Talox gently picked Venna up and swung her over his shoulder.

"What are the wraiths sending?" she asked Denan.

"Something bad." He turned his back on them. "Tam, range ahead and play the songs to clear away the"—he growled in frustration at being unable to say the word he wanted—"*beasts*." He spared a glance back at Larkin and Alorica. "If we don't reach the river before nightfall, we're all dead. Fall in."

Larkin trekked through the forest for hours. Her chest heaved, and she had to fight to make her legs bear her weight. She concentrated on putting one foot in front of another. When her knees buckled, she glanced toward the sun dipping toward the western horizon. *Wraiths rising from shadow, infected eyes, smoldering blades.* She forced herself to keep going.

Finally, they wove through the last trees, coming onto a dark stretch of rock pockmarked with deep, narrow pools filled with stagnant rainwater. In a former life, she might have peered into the pools coated with moss or examined the porous rock. As it was, she simply stood at the edge of a deep ravine, the river running swift and white far below. The river's roar came to her; she'd been so exhausted she hadn't noticed before.

The taste of coin on the back of her tongue, she collapsed into a heap, not sure if she could summon the strength to rise again even if a wraith lunged at her from the shadows. Alorica staggered a little way down and collapsed as well.

Crouching beside Larkin, Denan offered her warm water, which she drank thirstily, and some dried bread that tasted like ashes. He tugged at her bandage. "Let me check—"

She shoved his hand away. "Leave it!"

"I need to check—"

"You would have murdered my friend!"

He gave a frustrated growl. "Killing Venna would have been a kindness. What she will become ..."

She slapped him, her hand stinging. "Never!"

He reeled back, seeming to understand she meant much more than her letting him tend to her. Jaw tight, he pivoted. He and Tam busied themselves unloading rope from their packs and speaking in low tones.

Larkin watched the unwavering line of trees, as she waited for Talox to come through with Venna, knowing he was racing against the sun and his own body. If her guess was right, he had less than half an hour of light. And Denan had hinted at another danger—something the wraiths would send after them.

"Larkin?" Alorica said, her voice a dry rasp.

Larkin couldn't look at her. "It's your fault." If only she'd listened when Larkin had tried to warn her.

Alorica choked on a sob. "I know."

Denan and Tam continued to work. Larkin didn't watch them, didn't know what they were doing other than that it involved rope and a grappling hook.

Finally, Talox appeared. "They're hunting us, but they don't know where we are yet," he panted to Denan and Tam, who picked up their pace.

"What is hunting us?" Alorica asked.

"Something worse than gilgads," Tam said.

Larkin forced herself up against her body's protests. She took the pack from Talox as he set Venna down. With the ravine to her back, Larkin knelt next to her friend, Alorica on the other side, Talox at her head. The jagged black lines had crawled up Venna's neck to stain her cheeks. Her breathing was rapid and shallow, her skin hot and paper dry.

"Please," Larkin begged Talox. He sagged, his shoulders shaking in silent sobs. Tears welled in her eyes, the hope dying in her. "There has to be something."

He looked up at her, unashamed of the tears streaking down his face. "There isn't."

Sobbing, Alorica pushed to her feet and staggered away.

Larkin and Talox's gazes locked. "You care about her."

"I love her," he responded.

"You've only known her three days!"

"I would have lived or died for her—what is love if not that?"

Larkin stared at him, not knowing what to say.

"Larkin," Denan called. "Time to cross!"

Larkin looked at the single line of rope running from one side of the ravine to the other. No one could carry Venna across that. "What about Venna?"

"Larkin," a raspy voice said.

Larkin started and looked down. Venna looked up at her, her irises sickly yellow shot through with red. "Venna?"

"Larkin … run."

Before Larkin could comprehend what Venna meant, black wisps streamed into the whites of her eyes, turning them gray. Her lips pulled back in a snarl. She lunged for Larkin and knocked her onto her back, her head dangling over the precipice.

Acting on pure instinct, Larkin locked her arms and held Venna's snapping teeth at bay. In her periphery, she was aware of shouting, scrambling movement. Venna wrapped her arms around Larkin's throat and squeezed so hard the world started to go dark, her arms losing their strength.

Venna suddenly disappeared from above her. Larkin rolled to the side, coughing and choking in a breath. She glanced to the side, seeing nothing below her but the distant river. Hands snatched her shoulders and hauled her back. Denan deposited her into a heap a safe distance away. He jerked his ax and shield free and ran toward where Venna had taken a defensive stance before the ravine. Larkin reeled back and staggered to her feet. She shook her head over and over, unable to stop.

With inhuman strength, Venna lunged at Talox. They rolled, Venna somehow ending up on top. He braced his arms and held her back as she gnashed at him. Suddenly, an arrow bloomed from her shoulder. She shrieked, and Talox threw her off. Venna jerked out the arrow, thick black blood oozing from the wound. She held the arrow like a weapon. Her gaze split between the three pipers converging on her, pinning her against the cliff's edge.

Larkin didn't understand what was happening. She took a single step toward her friend. "Venna?"

Venna glared at Larkin. "You should have let me die!"

"Larkin, stay back!" Denan cried.

"Venna," Talox said gently. "You are not yet lost." Something passed between them—something that looked like regret and loss—but even as Larkin watched, Venna's eyes went completely black. She dropped into a crouch, teeth bared, hissing like a cornered animal.

"Tam," Denan commanded. "Put her down!"

Tam lifted his bow but hesitated. Larkin felt paralyzed by what she knew was coming. Venna wasn't. She threw herself off the cliff, screaming as she fell. Larkin cried out and ran for the edge. Denan intercepted her and wrapped his arm tight around her chest.

"No!" Alorica screamed. "No!" Tam reached for her, but she shoved him back. "How could you do that? How could you hurt her?"

Tam flinched. "She would have killed Talox!"

She beat at him with her fists, and he let her. "I don't care about Talox!"

Talox sank to his knees. Larkin threw an elbow into Denan and broke free. She looked down the sheer drop-off, the updraft blowing back her hair. She peered downriver, searching for any sign of Venna. Nothing. Denan came to stand beside her, not touching her, but tense as if he expected her to jump.

Alorica crept to the edge and looked down. "There's no way she survived that fall."

Larkin closed her eyes. "Is this the river Weiss?"

"Yes," Denan said.

Maybe Venna was going home after all. "What happened to her?"

Denan watched her, his whole body tense. "Poison from a wraith's blade turns a person into a mulgar—a creature possessed by dark magic and by the wraiths themselves."

So, Venna was part wraith now, part of that evil darkness. Larkin wrapped her arms tight around herself.

"You couldn't have told us that before?" Alorica shot at Denan.

"He couldn't," Larkin said. "Just like I couldn't tell you about the wraiths, though I tried."

Denan shot her a surprised look, probably because he thought she was defending him, but that wasn't her intention. She was accusing Alorica.

Alorica turned and walked away, Tam right beside her.

Larkin observed the three pipers. "You've been cursed, haven't you?"

"We all have," Talox said, his voice like broken glass. "You just didn't know it until now."

Larkin didn't bother asking who had cursed them or why—they wouldn't be able to answer.

"That scream will lead the mulgars right to us," Tam said.

"I will cross first." Talox shouldered his pack and approached the rope that stretched across the ravine. He rolled onto his back, hanging upside down on the rope, hands and feet crossing each other. About halfway across, the rope dipped and swayed, but Talox didn't pause.

Tam approached Larkin warily. "Please, help her."

She followed his gesture to see that Alorica had fallen to her knees next to the ravine, her arms wrapped around her middle, shoulders shaking with sobs.

"She deserves it," Larkin said.

Tam's face reddened. "Have you never made a mistake, never unintentionally hurt someone?"

Hadn't she let Sela wander into the Forbidden Forest alone? Her anger toward Alorica wavered.

"Please," Tam said. "She's refusing to cross. I can't carry her."

She saw genuine fear in his eyes. "Why can't we spend another night in the trees?" It would be awful with the wraiths prowling around below, but wouldn't they be safe?

"Our magic can misdirect patrols," Denan said, joining them. "And we can fight off a few mulgars and still manage to slip through unnoticed, but now the wraiths know we're here, they'll have sent a garrison of mulgars after us. Our only chance is to cross the river, forcing them to use a land bridge. It won't stop them from coming after us, but it will buy us time."

Larkin glanced toward the sun, already slipping below the horizon. She stepped around Denan to stand beside Alorica. "Alorica, we have to go."

"Leave me alone!"

"It's just as much my fault as yours," Larkin said.

"How?"

"I should have told the pipers what you were planning to do."

"That's not the same!" Alorica burst out sobbing harder than before.

Larkin was shocked to see cocky, cruel Alorica brought so low. She looked back at Tam for help, but he was too busy pacing, his hands on his head. Arrow nocked, Denan watched the line of trees, but he turned as if feeling her scrutiny. He nodded encouragingly.

She didn't want his encouragement. "If you don't stop," Larkin said to Alorica through gritted teeth, "we're going to have to leave you behind for the wraiths. Pull it together."

Alorica hiccupped on a sob. "Don't talk to me that way."

The sun inched lower—nearly a quarter gone now. They were running out of time. From within the forest came a triumphant shout. The mulgars had spotted them.

Larkin leaned closer. "You failed Venna. Are you going to fail me too?"

"Like I care about you."

Larkin huffed. "Why do you hate me so much? What did I ever do to you?"

"You took Bane!"

Larkin threw her hands up in exasperation. "You never had him!"

"We used to meet at the river at night. I thought he meant to marry me. I was so relieved to be free of the worry of the forest, right up until he told me there was someone else." Glaring, Alorica wiped her nose on her sleeve. "A few months later, he announced his engagement to you."

Larkin blushed and wondered exactly how far things had gone. Maybe Larkin didn't want to know the answer. "I didn't know," she whispered. "I'm sorry."

She glanced toward Denan and Tam. They whispered to each other, bows in both their hands, gesturing wildly. The setting sun was now more than halfway gone. "Alorica, if you stay here, you'll die. I don't want you to die."

Alorica wiped her cheeks. At least she wasn't sobbing anymore. "You don't mean that."

Something crashed through the forest toward them. Larkin stood with difficulty, muscles groaning in protest, and held her hand out to the other girl. "You're all I have left."

Alorica stared at Larkin for what felt like forever, but she finally gripped Larkin's hand and let her pull her up. Tam and Denan stopped whispering and hurried over.

"Larkin," Denan said. "You go first. Hurry."

"No," Larkin answered. "Alorica goes first."

Denan wavered, but Tam was already tying a cord with a pulley around Alorica's waist and wrapping her hands with bandages. "Keep your gaze on the opposite side," he instructed her. "There's no chance you'll fall. Hand over hand and foot over foot. Go quickly."

Swallowing hard, Alorica nodded and eased out onto the rope.

Tam hurried to Larkin, wrapping the bandages around her hands. "You go next. Then Denan."

"No," Denan said. "I'll stay—"

"I'm better with a bow," Tam interrupted. "And I'm replaceable. You and Larkin aren't."

Denan pulled up, letting loose an arrow. A mulgar fell forward onto the barren rock. Unlike the wraiths, at least the mulgars could be killed. "Tam, I need you on the other side of the ravine, taking down the mulgars here so Larkin and I can cross."

Without any more arguments, Tam dragged her toward the ravine. He attached a cord to her waist, which he tied with a loose loop around the rope.

"What about the pulley thing Alorica had?" she asked.

"There isn't time for them to send it back. I'm going first. You'll go right after me."

She looked down, down, down. "Why aren't we replaceable?"

"Because you have magic," Tam answered.

"And Denan?"

Another mulgar broke free. It wore rudimentary plate armor and carried a rectangular sword with an angular tip. Denan brought it down.

"Hurry," Denan called.

Tam knelt, took the rope, and started shinnying across.

Larkin couldn't seem to catch her breath. "What if the rope can't hold both of us?"

From across the ravine, Talox and Alorica were waving her onward.

Behind her, she heard an arrow's thunk as it hit its mark. "Go, Larkin!"

Trying to shut off her brain, Larkin rolled to her back, gripped the rope between her hands and the backs of her calves, and started across. After only a dozen hand over hands, the wrapping around her hands shifted. She wasn't even halfway across before her palms burned and her arms shook. Her scabs ripped free, leaving smears of blood on the rope.

After the halfway mark, the rope sagged, and she had to climb upward. After an entire night holding on to Venna, her fingers didn't want to close around the rope, no matter how much she tried to force them. The line bounced, making her heart pound. Letting her forearms take her weight so her hands could rest, she tipped her head back. Tam scrambled off and sighted down his bow.

Talox cupped his hands around his mouth. "Go, Denan!"

She looked past her feet and watched as Denan slammed the side of his shield into two mulgars and chopped down a third. Attaching his weapons to his pack, he dropped to the rope and started across. Immediately, arrows came from behind Larkin, cutting down the two mulgars sprinting from the forest. Those mulgars were immediately replaced with four more, and these mulgars had bows.

"Hurry, Larkin." Alorica sounded panic-stricken.

Ignoring her burning palms and aching muscles, Larkin stretched her arms and legs. Still, it wasn't long before Denan reached her. He panted, his face red. Arrows clattered on the ravine behind them, coming dangerously close. Before she could process what he was doing, Denan climbed under her, took a portion of her weight on himself, and kept going. Larkin worked with him, while Tam and Talox provided cover. It didn't seem to matter how many mulgars there were, more always came.

Larkin was so focused on the ravine's edge that she didn't notice the sun disappearing along the horizon. She didn't notice anything at all until she felt a sudden absence inside—like all the color and life had been sucked out of her. The four wraiths stood at the edge of the rope, wicked swords trailing from their armored hands. They hid behind long rectangular shields.

She gasped as the wraith with the crown lifted a black bow, sighted along it, and drew back. In an instant, she'd grabbed her amulet and held it before her, calling up the barrier. The black arrow slammed into it—clashing light and dark, shadows withering and dying.

Larkin peered down the rope and shot a triumphant look at the wraiths. The mantled wraith screamed in rage, lifted his sword, and cut through the rope. Larkin had a moment of weightlessness, and then they were falling. Their weight caught, and the rope swung them toward the opposite ravine, which grew in size and detail as they careened toward it.

"Hang on!" Denan cried.

Larkin braced herself. Denan hit first, taking the brunt of the impact. Larkin tried to hang on, but her hands gave out. The rope burned her palms as she slid down.

"No!" Denan cried—a cry that echoed from both sides of the ravine.

Denan's hand snapped out, catching her by the hair. Larkin yelped in pain, but it helped her hold on. "Find a foothold on the ravine," Denan said through gritted teeth. He strained, every muscle corded and exposed, the veins in his neck standing out as he struggled to hold them both.

She swiveled and found a ledge big enough for the balls of her feet. She grasped onto a few straggly plants with one hand and tugged to make sure they would hold her before releasing the rope. Denan dropped down beside her.

"What now?" she asked breathlessly.

"You worry about the shield. I'll worry about getting us out of here." He tipped his head up. "Pull us up!"

"Hang tight. I'll rework the pulley," Talox called back.

Luckily, the amulet was still hanging from her neck. Her hands were raw and bleeding as she took hold. She shot a glance at the other side of the ravine. The mulgars and wraiths were gone. "Denan."

He glanced over his shoulder, his features shifting from surprise to grim acceptance. "They're looking for another way across." He tugged back her hand, wincing at what he saw, though his hands didn't look much better. "Have you enough hand strength to hold on?"

She flexed her fingers. Between holding Venna all night, running all day, and supporting her weight over a rope, they were slow to obey. Seeming to take that as answer enough, Denan pulled up a length of rope, tying it around both of them. "I need you to turn around and straddle my waist."

She shot him an incredulous look.

He rolled his eyes. "You have a better idea?"

"No," she admitted.

"Give me your wrappings."

She obeyed. He wrapped his hands, grimacing as he pulled the cloth tight. The rope above them went taut. She turned around and wrapped her legs and arms around him. Talox and Tam pulled them up while Denan braced them against the side of the ravine.

When they reached the top, Larkin collapsed. She was alive. Thank the ancestors, she was alive.

But Venna wasn't.

Larkin closed her eyes tight and whispered, "Wherever you are, Venna, I hope you're free."

CHAPTER 22

THE ALAMANT

G rief came over Larkin like winter, slowly stealing away her ability to feel anything but a numb heaviness. It wasn't just Venna's death. It was the loss of her home and family—of Bane. The days always looked the same—trees and walking and river crossings. Her only thought was to put one numb foot in front of the other.

She ate when Denan insisted, and she didn't protest sleeping in the pod with him. Except to change her bandages and remove her stitches, he never touched her, and she never sought out his touch. But by morning, their combined weight always drew them together—her back against his warm side.

In the dim light that ended and began each day, he would pull out his pipes and play a song for her, soft and low, and for a little while, the frozen center of her chest thawed, and she wept silently. In the mornings, when he helped her out of the pod, he would study her chapped cheeks with such kindness it made her chest ache, but she would always look away, the grief of winter creeping back over her heart like frost over a pane of glass.

Three days after Venna's death, a boat waited for them on the river—all white with delicate lines and a curving prow like the curls on a pea vine. The wood was smooth as velvet under Larkin's fingertips. The others climbed inside; Alorica stuck to Larkin's side like a burr, refusing to look in Tam's direction. Talox hadn't spoken a word, but his grief was evident in his heavy movements and stricken face.

Denan helped Larkin inside and then pushed off the muddy bank. The boat shifted under his weight as he positioned himself at the front. All three men took paddles and started up the slow-moving river. Larkin spread out a blanket on the boat's floor and slept with Alorica beside her. While she slept, she dreamed. She was a child, held in her mother's loving embrace. Her mother sang in a language Larkin couldn't understand, the vibrations soothing against her cheek. She was loved and safe and, best of all, *home.*

Larkin woke with a start to Denan's hand resting on her shoulder. She didn't want to wake up. The warmth of the dream still curled around her, the echoes of her mother's heartbeat fresh against her cheek. For the first time in days, her cold grief felt distant.

Denan pointed to something ahead. What she saw made her gasp. They were no longer in a river, but some kind of lake. Before them was a stately progression of enormous trees. But instead of growing in a circular shape, the trunks had flattened and joined together, fusing to create one continuous wall. The lower boughs formed arches that wove into a parapet shaded by smaller branches, all of which were covered in thorns and bright yellow leaves.

Those leaves drifted down, coating the water like floating coins. Larkin reached to pick one up, but a flash of color and light in the turquoise water made her draw her hand back.

Twisting around, she shook Alorica awake. "You have to

see this."

Alorica blinked up at her, face shifting into a scowl, but then she caught sight of the wall and gasped. "Where are we?"

"The Alamant," Denan answered.

Larkin startled as a horn sounded. Sentinels atop the wall moved. They wore beautifully wrought armor, enormous bows strapped to their backs and spears in their hands. This wall wasn't just beautiful—it was a place of defense. As they came closer, she caught sight of an older man watching them, one of his sleeves pinned up in a crisp fold, highlighting his missing right arm. He was not the only one. There were missing arms and legs everywhere. Scars visible through helms. Though beautiful and polished to a mirror shine, the armor showed signs of carefully hammered-out dents and scars so deep they couldn't be buffed out. Larkin's eyes narrowed.

Venna had begged Larkin to cut off her foot to stop the poison's spread. Had these men done the same? "Would it have saved her—if I had helped her amputate?"

Denan's head whipped back in surprise, and he followed her gaze to the men on the wall.

"She would have bled to death," Talox answered.

Larkin hung her head. *Better than becoming a mulgar.*

An enormous arched gate pushed outward, large eddies sucking the leaves in and down. Larkin looked from the impenetrable wall to the sentinels patrolling the top. Were they there to keep the mulgars out or the women in? Probably both. Though beautiful, this wall was a prison as much as a protection.

"Will I ever come out again?" she asked.

The men's silence was all the answer she would ever need.

"Larkin, take out your amulet," Denan said. "You and Alorica grasp it so the branches pierce your skin."

Larkin was tired of her hands always being bloody and sore, but she did as she was told, holding the other half out to Alorica, who looked at the amulet as if it might bite her. "Why?" the other girl asked.

"Your town isn't the only one with a barrier around it," Tam answered.

"You don't get to speak to me," Alorica snapped.

Larkin studied the empty space the gate had left. She could make out a golden sheen, like light reflecting off glass. It was like the shield Larkin had made before. She took hold of Alorica's hand, maneuvering it against the amulet, and squeezed. Alorica hissed as the branches pierced her.

Larkin looked up as they passed through the shield. For a brief moment, crystals sang, and something abrasive, like sand, scraped against her skin. Then it was over. Alorica worked her jaw like she was trying to pop her ears, let go of the amulet, and rubbed at the blood welling on her palm. Larkin's hands were still bandaged from the rope burn, so she didn't bother.

They came out on the other side of the archway, and the whole world changed. Trees grew out of the lake—trees so large and wide her family's entire farm would have fit across the canopy of one. She looked closer. Not one tree, but hundreds. They twisted to form a single tree supported by great buttressed roots. Rooms had been cleverly integrated into the tree's natural shape. Larkin stared above her as they passed beneath a flat bough that spanned the distance from one tree to another. *A bridge*, she realized. She'd seen them before—dove off of them in her dreams. But how was that possible?

They crossed to the other side. More trees grew here, covered platforms and stairs circling the trunks, connected by bridges between them. People watched them from those platforms—women and children mostly, all of them dressed and groomed to perfection, hair and skin glowing with health, yet an air of sadness clung to them. Men and women alike wore simple garments—long tunics, robes, and loose pants with belts at the waist. The people called out a greeting to the three pipers.

Something bumped the boat. She looked over the side to see

something slick and gray crest the water, something five times the size of an ox. She drew back with a whimper.

"It's a melangth," Talox said. "They won't harm you."

"It's beautiful, isn't it?" Tam said hopefully from behind.

Alorica turned her glare on him. "Would you trade your freedom for beauty?"

He looked at her with reluctant devotion. "I already have."

Alorica muttered to Larkin, "Can I kill him?"

Larkin shrugged. Alorica had been threatening Tam's imminent demise ever since she'd met him. "Let me know when you want help."

Tam muttered something miserably.

They crossed under one of the trees, the green leaves edged in crimson. The boat bumped against the buttressed roots. A dock had been built onto one of those roots. Thick white scales that looked like crystallized salt covered the bark under the water.

Denan stepped from the boat onto the dock, tied it off, and turned back to offer Larkin a hand. She stared at it, still bandaged like hers. This would be her first step into the Alamant, the first step into the life she would never have chosen. "What happens now?" she whispered.

"I'm taking you somewhere you can prepare for the ceremony tonight to induct you into our people."

Larkin didn't like the sound of that.

"We don't want to be 'your people.'" Alorica said through gritted teeth.

"You don't have a choice."

Larkin looked up at Denan defiantly. He sighed and tugged out his pipes. Behind her, Tam stood up. If she wouldn't go willingly, they would force her. She stepped out on her own, turning to help Alorica, then she faced Denan. "Just when I start to think maybe you're not all bad, you do something to remind me."

He tucked his pipes away and started unloading the boat.

"Think we should push them into the lake?" Alorica asked under her breath.

Larkin barely heard her. The tree called to her—a softer version of the piper's song. Unable to resist, she started toward the trunk.

"Where are you going?' Alorica asked. When Larkin didn't answer, she huffed and fell in behind. Larkin hesitantly laid her hand against the smooth, paper-like bark. A wash of feeling came over her—welcome and anticipation and need and desperation. She pulled back as if stung, not understanding what had happened.

"Did you feel something?"

She started and turned to find Denan behind her. "What?"

Tam came over from the boat, his pack slung over one shoulder. Talox waited on the dock, watching another boat come in—a boat filled with soldiers.

Denan laid his hand where hers had been moments before. "I thought—The look on your face ... Did you feel something?"

Alorica crossed her arms over her chest. "She said she was going to throw up earlier. It's probably the sight of you that does it."

Denan and Tam held perfectly still, breath held, like Larkin's answer was incredibly important. "I didn't feel anything," she said too quickly.

His eyes narrowed as if he didn't quite believe her.

"How can the trees grow in the water?" she asked in hopes of distracting him.

He turned away from them. "Come on. They'll be waiting." He started up a set of curving stairs that grew out of the trunk and spiraled up the side. Tam waited for them, ready to take up the rear as always.

Larkin looked back at Talox, who was handing his pack to the soldiers in the boat. "Isn't he coming with us?"

"No," Tam said softly. "He must answer for disobeying his

commander."

She took half a step toward him before sending a pleading look to Denan. "But he was trying to help Venna."

"Without rules, we wouldn't survive," Denan said.

"Talox, wait." She crossed the tree to stand before him. He looked down at her, his expression so full of grief it nearly choked her. "You loved her?" she whispered so the others wouldn't hear.

Talox stared blankly at the ever-changing surface of the water. "A piper's music always calls to the one who will love him. You already know it. You have from the beginning."

She stiffened. "I do not love Denan."

"You will." Talox stepped into the boat. She watched him for a moment, wanting to protest. She could never love a man who forced her from her home. The boat pulled away. Talox looked back at them and lifted a single hand in farewell before turning away. Denan had said Talox would face court martial for disobeying orders.

"Where are they taking him?" she asked as Tam came to stand beside her.

Tam looked after the boat. "To face judgment."

"You should all face judgment," Alorica said.

Of all of them, Larkin liked Talox best. "Will he be all right?"

"The incident involved his heartsong, so leeway will be given. And Denan will protect him." Tam shrugged. "He might lose rank. Maybe even spend some time in confinement."

"You all deserve worse," Alorica said.

"Come on." Denan was nearly out of sight around the curving staircase.

Alorica rested her hand against the trunk. Frowning, she pulled back and started toward the stairs. Larkin fell in beside her. Alorica glanced back at Tam and said under her breath, "What *did* you feel?"

"Nothing," Larkin had to lift her skirts to start up the stairs. Moss with tiny white flowers grew in the dips and bends of the tree. In pockets of water, beautiful flowers the size of Larkin's chest were curled up tight in the shape of teardrops.

"Who will be waiting for us?" she asked Denan when they caught up.

Alorica grunted. "It's a surprise, apparently."

"Don't tell us we have to figure it out for ourselves," Larkin muttered. "There's no way we could possibly know."

"I think I liked you two better when you hated each other," Tam muttered.

"That's because you know that if we'd been working to-gether before, we would have escaped," Alorica said. She was probably right. "Or just killed you all in your sleep, which is still a possibility."

Larkin studied Denan. She felt more conflicted about him than ever. He had kidnapped her and been so eager to hurt Ven-na, and yet he was not all monster. He was also a strong, selfless leader who'd been willing to die for her more than once. Killing Venna really would have been a kindness—one she suspected would cost him dearly—and yet, none of this would have hap-pened if he hadn't taken her in the first place. It always came back to that.

Something flitted past her face—a little bird with a mousy brown body and brilliant copper beak. She gaped at it. She'd seen it before, when she'd followed an overlapping vision of the bird out of the pitch-black river. She followed its flight, losing sight of it in the vast canopy.

Hundreds of birds in every color and size imaginable perched on the branches. Larkin passed a branch, catching sight of a nest filled with eggs of mottled brown rust. Tiny lizards darted, one skimming across the surface of a little pond, which was crusted in white like the large lake below.

Larkin's legs burned by the time they reached the place

where boughs spread from the main trunk, creating a flattened expanse the size of a small field. The roof was beautifully crafted with supple lines, attention given to the slightest details, like the curving vines along the arches and stars in the peaks. The ground beneath her feet was springy with moss. Potted plants graced the space, as well as benches that grew from the trees.

It was as different from her hut surrounded by muddy fields as a candle flame was different from the sun. Shame for her ragged clothes and her even more ragged upbringing had her straightening her shoulders in defiance. Beautiful as all this was, it was rotten at its core.

Two women stood on the other side of the platform, their heads bent together in conversation. One of them was enormously pregnant.

Denan turned to face them, Tam beside him. Denan's expression was conflicted—hope and fear twined together with longing. So many emotions she had no answer for. She stepped closer to Alorica, knowing something was happening, but not sure what.

"I've already told Tam and Talox," Denan said. "And now I'm telling you. No one outside the five of us is to know of Larkin's magic—not until I say so."

Alorica narrowed her gaze. "Why?"

"Because she doesn't need to deal with the repercussions of women's magic coming back for the first time in over two hundred years, not while trying to adjust to the Alamant as well."

Larkin rubbed at the prickling on her arm. "What repercussions?"

"The kind that change everything." Denan faced Alorica. "I will have your word."

Alorica hesitated, but only to make the pipers nervous.

"I have the authority and ability to make you forget the magic ever happened."

Alorica blanched. "Fine."

"Then this is where we leave you," Tam said, his gaze on the mud caking Alorica's boots.

Alorica lifted her head. "I hope I never see either one of you ever again." But Larkin could tell by the way the other girl fiddled with her bracelet that she was nervous.

Why does Denan always get me where he wants and then abandon me? "What happens next?"

He gestured to the two women waiting on the other side of the platform, and they started coming over. "These women will prepare you for the ceremonies tonight."

Alorica folded her arms. "What ceremonies?"

"One to test you for magic."

"And the other?" Larkin whispered.

"You already know," he said softly.

She did. They had been building to this moment for days. He meant to marry her. Larkin flushed hot and then cold. She had to close her eyes against sudden dizziness. Alorica let out a shriek and attacked Tam. They rolled around twice before Tam pinned her, eyes closed against the threats and insults she lobbed at him.

Larkin stared at Denan as he stared back. She knew all the things he wasn't saying—that she didn't have a choice in this, that he was sorry for her pain, but he wouldn't change anything. There was one question she didn't know the answer to. "How do you expect me to ever forgive you?"

"By giving more than I took." He stepped closer. "For the rest of your life, you will be judged on how you behave today. Do you want to be remembered as Alorica will?" Denan took out his pipes and played a few notes that took all the fight out of the other girl. Shaking, Tam eased off her as she stared blissfully up at the boughs.

"I don't know if I can do this, Denan," Tam said.

Denan tucked his pipes away. "She'll come around." The other women had already halved the distance between them.

236

Alorica pushed herself to her feet, refusing to look at Tam, which was better than attacking him again.

Tam stretched his arms out at his sides. "Alorica, you will be happy again. I swear you will."

"Just go," she said, voice shaking.

Head hanging, Tam turned and left without another word. Denan lingered. He was still looking at Larkin, his expression unreadable. "I will see you tonight. Until then, you will be well cared for." He nodded over her shoulder at the same time Alorica let out a cry and ran toward one of the women—Atara, Alorica's older sister.

Startled, Larkin's attention shifted to the second woman. Like her brother, she had raven hair and a hooked nose, though hers was covered with a smattering of freckles.

"Caelia," Larkin breathed. She cut the distance between them and enveloped Bane's sister in an enormous hug, the other woman's belly a hard mound between them.

"Larkin, is it?" Caelia patted her back awkwardly. "It is good to see you."

Larkin pulled back, the relief she'd felt moments before eclipsed by embarrassment. Bane hadn't talked about Caelia much, but she was always there—a ghost in the periphery of his thoughts. Caelia would only know Larkin as the poor, dirty child who lived on the other side of the river. Larkin swiped at the moisture building in her eyes and tried to get a hold of herself. "We thought all the Taken were dead."

Caelia gestured grandly to herself. "Yes, well, you can see that we are not." She stepped closer, looking eager. "Tell me of my father and brother."

"They're fine." Larkin couldn't tear her gaze away from the mound that was Caelia's belly. "You-you're pregnant?" Her hands wrapped around herself protectively.

Some of Larkin's fear must have shown, for Caelia's expression softened. "Nothing will be forced upon you."

Larkin glanced back to find Denan gone, but he would be waiting for her. She whirled back to Caelia. "You *let* one of them touch you?"

Caelia lowered her voice to a conspiratorial whisper. "That man can touch me as much as he wants."

Larkin's mouth fell open. "He's your kidnapper!"

Caelia laughed. "He is my heartsong. The father of my three children."

"Heartsong," Larkin said bitterly. "It's a spell to lure us from the town. It tricks us into feeling lies."

Caelia tipped her head to the side. "Why does it take you and no one else?" Larkin didn't have an answer for that, and Caelia knew it. "I understand how you feel—cheated and wronged and trapped. I felt all those things, and honestly, you're dealing with it better than I did." She gestured to Alorica, who sat on a bench, deep in conversation with her sister. "I dealt with it more like she did—kicking and screaming and threatening—but in the end, I understood. The heartsong isn't a spell; it's what your heart desires."

"I know my desires better than anyone else."

"Not better than the magic does."

"You act like the magic is alive, like it has a will and purpose!"

Caelia looked at her with the same look Denan always gave her—the one where he was waiting for her to figure it out on her own.

"The magic is alive?" Larkin whispered.

Caelia smiled. "Of course it is. And today, you get to meet it." She studied Larkin, her brow furrowing. "Is that my dress?"

"Bane and I ... We were to be married."

Caelia sucked in a breath. "Ancestors take me! As if Bane hasn't lost enough."

Larkin blinked back tears. "Losing you wrecked him and your father. There has to be some way to let them know you're all right—that you're still alive."

Caelia's eyes grew distant. "If there was, don't you think I would have found it?" She wiped a single tear that strayed down her cheek and took a deep breath. "Come with me. There's still much to do." She turned on her heel, waddling to the other side of the platform.

Larkin paused when she drew even with Alorica. "Will you be all right?"

Alorica looked up at her with shining eyes. "Atara, this is my friend, Larkin."

Atara gave a little bow. She had the same dark skin and hair as Alorica, but where Alorica's features were lithe, Atara's were round. Atara noticed the bandages on Larkin's hands. "What happened?"

Larkin and Alorica shared a look. "Rope burns," Alorica said. "Some … puncture marks."

Atara reached for a bag Larkin hadn't noticed before. She pushed things around and came out with a little wooden jar. "Rub this on it after you clean it. Do you need me to help you bandage it?"

Larkin took the jar and shook her head. Caelia waited a few steps ahead. "Didn't either of you try to escape?" Larkin asked.

"Most girls try it," Caelia said. "The pipers expect it."

Atara shook her head. "Not me. I've seen what the wraiths do to the pipers." She looped her arm around Alorica's. "We'll see you two at the ceremony. I work as a healer, Larkin. You should come see me at the healing tree. I can teach you and Alorica."

The two of them started away.

"Alorica …" Larkin trailed off.

The other girl gave a small smile. "I'll be all right. I have my sister now."

Larkin felt a pang of jealousy. She had no family here. Of the sisters she did have, one had betrayed her.

"Come on," Caelia called. "You'll see Alorica again at the ceremony."

Larkin crossed the platform and caught up to Caelia as she started up another staircase. She wanted to ask her something, but she wasn't sure she could trust her. In the end, she had to trust someone. "Once I get past the wall—"

"You won't."

"But if I could—"

"Then you would face the wraiths and mulgars."

"You're under the piper's spell!"

Caelia whirled on her, face red. "Do I look like I'm under some kind of spell?" She lifted her arms. "Do you hear any music forcing me to say this to you? Do you see any pipers monitoring my words?"

"How would you even know?"

Caelia stepped closer. "You already know the answer."

She was right. Larkin remembered every time Denan had used his pipes on her. The magic temporarily enthralled her, but it didn't affect her memory.

Caelia whirled back around with a huff. "If you must try it, don't hurt anyone, and don't harm any tree. The pipers won't forgive either."

The two of them stepped into a room three times the size of Larkin's home. Scrolling vines and leaves graced the windows and roofs. Arches stood open to the air, letting in the sound of birdsong and a breeze that smelled of growing things. A beautiful vanity and mirror sat off to one side, next to a curtained corner.

"Women are treasured here," Caelia said, softer now. "Denan will give you anything in his power to make you happy, and he's one of the most powerful men in the Alamant. There are schools. You can learn to read and write. Chose a profession—healer, weaver, carpenter, cobbler, whatever you want. Yes, we were forced from our families"—her voice shook a little—"but if

I had known I could have this kind of life, I would have left on my own."

"None of that justifies what they did."

Caelia looked up at her. "You still don't know the pipers' reasons for taking us."

"And you can't tell me?"

Caelia tried, her mouth forming soundless words. She shook her head. "After you figure it out, come talk to me. Maybe it will change the way you look at things."

Caelia went to an arched window and waved her hand before it. The view of the lake clouded over, as if a sudden mist had come up. She went from one archway to the next, obscuring the view.

"What are you doing?"

"What do you think I'm doing?" she prompted.

Blasted curse. Larkin stepped up to it, her fingers pressing against the mist like glass. "How was the women's magic lost?" Caelia gave a helpless shrug. "It had to do with the curse?"

"Yes."

So the curse probably caused the loss of magic. It also bound people's tongues so they couldn't talk about it. Larkin wondered what other things the curse had done. "If women's magic was lost, how are you still using it?"

"As long as the magic lives, the spells will. Just no new ones—not for over two hundred years."

Larkin sat down on the bench at the vanity. Her reflection caught her attention. The wild, matted hair and filthy clothes were familiar. But the angry, ugly slash across her throat was new. She ran her fingers along its lopsided path. It was hard and lumpy, with scabs where the stitches had been.

Hunter flipped her, pinning her body with his own. Not murder in his eyes, but pity. "I am sorry." And then his blood had sprayed across her, his eyes going wide with shock.

Larkin sagged against the vanity, her head between her

arms.

"Larkin?" Caelia asked.

"The curse," Larkin asked, trying to distract herself. "Where did it come from? Why does it care?"

Caelia came to the vanity and pulled out a towel and a bar of soap. "Wash yourself with this, including your hair." She pulled back the curtain and demonstrated how to pull a lever to release a sluice of water. "Wet yourself, soap off, and then rinse. It's collected rainwater, so it's not heated, but it is clean. I've left you a tunic and pants to dress in. I'll be back to check on you shortly." She walked to the arch they'd come through, turned back, and held her hand up to the surface until it too went opaque.

Larkin stared at the misty barrier as if trying to see the magic it contained. She stepped forward, hesitated, and then pushed her palm against it. It grew harder the more she pushed. She yanked back her hand. She was trapped. She retreated to the vanity and began stripping off her battered clothes. Her many bruises were fading to greens and yellows.

It had been days since she'd had a proper bath, so she soaped up twice. Finished, she wrung out her hair as best she could and wrapped herself with the towel. Cream-colored tunic and trousers waited for her on the bench, as well a sleeveless robe of turquoise. Her own clothes were nowhere to be seen. No, not her clothes. Caelia's. Which made her think of Bane. She closed her eyes, her chest aching and eyes burning with the tears she refused to shed. For a moment, she considered refusing to wear them. But what then? Walk around in nothing but a towel? She glared at the tunic, picking it up and jerking it over her head. The fabric settled against her skin, soft as a rose petal.

Gah! How am I supposed to hate something so soft? Utterly defeated, she dressed and searched the vanity, finding vials and soaps, combs and brushes. She set about attacking the snarls of her hair.

"Oh, no. Not without the oils." Larkin started to find Caelia stepping through the banished barrier. Larkin gaped at the potted plant the woman held. It contained three white flowers, shining with an amber light. Larkin hadn't realized how dark it had grown.

"What is that?"

Caelia set the flower on the table. "A lampent. Fire is forbidden within the Alamant, but the White Tree is generous. She has given us light to guide us through the darkness." Caelia rummaged around in the drawers and pulled out a vial. She poured some oil, rubbed it between her palms, and massaged it into Larkin's hair. The woman went through nearly the entire bottle. Afterward, Larkin had to admit the comb glided through her hair much easier than before.

"Why did you lock me in?" Larkin asked warily.

Caelia's brow drew down in confusion. "You mean because I closed the barriers? They're created for privacy, as well as to keep out the weather, so they're incredibly strong. You have to know how to turn them on and off. Here, I'll show you."

At an archway, Caelia took hold of Larkin's wrist and pressed her hand into the strangely textured surface. "Push in until you feel it hardening, then draw your fingers together, grasping it gently and pull back."

It felt like a film on Larkin's hand. She drew back, and the barrier disappeared slowly, revealing the twilight outside. Larkin gasped at what she saw. Trees lit up as if they were graced with a thousand golden stars. Below, the water was black as ink, but in the depths, fish of all different sizes pulsed with rainbows of color. It was the most beautiful thing Larkin had ever seen.

"Wait until you see the White Tree." Caelia led Larkin back to the vanity and set about weaving Larkin's hair into a complicated set of braids, which she set off with tiny glowing flowers. Last, she placed a tapering mantle that draped down Larkin's right side. On the apex above her breast, a three-headed snake had been expertly tooled into a single circle. Below the snake was a peak, from which hung a polished teardrop turquoise stone that matched the robe.

Larkin took the piece of turquoise in her hand. "This mantle—it means something, doesn't it?"

"This is the insignia of Denan's house." She touched each snake head in turn. "Bravery, loyalty, intelligence. The stone is a wedding gift to you."

She stiffened. His insignia on her breast—his ownership.

Caelia's mantle had four glittering jewels. Larkin reached out and took a piece of onyx in her hand.

Caelia smiled. "My wedding jewel."

"And the others?"

"Mothers are greatly honored among the pipers. My husband gave me a jewel for each child I gave him. A diamond for my eldest, an emerald for my second. I'm hoping for a pearl for my third. And this one"—she held up an amethyst—"for mastering weaving."

"So much wealth," Larkin breathed. One of these jewels would have been enough for Larkin's entire family to live off for years.

"The pipers have a rich heritage," Caelia said, her expression turning inexplicably sad. She shook herself. "The last touch." She brought out a leather belt, studded with more turquoise, helping Larkin tie it on the right side. It was fully dark when she was finally finished dressing.

Caelia turned Larkin around so she faced the mirror. "There, now look."

Larkin peered into the mirror, hating how pale her skin looked against the thick freckles on her face, but her riot of copper hair was for once tamed into braids and curling waves instead of frizz. Dressed in such finery, she looked wealthy and pretty.

Larkin closed her eyes. "And if I refuse him?"

"You can try."

Larkin considered her chances. It wouldn't be hard to overpower Caelia in her present state, but then what? Would she flee back into the forest full of wraiths and mulgars? And that's if she could get past the wall and its sentinels. No. If she were really going to escape, it would take careful planning, and she would not leave without Alorica. They were allies now. Tears of frustration built in Larkin's eyes.

With an apologetic look, Caelia crossed to the opaque barrier and removed it. A young boy of around seven waited for them. He looked so like a younger version of Denan he could only be his brother. He carried a beautiful cloak in the same turquoise as the robe.

"Mother has been working on your clothes for days," he said matter-of-factly. "She wouldn't even take me swimming." He seemed to expect an apology for this affront.

Larkin wasn't sure what to say. "I, um, I'm sure she'll take you swimming now." It came out sounding more like a question.

His gaze narrowed. "I'm supposed to take you to the boat." By the tone of his voice, it was clear he thought this task unpleasant.

"This is Wyn, Denan's younger brother," Caelia said. "The pipers weave the cloth from tree bark. It will last for years without showing wear, and the color will never fade. The clothes are a gift from Denan's mother, Aaryn, to welcome you into the family."

Larkin hesitated before taking the cloak. It wasn't cold—in fact, it was perfectly temperate—but it seemed she was expected to wear it. "Was she taken from the Idelmarch as well?"

"We all were," Caelia said.

"I will take you to him," Wyn said.

Larkin considered fighting, but she didn't see how it would do any good. Heart heavy, she followed him, Caelia beside her. Little white flowers in the moss gave a gentle, warm light as she descended the stairs and came out on the platform. Shifting his weight impatiently from one foot to the other, Wyn opened the door to what looked like a decorative birdcage that dangled over the darkening water. He stepped inside and waved for them to hurry up.

Larkin hesitated to step into the cage, but Caelia tugged her forward.

CHAPTER

CEREMONY

Caelia pulled a lever, and they descended smoothly and rapidly. Before Larkin could catch her breath, they reached the dock where a boat waited, manned by four men wearing the snake insignia. Wyn lifted the latch and dashed out and into the boat. A little shaky, Larkin stepped onto the dock. Caelia pulled another lever, and the cage glided back up and out of sight.

The men helped Larkin and Caelia into the boat and moved to take their positions. Wyn had his arms wrapped tight around his waist, as if to keep himself from snatching a pair of oars he was eyeing, though it didn't stop his short legs from swinging restlessly. Caelia gave him a look, and his swinging feet stilled—mostly.

The men pushed off from the dock, their oars dipping. Color caught Larkin's eye, and she turned. The boat left a trail of glowing violet behind them. Wyn must have noticed her perplexed look. He reached out to the water and splashed, the water turning violet. He shook out his hand, water spraying her face.

"Wherever the water is disturbed," Caelia explained, "it changes colors."

"What is this place?" Larkin breathed.

"The Alamant," Wyn responded as if she were dense.

"Anything that feeds off the trees glows golden," Caelia said. "Anything that feeds off something that feeds off the trees gleams in different colors."

Larkin cupped her hands and brought up some water; tiny violet creatures so small she could barely make them out swam in her palms. Acting on impulse, she tossed them into the water. Violet spread like an ink stain.

At the boat's edges, a frilly creature nearly the size of their boat glided through the water beneath them—almost like it was carrying Larkin to her heartsong. The frills broke the surface, undulating edges flashing with color. Larkin reached out, her fingers dipping beneath the surface. The creature was spongy and slick, like a hard-boiled egg.

"A mandrill—a good sign," a man breathed.

As it faded from view, golden-white light caught Larkin's attention. Between massive overlapping trunks, a new tree came into sight. It glowed like a fallen star, piercing the dark waters with luminosity. An elegant staircase rose from the water. People lined its sides, all of them holding thin branches. At the top of the stairs, under a golden arch, Denan waited.

He brought his flute to his lips. The music breathed her in. Larkin turned liquid, a trembling form held together by nothing more than a melody. Every bit of her longed for her source, for the warmth and comfort of her heart. It was so much stronger here—so strong she was powerless to resist.

The boat glided to a stop at the base of the stairs.

"From here, you must go alone," Caelia said.

"I'm afraid." Larkin didn't understand her fear. Her heart waited at the top of the stairs, a fiery pulse that called to everything in her.

"We all fear the moment everything changes," Caelia said softly.

Larkin took a steadying breath. Caelia held her hand and helped Larkin step into the water up to her knees. As soon as her feet touched down, she was in another time and place.

Before her was another tree, another group of people superimposed over the ones before her now. Another man looked down at her in Denan's place. He was beautiful, with brilliant blue eyes and a shock of blond hair.

The vision faded as quickly as it had come. Larkin shook her head to clear it, not understanding what it all meant. The heartsong drew her back in, making her shimmer to liquid and back again. The music called her out of the water and through the archway of held branches. The wind picked up. Falling leaves fluttered against her face and onto the steps. Teardrop-shaped leaves that had faded to a silvery green clung to her bare feet. Beneath her, rainbow lights pulsed deep inside the tree.

All of it led her up, up, up, toward the man who made her heart sing. Denan wore a mantle with a snake on the front and a golden circlet of woven branches. An emerald the size of a child's fist dangled from the end of his mantle. On the final step, her hand came up, already reaching for him. Instead, he pushed a two-handled goblet into her palms, nodding for her to drink.

She tipped the cup to her lips, a single mouthful of golden sap slipping down her throat. Warmth spread through her, turning her head tingly and light. She recognized the sensation from when Denan had stitched her neck. He released his flute, letting it rest against his chest.

She stepped toward him, tears of love in her eyes. "Denan."

Four men came to stand beside them. They held beautiful metal bracers with opalescent branches studded with thorns woven throughout. Denan pushed his hands in the bracers up to the bend of his elbow. "Take hold."

As the song's effects faded, Larkin grew uneasy, but whatever she'd drunk had dulled her sense of fear, painting the world with rainbows. The bracers extended out long past his fingertips, which left plenty of room for her to reach inside and grasp his hands. With a simultaneous pull, the men tightened the clasps. The bracers bore down on Larkin's skin, the wood coming together to form intricate patterns. She gasped and tried to pull back, but Denan held fast.

She blinked at him as if waking from a dream. She glanced around at the hundreds of people watching them—most of them men. "What ..." Light like moonlight on rippling water came from their bound arms, trailing lines up Larkin's skin. The pain flared against the drug they'd given her. She whimpered and tried to pull free.

"Steady," Denan said. "It's almost over." Even as he said it, the lights began to fade.

"What's almost—" And then she knew. This barbaric ritual was her wedding.

The men released the bracers. She gasped in pain as they came free, leaving welts and broken thorns that twined from her skin to Denan's. She tried to jerk back again, but Caelia and another woman were at her side, wrapping her arms in pure white cloth covered in salve. The women worked quickly and quietly, the burn easing.

"What next?" Larkin hissed to Denan. "Will you flay me? Throw me in a cook pot?"

A man wearing a bigger crown and a boar on his mantle stepped forward. He placed a gold circlet around Larkin's head and called out, "Prince Denan and his wife, Princess Larkin!"

The crowd cheered, their branches waving in the air.

Larkin gaped at them, then Denan, then back at them. "You're a prince?"

He bowed to the crowd. "And now you're a princess."

She cocked back her hand to slap him. He caught her wrist,

which set her eyes to watering with the burn. "Everyone is watching. Remember the impression you want to give."

"I don't care about—"

"It's done, Larkin—sealed with women's magic. No power save death can break the bond between us now."

He released her, and she stumbled back, her head shaking. "No. You tricked me. You—I hate you!"

"Calm down, Larkin," Caelia warned.

"I will not! I …"

Denan played his pipes again. Her anger and resentment slipped away like water through her fingers. She took a step closer to Denan. He led her behind the archway, across a platform to the other side of the tree. He let his flute drop. She went into his arms, the feel of him under her hands … repulsive. She shoved him back and drew a breath to berate him.

He interrupted her coming tirade. "It's time for the second ceremony. You need to decide if you will participate of your own free will or if I force you."

"Like you already forced me?" she spat.

"I did, and I would do it again. Now make your choice."

She swallowed all the angry words—as she did when her father threatened her—burying them deep. For all its beauty, the Alamant gave her no more freedom than she had at home. At least there, she had Mama and Sela. "What is this ceremony?"

"It's really more of a tradition at this point, to see if you have magic, but I think we'll find you do—the first enchantress in over two hundred years."

He was still handsome, his face chiseled with sharp cheekbones and a strong jaw. His good looks felt like a trap—just like this place.

His expression softened. "I know this is hard."

"Don't apologize for hurting me while you're doing it. It's hypocritical."

He took a step back. "Follow me."

She glared at his back as she followed him back to where they'd been married. The people had gone, leaving a neat pile of branches. She picked at the bandages around her arms. "What was that thing you put on me anyway?"

"The marriage binding. Those branches came from the White Tree. The thorns will graft inside you and me, binding us with magic."

She gritted her teeth. "I don't accept this. I won't."

"Your acceptance isn't needed."

The pit she buried her anger in trembled and spilled over. "You're a monster."

"I do what I must."

On the other side of the wide platform was another set of stairs that wound upward. Like in the other tree, pools of rainwater gleamed in little hollows, flowers of multitudinous colors pulsing through them. The air had a mineral taste.

Larkin couldn't help but peer into the translucent White Tree. She recognized it instantly—the hard, smooth surface filled with flakes of color. The amulet and the pipers' weapons were all made from the opalescent wood of the White Tree. Movement within caught her attention. It was like looking into deep water. She could only see so far, but beyond the pulsing colors, formless shapes shifted.

She faltered. "There's something in there."

"Yes." He tugged at her elbow, pulling her forward.

"What is it?"

"So much of what we know has been lost, knowledge locked inside the White Tree, and us, unable to retrieve it."

"Why can't you retrieve it?"

"That was part of women's magic." He nodded to the archway marking the end of the stairs. "Perhaps questions left for another time."

She heard the murmurs of a large crowd, and her thoughts flashed back to facing the mob. She froze, hand covering her throat. Denan watched her, waiting.

"What happens now?" she asked.

"This ceremony is sacred to our people, Larkin. When I went through it at sixteen, my whole life changed."

Colors pulsed through the tree, disappearing before reappearing again. "Why?"

"I saw a vision." She glanced at him, startled. He shrugged. "Visions don't happen often—not since we lost the women's magic. It costs the White Tree too much."

But Larkin had seen many visions—not that she understood any of them. Denan bent down, picking up a crushed tear-shaped leaf. "Haven't you wondered why the leaves are changing? It's spring, after all."

She shrugged. "The trees grow out of the water. How do I know what's normal for this place?"

He let the leaf slip from his fingers. "The White Tree is sick."

Larkin folded her arms. She was stalling. Denan must know it too, but he wasn't pushing her. "Why?"

"What makes trees sick, Larkin?"

The curse—he couldn't answer her. "Disease, pestilence, and age." She studied the tree, seeing no sign of pests or rot. "I'm guessing a magical tree isn't vulnerable to the first two, so that leaves age. Why don't you plant another?"

He couldn't tell her, and she couldn't think of a reason why.

"What was your vision?" she asked.

"A copperbill—the birds with the red-gold beak—have you noticed them?" When she nodded, he went on. "It landed in my palm. If I closed my hand around it, it died. But if I left my hand open, it always came back."

Her brow furrowed. "What does that mean?"

He looked down at her. "I think that bird was you, and I think it means you will always find your way back to me. You have a purpose, Larkin—one important to the White Tree and the pipers."

"Is that what makes you think it's okay to kidnap me and force me to marry you?"

He faced the top of the stairs. "It's time to go."

She felt for the amulet under her clothing. "You think my purpose has to do with women's magic?"

"Yes."

A thrill darted through her. She wanted magic, wanted the power it gave her. She wanted to escape the pipers, to never be weak and at the mercy of others again. They climbed the last few steps and paused at the top of a bowl-shaped platform that contained nearly a hundred people—most were men with snakes on their mantles. A few had full heads of hair, but most had shaved scalps, a knot of hair behind their right ear.

Her breath came faster, harder. The last time she'd faced a crowd, they had been calling for her death. She finally caught sight of Alorica off to one side, Tam beside her. They wore similar fine clothes, though in emerald green, their mantles emblazoned with some kind of fish. Alorica's face was flushed with fury.

Larkin felt dizzy.

"My uncle told me Alorica cried through the whole ceremony," Denan said, a challenge in his gaze for her to be better than that. She forced herself to take slow, even breaths. He held out his arm to her. "You look like you're about to fall over."

She was, but she'd never admit as much. Though he had helped her through her grief these past days, they were not friends. She squared her shoulders and stepped past him. He fell in beside her. Together, they moved into the bowl-shaped depression. People moved aside to let them pass. In the center of the platform was a font surrounded by jagged crystals that ended in needle-like points. Behind the font, a man with angular features, a powerful build, and gray at his temples waited for them. His square mantle completely encased his shoulders and ended at five points, gems dangling from each. In the center, widest point, was an embossed painting of the White Tree, a large crystal star embedded into the leather above it. In his hand was a staff made of the same material as her amulet—the wood of the tree.

"Larkin of Hamel," the man said as they came to a halt before the font. "I am Arbor Mytin, steward of the White Tree and Denan's father. You have come to see if you are one of my people's true daughters. You may approach the font."

He was a handsome man with golden skin and brown hair and eyes. She could see where Denan got his muscular build and angular facial features, but his eyes must be his mother's.

Larkin cast a nervous look at the assemblage. Denan looked pointedly at Alorica, then back at her. Lifting her chin, she marched to stand on a little platform on the other side of Mytin. Inside the crystal font was a liquid the color of pale honey.

Mytin gestured to the needle-like shards. "Break off a thorn of the White Tree."

Eyes wide in disbelief, she looked at the thorns more closely. On second inspection, the sides didn't look sharp, only the tips. She reached for the smallest one she could find.

"Choose wisely, Larkin of Hamel," Mytin warned.

Larkin withdrew her hand. Mytin stepped back and gestured to his side of the font. She circled it, waiting for a thorn to call to her. Nothing happened. So she circled again. This time, ribbons of color coursed through one. She reached down very carefully and snapped it off. Sap leaked down the broken side, tingling as it ran down her wrist and lit an intricate band around her left forearm.

She felt someone approach and turned to see Denan hold out his hand for the thorn. "Alorica passed out for this part," he said under his breath, again with that challenge. She gritted her teeth, knowing what he was doing and hating that it was working. He pulled her sleeve up and wiped her left upper arm with something that smelled of alcohol.

She pitched her voice low. "Why do I need a thorn when I already have ..." She looked pointedly at the hidden amulet.

"Do you want to pierce yourself every time you use magic?" he whispered back. The thorn meant she wouldn't need the amulet anymore?

"The magic will be inside me?"

He held out his arm, displaying the raised lines across his skin. "Hopefully, it will give you one of our markings—a sigil. Ready?" Denan had positioned the thorn flush with her skin. This was going to hurt. She gritted her teeth and turned away. He hummed something soothing and sweet. She immediately relaxed. He was using a touch of his magic. Though she would never admit it, she was grateful.

He pinched her skin and slid the thorn inside her. She gasped, a layer of sweat broke out over her whole body as it dug in deeper. It felt like the worst bee sting she'd ever had. She bit her lip, knowing she was making a face but unable to stop.

"Done," Denan announced.

Trembling, she stared at the mound under her skin, which pulsed a deep red. A thin line of blood painted a garish streak around her arm.

"Now what?" she asked.

Wiping up the blood, Denan wrapped a clean bandage around her throbbing arm. "Now, we wait to see if the thorn takes root or withers and dies."

Takes root ... inside my body. She shuddered. "How long will that take?"

He pulled down her sleeve. "A few days to a couple weeks. The longer it stays, the better chance it will take root. It won't always hurt this much. The thorn softens before it spreads."

"I hate you," she murmured.

"No, you don't," he murmured back.

She refused to argue with him.

"Larkin," Mytin said. "Kneel before the font."

She reluctantly obeyed. He dipped his thumb into the font and drew a line across her forehead. Someone handed him a golden crown of leaves. Mytin placed it gently on her head. "I name you Princess Larkin of the White Tree. Rise." The crowd bowed.

Princess? I am no princess. She never would be, no matter what Mytin said.

From off to one side, a group of pipers started playing. The music twined through her, joy and elation staining her soul. This was men's magic, twisting her emotions. "You have no right to make me feel something I don't want to feel."

Denan studied her, arms folded across his chest. He motioned for her to follow him. Teeth gritted, she trailed after him as peace and contentment slowly snuffed out her anger and resentment. She wanted to dance, to sing and sway and be at peace. She drifted away from him and insinuated herself with the crowd, dancing with Denan's little brother, the boy who had escorted her here. *Wyn,* she remembered.

A hand came down on her arm. "Larkin, come with me."

Denan stood behind her, and she couldn't remember why she'd been upset with him. He was so handsome and kind. She left Wyn and pressed herself to Denan. "I'm sorry I was so angry before. It was silly of me."

He stiffened and then relaxed against her, pulling her in tight and breathing deep the scent of her hair.

"Dance with me," she whispered in his ear, her eyes begging.

He took her cheek in his hand. For a moment, she believed he would. His eyes shuttered closed. "When you truly want it, I will dance with you until the stars fall." He took her hand and practically dragged her through the crowd.

"But I want to dance with you now," she protested.

Some of the crowd chuckled. She flashed a smile at them, eager to lose herself to the music, the light, and the energy pulsing around her and through her and in her.

He pulled her down the magical stairs with their glowing flowers and ribbons of light until they reached a small boat. He bundled her inside, though she tried twice to head back to the dwindling music. When the boat was finally away, she stared at the tree, longing to go back, wishing he wouldn't take her away.

They came to one of the smaller trees that circled the White Tree. Denan tied the boat up on the dock. She didn't turn away from the music, every part of her straining to go back.

Denan rubbed his forehead as if he had a headache. "The nectar makes it worse. It always does." He pulled off his cloak and tugged hers from her shoulders, the night air kissing her skin.

She turned toward him. "If we can't dance there, why not here?"

He reached up and rubbed the back of his knuckles against her cheek. "If I did, you wouldn't thank me in the morning, little bird."

"Please," she begged even as she reached for him. He held her hands together with one of his own. With the other, he pulled out his flute and played a song of dreams and softness and falling. Her eyes slipped closed, unable to resist. He caught her, his muscles cording and bunching as he swung her up. She rested her head on his soft tunic as his humming vibrated against her temple.

CHAPTER 24

THE WHITE TREE

The next morning, Larkin found herself in a soft bed in the center of a room about the size of Bane's dining room. From one side, rays of light streamed through boughs and leaves. Beyond, the White Tree sparkled with color in the morning light. Beside her was a small desk with a chair, upon which lay her mantle and cloak. Toward the tree's heart, an armoire and washbasin had been built into the tree, a spout above it.

She studied the other side of the bed, relieved it didn't appear disturbed. So, Denan didn't expect her to share his bed—at least not on their wedding night. She shuddered, wondering when that was coming.

She sat up. She was still dressed in the tunic and pants from yesterday. Her arm throbbed, feeling tight and hot. Hissing, she lifted her sleeve to reveal a scab and bruising around the thorn Denan had inserted into her arm. She unwound the bandages around her hands and wrists, revealing scattered, pale markings.

Sigils.

The realization that she was actually married to Denan hit her. With a groan, she flopped back onto the bed. How could she be married to that manipulative, self-centered, boorish man? And now what? She was supposed to turn out like Caelia, pregnant and gushing about kissing him whenever she wanted?

"Never," she promised herself. For now, she would play Denan's game, get him to let his guard down. She would learn magic, and then she would take down the pipers from the inside out. One day, she would free the women of the Idelmarch and return them to their homes.

She went to the armoire and pulled open the double doors. Inside was a scarlet nightgown, a rich brown tunic, and trousers. She stripped out of her finery, hanging everything carefully, and put on the plain clothes, which were so soft against her skin. She turned on the spout and cleaned her teeth and face, undid the complex braids and pulled her hair back in a tail.

She left the bedroom, descending toward the main platform. Halfway there, she heard scuffling sounds off to her left. A horizontal walkway led in that direction. She hesitated before following the sounds that grew louder the farther she went.

At a bend in the tree, she paused, peering around a smaller branch. His chest bare, Denan practiced with a wooden ax and a shield on a platform shaped like a keyhole. It was open on all sides but one, a drop-off straight down to the water—not too far, but enough to sting if someone fell. There was no roof above it, though the canopy provided plenty of shade. In the keyhole-shaped section were various trunks.

Denan twisted and lunged, his body slick with sweat, his muscles sliding under his skin. A White Tree sigil covered his entire chest, intricate designs of angles and sharp points that were both beautiful and strong. On the center of his back was another sigil, a twisted three-headed snake insignia of his family. He dodged and struck with the grace of a cat.

She watched until he paused and wiped the sweat that streaked down his bare head. He took a cup, tipping his head back to drink. "Hello, Larkin."

She jumped, her eyes flashing to his. He cocked an eyebrow at her, and she felt a blush staining her cheeks. All thoughts of playing along with Denan flew out of her head. "How dare you marry me without my permission?"

His gaze held steady. "It can be a marriage in name only, if you want." She stiffened, surprised at the offer. "After a year, you'll be free to divorce me and remarry someone else. Or you could train with one of the other women, learn a trade. Support yourself."

She held out her hands and wrists, the sigils already forming there. "What about the binding?"

"It will remain, though you do not have to honor it."

She studied him for a while. "And the heartsong?"

He spread his hands. "It was a gift the tree gave us to fight the curse—a way to find women who would be happy here with us."

"And have women chosen to divorce the man who played their heartsong and bear their sigils?"

He didn't answer for a moment. "Yes. Not many, but yes."

So she was stuck with him, but maybe not forever. "What do you want from me, Denan?"

He sat on one of the chests. "I don't want to fight. I want us both to be happy. We barely know each other, but I think it's safe to say we've seen each other at our worst. I would like to show you my best."

She tried to calm her anger—after all, hadn't she determined to make Denan drop his guard? "It would help if I knew why you took me."

"Did you notice anything about the crowd last night?"

Most people had been wearing his insignia. "They were your family."

He nodded. "What else?"

"Some of them had full heads of hair. Most didn't." He pointed behind his ear, turning his head so she could see the missing queue.

"You cut it off last night ... after we were married?" The men with full heads of hair—they'd all had a woman with them. "Married men grow their hair." He nodded encouragingly. "The rest of the men—most of them aren't married. And all the girls—they were all Idelmarchians." She blinked at him. "Where are all your women?"

He let out a long, relieved breath. "No woman has been born to us since the magic disappeared two hundred and forty-three years ago."

Her jaw dropped. "Not even one?"

He shook his head. "If we didn't bring women in, there would be no more children. Our people and our way of life would die out. As would the White Tree—for we are the ones who defend her."

So that's why the pipers stole girls. She grudgingly stepped onto the platform. "Why not ask?" She spread her hands to their surroundings. "With this kind of wealth and beauty, girls would flock to you willingly." If not for Bane and her family, Larkin might have come on her own.

"I bind your tongues so no woman shall willingly come into the forest," he said as if by rote.

"Who bound you?" Larkin asked. Denan only looked at her. "You can't say. That isn't going to get old. And we have another *tiny* problem. I love Bane."

He shrugged. "Maybe we could be friends." Setting the ax down, he rose to his feet and rummaged through another trunk.

She relaxed a fraction, considering this. She didn't want to fight either; fighting was exhausting. For a moment, she considered thanking him for bringing her back last night instead of letting her get lost in emotions that were not her own. But he didn't deserve any of her apologies. She sighed, frustrated that she found it hard to hate him. Like when he'd offered to kill Venna—he'd been doing the wrong thing for the right reason. Memories of the wraiths overwhelmed her. She'd forgotten something. "When you fought off the wraiths, one of them said something about finding 'her' and pleasing the king. She seemed to know you."

Denan went very still. "If a wraith can't kill you or turn you with its corrupted blade, they will try to poison you in other ways—lies mixed with truths, truths mixed with lies."

He knew more than he let on. "What is the truth mixed in with the lie?"

"I hope you never find out." He found what he'd been looking for and approached her, box in hand.

Get him to drop his guard, she chanted in her head to keep from snapping his head off. "What are you doing?" she said through gritted teeth.

"Let me tend your wounds." She forced herself to hold still as Denan stepped closer and tipped her chin back to look at her neck. "It's healing well."

She reached up, fingers touching the uneven surface. "It's ugly."

"Alamantians have a lot of scars." He bent in half, lifting his trousers to reveal a pitted, jagged scar on his upper thigh. "It means your body can heal."

She dropped her hands. He was right. She was being vain. "How did you get that?"

"Mulgar's spiked club took a chunk out of me." Dropping his pant leg, he fingered the mess of pale markings on her arms that matched the ones on his. He unwrapped and inspected her thorn. "You haven't rejected your thorn yet. That's a good sign."

She felt a thrill of anticipation. It would be a relief not to pierce her hand every time she needed access to the magic, and she craved the knowledge of how to defend herself. "Will it always hurt?"

"No."

"How will you know if it does take?"

He gestured to the geometric lines all over his body. "It will begin to grow."

Something growing beneath her skin? She shuddered and studied him. He opened the box and removed some bandaging and ointment. "Where did the mulgars come from?"

"Long ago, the wraiths made them of their own people. Now, their poisoned blades turn anyone they pierce."

Denan had said Venna was possessed by dark magic and by the wraiths. "I still don't understand it."

Denan became distant, haunted. "I've lost friends to the wraiths. The darkness strips away all that is moral and robs them of their ability to choose good."

The humanity had leached from Venna's eyes, replaced with hatred and destruction. Death really would have been a kindness. "Unless they have the limb amputated before it spreads?"

"Which can be done if a master healer is in the unit and can get to them in time."

"And if there is no healer?"

Anguish swept over Denan. "We do what we must."

Ancestors, what had he been forced to do? Denan turned from her, going back to the platform. She followed slowly. He picked up the wooden ax again, holding the haft out to her.

She eyed the ax warily. Surely this was a trap. "What's this?"

"An ax."

She rolled her eyes. "You know what I mean."

"All Alamantians train with weapons."

"Even the women?" she baited him, sure he would tell her no.

"Especially the women."

This surprised her. "Why?"

"The smallest among us have even more need to protect themselves."

She straightened to her full height. "I'm not small."

"Average, then." Denan lifted her hand and closed her fingers over the haft. "I thought you'd be thrilled at a chance to hit me with something."

A sigil covered the inside of his right forearm—a geometric flower with angular petals. A vision superimposed over the sigil, the real flower. The petals curled up and fell away, leaving a single black seed the size of Larkin's fist. Her hand reached out, capturing his wrist and tracing the place where the seed would be, marveling at the dichotomy of the sharp curving lines.

"The ahlea," Denan said, voice husky. "Symbol for women's magic."

"Why would you have the symbol for women's magic?" She looked up to find something unreadable in his gaze. He touched his lips, his expression indicating he couldn't tell her. She looked down to where her hand caressed his arm. They were so close.

She lifted the ax and chopped at his shoulder. He ducked and spun. She swung again. He caught her wrist, twisting it so she had no choice but to release the ax. Her chest rose and fell as she stared at him, waiting for his anger.

He gave her a wicked grin—as if he enjoyed this—and went for another shield and ax from another trunk. Watching him warily, she picked up the ax he'd forced her to drop. When she straightened, he tossed a shield at her, which she promptly fumbled.

Embarrassed, she bent down to pick it up. When she straightened, he was there, showing her how to slide her arms through the loops and hold on to the handle. "Now, I need to get an idea of your skill level. So come at me with all you have, and we'll place you from there."

She'd been wanting to hit him for weeks. She lunged, swinging with everything she had. The ax hit his shield with a resounding crack, the reverberations jarring her arm. She pulled back and stabbed with the sharp tip. Again, he easily deflected it. Changing tactics, she aimed for his knees. His shield swept her ax out and up. He stepped forward, twisted to catch the joint of the ax on the top of the shield, and jerked it from her hands.

They went another round, which ended with her flat on her back. She blinked up at him as he watched her disapprovingly. "You've really had no training?"

"Women don't fight in the Idelmarch."

"My mother nearly killed my father with a sharpened stick. She still handles a sword better than my father."

Larkin had never heard of such a thing. "Good for her." She pushed to her feet, throwing her ax. He deflected it with his shield. She kicked his leg with the top of her foot. The pain dropped her. For half a moment, she wondered if she'd broken her foot.

He knelt next to her, gently bending her ankle. "Well, you certainly have the aggression for it." He took her ax and shield, settling them inside the beautifully carved trunk. "But we're going to have to start from the beginning."

Her gaze fixed longingly on the trunk. "I like the ax."

He chuckled, surprising her again with how much more open he seemed since they'd left the Forbidden Forest and entered the Alamant. "As do I, but an ax thrust is really an extended punch." He reached down and pulled her up. She winced as the weight came on her injured foot, but the pain quickly faded.

He showed her how to stand—with her feet spread hip length apart, one foot cocked back—how to shift her weight, how to throw a punch. She'd seen her father take that stance, seen him ball up his fists ... felt those fists connect with her middle.

And suddenly, she was a little girl again, her father's hands clamping down on her shoulder and crotch as he lifted her above his head and pitched her headfirst into the river, like she was garbage, like she was already dead.

She staggered back from Denan, feeling sick. He froze, watching her like an animal he'd spooked. "What good does it do when your opponent is always bigger and stronger?" she cried. "Curse it, he was always so much bigger."

She hadn't meant to say that, hadn't meant to reveal so much, but the water had been freezing. It had closed over her head. *She clawed for the surface, her fingers breaking through, but never her face.*

Larkin couldn't breathe. She backed away, desperate to be free.

"Larkin, careful—"

She turned to run and came face-to-face with a long drop to the water below. She cried out, but her momentum dragged her forward. Hands grabbed her shoulders and hauled her back. As soon as she was safe, Denan backpedaled, palms facing her. "You have to watch the edges."

Eyes closed, she battled to control her ragged breathing, to rein in the fear clawing its way through her. Music slipped over her and around her and slowly pushed away her panic. The music changed, becoming the flitting of a bird through the trees as it easily evaded the predators locked to the ground—dodging and dancing and reveling in the strength of being free.

The music faded, leaving Larkin firmly in her own body.

"Who hurt you?" Denan asked softly as he lowered his pipes.

She hesitated. This wasn't something she talked about with anyone, but Denan wouldn't have her father in the stocks or gossip at the tavern later. "My father." Instead of panic and shame, loathing choked her. "I hate him and I love him. How is that possible?"

Denan was silent a moment. "The people we love leave the

deepest scars."

"Even when they don't mean to," she murmured, thinking of how much it hurt to be apart from her mother and younger sisters. The baby, Brenna, was she doing all right? How was her mother getting along without Larkin's help? And Nesha ...

Larkin and Denan's gazes met, their pain intermingling. Who had hurt him? She turned away, unwilling to share a sorrow with Denan. Instead, she tugged the amulet out from her shirt. "Where did you get this?"

He hesitated, and she silently begged him to let the conversation drop. He sighed and touched his lips, his way of indicating he couldn't tell her. "I will teach you how to protect yourself."

She shot him a flat look.

He shrugged. "Even from me."

CHAPTER

MAGIC

Denan went to the trunks, pulled a globular fruit out of a bag, and tossed one to her. She caught it at the last second.

"Gobby fruit," he said. "It grows from the trees no matter the season." He sat at the platform's edge, his feet dangling over the water. He peeled back the crimson rind and bit into the meat, juice running down his chin.

Her own stomach rumbled, and she sat down far away from him and peeled back the tough rind, revealing pale pink flesh that darkened to peach in the center. She bit down. Sweet and tart exploded across her tongue. Her mouth ached with the perfection of it. She ate the whole thing, spitting out the little black seeds and watching them fall. Sela would have loved to climb this tree, eat this fruit, see the White Tree in all its glory.

"For all your kindnesses, for all your promises that I'm free, you won't ever let me go home. Caelia, Alorica, and Venna"— her voice broke on the last—"their families won't ever know what happened to them."

"I can't tell them."

"Can't or won't?"

His mouth pursed in frustration. "Can't."

She looked down to the water below, calculating her chances of shoving him off. Denan scooted away from her. She closed her eyes, reminding herself again of her promise to get him to trust her. She tucked the anger away, deep inside. "You said you can't teach me how to use magic, but you must know something."

"The library that contained the records was lost in a mulgar attack decades ago. What I do know is that the magics were complementary. Men's magic controls thoughts, feelings, moods, but only temporarily. It works best when the subject is relaxed."

That explains why girls are always taken in the night.

"Women's magic has to do with the creation of different types of barriers—they all used to have a name and a function. Many of the larger ones have crumbled. But if they were made by a strong enough enchantress, the smaller ones can last for years."

"There were more?"

He nodded. "Bridges, dams, defensive walls ... The shield you made before, it's supposedly a simpler spell. You won't be able to access the magic until your sigil takes hold, which could be a couple weeks. Can you swim?"

She warily nodded.

Denan pushed to his feet, fetched a spear from a chest, and stripped off his pants, leaving him in only his underthings. "Come on. Let's get some fish for breakfast."

She had to admit, he was very nicely built—if she noticed such things. She was staring. She looked away, but not before she caught his broad grin. "What am I supposed to swim in?"

"Just your tunic." He focused on something she couldn't

see, and he launched himself spear first into the lake. The water enveloped him.

Larkin peered down, waiting for him to come back up. She waited a long time—long enough for her palms to sweat—before he broke the surface. "Aren't you coming?"

Feeling self-conscious, she tugged off her pants, exposing her legs from mid-thigh down. She caught him staring at her freckled skin. He turned away quickly.

Knowing he would tease her mercilessly if she hesitated, she took a deep breath and stepped off the edge. Surprisingly warm water enveloped her. She opened her eyes and found herself transported to another world.

A faintly glowing white crust surrounded the tree's roots, from which strange plants grew. Some were stiff, sharp even, under the pads of her feet. Others were like gently waving fans. Yet others were like weird bare-branched trees, and instead of birds flitting among the branches, fish of every color, size, and shape swam and darted. Far below, farther than she could see, the tree's roots speared down.

She turned in a circle and fought the need to surface as she took it all in. Denan motioned her up. She broke the surface, paddling and gasping in fresh air. "It's amazing!"

His eyes crinkled as he smiled at her, clearly pleased. "I'm glad you know how to swim. Not many girls from the Idelmarch do."

She'd been enjoying spending time with Denan, which felt like betraying the life she'd had before—a life that had spit her out like moldy bread. She frowned. "Bane taught me."

"He sounds like a good man."

She turned away. "He is."

"Would you like to see more?"

She nodded.

"Stay right behind me." He bent in half and kicked down. Taking a deep breath, she followed him as he swam around the tree's base. Denan pointed out a flat fish with a pair of eyes on the top of its head. It was burnt orange with bright blue spots that shimmered when she approached. Denan's hand came down on her arm, and he shook his head, warning her not to get any closer.

Farther out, translucent ropes floated lazily, carrying dozens of creatures shaped like cucumbers. Those, too, Denan steered her away from. But he let her hold a creature shaped like a flower. Its petal-like arms waved through the water, and its center glowed a pale yellow. They picked misshapen yellow lumps, which they placed in a pouch at Denan's waist along with some orange critters that looked like cockroaches. He dove deep, spearing a fish.

They approached the dock. Below it, piles of sticks tied with twine were tethered down with hooks, and Larkin wondered what they were for. Denan hauled himself up, Larkin half a beat behind. She slicked water from her face and wrung out her hair. Denan led her up a level to a platform she hadn't seen before, hidden on the opposite side of the buttressed roots. It was obviously a kitchen: a table and chairs took up the center, shelves filled with cooking implements built into the trunk.

Denan rested his spear against one wall and took down a bowl. He showed her how to roll the yellow fruit to release the juices, then how to cut it in half and squeeze the juice into the bowl. While she did that, he cleaned the fish and shelled the cockroach critters. He put all of it in the juice and then stretched out in the sunlight on the floor.

"Aren't we going to cook it?" she asked.

He yawned and scratched his stomach—he was oddly hairless for a grown man. "You must never light a fire in the Alamant, Larkin. The penalties are severe."

"Why?"

He gestured lazily to the trees all around them.

She couldn't imagine a life without fire. "But what about

heat?"

"It doesn't get cold."

"Even in the winter?" Winters in Hamel were always wet, dreary things, full of freezing rain. On rare occasions, they woke up to snow covering all the depressing browns, but it was mostly gone by afternoon.

"There is no winter here."

Had they really gone that far south? Larkin didn't think so. "What would happen if someone were to light a fire?"

He shuddered. "Imprisonment, at the very least."

She tried to imagine life without cold. Every day feeling much the same as today—no struggling for food or to keep warm in winter. Hugging her knees to her chest, Larkin watched the sunlight sparkling on the lake. The boughs swayed gently above her. This place was like an enormous garden; only, it didn't need plowing or planting or tending. "Is this what life is like for you? Every day as easy as this?"

He chuckled. "Honeymoon, remember?"

"And who's dealing with your princely duties?"

"King Netrish. He wasn't at the ceremonies. Tradition dictates he step down after your coronation."

Larkin was suddenly dizzy. "Coronation? I'm to be crowned?"

He nodded. "As soon as the prince's new wife has settled in, he becomes king."

She had to get out of here. "And Netrish will step down peacefully?" Stepping down wasn't something Larkin thought kings did.

"He doesn't have a choice. I have the military's loyalty, and the magic of leadership will shift to me." Denan's eyes darkened, making her think it wasn't as easy as he implied.

She studied the sigils on his skin, wondering which one marked him as king. "What do they mean?"

"The meanings are symbolic. This one"—he touched the

White Tree in the center of his chest—"named me as the future king."

He hopped up and brought her the bowl of fish, snagging a piece with his bare hands and plopping it into his mouth. Larkin was hesitant, as they hadn't cooked it, but if Denan could eat it, so could she. It was sour and fresh and delicious. She ate even more than he did. He handed her some bright red berries she hadn't seen him gather. They were sweet and chewy with a bitter aftertaste.

If not for the defensive wall, she could almost fool herself into believing she was safe here. "How much of a danger are the wraiths and mulgars to your people?" she asked.

"Every once in a while, the mulgars attack, but the walls have never been breached. Most are injured out on patrols."

They washed the bowls in rainwater. Denan flicked his fingers and headed toward the dock. "Come on. There's still so much I want to show you."

They went back to the keyhole platform and dressed, and he insisted she wear a hat. They climbed into the boat and paddled out onto the exceedingly calm lake. A huge melangth broke the surface, bland gray skin mottled on the underside. "It lives under our tree," Denan said. "So you'll probably see it a lot."

They paddled around the inner circle of trees, Denan pointing out people he knew. The children, all of them boys, waved enthusiastically back. They passed beneath branches woven into an elegant bridge. A little boy with wild blond hair pulled down his pants and peed off the edge, his little bottom pale and dimpled. His mother came out to scold him, waving embarrassedly at them as they passed. Denan chuckled and waved back.

Larkin wasn't sure what she expected, but it wasn't this ... normalcy—like these women hadn't been kidnapped and forced to marry their kidnappers, like these boys weren't being raised to do the same to some innocent girl in their future.

Little islands sprouted like mushrooms and boasted wavering fields of grain. Men and women tended the crops side by side, looking up to wave and call out greetings as they passed. In the shallows, a creature flared and contracted, dozens of fins arranged like a yellow-and-black pinecone. She pointed it out to Denan.

"Brackis," he said. "Don't touch them. Each fin has a stinger."

Larkin shook out her arms—she wasn't used to paddling so much. He steered them toward another large tree, where a woman crouched, washing out clothes in the lake. She had a scarf tied around her long dark hair, and she dressed in plain brown garments like the ones Larkin wore.

"That's my mother, Aaryn," Denan told her.

Larkin recognized her from the wedding, though she'd probably been at the magic ceremony too. They tied off, and Larkin climbed onto the dock.

Aaryn took Larkin's hands in her own, her rich skin a contrast to Larkin's. "I'm sorry for all you've lost."

Larkin blinked hard. "Where are you from?"

"A little town outside Cordova, smaller than Hamel." She tugged Larkin toward the tree. "You arrived just in time. Mytin should be about done with dinner, but first, I want to show you my weaving."

Mytin cooked? Larkin thought in amazement.

Aaryn took Larkin to a room filled with yarn and sticks like the ones she'd seen tied underneath the docks, which were in the process of being broken down to fibers. Aaryn showed Larkin how she wove those fibers into clothing.

"I could teach you, if you like." She sounded so hopeful that Larkin could only nod.

Smiling, Aaryn called for Wyn and led them to a kitchen only slightly bigger than Denan's, though this one was built directly over the water. Bowls were laid out, filled with fish, soggy greens, flat bread, and a creamy substance that Mytin drizzled honey on.

"Larkin, welcome!" Mytin still wore his mantle of authority, a collar that covered his shoulders and peaked at each corner, jewels dangling. "Has your thorn come out yet?"

Her hand strayed to her arm, still tender to the touch. "How would I know if it had?"

"It would come out, like a sliver," Mytin said. "Probably sometime in the next three days."

"It's an old tradition that should have ended years ago." Aaryn came up behind him and stirred something. "It does nothing but scare the new girls, and they always lose them."

"If there's even a chance a girl could have magic, we have to take it." The way the older man was looking at Larkin, the weight of his expectation—he knew she'd used magic. She forced her gaze to the ground, angry that Denan told her to keep a secret he himself hadn't.

"I don't think magic is ever coming back for women." Aaryn set down the bowl harder than she needed to. "Wyn!" she called, making Larkin jump.

A few moments later, Wyn pounded up the stairs, dripping wet and spear in hand.

"Dry off," his mother chided, tossing him a towel. "Mytin, will you close the barriers to the wind? The boy's going to be sick."

"It's hot out," Denan said. "He's fine."

Aaryn shot him a look.

"I'll do it," Larkin said hastily. She wanted to touch the magic again, if only for a moment. She lifted her hand, the magic stirring against her skin. She pushed and spread her fingers out, the breeze against her face dying out.

"I bet she can't handle a sword," Wyn said derisively.

"Wyn!" his mother said.

Denan smacked Wyn on the back of the head. "I'll teach her."

Wyn rubbed his head and glared at his older brother. "Mother nearly killed Father with a sword when she was new."

Mytin gave his son a sheepish grin. "Which is why we never take captives alone. It takes a unit."

"Mother was a rich man's daughter," Denan said. "She had time and money for lessons, and her father indulged her because he wanted her safe from the forest."

Aaryn clapped her hands. "That's enough. Wyn, you had better behave or Master Ritland will hear of it."

Wyn straightened in his chair.

Larkin hung back, feeling like the outsider she was. Denan spooned fish onto some bread, topped it with the creamy sauce, rolled it up, and brought it to her.

"I thought we could sit at the edge while my family takes the table." Denan must have noticed her discomfort, for there were plenty of chairs.

She took the plate in relief. She dangled her feet in the water, glowing fish nibbling at her heels as she ate.

"What is your father?" she asked soft enough his family wouldn't hear.

Denan looked at her, his brows drawn, then his head came back in understanding. "Oh, you mean his position. He's the Arbor. He represents the White Tree. It's a religious title."

"And does the king answer to him?"

"No, but my father does advise him. It's—"

Wyn stood behind her, looking sullen. "I'm sorry I said you were a bad fighter."

Larkin studied the boy. He'd clearly been sent to apologize and wasn't happy about it. "You don't like me much, do you, Wyn?"

His answering glare said it all.

"Wyn," Denan chided.

Larkin held out her hand to stop Denan. "Why?"

Wyn stuck out his chin. Tears filled the boy's eyes. "Why

are you more important than me because you're a girl?"

"Wyn," Denan said, gently this time.

The boy dashed tears off his cheeks, still glaring at Larkin. "You don't even like him, and he's spent all his time with you since he got back."

"We've decided to be friends." Or at least not enemies. "And you can spend as much time with my friend as you'd like." *Or all your time.*

Wyn considered this before he gave a curt nod and plopped down beside his older brother. Denan planted a kiss on the boy's tousled hair.

Larkin leaned across Denan and whispered to Wyn, "Maybe we could be friends too."

Wyn considered it. "Are you going to the king's party tomorrow? Father says I have to."

Denan shook his head. "The new girls don't go to parties—too much fuss."

Wyn shot her a challenging look. Larkin knew a test when she saw one. "I won't make a fuss."

Denan raised a single brow. "You'd have to pretend you actually like me."

Wyn folded his arms, eyes narrowing. "You said you were his friend."

She forced back a wince of guilt and lifted her hands in surrender. "I am! And I will!"

"There will be music," Denan said carefully. "Larkin, you might not like how it makes you feel."

A breath of unease fanned through her. "What will it make me feel?"

"It's a state dinner," Aaryn said. "The music will ensure everyone tells the truth."

Larkin shot Denan a look. "Don't ask me any questions you don't want to know the answer to."

Mytin laughed. "I'll ask for more seats at our table."

She busied herself eating and listening to Wyn tell Denan all about his classes. Clearly, the boy adored his older brother. Larkin missed her own little sister so much in that moment, and she grieved for the younger sister who wouldn't remember Larkin at all.

Denan must have noticed. "We'll see you tomorrow, Wyn. It's late. Time for everyone to go to bed."

"But I wanted to go swimming," Wyn whined.

Denan glanced toward the setting sun. "It's too close to dark."

"Why can't you go swimming after dark?" Larkin asked. That would be the best time to see all the glowing creatures.

He searched the waters. "At night, the waters belong to the lethan."

"What's that?" she asked.

"Let's hope you never find out."

CHAPTER

DANCING

The next day passed with more training and a midday swim to cool off and gather their lunch. In the heat of the afternoon, Denan began teaching her to read, though she wasn't sure why. She'd never be a merchant. When evening came, Denan handed her a towel, a bar of soap that smelled of lime, and a vial of oils that smelled of marjoram. "If you follow the path around the tree, the third space between buttressed roots is perfect for bathing. After you're done, put on your dress robes."

She bit her lip, anxiety twisting her middle. "I won't be able to tell a lie—that's all the music will do?"

"It also reminds us how connected we are."

She frowned. "The music—it affects you as well?"

"Not like the heartsong. Our sigils make us more resistant to the rest."

"I don't trust you when I have all my wits about me. Yet you expect me to make myself even more vulnerable to you?"

The night before, he'd played a lullaby that put her to sleep. And her day had started with music that had made her eyes spring open, eager to start the day. But what happened when he used his magic to make her do something she didn't want to? He'd done it before.

"I told you I wouldn't lie to you."

"Yet you told your father I had magic, after you made me promise to keep it a secret."

Denan rubbed his hands together. "My father knew you would have magic before I met you."

She didn't believe him. "How?"

"He was there when the tree gave me the amulet. He made the connection between my future wife and my ahlea sigil. I still did not understand. The day we met, I heard Sela singing and found her in the meadow. I stood far off, making sure she was safe and hoping she'd find her way back to your town on her own. And then you came, my heartsong, your hair as red as the beak of the copperbill in my vision."

She held out her hands in a helpless gesture. "What do you think I can do for you, Denan?"

"We'll worry about that when your magic manifests."

She rolled her eyes. "You're not even sure I have magic."

"I'm sure."

She rubbed her lower back. It had been aching all day. "What if you're wrong?"

"There's a way we can prove it." He said it like a challenge.

She wet her lips. "How?"

"Go back to the font. Ask the White Tree yourself."

She hesitated—but the more she understood, the sooner she could escape. "All right."

He let out a long breath. "The bathing spot is that way. Wave your arm to close the barrier." He inclined his head in the direction she should go.

Larkin removed her clothes and stared at the blood on her underclothing. Her insides hadn't been twisting with anxiety, but cramps. What was she supposed to do? There wasn't another woman around to ask about it, and she hadn't seen any rags in her room.

That left Denan. She didn't want to talk about such things with Denan, but who else could she go to for help? She washed her clothes out and scrubbed herself, then she carefully wrapped herself in the towel. There wasn't anything else for it. Face burning with humiliation, she went in search of Denan. She found him on the main platform, polishing a set of armor she'd never seen before. It was silver and embossed with the White Tree in the center, but even all his polishing couldn't remove the dents and gouges.

He looked up at her, but she couldn't meet his gaze. "I need rags."

"Rags? For what?"

"For …" She glanced up, hoping he'd understand. His brow drew down in genuine concern, but there was no embarrassment or horror. Not yet. Curse him, why couldn't he understand? "My monthly!" she blurted.

He was silent a beat. "Oh, that's why your back was hurting. We don't use rags for that. There's a sheepskin with a belt in your room. Bottom drawer."

She shuffled, knowing she needed to hurry or she'd have blood running down her legs. "I don't know where … ?"

He put his armor back in the trunk and closed the lid. "I'll show you."

In her room, he opened one of the bottom drawers in the armoire. Inside was a tooled belt and sheepskins, wool still attached.

"I can't use those." They were too clean and pretty. At

home, she'd used rags that were falling apart and stuffed them into knitted underthings. They weren't very effective, so she didn't go out in public on heavy days for fear of leaking.

"I made them for you," Denan said, sounding almost offended.

"I'll ruin them."

"You can't ruin them by using them for what they were designed for." When she made no move to take them, Denan sighed. "Larkin, why are you so upset?"

It happened. A drip of blood ran down her leg and skimmed the inside of her foot before soaking into the floor. She pressed her hands into her eyes to keep from bursting into tears.

"You're embarrassed?" He said it like a revelation.

She nodded, relieved she didn't have to say it.

"My armor was fashioned by the finest smiths the world has ever known, my uniform by my own mother. I've bled all over both. It washes out."

"This is different," she whispered.

"Blood is blood." He pressed the underthings into her hand and stepped back. "I'll go bathe, and then we'll go to the celebration."

"I can't go out in public! And there's no way I can wear the ceremonial robes. What if I stain them?"

He looked at her, genuine confusion on his face. "They wash." He left her alone, bleeding on the floor. She looked down at the undergarments in her hand. He'd made them for her monthly, like her bleeding wasn't an issue, like it was normal. Before she could talk herself out of it, she pulled the underwear on. It fit snug against her and was soft—unlike the soggy, ill-fitted rags she usually wore. She washed her legs off in the fountain and cleaned the floor as best she could, then she dressed in her ceremonial robes.

Denan came for her, looking handsome in his robes. He handed her a cup of tea he said would help with her cramps. She took it gratefully. They paddled the boat toward the gleaming amber tree. The wide staircase was covered with Alamantians, mostly men, all of them wearing the same fine clothes, though the mantles were all slightly different with different insignia embossed on the front.

All those strangers watching her ... Larkin chewed her lip.

"Are you sure you want to go?" Denan asked.

"I promised Wyn."

She hesitated before stepping onto the same stairs she had earlier. Would she see another vision? Gritting her teeth, she stepped down, and the vision instantly swept her up.

She hit the water hard, slicing clean through. There was something tight around her waist, pulling her down. The pressure from the water drove knives into her ears and made her scream until they gave with a pop. The pain receded, leaving her with a hollow ringing.

She gasped and came to with Denan holding her in his arms. Her ears were still ringing, the pain slowly fading.

"How many of these visions have you had?" he whispered.

People were watching them, looking concerned. She saw no point in lying to him. "Three. Maybe four."

He glanced around. "We'll talk about them later."

She pulled away from him and straightened. A woman approached them. Not much older than Larkin, she had glowing ebony skin and tight curls, which she wore short. Her cinnamon eyes swept over them, hardening on Denan before sliding away again. "Denan, does your wife need assistance?"

Larkin cringed at being called his wife.

He wouldn't meet the woman's gaze. "No, Magalia. She's suffering her monthly."

Larkin would kill him. Just as soon as they were alone, she would kill him. For now, she settled for pinching his side. Denan's mouth tightened, and he pulled her fingers free, covering the action by holding her hand. Reminding herself she needed to pretend to like him, Larkin allowed it.

Magalia's eyes narrowed. "I have a tincture that will help. Come see me at the healing tree?"

"I'll send a page," Denan said. He had pages? He bowed and tugged Larkin away.

Larkin glanced back to see Magalia glaring after Denan, something like hatred in her eyes. "What was that all about?" she hissed at Denan.

He only shook his head. After she killed him, he would tell her what was going on. Larkin scanned the crowd, many of whom watched her curiously. She realized Denan still held her hand and suppressed the urge to pull away. Halfway to the archway at the top of the stairs, a man stepped toward them. He was middle-aged, bald and portly, yet still Denan tensed, his hand slipping free of Larkin's.

"King Netrish." Denan bowed without taking his eyes off the other man. "May I present my wife, Princess Larkin."

Trying not to cringe at the title, Larkin gave a watery smile and bowed as well.

"Prince Denan, I'm surprised to see you out and about so soon." Netrish didn't seem happy about it. "Your wife is adjusting well?"

Larkin hated when people spoke about her like she wasn't there. "Perfectly well, thank you."

Netrish examined her from her bare head to her bare feet. "Wonderful." He placed a damp kiss on the back of her hand. "Such a fine thing to have you here, my dear." He breezed past them, heading toward a man in full armor.

"He's not happy about stepping down," Larkin whispered.

Denan watched him go. "No."

Larkin spotted familiar dark curls and a flash of dusky skin. For a moment, everything stilled. She let out a gasp and ran forward.

"Larkin?" Denan called after her.

She was already halfway up the stairs, darting around staring people. Alorica met her in the middle, and they enveloped each other in a hug. Knowing they had only a few seconds before Denan arrived, Larkin whispered, "As soon as I figure out my magic, I can keep us safe from the pipers and the Forbidden Forest. We can go home!"

Alorica stiffened. "We can't even leave our trees without an escort. How will we ever—"

"Where is your tree?" Larkin interrupted. "So I can find you when the time comes."

Alorica hesitated and pulled back. She jerked her chin to the right. "That way."

"That doesn't—"

"Larkin." Tam appeared behind Alorica. A look passed between the two of them. Alorica looked away first. He looked at someone behind her and bowed. "If I'd known you were to be in attendance, I wouldn't have come."

Larkin whirled on Denan. "Why shouldn't they attend?"

Denan stepped closer. "Because you and Alorica tend to plot." His hand came around her waist, tugging her away. "My family is waiting. The music will start soon."

Tam led Alorica in the opposite direction. "Why can't I talk to her?"

"You can. If you both promise there will be no whispering and no alone time." She stiffened before nodding. "I'll arrange it, then, but not tonight. We haven't the time."

Denan took her to a table that had been set up on a platform at the tree's base. His family was waiting for them, plates of food before empty chairs. Aaryn patted the chair next to her.

From the other side of Denan, Wyn eyed Larkin as if considering something. "Did someone try to kill you?" He pointed at her throat.

"Wyn," his mother hissed.

Larkin covered her scar self-consciously. "Yes."

He nodded approvingly. "I guess she's not so bad," he said to his brother.

Denan choked on a laugh.

Larkin decided she didn't like Denan's brother. "Someone almost killing me makes you like me?"

Wyn's brow furrowed. "No. You surviving does."

She let out a long breath. Maybe he wasn't so bad.

Wyn's feet kicked under his chair. "I'm going to be commander general someday. I haven't had my ceremony to choose my path yet, but I know what it will say. Then I'll kill all the mulgars and wraiths. Although I wish I could have one of the women's magical swords—their magic is so much better than enthralling a girl with pipes."

"Wyn!" Mytin's voice held an undercurrent of threat.

"What? All the other boys say it too." Wyn continued to kick his feet as he turned to Larkin. "Do you like being married to Denan?"

Everyone at the table froze.

The music hadn't started, but Larkin wasn't going to lie to smooth things over. "No."

"Why?" Wyn asked. "He's going to be king, and he always beats Tam in wrestling. Tam is pretty good too, but no one can beat Talox."

No one would look at her. "Because I was forced to marry him."

"Why does that matter?"

"Wyn," his mother begged.

"But I don't understand," Wyn went on. "If she could've, she would have chosen him. All the women say it." He turned back to Larkin. "Denan can hit a target from the other side of the clearing with an arrow *and* a knife. He's not as good with his ax, but they're not the throwing kind anyway."

Determination obviously ran in the family. "I was to marry someone else."

Wyn waved away her comment. "Denan is better." He continued enumerating Denan's virtues between bites of fish, flatbread, sugared berries, and crunchy, salted seaweed. Twilight came on, the tree's inner light casting a pleasant glow. When a young man came to take Wyn home, Larkin wasn't the only one to breathe out in relief.

"The music will start soon," Aaryn said. "I'm orchestrating."

Mytin rose to his feet to follow her.

Denan stood to block him. "I wonder, Father, if Larkin might see the font again."

Mytin shot his son a questioning look. Denan gave a slight nod. Mytin patted his wife's hand. "Proceed without me, my dear. We'll be along shortly."

He led them to the stairs that wound up the tree. Two men in ceremonial armor blocked the way, halberds crossed over the stairs. When Mytin approached, they uncrossed them and snapped to attention. Mytin climbed past them without looking back.

Larkin eased nervously past the guards. At the archway at the top of the concave space, she couldn't take her gaze off the font.

"So her thorn has taken?" Mytin said.

"Not yet," Denan answered.

"Then what are we doing?" Mytin asked in that mild way of his.

"Larkin wants to choose her path," Denan said. He turned to her. "I was marked as the future king when I was twelve. When I was twenty-one, the tree marked me with the ahlea—the insignia of women's magic. From the font came the amulet, which bore the figure of the White Tree—the mark of the Arbor."

Larkin shook her head. "I don't understand."

"Before women's magic was taken, all Arbors were women," Mytin said. "They communicated with the White Tree in ways we haven't been able to since."

"You think I'm the Arbor?" Larkin asked.

"Yes," Mytin said.

She pursed her lips. "And if I refuse it?"

Mytin chuckled. "You can't refuse the calling any more than you could refuse your hands or your eyes. It's a part of you."

Denan spread his hands toward the font. "You have to ask her."

"Her?"

"The White Tree has always been female."

"How do I ask?" she said softly.

Mytin led the way, pausing before the largest thorn. "Push your hand onto the thorn."

She flinched. "What?"

Mytin's eyes were gentle. "You don't have to do this, Larkin—not if you aren't ready."

Biting her lip, she examined the thorn and noted what she'd missed before—the tip was hollow. A drop of sap dripped from the tip into the font. It wouldn't be any different than squeezing the amulet. Before she could change her mind, she gripped the thorn, feeling it slide into her skin.

Her blood swirled inside the point, mixing with the sap in mesmerizing patterns. Warmth swept through her hand, the pain gone in an instant. The sap spread through her, just as her blood spread through the sap. Within her, something foreign quested, searching, niggling.

"What do you want from me?" she cried.

The vision sucked her in.

Ahead, the White Tree's light outshone the stars and even the moon. She stood at the head of a boat, her hair long and wavy down her back. She wore a headdress of gold and amber. Behind her, the women pulled up their oars, the boat bumping against the stairs.

Pulling up her gown of gold and white, she stepped into the water. Her bare feet touched the bark. Joy and sadness and longing curled up inside her, lighting her sigils so they burned gold. She climbed the stairs to a wide bough. She crossed its wide expanse, the water gleaming turquoise from the tree's inner light.

As she walked, she dropped her cloak, mantle, tunic, and trousers, so she stood in only her underthings, a weighted belt, and a necklace. Only then did she turn outward. Beyond the trees branches were hundreds of boats, all filled with her people. She took a pendant in her hand, the seed inside rattling against the metal.

She stepped to the edge, the bough swaying gently with the breeze. Swallowing her fear, she pointed her hands over her head and dove. Falling. Falling. Falling. She hit the water and sliced deep into the dark abyss, the weighted belt forcing her deeper.

Larkin wrenched free of the vision with a gasp, coming back to herself one breath at a time. She still held the thorn, her blood turning the sap pink. The tree wanted her help to plant a seed deep in the water. "Help me save my people from the pipers, and I'll help you," she whispered back.

A metallic hum started in her chest, like the singing of crystals. A feeling swept over her—need, desperation, a sense of time running out. Denan asked her something, but she couldn't hear him over the singing crystals. She followed the sound to the other side of the font.

Her fingers brushed over the tips of the crystals, the points sharp, but not cutting. Her finger grazed one, and the singing stopped. Her breaths sounded unnaturally loud. She broke the thorn off, her right hand buzzing with need. She was aware of movement in her periphery, but she didn't look up as she slid the thorn into the skin behind where her thumb and first finger met.

Sweet release flooded her, the pressure in her chest popping. She staggered, only to have another crystal start singing. This one she pushed into her left forearm. Another crystal sang, the thorn longer and wider than the others. The moment she touched it, the singing stopped, a hollow ache pulsing at the back of her neck. She swept her hair aside, positioning the thorn where it needed to be.

"Let me." Denan took the thorn from her, sliding it into the skin of her neck.

Only then did the humming stop altogether, replaced by the pain. She came back to herself fully, staggering with dizziness. Mytin wrapped her welted wounds with a soft cloth smeared with salve that took away a little of the ache. He handed her a simple wooden cup filled with sap from the font. She drank it eagerly.

"What did the tree show you?" Mytin asked.

"It wants me to plant a seed."

Mytin and Denan exchanged a weighted glance. "We'll find a way," Mytin said.

"A way to what?" Larkin asked.

"The White Tree is dying," Denan finally answered. "Our people and yours are in danger."

"My people are in danger? From what?"

"The barrier around the Idelmarch is failing," Mytin said. "And when the tree dies, it will be completely gone."

When the barrier fell, mulgars and wraiths would have free reign over her people. They'd all be slaughtered! "Can I plant another?"

"Perhaps," Mytin said.

From below, music twined through the boughs, spinning around Larkin like a whirlwind before sinking deep inside her. Peace and contentment settled into her body like a pleasant drowsiness, chasing away the worry and constant fear.

When she opened her eyes, Mytin was gone. Denan held out a hand. "Dance with me?"

It took all her will to hold back. "You're my enemy." The moment she said it, she realized it wasn't true—not anymore.

"Do you really believe that?"

She chose not to answer.

"You'll be expected to know the steps when we go down."

Her resistance evaporated. She placed her hand in his, for once not cringing away from his touch, even when he placed his hand on the small of her back. He didn't have to teach her anything. She followed his lead, the music becoming one with her body. The music melded from one song to another. They moved together in perfect step, effortless and dreamlike. Larkin had always loved to dance, but this was more than just dancing. This was its own kind of magic.

When the music finally trailed off to nothing, Larkin came back to herself slowly. Her head rested against Denan's chest as if was meant to be there. His arms cradled her against him. She pulled back. He tucked her hair behind her ear, the backs of his fingers trailing down the side of her face.

"It's the music," she said breathlessly.

"The music stopped," Denan answered.

He was right. It had stopped. And she still didn't want to move. It felt … good to be held by Denan. When had she stopped hating him? Or had it been so gradual she hadn't even noticed? "We barely know each other," she echoed his own words back to him.

"I know you're smart and brave and incredibly tenacious. I know you don't trust easily, but when you do, that person has your undying loyalty for the rest of their life."

She studied his eyes, black in the dim light. She knew things about him too—his endless patience, his leadership and high morals, and, most of all, his devotion to his family and people.

"Can I have a lock of your hair?" he asked.

"Why?"

He reached out, running his fingers through it, and she shivered. "A keepsake."

He'd given her so many fine things that she could not deny him this. She nodded. He eased a small knife from his belt and stepped closer. She could feel the heat of him shimmering between them, his skin gleaming in the soft light.

He pushed her hair back from her shoulder. "Tip your head to the side."

She exposed the length of her throat. He pulled out a tendril of her hair from the nape of her neck. The knife sang through it, leaving a long rope of copper in his hand. He tucked the knife away, wrapped the hair around his knuckles, and slipped the tendril deep in his pocket. She rubbed at the short, tightly curling strands hidden beneath her thick hair and glanced up to see him watching her with such intensity and longing that it took her breath away. He reached up, his movements slow and deliberate as if she were a bird he might startle away.

Instead, she held very, very still.

He cupped her cheek, and she felt the tremor start beneath his skin, as if he were touching something precious and rare instead of simply her freckled cheek. Something in her swelled, begging to rise and meet him. It was getting harder and harder to hold it back.

"Why are you looking at me like that?" she asked breathlessly.

"Let me kiss you," he asked.

A sweet pang shot through her lower belly. She had to look away—or risk being lost forever. "Don't."

He stroked her cheek, his fingers trailing down her neck before starting back up. She wanted this man, wanted his arms around her. To feel the press of his hard body against her soft one, his heart beating against her chest, his lips on hers. That longing dragged her gaze back to his eyes, the love in their depths tugging her upward, his full lips beckoning. Were they as soft as they looked? His hand slipped through her hair, cupping the back of her head and tilting her mouth toward his. She rose up to meet him, their lips a mere breath apart.

"Bane."

Arms wrapping around herself, she whirled away from Denan. He let her go without a fight. How could she have forgotten Bane? It had only been a week. "The music, you promised it wouldn't trick me."

"It only strips away the lies we tell ourselves, the walls we build to protect and isolate us."

Ancestors, what had she nearly done?

A hollow note sounded, cutting through her like a knife. She staggered back. She searched for the danger that had to be there, though she wasn't sure where or how she knew it.

Denan snatched her hand. "Come on."

She hurried after him. "What's wrong?"

He didn't have to answer. Through the boughs of the White Tree, she caught sight of something rising in the distance—brilliant gold and red, like a serpent's tongue.

Flames.

A tree burned.

CHAPTER 27

FIRE

L arkin followed Denan down the winding staircase, past the startled sentinels standing guard at the entrance. She followed the men's gaze through an opening in the branches. The tree burned, tongues of flame devouring the branches. On either side, men chopped at the connecting bridges in an attempt to keep the other trees from catching fire.

"No!" Denan cried, and he took off at a full sprint.

"Denan?" Larkin tried to keep up, but he was so much faster. The single long note of warning echoed across the waters, and she could swear the trees groaned. He passed the archway and sprinted past servants cleaning up the mess—they couldn't see the burning from here. He reached the dock and pulled the mooring line free.

"What are you doing?" she cried as she reached the stairs.

He jumped into the boat. "That's my family's tree!"

Larkin thought of Wyn and his unyielding love for his brother, of Aaryn's kindness, of Mytin's adoration for his wife.

Denan pulled away from the dock, his oar digging deep into the dark water. Larkin dove after and grabbed the gunwale, nearly capsizing the boat. Denan pulled her in and threw her an oar. They paddled hard.

As they came closer, burning leaves sifted through the air, sizzling as they hit the water. Smoke burned Larkin's lungs. They had nearly reached the tree—the heat of it blasting her face—when another boat pulled away, Mytin paddling. Aaryn was hunched over, sobbing with pain. Much of her clothing had burned away on her left side, the skin bright red and blistered.

"Where's Wyn?" Denan called.

"I looked everywhere," his father choked out. "I have to get your mother to healers."

"You have to find him," Aaryn wailed. "Please, Denan!"

"I will." Denan dug in with his oar. As soon as they slammed into the dock, he shot out of the boat. Half standing, Larkin stumbled and went down to one knee. She pushed herself up after him.

"Stay by the boat in case he comes," Denan said as he tied the craft off. "If he does, get out before the boughs come down."

"But—" she began to protest, but Denan was already gone. "Wyn!" she called, hands cupped around her mouth. "Wyn, where are you?"

Denan's call echoed from above. A mighty crack followed by a groan, and then something fell toward her. Larkin didn't have time to think. She dove forward. She must have blacked out, because when she awoke, she was smothered in smoldering branches that should have burned her to a crisp—and they would have, if her shield hadn't sprung up between her and the branch.

Left arm buzzing painfully, she kept her shield up as she wriggled out from under the burning branches and staggered farther up the dock. She patted herself, expecting to find charred clothes, singed hair, and burned skin. Besides her throbbing arm, she wasn't hurt. The shield had protected her.

Swallowing a sob of relief, she tried to think where a frightened little boy would go. Unbidden, an image popped in her mind of herself beside the loom with Aaryn yesterday. Choking on smoke, she ran to the main trunk and climbed. A couple dozen steps later, she was on the platform, which was filled with yarn, thread, and sticks.

"Wyn? Wyn, are you in here?"

Nothing. She forced herself to be still and listen—beneath the hungry crackling of the fire, little whimpering breaths. She turned her head toward a pile of soft yarn, illuminated by the flames from above. She pushed the yarn aside. The boy looked up at her, his hands wrapped around his knees. She snatched him up. He didn't resist, wrapping his little arms around her neck. He reminded her so much of Sela in that moment, of the time she had run for her life with her sister in her arms.

"Denan! I found him!"

She turned to leave but another branch fell, blocking their entrance with a wall of flame that flared into the room, catching the dry sticks and brittle pieces. She had seconds before the whole space went up, but she would not let the fire hurt this little boy. She held him fiercely and called up her shield, forcing it to grow bigger, wider.

Gathering herself, she leaped across the crackling tinder and prayed her clothing wouldn't catch fire. She drove through the wall of flame and used her shield to push through the burning branches. When she came out on the other side, she turned back, amazed both of them were still alive—even more amazed her skin wasn't blistered and melting. Wyn coughed, his body convulsing.

"Denan! I have him! Denan!"

There was no answer. Another branch fell, and she looked up, into fire and smoke. There was no way Denan could survive that inferno. Fear like she'd never known pulsed through her. The little boy's fingers were knotted in her hair, pulling hard.

Ignoring the pain, she looked about, trying to find the boat, but it was buried under the branch that had hit her earlier. More branches fell, the whole tree coming down around her.

That left one option.

"Hold your breath," she instructed Wyn. She sprinted and dove headfirst into the black water. Kicking for all she was worth, Larkin tried to get as far away from the falling branches as she could. She could only hope she was going in the right direction, as all the fish had fled, taking their lights with them. She swam until her lungs screamed for air before breaking the surface. She took a great gasping breath. Wyn's weight pulled her under again. Her wet clothes bound her limbs. Wyn pushed against her like he wanted her to release him. It was hard to let go, but she made herself do it.

"Follow me," he said as he rolled onto his belly and started kicking away from the tree. He was fast, shooting ahead of her.

A little relieved, she started after him. Moments later, a great groaning sounded. Above her, the tree buckled, and limbs speared toward her.

"Wyn! Dive!" she screamed in warning. He ducked under. She sucked in a breath, bent herself in half, and swam hard for the bottom. A moment later, something fell on her and shoved her deeper. In the blackness, she had no concept of which way was up or down. She writhed to free herself from the branches dragging her down.

Her shield! She formed it, amber light slicing through branches. Tangled branches hissed smoke above her. She couldn't surface through that mess. She swam out. She'd reached the outside edges of the branches when the urge to breathe overpowered her fear of the burning wreck above her. She kicked upward, pulling herself between hot, bubbling branches that grabbed at her clothes.

She kicked and struggled, her lungs screaming for air, her body losing the fight toward unconsciousness when a hand reached down, grabbed hers, and hauled her to the surface.

She stood on a floating, steaming bough, and gasped for breath, slowly coming back to herself, to the arms wrapped around her as if they'd never let her go.

Her body shuddering, Larkin gripped Denan's tunic and held him like an anchor. "Wyn?" she managed.

"You saved him." His voice shook.

Her magic had saved them both. "How did you get out?"

"I saw you escape. I jumped and swam for a boat."

She dropped her head to his wet chest. "How did you find me?"

"Wyn pointed to where he'd last seen you." She looked into his eyes as ash fell around them like dirty feathers. He took her face in his hands. "I could see the light moving under the water, and then I saw it stop. I couldn't get to you. Couldn't—" His voice broke, tears running down his sooty cheeks.

She'd felt the same way when she'd looked into the inferno above and known he was up there somewhere and that he might not ever make it out.

"Larkin, what would I have done if you'd—"

She rose up, silencing his fears with her mouth. He froze in surprise, and then he kissed her back, lips desperate and relieved.

"Denan!" a voice called.

They broke apart. Denan tucked her head under his chin and held her, arms trembling. "We're here!"

Through the steam and smoke, Mytin appeared in a large boat with several more men. Because of the debris in the water, the men couldn't reach them. Larkin and Denan navigated burning branches until they reached a place where the boat could pull alongside them.

Mytin hugged Denan, his relief palpable. "You found Wyn."

"Where is he?" Denan asked.

"Safe with Demry," Mytin said.

"Larkin found him."

Mytin wrapped her up as tight as he had his son. "I will forever be indebted to you."

"Mother?" Denan asked.

Mytin drew back and passed a hand down his face, looking around helplessly. "She's with the healers."

As the boat rowed away from the steam and smoke, they passed a dozen more boats. Men and women threw water onto the branches or stood in the neighboring trees, vigilant with axes and buckets.

"I'll make sure the fire stays contained," Denan said to his father. "Go to her."

His father didn't hesitate to call over another boat to take him to his wife.

CHAPTER 28

BURNING

The sun rose in a bloodred sky. Covered in soot, Larkin and Denan staggered out of the boat and onto an unfamiliar dock. Squinting through stinging eyes, Larkin looked up into the boughs, covered with dozens of small rooms. She held her right arm protectively in her left; it was too sore to move much. And the other thorns weren't feeling much better. Pipe music came from somewhere, its soothing effect easing Larkin's hurts a bit.

An older man in dark-brown robes with a short mantle stepped out to greet them. He pointed to a room directly above them. "She's in there."

Denan nodded his thanks and hurried up the winding stairs on the main trunk. Larkin followed him inside a wide room. Aaryn lay on a bed. Bandages covered the right side of her body from her jaw down to her arm before spreading to her ribs and stomach. Mytin sat beside her, playing his flute. He glanced up when they approached.

"Oh, Mother ..." Denan breathed.

Aaryn reached for Denan, who immediately went to her side and took her hand. "I'll be all right."

Feeling out of place, Larkin hung back by the door. Unable to watch their tearful reunion, she looked instead at the healers beside Aaryn. Magalia and—"Alorica?" she gasped.

"Hush, Larkin," Alorica said with a meaningful look at Aaryn, who moaned as Magalia pressed bandages on her weeping skin. Denan pressed his mother's hand to his forehead.

"What are you doing here?" Larkin whispered.

"I'm apprenticed to Magalia."

Magalia motioned Alorica closer. "Wrap them firmly. It will help with the swelling," Magalia said as Alorica watched, enraptured. "There was quite a bit of weeping, so we decided to change her bandages. I've given her something for the pain, and the music is helping." Magalia settled the last bandage. "The burns were not as deep as they could have been. Barring infection, I expect Aaryn to make a full recovery, but she needs her rest." Magalia's eyes narrowed on Larkin. "Did you hurt your arm?"

Everyone's gaze swung to her.

Uncomfortable with the attention, Larkin shrugged. "A burning bough fell on me, but it's getting worse."

"Why didn't you say something?" Denan asked.

Magalia went to Larkin's side and pulled up her sleeve, revealing swollen, bruised skin over the new thorn in her forearm. Magalia prodded the swelling gently. "She's probably losing her thorn."

Sharp panic lanced through Larkin. But then, the magic had worked last night. She must have just used too much too soon.

Magalia took a long strip of cloth and wrapped Larkin's arm, placing a pungent poultice inside. "A tree branch landing on the site didn't help much. Some feverfew should help too. I'll bring you some. Just be careful—it can upset your stomach if you have it too often." Magalia motioned for Alorica to follow her out.

"Alorica," Larkin said. "Can I speak with you?"

Alorica paused, looking for permission from Magalia.

Mytin pushed himself up and came to stand by Larkin. "Actually, if you two could excuse us, I would like to talk to Larkin for a moment."

"You should let Aaryn sleep," Magalia said. "She needs to rest."

Alorica shot Larkin an apologetic look and followed the other healer out. Mytin shut the door behind them and ushered Larkin into a corner while Denan took over playing something soothing for his mother.

Mytin unwrapped the bandages Magalia had placed over her forearm. "Wyn told me what happened. You didn't have time to use your amulet, did you?"

Larkin's eyes widened. She hadn't. She didn't need the amulet at all.

Mytin nodded. "Your sigil protected you and my son."

"You said they would take weeks to come in."

"Sometimes magic comes quicker for those who wield great power." He rested his hand on her shoulder, eyes shining with gratitude. "Thank you for what you did."

Reeling in her excitement, Larkin nodded.

"I would like to talk to Larkin as well … alone," Aaryn said softly.

Denan and Mytin exchanged glances but quietly filed out. Larkin hovered in the corner.

"Come closer, please."

Larkin hesitated but obeyed, sitting in a chair by the woman's bed. "Are you in a terrible amount of pain?" she asked.

"No," Aaryn said, her voice sounding disused. "Magalia gave me something." She swallowed hard a few times. "I want to thank you for saving my son."

Head down, Larkin nodded.

After a moment of silence, Aaryn said, "Has Denan been good to you? Because if not, I'll break his neck."

Larkin choked on a laugh. "How have you—all of you—come to accept this?"

Aaryn grew distant. "At first, I hated Mytin and everything about this place. As time passed, I came to understand that had I been given a choice to leave my family forever in exchange for this life, I would have. Now I hurt more for those I've left behind, for the drudgery and oppression of the women I love, and I grieve for the daughter I will never bear."

Larkin felt like crying—probably stress. She hadn't slept all night. "Did you never try to escape?"

Aaryn chuckled. "Of course I did, but no girl has ever made it past the sentinels. Sometimes … Sometimes I wish one of my sisters would be taken, just so I could see them again."

Larkin saw her future roll out before her. She would fall for Denan—was already falling for Denan—and as hard as she tried, this place was impossible to hate. And the magic … She'd never had power before, never had the chance to change the world for the better. Could she really walk away from that?

"I told all of you to let her rest." Larkin turned as Alorica and Magalia stepped into the room. Magalia held two cups in her hands. She tipped one to Aaryn's mouth. "This will help you sleep."

Aaryn finished the drink, her eyes heavy. Magalia handed Larkin the other cup. "Best to down it all in one go."

Larkin drank the concoction, the sweetness of honey lingering as the bitterness faded. "Thank you."

Magalia took the empty cups and motioned Larkin out. Turning sideways, Magalia shuffled past Larkin. "If it becomes infected, make sure you come back. Sometimes they have to be helped out."

Larkin blocked her path. "Did you ever try to escape?"

Magalia paused, her arms folded impatiently. "I have patients to tend to." She started around Larkin, who moved to block her again. Magalia's eyes narrowed. "I left behind a fiancé too. I loved him so much, more than anything. But my husband, Serek, was right—I loved him more."

Larkin's head fell. "Would you have chosen this life freely?"

Magalia heaved in a breath. "My husband died beyond those walls. He was captain of the prince's guard. No one could best him with any sort of weapon, not even Denan. But a wraith pierced his arm, and I wasn't there." Moisture brimmed in her eyes. She turned away, swiping at her cheeks. "And still, even knowing he would die, I would have come. Accept your life here. Appreciate your husband with what time you have. Because it won't last forever."

Magalia pushed past her, starting up the stairs at the trunk.

Larkin grabbed Alorica's arm before she too could disappear. "And you? Would you stay?"

Alorica brightened. "I've always wanted to be a healer. It's fascinating. They have books. Tam is teaching me to read them."

"What happened to you?"

Alorica held out her hands. "This place happened to me. Have you ever seen such wealth? I mean, I had my eye on Bane—he was the richest boy in town—but he's a pauper compared to Tam. I have my own bed—no sisters kicking me. Have you tried all their sweets? And the clothes ... Tam's having an entire wardrobe made up. I have an amethyst pendant the size of my thumb."

Larkin's mouth fell open. "You were the one who was so set on escaping."

"Well, of course. We were traipsing through the woods, eating lizards over campfires, and running for our lives."

Larkin shook her head in disbelief. "What about your family?"

Alorica rolled her eyes. "Don't tell me you aren't enjoying being spoiled—after that pit you climbed out of."

"Alorica!" Magalia snapped from the stairs.

Alorica cast Larkin an apologetic look and hustled out. Larkin watched her go.

For the first time since she'd arrived at the Alamant, she was alone. Wondering what to do with herself, she looked around. Not seeing Denan, she started toward the main trunk when a thump followed by muttered cursing sounded above her.

She hesitated, but what if someone needed help? She followed the sound to a room just above Aaryn's. Inside, a young man was trying to pull himself up from the floor with one hand on his cane, the other on the side of the bed. He had golden skin and angular eyes.

Larkin hurried to hook one arm under him and lift. He looked up at her in surprise before heaving himself onto the bed. He was sweating and red-faced, his leg ending in a stump above his knee.

Feeling awkward, she stepped back. "Is there something I can do for you?"

He nodded to a pitcher and washbasin. "Bring me a wetted cloth. I don't think I'm up for standing again."

She did as he asked. He washed his face and neck before catching her staring at his stump. "Wraith blade. Luckily, I was close enough to come in for an amputation before the poison spread." He rubbed his shaved head nervously. "Were you in the fire?"

"How did you know?"

"You still have ash in your hair. You must be Denan's wife."

"I'm not his wife," she ground out.

His eyes narrowed in disapproval. "Denan is the best man I know. He's my commander—or *was*."

"Was?"

"When a prince is called, he learns to lead the military first. That way he knows how to lead men, fight in a war, and he has the support of the army. He steps back from that calling when it's his turn to search for a wife."

"So, your leg ... it wasn't that long ago?"

He shrugged. "A couple months. I was doing better, but then it got infected."

"What happened?"

His eyes grew distant. "We were driving off a group of mulgars. They were getting too close to the wall. It was a trap. The wraiths ambushed us, Hagath leading them. Denan himself would have died if Serek hadn't taken a wraith blade for him."

Serek ... that was Magalia's husband. "Is that why Magalia hates Denan?"

The man shifted uncomfortably. "I shouldn't be telling you this."

He didn't want to tell her something; she could see it in the way he turned away from her. "Did Denan ..." Closing her eyes, she steeled herself. "Did he kill Serek?"

The man went very still. "You need to go."

So that's why Magalia hated Denan. Larkin would have too, except she'd seen what the poison did to Venna. She felt a rush of compassion for Denan. He'd been so patient with her, all while bearing his own grief. Guilt squatted on her chest, making it hard to breathe.

She backed out of the room, went to the dock, and sat with her feet in the water, wondering when Denan would come for her. She didn't have long to wait. He came down the stairs, his tension easing when he caught sight of her. He jumped into the boat without a word.

"Are you all right?" she asked as she climbed in behind him.

He took up his oar, and they rowed in silence. At Denan's tree, a familiar man stood at the dock, waiting for them, his robes still covered in soot.

"My Uncle Demry," Denan said.

"Wyn's in the kitchen. I can't get him settled," Demry said as their boat approached.

Denan peered into the boughs above them. "My men cleared the tree?"

"Yes."

Larkin followed his gaze, shocked to see sentinels in the branches. Denan helped her out of the boat, his touch perfunctory. "I'm going to need you to stay here. Look after my brother. Can you do that, Larkin?"

She nodded. "Where are you going?"

"I have princely duties." There was anger in his voice. He made to push off the dock.

"Wait," she said.

He paused. She hesitated, shooting an embarrassed look at Demry. Denan waved him off, and he retreated to give them some space.

"What aren't you telling me?" she asked softly.

He sighed, his shoulders falling. "Someone set that fire."

Her mouth fell open. "How can you know?"

"My father saw someone leap from the boughs of his tree into the water and swim away."

"Who?"

Denan shook his head. "When I find out, they will wish they'd never been born."

It didn't make sense. "Why would anyone want to hurt your family?"

"Probably because they can't get to me. The only way to reach my tree is by boat. I have sentinels posted in every tree around ours."

And now, apparently, sentinels in the tree as well. "You think Netrish did this?"

Denan started rowing away. "I'll be back as soon as I can.

Clean up and rest."

She rubbed her tired eyes, getting soot into them and setting them stinging. "You have to do this now? You haven't slept all night."

He turned the boat. "You're safe with my Uncle Demry and the sentinels."

Demry stepped beside her, and for the first time she noticed the ax and shield strapped to his back. "I will defend her with my life."

"Don't go," Larkin said softly, not wanting to admit she was frightened.

A memory of a smile touched Denan's lips. "I'll be back as soon as I can."

Larkin watched as he rowed away. She touched her mouth, remembering the kiss they'd shared last night. Shame and sadness overwhelmed her. Steeling herself, she went to the kitchen, Demry trailing behind her.

Tears streaking through the black on his face, Wyn paced from one side of the kitchen to the other. "How's my mother?"

"Sleeping. How are you?"

"Hungry."

She looked back at Demry. The man shrugged. "We've offered him food."

"I want to catch my own!" Wyn shouted. "I always catch lunch."

"Then let's catch lunch," Larkin said.

Wyn looked up at her, distrust in his eyes.

"Do you know where Denan keeps his spears? He hasn't shown me yet."

Wyn raced away, returning with a spear.

The two of them went for a swim, and Wyn taught her what was edible and what wasn't. By the time they came back, most of the ash had left their clothes, though Larkin feared her beautiful robes were ruined.

"Now," Larkin said. "You take a bath while Demry helps me prepare this."

Wyn agreed reluctantly. Demry taught her how to assemble the ingredients. The three of them ate in companionable silence, Wyn's eyes growing heavy. On his second helping, he fell asleep on the table, his arm stretched out.

"Put him in my bed," Larkin said. Demry followed her up, and she turned back the sheets and tucked Wyn in. She gathered her simple tunic and pants from the armoire. She went to the place between the buttressed roots, activated the barrier, and stripped to her bare skin. Half submerged, she worked up a lather and scrubbed away layers of soot. To rinse, she dove into the water and floated at the surface, staring at the strange opacity of the barrier that shifted like storm clouds.

In the stillness, the events of the day washed over her—the way Denan's family had loved and cared for each other … An ache of loneliness started in Larkin's chest for her own family. She shifted, the pain of her thorns drawing a sharp inhale from her lips. She glanced at the thorn on her upper left arm, surprised to see raised lines a shade paler than her own skin. They formed the center of a geometric flower.

Larkin forgot to breathe. Her heart stilled in her chest. Tears welled in her eyes—tears that spilled down her cheeks when she blinked. She took a ragged breath and drew upon her magic. Her forearm tingled. A shield formed before her, with darker lines in the shape of a tree. A smile bloomed across her face.

There was no denying it. She had women's magic.

At a sound like hail on a rooftop, the barrier's surface scattered like disturbed water. Nervous, Larkin swam back out, dried off, dressed in a clean tunic and her underthings, and dissipated the barrier. She looked high into the trees and didn't see the sentinels, though she still felt like she was being watched. She climbed out, moss sticking to her damp feet.

Denan sat at the dock, scrubbing the sooty clothes they'd

been wearing the night before. She gaped at him. She'd never seen a man do laundry before. "You're back."

"I sent Demry and the extra sentinels away."

"You think that's a good idea?"

"They're looking after my parents."

She nodded. "Is Wyn awake? I thought I heard something."

"Probably just the birds."

"I'll check, just in case."

"You're just trying to get out of doing laundry," Denan teased.

She wrung out her hair, trying not to notice the way Denan eyed her bare legs. "Obviously."

In her room, Wyn was curled on the bed, sobbing. She thought he would demand Denan, but he simply crawled out and collapsed in a heap in her arms. Missing her family more than ever, Larkin settled in the chair and held him close, rubbing his back and humming her mother's lullaby.

Denan came in moments later, their wet clothes in his hands. He laid them out over some branches. "Play a lullaby for me, Denan," Wyn said.

Denan sat on the bed and pulled out his pipes. He played as the sun set and the colors of the night came out. For the first time in a long time, Larkin felt content, and she didn't care if it was the music's doing. With a sigh, she closed her eyes, the events of weeks melting from her body.

She awoke when Denan bent over her, tugging Wyn from her. He settled him into the bed. "How's your arm?"

She almost considered telling him. Almost. "A little less swollen, I think."

Denan stroked his brother's hair. "I can sleep in your room if that makes you feel safer."

Larkin leveled him with a flat look.

He gestured helplessly. "I'm happy on the floor."

The room was so open to attack. "All right," she relented.

She took the vial of oils from where she'd left it on her desk, flipped her long hair over one shoulder, and rubbed it through her tresses, enjoying the smell of the herbs as she looked out over the sun skimming through the trees and atop the water in a long column of light.

She started when Denan reached past her—she hadn't realized he was behind her—and took the brush. Careful of the thorn at the base of her skull, he ran it through her hair, starting at the top and working his way through the length of it in soft, even strokes. Her eyes slipped closed at the pleasure of having her hair brushed.

Eventually, Denan's hands shifted to her shoulders, his thumbs kneading at the muscles between her shoulder blades. His fingers stroked her shoulders and brushed lightly over her neck. Heat built in Larkin—heat and longing and ... desire.

She jumped to her feet, darting out from his touch, and turned an accusing stare on him. "What are you doing?"

Hurt flashed in his eyes. "Touching you."

"Well, don't."

He stalked toward her until her backside came up against the desk. He stopped before her, the heat from her body scorching the gap between them. "How much longer are you going to fight this? How much longer are you going to deny yourself happiness?"

"I could never be happy here."

"You would be if you didn't fight that happiness at every turn."

"Why do I deserve to be happy when my mother and sisters are suffering? They need me!"

His expression softened. "You suffering needlessly won't change that."

"I have to get out of here! I have to get back to them!"

"And if you could, what then? Your townspeople would never let you stay. You'd be driven out. If your family came with you, they would lose their land, their means of support."

A sob bubbled up in her throat; she tried to swallow it down. "Denan, last night, I was so relieved you were all right. I shouldn't have kissed you, and you shouldn't have kissed me back."

"Larkin, I will *always* kiss you back."

"A week ago, I was on the cusp of marrying Bane, a boy I've loved for as long as I can remember." She studied Denan's nearly black eyes—the eyes of the man she had kissed last night. What did that make her? Unfaithful, certainly. For she'd never given up on her plan to go back to the Idelmarch, back to Bane. "I'm still engaged to him, and I was untrue."

Denan cupped her face in his hands, brushing at the tears streaking down her cheeks. "Help me break the curse. Help me free both our peoples. Only then will you be able to save your family and Bane ... and decide where you truly want to be."

He was right. The tree was dying, and when the magic was gone, so would the barriers that protected and entrapped her people. The best way to help her family was to banish the curse. Slowly, she nodded.

Denan eyed her. "You still don't believe in the heartsong?"

"Never." But even to her own ears, she didn't sound convinced.

He took another step toward her, so she had to lean back over the desk. "I dare you."

Every part of her stiffened at the challenge in his voice. "Stop trying to manipulate me."

"It's not a manipulation." His hands came under her knees, lifting her onto the desk. "You already kissed me once. Now it's my turn."

"I was just glad you were alive."

"One kiss, Larkin. Prove me wrong."

She opened her mouth to protest but paused. "Fine. One kiss. Just to end this once and for all." She hardened her lips and turned her mouth toward him.

But it wasn't his mouth that touched her, but his hands, stroking down her arms. She opened her eyes to see him studying his hands as they skimmed down her shoulders and disappeared into the sleeves of her tunic. "So soft," he murmured. "Your skin is so soft."

She swallowed heavily. Any girl would have a reaction to Denan—even one who wasn't attracted to him in the least.

His fingers trailed back down her arms before skimming along her hips. His fingertips touched the bare skin of her outer thighs, trailing fire that started a slow burn in her lower belly. He grasped her by the back of her knees and slid her closer. One hand trapped her legs behind him, the other took her by the side of the head, turning her jaw up. Denan brushed his lips across her collarbone, pausing at the frantic pulse in her throat, before skimming across her jaw.

His other hand came around, trapping her jaw between his hands. His mouth hovered just above hers. "Larkin." His whisper caressed her lips. "You're trembling."

"No, I'm not."

"Your heart is racing."

"No, it isn't."

"Look at me and tell me you don't want to kiss me."

She considered his eyes, rings of black surrounding the darkest brown. "I don't."

One side of his mouth quirked up. "Liar."

He was taking too long. Her hands pushed through the soft bristle of hair on his scalp to pull him in. The moment his mouth met hers, Larkin's core trembled, shifted, found a new home. Their lips moved as if in a dance they'd done a thousand times before and only forgotten before now.

There was too much space between them. She pulled him closer. He pulled her closer. She opened her mouth to him. He responded, deepening the kiss, his tongue brushing against hers.

Larkin moaned, and he pulled her so she fit snug against him. She pushed her tongue into his mouth, and he sucked gently. The fire in Larkin's belly transformed to a raging inferno. Her hands skimmed across his broad shoulders and then to the front. She wanted to feel his skin—had to touch it.

She tugged his tunic up, hauling it off his head and discarding it on the floor. Her hands skimmed across his smooth chest, feeling the muscle and the scars. Denan's hands slid up under her tunic, rucking it up against her thighs. He wasn't going fast enough.

Larkin reached for the hem, intent to pull it over her head, when Denan paused. "What about Wyn?"

Who was Wyn? Denan pulled back a little farther. She blinked up at him in confusion.

Wyn.

In the bed next to her desk.

She turned quickly, but the boy was still fast asleep. And then she saw herself, her legs locked at her ankles around Denan's waist, their bodies so tightly entwined she wasn't sure where hers began and his ended. His lips were swollen from her kisses. By the feel of it, so were hers.

She slowly released him, her legs falling to the side. Her head dropped in shame. Denan captured her jaw and tried to lift her head. She pulled away from him. "I'm weak."

"To let yourself feel a little happiness? To let yourself love someone?" He tipped up her jaw and looked her in the eye. "You are the very opposite of weak."

"I thought we were going to be friends," she whimpered.

His grin turned wolfish. "Larkin, that was never going to happen." He wrapped her in his arms, holding her tight. "I love you." She stilled, not believing she'd heard him right. She hugged him back, ignoring the urge she had to pull his mouth back down to hers.

"Still want me to sleep on the floor?"

She chuckled. "Wyn will protect me from your advances."

"He already has," Denan muttered. He turned from her, reaching for his discarded tunic.

Larkin hopped off her desk and opened the drawer to put the brush away. What she saw made her freeze. A ruby ring. Heart pounding, she picked it up, recognizing the tone of the jewel as well as the vines twining up and down the band.

But ... she'd left the ring on the nightstand in Caelia's room before she'd ever been taken into the forest. How had it gotten here? Or more accurately, who had brought it?

"The forest take me."

"What?" Denan had set his tunic on the chair. Wearing his trousers, he slid into the bed on the other side of Wyn. She tucked her hands behind her. "Nothing. I just—" She scrambled to come up with some excuse for leaving for a while. "I need to take care of something." She reached into the armoire drawer and grabbed some of the woolen underwear.

He lay back on his blankets. "I washed out the other ones and hung them to dry."

He washed my underthings? She cringed. "You shouldn't have done that."

He shrugged as he tugged the blankets back over him. "No worse than washing out bandages."

She hurried out of her room, looking around for something out of place. She was almost relieved when she reached the main platform and saw nothing. But then ... a lampent petal lay on the steps of a bough she'd never gone up before. Heart pounding, she bent to pick it up. It pulsed, colors chasing up and down the edges of the petals. She looked up. Through the branches, she could see another.

She started up a set of stairs. Here were smaller rooms, all of them empty. She picked up another lampent, colors dancing at her touch. And a little higher, more light. She hurried toward it, finding petals every dozen or so steps. She was moving fast now, eventually leaving the stairs behind. She practically flew up the tree. Sweat gathered to run in streaks down her back and temples. Far below, the water looked almost like the sky with glowing stars.

Finally, she caught sight of a lone lampent sitting in the middle of the branch, but she didn't see anyone. Was she so desperate for home she was imagining things? The heavy weight of the ring in her hand convinced her otherwise. Kneeling, she cupped the blossom in her hands and leaned forward, inhaling the light, sweet fragrance.

"Larkin," came the voice moments after she felt his presence directly behind her.

She was already spinning, launching herself toward him. Bane grunted as she landed in his arms, and the branch they were on swayed with the weight of them.

"Easy," Bane said, but his voice held no trace of scolding. "You'll send us both toppling."

CHAPTER

LETHAN

"**B**ane," Larkin whispered. The familiar smell of freshly tilled earth and mist washed over her. He was dozens of early mornings in the river, fresh baked bread when she'd had nothing to eat all day, her ally when the other children teased her threadbare clothes. He was her best friend.

And she'd betrayed him.

Forcing back the tears, she pulled back and leaned a little aside so the light from the lampent could touch the planes of his face. His cheeks were scruffy, his eyes hollow and sunken.

"Bane," she said again, this time with concern. "How are you here?"

His fingers skimming the scar on her neck. "Did he do that to you?"

"Hunter did."

"If he wasn't already dead, I'd kill him for scarring you like that."

"My family? Are they all right?"

"They were when I left."

She felt a wash of relief. At least Garrot hadn't hurt them.

Bane sniffed. "Do you have anything to eat?"

That hadn't even occurred to her. She searched the branches. It didn't take long to find some gobby. She picked one, tearing off the rind, and held it out. "Here, take this."

"I wasn't sure it was safe to eat them." He tore into the fruit, consuming it in a few bites. Larkin took him in. His once-fine clothes had seen hard wear, and his hair was knotted and dirty.

Larkin took the lampent and searched until she'd found more gobby. He ate it as quickly as the first. "Have you seen Caelia?" he said around a mouthful.

She pulled him behind a branch with thick leaves. "She's here." She steeled herself. He had a right to know the rest. "She's married and has three children."

Bane choked and coughed so hard she was sure Denan would hear it.

"Quiet," she hissed.

Bane swore violently. "I'll kill the monster that forced himself on her."

Larkin winced. "He didn't. She's in love with him."

Bane chucked his rind. "She's enthralled!"

"Shh!"

Bane put his head between his bent knees, his hands locked around the back of his neck.

"How did you find me?" she asked. Did he see her with Denan?

"I left not long after you were taken—gathered up supplies and weapons and followed you in. I lost the tracks in the stirring, but I found them again eventually. The trail was pretty confusing for a while, and I ran into a pack of beasts." He wiped his mouth, hands shaking. "Who knew giant lizards could run so fast?"

"The pipers call them gilgads."

He shuddered. "The other ones—the ones made of shadow—they were worse. Not animals at all but some kind of demon. They followed me everywhere I went, but they left me alone if I stayed in the trees at night."

"Wraiths are the hooded ones. The ones with black lines are mulgars."

"I didn't see any of those." He was silent for a time, his eyes haunted. "When I couldn't cross the river where you had, I lost them for good. The only thing I could think to do was stick to the river. I'd started to think I'd never find you when one night I saw the glowing trees."

Unable to help herself, she reached out and touched him again, just to reassure herself he was real. Ever since she'd been taken, this is what she'd wanted—Bane and home. But now ... "You should have forgotten about me like the rest of the men." Like her father had.

Bane took her hands in his. "I've been hiding out in this unnatural place for nearly a week. This lake drains into the river—our river. If we can steal one of these boats, we can float our way back."

She shook her head. "Bane, I can't go back."

He didn't seem to have heard her. "After we reach Hamel, we'll go somewhere no one knows us."

"And how would we live? What about my family?"

"We'll take them with us. We'll find a way."

To see my family again ... The thought was sweet and sharp as a knife. She could see Mama and the baby, Sela and ... But her thoughts stopped after that. She never wanted to see her father again. As for Nesha—Larkin loved her sister, but she would never trust her again.

"Denan would come for me." He would, but that wasn't the reason she had to stay.

Bane squeezed her hands so hard it hurt. "He won't have you. You're mine. You've always been mine."

Had he seen their kiss? She couldn't ask. She pulled away.

"I can't." Her voice hitched, and she had to stop for a moment. She couldn't get the image of the mob chasing her out of her head. "I can't risk it."

"You have to. Larkin, your family needs you. I need you."

"We'd never make it past the wall."

"I'll keep you safe. You go down to that room you sleep in. Take anything you think we'll need. I'll meet you at his boat. We'll find my sister and sneak out."

"Bane, there are things you don't understand. There's a—" Her mouth refused to form the word *curse*, no matter how hard she'd tried. She wanted to scream in frustration. She tried a different tactic. *There's a great evil here—something that's causing the girls to be taken and prevents us from speaking about it.* But she couldn't say any of that either. Finally, she held out her hands and formed the barrier between them.

Bane gasped and scrambled back. She watched him, waiting. He gaped at the shield. "You have magic?"

She nodded, relieved. "The pipers need my magic, Bane. With it, we have a real chance of saving both our peoples."

He frowned. "Larkin, the only thing we need saving from is the pipers!"

"No. The wraiths and mulgars—"

"Don't bother us."

"Only because of the barrier around Hamel. Barriers made by women's magic. Barriers that are weakening."

"The stirring?" He huffed in disbelief. "Larkin, that's the pipers' way of trapping us so we can't go after the Taken."

She shook her head. He wasn't going to understand—not unless he saw it, lived it, like she had. She pushed herself up. "I'm not going with you, Bane. I can't."

He stood, eyes hard. "I didn't come all this way to go home without you and my sister."

"She won't go with you either," Larkin whispered. "She won't leave her family."

"I'm her family!"

Larkin took a step back from him. She considered telling Denan that Bane was here, but she wasn't sure if the pipers would help Bane or imprison him—perhaps something else altogether. "I'll round you up some supplies, but you need to go."

She turned to leave, but Bane caught her arm. "Larkin, please trust me. You've been enthralled. These things the pipers have made you believe—it's all part of their enchantment."

"You need to trust *me*." She placed her palm on her chest for emphasis. "It doesn't work like that, Bane."

He looked at her for a long time. "At least help me get to the wall."

She hesitated.

"Get me Denan's cloak. They won't question him."

She finally relented, nodding. "What else do you need?"

"Some more arrows. Food."

She nodded. "There's some nuts and dried fruit in the kitchen. Meet me at the dock?"

They parted ways at the main platform, Bane heading down, Larkin up to the stairs she knew led to Denan's room. The first platform she came to didn't have a personal item in sight, but she knew it was his—from the bed made up with a precision to the chair tucked into the desk in exactly the center.

Holding the lampent aloft, she opened the armoire to the neat array of cloaks, tunics, and pants. She took Denan's casual cloak, tucked it under her arm, and hurried to the kitchen. She packed nuts, dried fruit, and some travel bread into a towel, tying up the corners. She would have liked a knife, but Denan always locked up.

Bane was waiting in the shadows by the dock. He pulled on the cloak, tugging the hood low over his eyes.

She bit her lip. "What if the sentinels don't fall for it?"

"As far as they know, no one else has come or gone from the tree." He had the voice he used when they were about to get in trouble—the one that sounded more confident than he was.

Hands shaking, Larkin slipped into the boat. "We'll head for the healing tree. They'll think we're going to see his mother."

Bane carefully untied the line and pushed them off. Almost immediately, their boat was surrounded by the purple glow from the tiny creatures that lived in the water, lighting them up like a beacon to the sentinels above. They started rowing, steady and smooth.

It took everything Larkin had not to search the boughs of the surrounding trees. With painful slowness, they eased beneath the branches of the trees. At any moment, Larkin expected someone to sound the alarm, but no one did. When she was sure they were out of sight of the sentinels, she turned the boat toward the outer wall. They were nearly halfway there when Bane steered them toward a tree and hopped out onto the dock.

"What are you doing?" she whispered. "They'll hear you."

"This tree is abandoned," he whispered back as he pawed through the contents of his pack.

"Bane—"

"Trust me." He trotted into the shadows.

She waited, tense, as the tree groaned above her. He was gone for what felt like a long time. Finally, he reappeared. "From here on out, we'll have to row more carefully so as not to set the water off."

Trying her best not to disturb the surface, they rowed back into the open water. By the time her arms ached in earnest, the city's living wall rose up before them. Larkin hadn't seen the walls since her first day in the Alamant. They left the cover of trees, moving methodically until the boat bumped into the wall.

"How are you planning to get through?" Larkin asked.

Bane pulled out an ax. "It's only wood."

"Besides the obvious fact they'll hear you, the tree has a barrier around it. You'll never get through."

He hesitated a second. "You have magic. Take it down. And

don't worry about them hearing it."

"What's that supposed to mean?"

"It means I've managed a distraction."

"What?"

He peered pointedly back the way they'd come. A faint tinge of orange flickered.

"What have you done?" she breathed.

As if in answer, the warning horn pealed out, Larkin's heart writhing at the sound.

"What I had to," Bane said as he fired a crossbow into the wood, burying the head of an arrow. "Hold on to that and keep us steady." He swung his ax, the sound drowned out by the warning horn. The boat shifted away from the wall, forcing Larkin to tighten her grip on the arrow.

Images flashed in Larkin's mind—pain and anger and warning. She shook her head, trying to dislodge the foreign thoughts. Behind her, tongues of flame licked up the boughs, as they had yesterday. Her mouth came open. "You're the one who set fire to Mytin and Aaryn's tree."

"I had to draw the sentinels away from your tree long enough to get inside," Bane huffed with effort. She could see light coming from the other side of the wall.

The burns on Aaryn's body. Wyn huddled in the yarn. The branches, hissing in the water beside her. Smoke so thick she couldn't breathe. Screaming for Denan, sure he was trapped and dying in the upper boughs. He would never forgive her for this.

Tears filled her eyes. "You could have killed them!"

"They're the enemy, Larkin!"

"Defenseless women and children are not the enemy!"

He whirled toward her, the boat rocking dangerously. "Their magic has twisted your mind. You can't see the truth."

She slapped him. "If you've hurt anyone else, I swear I'll turn you in to them myself."

Bane rubbed his cheek. "Larkin, this isn't—"

"Declare yourself!" a voice rang out sharply from above.

In answer, Bane whirled around and chopped into the wood again, opening it wide enough for them to get through if they crouched.

"Move away from the wall!" the same voice commanded.

A hail of something small scattered all around them. Larkin picked one of them out of her cloak—seeds. She didn't understand until the water gleamed purple, outlining their dark boat. A long low note rang out, followed by a flurry of footsteps and grinding gears. Boats swung out above them and dropped. Boats filled with pipers, close enough she could make out their hard faces in the light cast by the eerie purple water.

Their eyes widened when they recognized her, widened further when they didn't recognize Bane. They carried their spears at the ready, their bows tied to their backs. She hoped the fact that they weren't shooting at them meant they intended to take them alive.

"Stop now!" one of them commanded.

"Larkin!"

She whirled around to see Denan and his sentinels—one of them was Tam—coming after her in another boat. Her heart lurched within her.

"We have to abandon the boat!" Bane tried to push through the opening he'd made, but he came up against the barrier. He slammed his ax into it, sending out a rippling pulse. "Larkin! You have to get us through!"

If she didn't, the pipers would kill Bane for what he'd done. She was sure of it. Whatever wrong he'd committed, he didn't deserve that. She squinted at the open space, trying to see what held the barrier together. The thorn on her arm buzzed, and she could see it all—a tightly woven net made up of hundreds of strands of light in a dozen different colors.

Her right arm buzzed, and a sword made of light appeared in her hand. She turned it sideways and slid it into the barrier. It sliced through, the net fraying at the edges like it was made of some kind of fiber. Above her, men cried out in disbelief. Denan and the sentinels were nearly upon them.

"Go, Bane!"

He gripped her arms. "Not without you!"

"I told you, I'm not going!"

He shook her. "I'm not leaving without you. If I stay, they'll kill me."

"Larkin." Denan stretched toward her, his voice gentle. "Remember when I said we don't go swimming at night? The lethan is in these waters. The disturbances will bring it to us."

"We're not lying, Larkin," Tam said. "Please."

They had seconds before the boats reached them. Bane released her arms. "I came all this way, and you're going to let me die?"

The forest take him, he was right. She growled in frustration, pushed past him, grabbed the edges of the hole, and pulled herself through, gaining a dozen slivers in the process.

"No, Larkin!" Denan cried. "You don't—"

She dove headfirst into the water and swam hard, trying to get as far away from the wall as possible in case the guards decided to use their bows. When she finally surfaced, she gasped in a breath, shifted to a sidestroke, and glanced back. Bane was right behind her. Denan was halfway through the hole, Tam hauling him back.

"We'll lower the boats," Tam said in a strained voice.

"How did she get through the barrier?" the one who'd ordered them to halt asked. In the same breath, he lifted his face upward. "Lower the boats on the other side!"

"She had magic. I saw it," another voice said.

Within seconds, more boats eased down on this side of the wall. The current picked up, pulling them away from the wall. A wave splashed over Larkin's head. When she came up, Bane had caught up to her.

"Head for the forest!" he cried. "We'll have to go by land."

Larkin's heart sank. On the river, they had a chance of staying ahead of the pipers. On land, it would be nearly impossible, and they'd have to deal with the wraiths and mulgars, but it was too late to turn back now.

She swam hard, the water flashing purple with each stroke. All her focus was on the shore, so at first she didn't register the flash of movement beneath her. Not until it shot past her with enough force to send her spinning, water churning around her.

"Bane!" she cried a warning as she struggled to keep her head above water.

"What was that?" Bane asked.

Denan's warning pounding in her head, Larkin searched the water and found nothing, which made her more afraid. Some deep instinct within her warned she had to get out of the water. *Get out of the water. Get out of the water.*

Panicked, she spun around, looking for the closest way out, but no trees grew nearby, and the boats on this side of the wall were halfway down. The shore was farther still.

"Larkin!" Denan shouted, and the panic in his voice made the fine hairs all over her body stand up. "Come back to the wall! Now!"

The sentinels in the boats were frantically waving them back.

"Hurry!"

"It's coming!"

She hesitated. Going back wasn't any safer than here—at least not for Bane.

Denan jerked a spear from one of the sentinels. "Larkin!" he cried, and something in his voice told her he was terrified, but not for himself.

Sensing something beneath, she looked down. Wine-red tentacles bloomed beneath her, revealing a razor-sharp beak aimed right for her. She screamed as the tentacles snapped toward her and wrapped around her legs. Her scream cut off as it yanked her under. More tentacles wrapped her up in a too-tight embrace. She writhed, trying to pull her arms free. The tentacles twisted her around. She came face-to-beak with a creature that glowed red, its flesh textured like velvet. Its shining eyes fixed on her as it shifted her toward its open serrated maw.

She was going to be eaten alive. She called up her shield, which lit up the creature, but her arm was pinned uselessly to her side.

From the direction of the wall, a spear launched toward the creature, sinking into its bulbous body. A strong arm wrapped around her chest, knife stabbing into the tentacles that held her. The creature tightened its hold and sank deeper, into the blackness below. Larkin writhed, but the world was growing dark and shadowy. Her body shut down, refusing to obey her frantic orders.

Another spear launched into the creature, burying itself in its flesh.

It released her.

Strong arms hauled her upward. She looked up to see Bane holding her, his gaze fixed on the distant surface even as her eyes lost focus.

CHAPTER

SENTENCING

The sound of angry voices roused Larkin. She knew by the mineral taste she was underground. She could tell by the heavy weight of her limbs she'd been drugged. She struggled awake, finding herself on a narrow bed in a shallow cave lit by a single lampent on a carved table. A ladder stood sentinel in the center of the room, with a trapdoor above it. Everything had a hazy, over-bright quality. She pressed the heel of her hand into her eye, which throbbed, and tried to piece together what had happened.

All at once, she remembered wine-red tentacles blooming beneath her. She sat up with a jerk, the pain hitting her a moment later.

"Ah, you're awake."

Her vision swam, and she leaned forward, bracing herself against her knees. Her hands hurt. She could feel where the slivers had been. Someone must have removed them while she'd slept. At the start of all this madness, she'd had a sliver too.

Careful hands took hold of her shoulders. "Easy, now. Take your time." After a few settling breaths, Larkin was able to look up. Magalia stood over her, expression concerned. "How are your ribs?"

Larkin tried a deep breath and winced at the pain. She wrapped her hands around her middle.

"You're terribly bruised."

A pitcher of water sat on a side table. Thirst hit Larkin instantly. Following her gaze, Magalia poured her a glass. Larkin drained it and then shifted her feet out of the bed, surprised at the dark circular bruises marring her pale skin. She pushed herself up, which sent a pulse of pain through her. She wavered on her feet.

Curious, she went to the pitcher, poured water in the bowl, and peered into the rippling surface. The whites of her eyes were bloodred, bruises coursing up and down her neck. Wincing, she peeled off her tunic and studied the bruises that covered her entire body. "This should hurt more," she told Magalia.

"I've given you something for the pain."

She took little steps to correct her balance as she made her way back to the bed, sat, and held her spinning head in her hands.

"Your sigils are forming nicely."

Her wedding sigils curled like vines around her hands and wrists. The flower on her upper arm was almost finished. She could make out markings on her right hand and left forearm too. "What happened to Bane?"

Magalia hesitated. "Is that his name?" Larkin simply waited. "He's alive."

"And will he stay that way?" Her voice trembled.

Magalia smoothed out invisible lines in her long tunic. "That hasn't been decided yet." She headed toward the ladder. At the top, she rapped her knuckles against the trapdoor. Hinges groaned, and light shone down. She looked back at Larkin. "I'll be back with something for you to eat."

Larkin curled around the blanket, trying not to think, to worry. Whatever medication Magalia had given her made her drift. Larkin wasn't sure how much time had passed when the other woman returned with steaming soup and some tea.

Larkin eyed the food warily. She didn't feel hungry. "I thought you couldn't cook in the Alamant."

"You can on the islands."

"I don't want any more of that medicine."

"This one isn't as powerful as before," Magalia said. "And you'll need your strength."

Something about the way she said that made a well of dark dread rise within Larkin. She forced herself to eat the soup and drink the tea, and she had to admit she felt better afterward.

When she was finished, Magalia handed her trousers and rose to her feet. "Come with me." She started up the ladder.

Larkin didn't move from the bed. "Where?"

"The king is waiting."

Larkin's throat went dry. "King?"

Magalia gave her an encouraging look. "There's no reason to drag it out any longer than necessary."

There were plenty of reasons.

"Bane will be there."

Larkin put on the trousers and hurried up the ladder, coming out to blinding sunshine. After she blinked away her tears, she found herself on a small island inside a copse of trees. A man stood guard a little ways off—Tam. She hadn't recognized him with his mantle and beautifully carved spear.

He offered her an encouraging nod.

"Larkin," Magalia said with a touch of impatience.

Larkin turned to find the other woman waiting for her a little ways down the hill. Wiping her damp hands on her tunic, Larkin wound through trees covered in pink and white and purple blossoms, the air heady with their sweet fragrance. Petals drifted down whenever the wind blew, catching her hair and carpeting the ground beneath her feet. Tam stayed right beside her, his steady presence surprisingly comforting.

"Where's Denan?" she whispered to Tam.

"Waiting for you at the king's tree," he whispered back.

They left the trees and climbed into a waiting boat manned by four sentinels. As soon as they were seated, the men unmoored and paddled toward a large tree on the opposite side of the inner circle from the tree she shared with Denan. Larkin had to squint at it in the sunlight, the iridescent flashes of color blinding her.

When the boat docked, Larkin glanced up where she knew the platform would be. She couldn't help but wonder if they hung people from the great boughs spreading above her. Her dread grew so strong she couldn't make herself climb out of the boat. Her breaths came hard and fast, sweat collecting to run between her breasts.

"What will they do to me? To Bane?"

Tam's hand on her shoulder was gentle. "I'm right behind you, Larkin."

"I'm frightened."

"Denan won't let anything bad happen to you." He didn't say anything about Bane. The boat shifted around her. Tam took hold of her arms and pulled her to her feet. "One step at time."

She nodded, leaning on him as he helped her out of the boat. She did as he suggested—one foot after another she ascended the steps circling the king's tree.

One hundred and twenty-seven steps later, Tam paused. "From here on out, I can't walk beside you. Keep your head high. It will be better for you and Bane if you remain dignified."

She cast pleading eyes up at him, silently begging him to help her.

He looked frustrated, even a little annoyed. "If you're so afraid of the consequences, why did you run?"

"I wasn't planning to," she whispered. "Bane wouldn't leave without me. I didn't know what you would do if you caught him."

Tam squeezed her arms. "You didn't let the druids beat you. You didn't let a mob beat you. Ancestors, you didn't even let us beat you. Are you really going to crumble before the king?"

His words soaked in drop by drop. She took a deep breath and rose to her full height, chin out.

Tam nodded approvingly. "Good. Now, march up there."

She turned on her heel, took a steadying breath, and strode up the incline. She paused to look around her. A small crowd of a few dozen people had gathered. On the other side of the platform, the king sat on his raised dais. He eyed her disdainfully, his fingers interlocked and resting on his large abdomen.

Denan stood behind the king, his hands at his sides, feet spread like he was ready for a fight. He'd promised whoever had hurt his mother would pay.

"Larkin!"

Despite everything Tam had told her, her head whipped around, finding Bane on his knees to the right of the king. His hands were bound, and two sentinels held him down as he struggled. Her gaze raked him for injuries. He seemed fine, better even, as his hair had been cut and his scruff shaved. His clothes had been washed, and it appeared he'd had a bath as well.

A gentle hand settled on the small of her back. "Don't," Tam warned from behind.

Larkin gritted her teeth and silenced every instinct in her screaming to run to Bane. She forced her gaze away, and after a moment, Tam stepped back. She scanned the gathering of people. Aaryn was there, the bandages along her neck and face the only ones visible. Mytin stood beside her, a look of betrayal on his face. Larkin was glad Wyn wasn't here. She walked through the crowd and came to a stop before the dais, five or so steps from Bane.

"Bane of Hamel," Netrish said. "How did you come to invade our sanctuary?"

Bane stiffened and said nothing.

Netrish leaned forward. "Answer or you will be forced to answer."

Bane stuck out that stubborn chin.

Sitting back, Netrish waved at a sentinel standing off to the side. He brought his flute to his lips and played, the notes clean and sharp, demanding truth and promising safety.

Larkin immediately covered her ears. "Bane," she warned.

He gave her a confused look, his eyes already glazing over. His face went slack. Despite her efforts, the music wormed into Larkin.

"Bane, tell us, how did you come to the Alamant?" Netrish asked again.

"I sneaked into a boat while the men were off on patrol."

"And were you the one who set our trees on fire?"

Still fighting the pull of the music, Larkin's head snapped up. Her gaze locked on Bane, silently begging him not to admit to it.

"Yes."

Netrish's fat chin lifted, his mouth tight. "Did you know there were people in the tree—a woman, a child?"

Bane shrugged as if it didn't matter. "Just another boy who will grow into a man to kidnap our sisters and daughters, and any woman willing to birth more monsters deserves to burn."

Larkin couldn't seem to get enough air. Dreading what she would see but unable to stop herself, her gaze slid to Aaryn. Tears ran down her cheek as she stared at Bane. Mytin's hand rested on her good shoulder, but his gaze was fixed on Larkin, his expression unreadable. She looked away, closing her eyes so she wouldn't have to see the pain Bane's words had caused.

"And the fact that Larkin nearly died in the same fire?" Netrish went on.

Bane's gaze snapped toward her. "What?"

"It's a miracle she survived," Denan ground out.

"Larkin," Bane said softly. "I would never hurt you."

She couldn't look at him, couldn't deal with feeling like she was being torn in two.

"Fire is forbidden within the Alamant." Netrish's voice rang with finality. "But to willfully set one, hoping to kill the innocent, is unforgivable."

"Please." Larkin's body softened with pleading, her arms outstretched. "He lost his sister, and then me. He was trying to save me. We were to be married. He's been my best friend since we were children. What would you do if someone took your wife from you? What lengths would you go to get her back?"

"He is not being punished for coming after you. He is being punished for setting fire to a tree and nearly killing five people," Netrish said.

"Please, just let him go home," she said.

Netrish's gaze shifted back to Bane. "What would you do if I let you go?"

"Come back with an army," Bane said.

Larkin winced.

The crowd murmured. Netrish turned to Larkin. "Larkin, did you have any knowledge of the fires before they began to burn?"

"No." She couldn't have held back her answer even if she'd wanted to.

The whole room relaxed. "And did you," Netrish went on, "ever strike the wall with an ax?"

"No."

Netrish sat back in his chair as if disappointed by her answers. "By all reports, you were settling in beautifully. You seemed content, happy even. Why did you try to escape?"

"I wasn't trying to escape. I was trying to help Bane, but he wouldn't leave without me." The words were out of her before she could think to stop them, drawn out by the music.

Netrish rubbed his chin thoughtfully. "Escape attempts are not unusual—indeed, they can be expected from strong-willed girls—but we cannot tolerate when a girl puts herself at unnecessary risk. The lethan nearly crushed and drowned you."

Larkin gripped her hands together to hide their shaking. "I wanted to help Bane."

"Larkin, no girl has ever escaped the Alamant. Even if you did, wraiths and mulgars lie in wait beyond the gates. You must accept that you have a new family now, a new life, where you are loved and valued."

She lifted her chin, looking him in the eye to let him know she wasn't afraid, though she trembled on the inside. "But never free."

Netrish sighed and waved his hand. The music trailed off. "I sentence her to underground confinement for a week."

"She's done what any decent person would have in her circumstances," Denan said. "It is unjust to punish her for it when the other girls are not."

Netrish looked over his shoulder. "You aren't king yet. Now, take her back to the island."

The effects of the song were wearing off in earnest. It was over. Bane had been found guilty. Only his punishment awaited. "What are you going to do to him?" she asked.

"That is none of your concern," Netrish said.

"This isn't right," a voice rang out.

Larkin started at the source—Aaryn. "The boy thinks you all monsters. And who can blame him? You stole his sister and his fiancée. He was only trying to take her home."

Larkin couldn't wrap her mind around the woman protecting the man who had nearly killed her and her son.

Netrish's face turned red. "He nearly killed your son!"

Mytin tried to pull her back, but Aaryn shook him off. "For the Idelmarchians, this is war! He was fighting the pipers on the terms you all set."

Netrish's face darkened to an alarming shade of purple. "You know very well the Alamant is all that stands between both our peoples and ruin. Our men die out on the battlefields while the Idelmarchians only lose a few daughters a year. Forgive me for not pitying them."

"We didn't know that," Larkin spoke up. "To us, the pipers are the monsters in the stories our mothers tell us to keep us in line."

Netrish sipped from a goblet a servant brought him. "Denan, take your wife to the island. Mytin, take your wife to your tree. If you cannot manage, some of my guards can help you."

Denan leaned in and said something to his mother before coming to stand beside Larkin, gesturing for her to precede him back the way she'd come.

She backed away from him. "Wait," she cried, unable to meet his gaze. "What will they do to Bane?"

Denan took hold of her arm, his grip gentle but firm. She finally met his eyes, noting a new hardness, as well as worry and fear. "You'll make things worse for him, Larkin."

"How?" she demanded.

"If they think Bane has ruined your chances for integrating in the Alamant, his sentencing will be harsher."

All the resistance leaked out of her. She allowed herself to be led away. She locked gazes with Bane until the crowd moved in, blocking her view.

CHAPTER 31

A FINAL GOODBYE

L arkin paced back and forth in the small cave, six steps in each direction. Arms crossed and leaning against the ladder, Denan watched her, face expressionless.

"What will they do to Bane?" she asked again.

"I don't know."

"You have to help him." When he didn't answer, she looked up at him. "Please." Still, he didn't answer. "The law about never lighting fires, he didn't know!"

"It's still the law."

"Please, there—"

He stalked toward her, and she staggered back from him. "He nearly killed my entire family, Larkin! He'd seen me with them earlier and knew it would draw me—and you—out into the open. He did it on purpose, and he didn't care who he hurt."

"Do you blame him?" she choked out. "The pipers took his sister and his fiancée! What would you do in his place?" At his frustrated look, she softened her tone. "Denan, there has to be

338

something you can do."

Denan let out a long sigh. "I'll try. For you, I'll try."

She nodded, latching onto his words like a drowning woman to an offered hand.

"I'll be back to let you know as soon as they decide."

She went back to her pacing, from one end of the room back to the other, ignoring her aches and bruises. It was hours before Denan returned, looking haggard.

"What? What did the king decide?"

Denan lifted his eyes, and the look in his gaze—the terrible knowing.

She reeled. "What are they going to do to him?"

His gaze slowly softened. Sick horror spilled from the top of her head down her limbs. She shook her head, wails bubbling up in her throat. "You can't! You can't!"

He held his hands out, palm up. "I'm not doing anything, Larkin. I—"

She grabbed the front of his tunic in her fists. "You have to stop them, Denan! You can't let them kill him!"

He gently covered her hands with his own. "I already tried."

"Please. I love him." Hurt flashed across Denan's eyes, and he turned away. She forced herself to release her hold on him. "I'll do anything you want. I'll act like a wife. I'll bear your children. Please."

"I wouldn't want you like that," he said softly. "Not as payment for some kind of favor."

"If you don't," she said, voice trembling, "I'll never forgive you."

He took a step back, and she knew that he wouldn't help her.

"No wonder Magalia hates you. Instead of saving her husband, you killed him."

Denan went ashen. He staggered back and leaned against the ladder, his eyes screwed shut. She'd hurt him. She'd wanted to hurt him—to lash out and hurt someone like they were constantly hurting her. She was not sorry, even though her pain wasn't his fault.

"The best I could do was make sure my men were guarding you two," he said, his breathing haggard. "So you could say goodbye. He deserves to hear his sentence from you."

They hadn't told him? Her hands covered her mouth. A wave of dizziness washed over her, and her legs buckled. She collapsed into a boneless pile on the dirt floor. She was cold and hot, sweating and shivering. She tried to picture a world without Bane in it—a world where his gentle teasing and raven hair didn't exist, a world where he would never take her in his arms, the smell of earth and mist washing over her with the sure knowledge that everything was going to be all right.

Denan crouched before her, watching her with a helpless look in his eyes. When the wave of grief had spent itself, she felt numb and distant. She pushed herself up. Denan turned away from her and climbed the ladder. Forcing herself to focus on the fact that she was about to see Bane, she climbed after him. A mere dozen steps away was another trapdoor, Talox beside it.

She hadn't seen him since they took him away in the boat.

Talox took one look at them and groaned. "Denan, I already lost rank and just got done running patrols for a week straight."

"I'm your commanding officer, not Netrish." Denan rested a hand on Talox's shoulder. "She needs to say goodbye. It's a kindness."

Talox looked between them and nodded reluctantly. Denan opened the trapdoor and nodded for her to go.

"What do I say?" she whispered.

"The truth."

Shocked he was letting her go alone, she hurried down. Bane was in a room almost exactly like hers. He was propped up on the bed, one leg stretched out in front of him, the other drawn up, one hand wrapped around it. He looked up when she came down but made no move toward her. She halved the space between them and stopped, her arms wrapped protectively around her middle.

"Bane?" She wasn't even sure what she was asking.

He looked away and wiped surreptitiously at a tear spilling down his cheek. "Do you know what they're going to do to me?"

Something wrenched within her. The beast take her, she couldn't tell him.

Bane read everything he needed to know from her expression. "I'm going to die for burning down a couple trees."

"You almost killed three people, Bane."

"Almost and dead are different. I needed a distraction." He wiped his nose with his sleeve. "They're the enemy, Larkin, or have you forgotten that?"

"The woman who defended you to King Netrish—you nearly killed her and her son. She'll bear the scars of it her entire life. How is she your enemy?" Her legs felt weak and her head light. She slumped down where she stood. "I almost died too."

"Larkin, I never would have done it if I'd known you were going to be there." When she didn't respond, he hauled himself up and came to sit beside her, resting his forehead on the point of her shoulder, a reversal of the way they'd sat as children.

"There has to be a way out of this," she said. "A way to get you home."

"Not without you." Pulling back, he looked at her. "And not without my sister. Have you seen her?"

Averting her eyes, Larkin shook her head. "Not for a few days."

"She probably doesn't even know, and they'll never tell her." Bane's eyes hardened with fury. "It's the spells they weave with their music. They have her under their thrall—like that damned piper has you under his."

She winced but didn't argue. What was the point?

Bane took her hand. "If something happens to me, you have

to promise me the two of you will escape."

It bothered her that he'd brushed aside Caelia's children as if they didn't exist. "No girl has ever escaped them."

He made a half-strangled sound. "Larkin, I can't leave you with them."

Above them, the trapdoor squealed open. "Time's up, Larkin," Denan said.

Bane jumped up and was halfway up the ladder when a spear point appeared, pointed right at his throat. "She's not yours," Bane seethed. "You stole her."

"I want you to know I spoke up for you," Denan said.

"Is that what you're telling Larkin so she won't hate you?"

Denan sighed. "Larkin, someone is coming. There's very little time."

She glanced up to see Bane looking at her with such possessiveness that something inside her recoiled. He strode across the room, wrapped her in his arms, and claimed her, his lips bruising against hers, his arms too tight around her bruised ribs.

She tried tell him no, to push him back, but he was beyond listening.

Half a second later, he was ripped away from her. Denan held him, one arm across his shoulders, one under his arm. Bane struggled and cursed. Larkin couldn't catch her breath. She staggered toward them, not sure what she meant to do.

Talox approached her, gently steering her toward the ladder. "Magalia is coming back with your supper," Talox said. "And if she catches you here, she could report on all three of us. It won't go well for anyone, especially Bane."

"What more could they do to him?" But she forced her legs to move. Bane whirled and kicked. "Stop!" she chided him. He bucked and threw his elbow back at Denan. "Stop it!"

Talox pushed her up the ladder. "Denan can handle him. Let's go."

Bane went limp. Larkin cried out in horror.

Denan looked up at her, face red, blood leaking from the corner of his mouth. "He's unconscious, not dead. Now, hurry up."

Not dead yet. Tears streaking down her cheeks, she hustled up the ladder and peered through the trees, making out a hooded figure in the distance. Larkin hurried back to her own cell. Denan lifted the trapdoor to shut it but paused when he saw her watching him.

"When?" she asked.

"Tomorrow morning."

At the sounds of a struggle coming from above, Larkin shot out of bed. Though it was the middle of the night, she hadn't been able to sleep. She hurried to the ladder and looked up as the trapdoor swung open. A shadowed face looked down at her. "Larkin, come on."

She blinked in disbelief. "Alorica?"

"Hurry up!" the other girl hissed.

Larkin shot up the ladder. It was darker than she'd ever seen it in the Alamant, the stars hidden behind black clouds. Alorica hurried through the copse, gleaming blue and green flowers lighting the way.

Larkin ran after her. "What's going on? Where are we going?" She stopped short at the sight of two more cloaked figures.

"Larkin," Bane said in a relieved voice. He pulled her into his arms and squeezed, her sore ribs barking in protest.

"What is she doing here?" a fourth person said from behind them. Larkin could make out the planes of her face in the light of the lampent she held. At first, Larkin didn't recognize her, but that pale skin, the raven hair. "Caelia?"

She glared at her brother. "Denan won't ever stop hunting her. If you want your freedom, you have to leave her behind."

Bane crossed his arms over his chest. "I'm not leaving without her."

"You foolish, stupid—"

"I'll go with him and protect him. Make sure he reaches Hamel safely." Larkin at least owed him that. "Then I'll come back with Denan."

Caelia threw her hands up in frustration. "And what makes you think you can protect anyone?"

Larkin let her shield flare, her sword materializing in her hand.

Caelia's mouth fell open. "Every piper in this place will come for you once they know about this."

"And I'll return with them willingly." Larkin expected Bane to argue. He didn't.

Caelia considered her a long moment. "Your mother saved my life once. After this, we're even."

"Saved your life? When?" Bane asked.

Caelia's head dropped, and she turned away from them.

Bane grabbed her arm and pulled her around. "Saved your life from what?"

Caelia tried to squirm free, but he wouldn't let her. "I was pregnant!" All the fight drained out of her. Shocked, Bane let her go and stepped back. "I didn't know who the father was. I started bleeding, and the bleeding didn't stop. Papa found me like that. After everything I'd done to him, he didn't turn his back on me." Caelia wiped a tear from her face. "Pennice never told a soul."

And when Larkin had been in trouble, Mama must have called in the favor. Feeling uneasy, Larkin turned to Bane. "Did your father tell you to marry me?"

Bane shrugged. "He asked me if I wanted to."

She breathed out in relief.

Caelia spun on her heel and marched away. "I won't let my brother die," she muttered to herself. "They're fools to think I would." She led them through the trees, quick on her feet despite her enormous belly.

Still reeling from shock at the revelation, Larkin hurried to keep up. "What about Tam? Denan?"

"I took care of Tam," Alorica admitted. "Wasn't as hard as you might think."

When Larkin looked back at her, Alorica shrugged. "All I had to do was kiss him. He completely forgot he was on guard duty."

"You darted him, didn't you?"

"I did," Alorica admitted gleefully. "Fool smiled and said in the end he came out the winner, whatever that means."

Caelia laughed. "The kiss—that's how they get you. This time next year, you'll be having his babies."

"We're not all as soft as you."

"We'll see," Caelia said. They reached the docks and climbed into a waiting boat. "Keep your movements smooth and even. We don't want to agitate the water."

They pushed into the lake and started paddling. Larkin stared at the black water with flecks of glowing colors, waiting for the bloom of red tentacles beneath them. She broke out in a sweat, her breathing coming faster and faster until her head was spinning.

"The lethan doesn't attack boats," Caelia said.

Larkin still couldn't calm down. At the first tree they came to, they pulled up at the dock, and Larkin practically jumped off the boat.

"Follow me. Stay silent," Caelia said. "Don't touch any flowers."

They hurried up the stairs, careful to keep their garments from brushing against the plants and setting off a ripple of color. When they were halfway up the tree, they stepped onto one of the bridges.

Caelia pulled out a handcart loaded with flatbread. "Alorica, take the boat at the dock back to your tree and then push it into open water."

"Why?" Alorica said in a bored tone. "It's not like Tam doesn't know it was me."

"He won't tell," Caelia said.

"Alorica's not coming with us?" Bane asked in disbelief.

Larkin couldn't make out Alorica's expression in the dark, but she was sure it was scathing. "And leave this place? I'm free to learn my own trade—one that pays quite well, once I'm past the apprenticeship. Tam treats me like a queen. He's already given me a ring with five different gemstones, and the finest cloth makers in the Idelmarch couldn't come close to matching the luxury of their fabrics."

"Ancestors, you're shallow," Bane said.

Alorica shrugged. "You're just mad you're no longer the best catch around."

"What about your family?" Larkin asked softly.

Alorica hugged Larkin goodbye. "Tell them Atara and I are happy. It's all my father ever wanted for us."

Larkin didn't know what to say to her enemy turned ally. What would the king do to her if he discovered she'd helped them? "Will you be all right?"

"She'll be fine," Caelia answered. "Tam will make sure of that."

Still, Alorica hesitated. "I want you to know I'm sorry, Larkin, about Venna. I should have listened to you."

Larkin couldn't get any words around the hard knot in her throat. Alorica turned and slipped back into the shadows.

"This next part is the riskiest," Caelia said. "Use your magic to cut through the wall. There's a boat waiting for you on the other side."

Bane took hold of Caelia's arm. "You're coming with us."

She rested her free hand protectively on her belly. "No, Bane, I'm not."

He stepped closer. "I didn't come all this way just for Larkin. I'm not leaving without you."

"I have two sons." Caelia's voice wavered. "I won't leave them."

"Bring them with us." Bane's voice was far too loud.

Caelia shushed him. "I know this will be hard for you to understand, but this is my home now. I love my husband. I love my children."

"What about Papa and me?" he said, voice tight. "Don't you love us?"

"Of course I do. But that isn't my life anymore. Besides, I have to distract the guards so you can make your escape."

"This is ridiculous!" Bane growled. "You're coming with us."

Caelia jerked free from his grip. "Head for the mouth of the river and don't stop. You'll need all the lead I can give you."

"Caelia—"

"I've made my choice, Bane. If you try to force me, you'll only get yourself caught."

Bane ground his teeth.

Caelia hugged him hard. "Don't stop in Hamel. Find another town, change your name, and start over." She ushered them into the handcart, covered them with a blanket, and settled a basket filled with loaves of bread on top of them. "If they do catch you … Bane, do whatever you must to escape, but, Larkin, don't fight them. They only lock up the girls who try to escape, but if you hurt someone or one of the trees … Just don't."

Before either of them could respond, Caelia started off, the wheels moving in oiled silence. Through a crack in the blanket, Larkin watched as they crossed bridges that connected the trees, sweat running in streaks down her face.

Finally, they came to a bridge that led to the outer wall. She reached out for Bane, and he took her hand in his. Caelia stepped into the light of the bridge and started across.

She'd reached the halfway mark when a voice rang out from

the tower. "Identify yourself."

"Caelia. I've come with food for my husband, Gendrin, and his company."

"You may pass," the sentry replied, clearly pleased.

Caelia started back across. As soon as they were under the tower, she jerked off the blanket, pulled out a rope from the base of the handcart, hooked it around an arch, and let it drop. "Hurry."

Bane took hold of her arm. "Caelia—"

She hugged him hard. "Go." She led the handcart away.

Larkin looked down, down, down. If she fell into that water … *The lethan rising toward her, red tentacles spreading.* Closing her eyes, she swayed unsteadily.

Bane pushed Larkin to the rope. "Go."

Steeling herself, Larkin swung out over nothing, hands slick with sweat, and started down, Bane right behind her. The light was so low she had to make her way mostly by feel. By the time they'd neared the bottom, her arms were shaking and her ribs were on fire.

When the water was nearly lapping at her feet, Bane said, "The boat should be waiting on the other side. Use your magic."

Larkin concentrated on the thorn in her right hand and the one on her arm. The barrier bloomed into her sight as the sword formed in her hand. It sliced through, and the wood curled away, leaving a circle large enough for them to crawl through.

Bane climbed through first, then held the boat steady while she climbed in after him. She took up one of the leaf-shaped oars. "No splashing. It will make the water glow."

Slow and steady, they inched their way across the lake toward the river. The current took hold. Larkin looked back, at the trees with glowing flowers like stars between their branches, at the water that gleamed with life. Beyond the wall, the White Tree glowed in the night. A pang sounded in her chest like a tuning fork, longing vibrating through her limbs.

"Larkin?" Bane asked.

She turned her back on the Alamant.

CHAPTER 32

RIVER RUN

L arkin and Bane spent the entire night paddling through the lazy, fat river. She couldn't help looking behind them every few minutes, convinced the pipers would appear at any moment. They never did.

By midday, she was so exhausted from lack of sleep over the last three nights and her muscles were so overworked that she could barely hold up her head, let alone the paddle. The thorn in her arm was a dull throb she was starting to think would never go away. Thankfully, the current picked up, and the paddles weren't as necessary.

"We have to rest, or we won't have any strength if they do show up." Bane jerked his chin toward a chest tied to the bottom of the boat. "What's in there?"

Larkin barely had the strength to lift the lid. What she saw made tears inexplicably well in her eyes. She held up the irregular fruit. "Gobby." She tugged out something that was wrapped up, pulling back the cloth to reveal the dense travel bread of the pipers. "There's a hooked spear for fishing too." Not that Larkin had any idea how to use it. She lifted out a beautifully carved water gourd.

She passed him some food and water and settled down to eat. Bane bit into his bread, his gaze dark. Larkin knew him well enough to know what he was thinking. "Caelia had her reasons."

His jaw bulged. "She's still under their spell. It's the only explanation."

"I told you before, it doesn't work like that," Larkin said gently.

He cast her a suspicious look. "You would say that if you were still under their spell, wouldn't you?"

She wasn't, but she didn't feel like arguing. She would see him safely back to Hamel, then she was returning to the Alamant.

As if he knew what she was thinking, Bane chucked the gobby rind into the river. "Finish eating, then we better paddle some more if we have any hope of outrunning them."

Arms aching, Larkin lifted her paddle again. The river narrowed, the gently sloping land rising until walls of rock encased them on every side. White caps crested the waves, boulders lying in wait beneath. Larkin pushed off from a boulder and frantically paddled for the center channel. The prow dipped. A freezing wave slapped Larkin, leaving her gasping and soaked. The boat surged upward, heading toward another rock.

She lifted her paddle to push off, but her sluggish arms didn't move fast enough. They slammed into it so hard her teeth rattled. She tensed, waiting for the boat to come apart. Instead, the craft careened sideways, tipping dangerously.

"Lean to the right!" Bane cried.

She held on to the opposite gunwale, arms shaking with exertion. For a moment, the boat hung precariously. Helpless, Larkin lifted her head to the heavens, praying to her ancestors for help. Far above, a rope stretched down one side of the ravine.

This was where they had crossed to escape the wraiths, where Venna had fallen to the river.

The boat slammed back down, sending another freezing wave over them. They spun, careening off rocks and bouncing over waves. Larkin paddled with all her remaining strength. She'd finally aligned the prow downriver and back in the center channel when Bane shouted, "Larkin!"

She followed his pointing finger to see the river disappear in the distance—a waterfall.

She'd sat beside the falls while Denan told her about the curse. How could she have forgotten? She desperately paddled backward, but the river had them now. The paddle slipped from her exhausted fingers, the river pulling it away from her. It spun and dipped before shooting off the edge. Gripping the gunwales, she watched helplessly as the boat tipped, open air beneath them.

"Venna," she whispered, the word like a prayer on her lips. "If you can hear me, please help us."

And then they were falling.

From the darkest recesses of unconsciousness, Larkin felt a sudden urge to cough. Her body seized, water pouring from her mouth. She gasped in a short, tortured breath, which mixed with the water in her lungs. She coughed again. Spots and blackness sparked before her unseeing eyes. On her third cough, she realized a hand was pounding her back.

She finally managed to draw a decent breath. The ringing in her ears subsided enough she could hear Bane swearing violently. "Larkin?" He shook her. "Larkin?"

She was too busy gasping for breath and coughing up water to answer. He shook her again. She shoved him off her.

He fell on his backside. "Are you going to be all right?"

She could only nod, her vision coming back gray and spotty.

"All right. I've got to try to find the boat. Stay here." He took off at a run.

Larkin spat out the last of the water, and her body relaxed from its locked position. She collapsed on the rocky bank, clarity slowly returning.

At Bane's shouting, she tipped her head to the side. He hauled at the submerged boat, fighting to get it out of the current before the river claimed it. Not having the energy to care, she closed her eyes.

Water splashed her, the cold making her gasp. Bane crouched over her, his eyes pinned on the forest. "Get in the boat." Something about the way he said it …

She braced herself, pushing up. He wrapped her arm around his neck and pulled her to her feet, water and dirt falling from her. He dragged her backward into the pool at the base of the waterfall, toward the boat, which was now floating.

She followed his gaze. There were … people staring at them from under the trees—people with black lines etched into their gray skin. Black eyes with sickly yellow irises spiked like thistle watched them. They wore crude black armor. One of them hissed at Larkin, its gums black as its eyes.

"Mulgars," she gasped. She fumbled to pull up her shield— this was the part she'd known was coming, the part where she had to use her magic to protect Bane—but the mulgars only watched them.

"Why aren't they attacking?"

"Get in the boat," Bane hissed.

She struggled to get inside, falling headfirst into the puddle of water at the base—a lot of good she'd be in a fight. Bane climbed in after her, took hold of their one remaining paddle, and pushed them away from the shore. He paddled furiously toward the mouth of the river.

Larkin kept her shield up, as big as she could manage. The mulgars silently watched them slip past and made no move to stop them.

"What are they doing?" Bane asked.

She shook her head, shivering and exhausted. "I don't know."

They finally reached the river, Bane easing up as the boat sped forward on its own. He found a bucket in the chest, which thankfully seemed intact. They bailed out, Larkin barely moving. Bane finally handed her a blanket from the chest. She wrapped it around herself and instantly fell hard asleep.

She started when Bane shook her awake. It was night, the stars hidden behind clouds.

"I've got to have some rest," he said.

She must have slept most of the day away. Blearily, she took her turn. They passed the rest of the night and all the next day this way, seeing no signs of mulgars or wraiths or pipers. The river kept up its relentless pace. They were making good time. Still, she couldn't help but check behind them every few minutes. She knew what the pipers would do if they caught Bane, but what about her? Lock her back in that cave for months? Banish her?

It didn't matter. Finding a way to stop this madness was all that mattered.

She was resting, watching the boughs arch over her like a roof, their leaves like lace against the gray summer sky, when Bane cried, "Larkin, look!" He sat up in the boat, his finger pointing to something ahead.

The never-ending splay of trunks and branches thinned, revealing fields beyond, and beyond that was Hamel. She blinked, surprised at the changes she saw.

A wall of black rocks nearly four stories tall had been built around the town. Gates were open to the north and south. In front of the druid house to the southeast, hundreds of tents had been staked in perfect rows and columns. In the pasture in front of those tents, men in black uniforms and armor drilled to orders she was too far away to hear.

Bane pushed her shoulder. "Get down. Keep out of sight." He covered her with the blanket. As they came out of the shadows and into the light, those in the fields spotted a boat coming out of the Forbidden Forest. They pointed, shouting in alarm.

Larkin's heart thumped painfully in her chest. She couldn't catch her breath. She peeked out of the blanket, watching the bank slip by. When she'd left, everything was the previous year's rot and mud. Now green had taken over the fields and trees. Flowers bloomed, and the air was warm with promise.

If only those promises had ever applied to her.

Bane picked up their remaining oar and paddled, his gaze fixed on the soldiers marching toward them at a fast clip. He steered toward a pocket of still water, running the boat partially aground on the bank. "Get to your house. I'll come for you when I'm sure it's safe."

She wouldn't be there. She'd done what she came to do— see Bane safely home. Now she would go to her family, let her mother know she was safe and well, kiss her baby sisters. Then she would go back into the forest to wait for Denan to come for her.

She threw off the blanket and gave Bane a quick hug goodbye. Trying to hide the tears welling in her eyes, she jumped into water up to her knees and pushed the boat back into the river. She watched as Bane paddled on without looking back. Would she ever see him again?

If she did, she hoped she'd found a way to protect their people from the curse. Glancing around to make sure no one had seen her, Larkin splashed out of the river and wove through the thick willows. Before leaving the cover of trees, she scanned her family's partially plowed fields. She was relieved her home had withstood the flooding. Weeds had been freshly chopped down, but she didn't see anyone. Perhaps they'd gone home for lunch? Heart light with hope, she broke into a sprint, coming down the hill.

"Mama! Mama!" Larkin called toward the house, hoping to catch sight of any of her family—even Nesha. The door opened, and Sela burst out, legs and arms flashing in the sunlight, and threw herself into Larkin's arms.

Larkin clutched her sister. The familiarity of the little girl's bony body vibrating with energy made her weep with relief. "Where's Mama?"

Sela shook her head.

"What's the matter?"

Sela pointed back to the house.

Gathering her tattered courage, Larkin pushed to her feet. "Show me."

Sela's hand fit in hers, much like Wyn's had, and her sister led her inside. Larkin had to drop her shoulder to open the warped, weather-beaten door. She stepped into the tiny space— she'd forgotten how small their hut really was, how dark and dirty. Her mother lay on the sleeping mat, the baby against her breast. A stew bubbled on the fire.

"Larkin?" Mama gasped.

"Mama?" Larkin's legs lost their strength, and she collapsed. Mama set aside the baby and lunged toward her. They embraced, holding each other so tight nothing would ever pull them apart.

"You're alive!"

"The pipers took me, but they've been kind and gentle. Mama, oh, I have so much to tell you."

Mama pulled her back. "You were safe? Then why would you come back?"

"It's just until tonight."

Mama embraced her again and started sobbing. "I'm sorry I couldn't protect you. I'm so sorry."

Larkin stroked her mother's hair. "You tried. You did everything you could."

"And it still wasn't enough," Mama wailed.

Sela wrapped her arms around them both. Brenna screamed in indignation for having her meal interrupted.

When they finally pulled back and wiped their eyes, Mama looked Larkin up and down, eyes widening in disbelief at the rich clothing she wore. "If the druids find out you're here …"

"I'll leave tonight. They'll never know I was here." Knowing the easiest way to explain was to show her, Larkin formed the shield. Her mother gasped, leaning away from the shield like it might burn her. "You have magic?"

"It's all right," Larkin soothed. "Mama, nothing is what it seems—not the pipers, not the druids, not the beast of the forest. My magic isn't the only kind. There are darker kinds, and they've done some horrible things. I can help stop it. I can make things better for everyone, but I have to go back to do it."

Mama blinked at her. "Go back to the pipers?"

Larkin shrugged, letting the barrier dissipate. "I have to change things. After I do, everything will be better—for all of us."

Her mother crawled back to Brenna, picked her up, and settled her against her breast. "Things have changed since you left, Larkin. The druids have brought their army."

The men in black uniforms. "Why are they here?"

Mama shrugged. "They've been building fortifications, drilling soldiers, stirring up the townspeople. Half the men have joined them."

Sela spooned up a bowl of soup and handed it shyly to Larkin, who took it with a smile. Sela fetched her own bowl and sat beside Larkin. Larkin brought the bowl to her mouth and sipped. She was surprised at the flavor—chicken and some early greens with bobbing dumplings. There were also hints of thyme and sage. Where had her mother found the money for such luxuries?

Larkin set the bowl down. "Where is Nesha?"

Sela pointed toward town.

"Why aren't you talking to me, sweetie?" Larkin asked.

"She hasn't said a word since you were taken," Mama said.

Larkin's eyes slipped closed. She had to make this right, so no other child would lose their sisters. "What is Nesha doing in town?"

Her mother wouldn't meet her gaze. "She got a job, remember? She cooks and cleans."

Larkin blinked in surprise. So that was where the money came from. "Someone hired her?" She left the other words unspoken—Idelmarchians didn't hire cripples.

Mama frowned. "She's been fortunate."

"When will she be back?"

"She sleeps in the servant quarters at work."

Larkin relaxed. If Nesha knew Larkin was here, the townspeople would be storming across the bridge, intent on burning her at the stake. Larkin considered asking after Harben, but she couldn't bring herself to say his name aloud.

Mama seemed to know exactly what she was thinking. "He lives in town with his new wife."

The words were like milkweed sap—all bitterness and poison. Larkin lifted the bowl to take another sip when a knock sounded at the door.

CHAPTER

GARROT

Larkin froze and carefully set down her bowl of soup. Sela's head came up, and she looked at Larkin, whimpered, and hid behind Mama.

"Larkin, it's me," Bane said.

Letting out a relieved breath, Larkin lifted the bar and opened the door.

"I went to Garrot," he blurted.

"You did what?"

Bane held out a calming hand. "They came to me right after you were taken. Told me if I managed to bring you back, they would protect you."

This couldn't be happening. Her mouth fell open, and she glanced behind him, relieved when she didn't see a mob storming her house. Was there time for her to make it into the forest before they came for her? "You can't trust the druids, Bane!"

He reached for her hand. "The druids—they're not what you think."

She jerked back. "They tried to kill me!"

He shook his head. "Garrot thought it was kinder than making you a slave to the pipers, but I convinced them I could bring you back, that eventually the pipers' thrall over you would fade."

"I'm not under their thrall!" She sensed movement beside the door. "What have you done?"

"I'd say he finally understands," a new voice said. Garrot slid into view. Larkin tried to throw the door shut, but his foot shot out, jamming it open. He forced his way inside. Sela's open-mouthed, silent screams joined the baby's vocal ones.

"I told you to wait, Garrot," Bane growled.

She'd been in this position once before with Garrot. Only then, she'd been defenseless. That wasn't true anymore. She called up her shield and her sword, glorying in the buzz from her arm and wrist. "Get out."

"Larkin, please—" Bane began.

Garrot eyed her magic with a desperate kind of hunger. "I have no desire to discuss anything here. You will come quietly."

Larkin shifted to the side, standing in front of her mother and sisters. "I'm done being quiet, Garrot."

He tilted his head. "Not yet, I think. I have your other sister in my care, Larkin. Come quietly, and she will remain safe."

"There's no need to threaten her," Bane said.

Larkin's head came up. "Mama?" she asked without turning.

"It's true," Mama said in a horrified whisper. "Nesha has been working for Garrot since before you left."

All that Nesha had done, and still Larkin couldn't let her come to harm. Though it warred with every instinct she had, she let her magic dissipate. Garrot stepped aside and motioned to a cart just beyond the door. "We're not ready for people to know you're here yet. Get inside and cover yourself with the blanket."

She wasn't ready for them to know she was here yet either. "I want Bane gone."

Bane took a step toward her. "Larkin—"

"He leaves or I'm not coming."

Bane took another step toward her. Garrot caught his arm. "There is time for the rest later. Go to your father. He's been worried."

She felt Bane's eyes on her. She held her chin high, refusing to look his way. Finally, he left. She waited until he had plenty of time to go before stepping outside. She climbed into the wagon and drew the blanket over her. She had no desire to peek out, no desire to know where he was taking her.

The blanket was pulled off Larkin's head. She sat up in the cart. She was in a large barn, a milk cow in one of the stalls. Her arm throbbed in time with her heartbeat. Garrot stood at the end of the cart. She scooted to the end of the wagon and hopped to the ground. "Where is Nesha?"

"In the kitchen, making our lunch."

Her sister had chosen this man over her. Why? What had she done to deserve such a betrayal? Someone else was missing from this little gathering. "And Rimoth and his mad daughter?"

"I thought this meeting should stay between us."

Larkin snorted. At least Maisy wouldn't be leading the charge against her.

"I would see you integrated back into this town," Garrot began. "Your family will receive a monthly stipend equal to that of a lower-level druid—enough to keep them comfortably in a modest house."

She blinked at him in disbelief. The last time she'd seen him, he'd been bent on killing her. Now, he wanted to help her? She didn't buy it. "What do you want in return?"

Garrot lifted an eyebrow.

"You wouldn't help me out of kindness, Garrot. It isn't in

you."

"I do what I must, Larkin." Larkin recognized the phrase—the pipers used it. "I protect my people, as the pipers protect theirs. So, now you need to decide: who are your people? The people of the Alamant or the Idelmarch?"

Her mouth fell open. "You know about the Alamant?"

"I am a Black Druid. We know the truth of the forest."

She wanted to hit him. "And yet you *allow* girls to be taken?"

"Allow?" he growled. "Your pipers haven't given us much of a choice."

"You've known all along what's been happening to the girls, and instead of telling us the truth, you let rumors of the beast take the blame. You let the families of the Taken think their children devoured!"

"Rumors we started over two centuries ago."

She gasped in disbelief and disgust. "Why?"

"You think the curse only affects the Alamant?"

Worried she was going to be sick, she covered her mouth with her hand. "You could find a way to tell everyone the truth."

"The truth that their daughters are stolen by men who possess magic, men we are powerless to stop?"

Men the *druids* were powerless to stop. "You would have lost all control over us."

He tipped his head in acknowledgment. "And I know the secret is safe with you. You literally cannot tell anyone. None of us can, once we learn the truth."

She gave him a hard smile. "I can show them."

His eyes narrowed. "I don't think you will. I think you will do what I tell you." He held out his arms in a gesture of abundance. "And in exchange, I will give you everything you want. It's not such a hard bargain, is it?"

He didn't have anything she wanted—except complete control of her family. "And in return?"

"First, tell us what you know of the pipers—their numbers, location, armor, and weapons."

She could only think of one reason he would want to know that. "You're going to war? How? The forest is crawling with wraiths and mulgars. And the pipers are inside a lake behind a magic barrier."

"None of that is your problem," Garrot said evenly.

Larkin leaned back, trying to pretend her shoulders didn't ache. She wouldn't mind the druids going up against the far superior pipers. Perhaps it would teach them some manners. Her mouth came open as the realization struck home. "The night you made me face the crucible—you came out of the forest. You'd just sold me to Denan."

"And then he didn't take you. Caused me all sorts of problems."

"Problems like the town turning against me. You knew I was innocent, yet you fed the townspeople's superstitions and fear. You wanted them to kill me."

"No," he said. "They would have done it anyway—there's no reasoning with a mob—but I needed their loyalty more than I needed you alive. You had been no end of trouble for me."

Until she'd called up her shield and he'd realized she had magic. "And now that I'm worth the trouble, you'll protect me." She shook her head in disgust. "What makes you think I would help you after everything you've done to me? You turned my own sister against me." Her voice wavered as she remembered the self-righteous loathing in Nesha's expression.

He frowned. "I saved her from going down with you. We have ways of making you comply." Her mother. Her sisters. "Really, Larkin, the choice is simple—happiness and prosperity or misery and imprisonment."

She wouldn't help him hurt anyone, but for now, she couldn't think of anything else to do except delay him. "First, show me you'll make good on your promises."

His eyes glinted with satisfaction. "Jump down."

She hated to come any closer to him, but she also needed him to believe her compliant. Dragging her feet, she stepped to the end of the wagon and hopped down. He took out a knife and approached. She balked.

He held her shoulder fast. "If I wanted you dead, I would have done it already." Bending far too close for comfort, he slipped the knife between the cords and cut her free. She backed away from him, rubbing her wrists.

She could kill Garrot now—pull up her shield and sword and end him before he could even scream—but he had hundreds of Black Druids. She couldn't kill them all. So, she would wait, bide her time until circumstances turned in her favor, then she would escape, taking her family with her.

Garrot pushed open the door, revealing the roofline of one of the houses amid the town. She stepped into the sunshine and blinked at the brightness, recognizing where they were. Old Widow Wensop's house, easily the second largest in the town, just a bit smaller than Bane's manor house. It had been sitting vacant for the last couple of years because no one could afford to purchase it.

Now, instead of weeds, the land had been plowed, vegetables and herbs spouting in neat rows. From off to the side of the barn came the clucking of chickens. Garrot started toward the kitchen door, pausing to whisper something to one of the two guards that stood to either side of it. That guard left at a jog while Garrot opened the door for Larkin.

Reminding herself that she wasn't powerless, she stepped past him into the kitchen, half expecting to see Nesha. Her sister was nowhere to be seen. Larkin scanned the room. There were three doors—one led to a pantry, another to a dining room. The last door was closed.

Bread baked in a pan over the hearth, and something savory bubbled in a pot. Garrot pulled out a stool, gesturing for her to sit at the table. She did so as he spooned out bowls of soup and set the steaming bread on the table. She waited while Garrot took his own seat across from her and began blowing across the top of his soup.

He looked up at her over the bowl. "You won't have another chance to eat until tonight."

Taking a towel, she upended the bread pan, sliced herself a piece, smeared it with butter, and began eating—the soup a creamy chicken like Mama had made them before the crop failures. The bread wasn't nearly as good as Venna's had been.

"Where is Nesha?"

"She doesn't want to see you."

"She betrayed me."

"You betrayed her first."

Larkin spread her hands. "How?"

Garrot grunted. "That's between the two of you."

If she was working in this house, she couldn't avoid Larkin forever. Larkin had nearly finished eating when a door out of sight groaned open behind her. Nervous, she pushed to her feet, ready to call up her shield if necessary. The guard from the back door came in first, followed closely by Mama.

Larkin rushed forward and wrapped her arms around her. "Are you all right?"

Mama pulled back, hands inspecting Larkin's face and arms. "Are you?"

Larkin nodded.

Mama stepped around Larkin and glared at Garrot. "Let her go."

Garrot sawed through the loaf, cutting himself another piece. "When she proves herself loyal to the Idelmarch."

"What must she do?" Mama said.

"Everything I ask." Garrot tore off a chunk of bread. "Now, Pennice, tell Larkin about the men I sent to plow your fields."

Larkin turned back to her mother, whose mouth tightened

into a hard line. "Men from the army showed up with a dozen plows."

"They'll have your fields plowed and planted in a few days. Consider it your first payment for information, Larkin."

Larkin swallowed hard. "Let me go home with my mother. You can post guards if you want." It might be hard to slip past them, but with the help of her magic and Denan's pipes, it was possible.

Garrot chuckled. "Not quite yet."

"When?" she asked.

He cocked his head. "After the wedding, of course."

Larkin stopped breathing, stopped thinking, stopped feeling. For a moment, she was bobbing helplessly in the river—the bruising imprints of her father's hands still pulsing against her skin. She stared at the too-bright surface, weightless and at the mercy of the river.

She gasped in a breath, feeling dizzy. "What wedding?"

Garrot watched her very carefully. "Your wedding to Bane."

Mama shored her up on one side. "Larkin?"

"I'm fine," she reassured her—or perhaps she was trying to convince herself. Marrying Bane ... Wasn't that what she want-ed? Here it was. She dragged her gaze up to Garrot's.

He tossed the bread aside. "Why, Larkin, I thought you'd be happy."

There was something about his expression—a kind of dis-gust that made her force a smile onto her frozen cheeks. "I am. It's just—I am already married to one of the pipers."

Her mother gasped. Garrot's expression revealed nothing. "The Idelmarch does not recognize forced marriages. Were you forced?"

"Yes," she admitted.

"Then you are wife to no one." He wiped his mouth with a napkin. "The wedding is tomorrow." Rising, he spoke to the guard. "See Pennice safely back to her home and make sure the men watching over the family know she's returned."

Mama squeezed Larkin's hand. There was a sheen of hope there—that perhaps they would all make it through this alive. Larkin hugged her, savoring the comfort of her arms. "It's going to be all right, Mama. I promise," she whispered.

"I should be comforting you."

"Hurry along. I'm a busy man," Garrot said.

The guard took hold of Mama's arm and tugged her toward the door. She went reluctantly, her gaze clinging to Larkin until the very last moment. Larkin wondered how many more times she would have to say goodbye to her mother, never knowing if she would see her again.

"What information do you want?" Larkin said in a harsh whisper.

"Come along." Garrot led her into a large dining room complete with a new table, over eighteen chairs, and an empty hearth. They climbed a narrow flight of stairs. At the top was a large bedroom.

"You'll find paper and pen on the desk. Write down the names of any girls you recognized in the Alamant. Their families should know they're alive. When you're done, slip it under the door."

That was information she'd happily impart. The families deserved to know what had happened to their Taken. He started to pull the door shut.

"What are you telling the townspeople about me?

He paused. "That you've come bearing the truth of the forest. Don't you think it's time the people of the Idelmarch learned it?"

Larkin clenched her fists. "After all this time, after all these lies, why now? What's your game?"

He shook his head. "Game? There's no game. My purpose is to protect my people." He shut the door behind him, the lock snicking shut.

CHAPTER

KILLING FROST

The next morning, Larkin lay curled on the bed, numb and exhausted, yet doubting she would ever sleep again. She listened to the sounds of cooking below her, the murmur of voices, and knew one of them was her sister's—a sister she wanted to strangle. Tears threatened. Nesha had been her best friend once. Why had that changed?

It wasn't long before the sounds of a crowd built beyond her window. She pressed her pillow over her ears, trying to calm the panic that demanded she hide under the bed. When she could stand it no more, she stood, calling on her sword and shield and standing like Denan had taught her. "If they come for me," she murmured through gritted teeth, "they won't find me cowering."

"Larkin," a male voice called from outside. That call was echoed by others. Her heart kicked in her chest—another mob come for her? Only, the voices didn't sound angry but pleading. She eased to the window that faced the street, lifted a corner of the curtain, and peeked out. Her gaze caught on a few familiar faces—Kenjin, Patrina, and Vyder. The families of the Taken. Garrot must have made some sort of announcement. They knew she was here and that she knew things about their daughters.

The door groaned open behind her. She whirled to face Garrot. "What did you tell them?"

He set down a plate of bread with jam and some cheese. "Put away your weapons." Instead, she pointed them at him. He folded his hands at the wrist. "Have you forgotten our arrangement?"

Her mother. Her sisters. She worked her jaw and let her magic subside. She missed the familiar buzz immediately.

"I told them what the curse would allow," he said. "You have returned, escaped from something much more intelligent and evil than any beast. You have word of their daughters."

"You're manipulating them."

He nodded to the washbowl in the corner. "Wash your face. I'll have the families brought to the dining room."

She took a step back. She wasn't ready to face the people who'd called for her death weeks before.

"My guards will be present at all times. As will I. You have five minutes to eat, then you better be downstairs."

She hesitated, wanting to defy him, but the time to escape was not yet—not until Denan came for her. She ate the food; the bread was her mother's recipe. The familiarity would have been a comfort, if Larkin didn't know who had made it. Face clean, she tried the knob to find it turned easily. Bracing herself, she started down the stairs.

Alorica's family was seated around the table, Garrot speaking with them in a low voice. Kenjin jumped to his feet at the sight of her. "Atara? Alorica?"

Trying to forget that this man called for her death, Larkin stood beside the hearth and told them the truth. Atara and Alorica were both healers, much loved and doted on.

"You mean the beasts that took them were men?" Patrina

said.

Larkin nodded.

"Why didn't you say that in the first place?" Kenjin demanded.

Larkin sighed in frustration and held her hand over her mouth.

"The men have stopped you somehow?" one of Alorica's brothers guessed.

"Magic!" the other cried.

His parents shot a silencing look, but Larkin nodded vigorously.

"But why were they taken?" Patrina begged.

Garrot leaned forward. "What reason would men take young, unmarried girls?"

"They need wives," Kenjin guessed darkly. Garrot nodded. Kenjin slammed the flat of his hand down on the table. "The forest take them! They can marry one of their own."

Garrot leaned forward. "I can promise you, Kenjin, we're doing everything we can to get your daughters back. For now, Black Druids are waiting in the tavern. Guess what you can, and my druids will confirm or deny. It's the only way to work around the dark magic binding us."

Larkin eyed him. "What are you planning?"

Garrot waved Alorica's family out. Once the door was shut behind them, he rounded on her. "You tell them about their daughters. Other than that, keep your mouth shut."

"You think you can get the Taken back? That you can defeat the pipers? You're wrong."

Ignoring her, he called in the next family. Each encounter went pretty much the same. The families experienced the gamut of emotions—elation, despair, confusion, anger. All of them had more questions than Larkin could possibly answer. At some point, the door to the kitchen opened, and she could make out her sister's uneven footsteps. Nesha was right on the other side of

371

that wall—so close and yet impossibly far.

Even as distracted as she was, she didn't fail to notice Garrot brought them in by order of their position in the community. She knew what was coming when Vyder opened the door. His hat twisted round and round in his hands, his shoulders stooped. He'd aged ten years since she'd last seen him. "My Venna?"

Dripping blood and black lines and falling. Larkin closed her eyes, trying to block it out. She didn't know what to say. How could she explain that Venna was gone and she would never come back?

She forced her eyes up. Tears streaked down her cheeks, snuffing out the hope in Vyder's eyes. His face crumpled. He shook his head, as if to keep her from saying it. He turned away, tugged his hat on, and pulled open the door,

"She was my friend," Larkin called after him. She couldn't let him go without something to take with him. "She died in my arms." Not entirely true, but Larkin would never tell him the full truth of what had happened to his granddaughter. As soon as she stopped speaking, Vyder closed the door softly behind him. Through the wavering glass of one of the windows, she watched as he faded from view as if he had never been.

"How did she really die?" Garrot asked.

"Wraiths killed her," Larkin responded, voice dead of the emotions that had been wrung out of her throughout the morning. She turned to the man beside her. "Why do you hate the pipers so much?"

Garrot's jaw hardened a fraction.

"They took someone you loved, didn't they?" Still no answer. "A sister? Friend? Lover?" He remained utterly unaffected. "If I saw her, I could tell you about her."

"I don't want to know," Garrot finally said, his voice husky with emotion that barely registered on his face. He always seemed so unflappable. She was beginning to wonder if his mask was just to cover a well-concealed rage.

A soldier opened the front door. Larkin sagged. She didn't think she could handle another grieving family. Instead, five Black Druids slithered into the room—one of them was Rimoth. It reminded her of the time when druids had stolen into Bane's house and Garrot had pinned her against the fireplace. She jumped from her seat, her shield and sword before her.

Ignoring her, one of the men laid a map on the table, weighting the corners down with polished stones.

"I know how to make her talk." Rimoth smiled his oily smile and disappeared into the kitchen. Remembering her sister, Larkin started after him. Before she could reach the doorway, Nesha appeared. She wore a new dress and a thick pleated apron, her hair tied back in a neat braid. Rimoth held a sword point to the small of her back. Larkin backed away.

Nesha was even lovelier than the last time Larkin had seen her—hollow cheeks filled out, auburn hair a glossy sheen. Her violet gaze flicked to Larkin and then back at the ground. Larkin wet her lips, not understanding.

"Put away your weapons, Larkin, and come draw everything you know on this map." Garrot said implacably. "And I'll keep Rimoth in check."

"Please," Nesha cried.

Garrot held up a hand. Nesha winced and fell silent.

Larkin straightened. "I don't believe you."

"Rimoth, take her into the back and have a little fun."

Rimoth leered at Nesha and grabbed her arms. Larkin took a step to stop him.

"You have two other sisters," Garrot said mildly. "And a very beautiful mother. Don't make me turn Rimoth loose on them too."

Larkin froze, caught between wanting to believe her sister hadn't really betrayed her and knowing she was still betraying her. In that time, Nesha was dragged out, guards coming to help. Muffled screams came from the backyard.

Larkin whipped the sword up, holding the point to Garrot's throat. "Leave her alone."

"Cooperate, and you can have everything. Fight me, and you lose everything." He pointed to the map. "Draw what you know."

She debated. One thrust and Garrot would be dead. She thought she could kill the other druids as well, make it into the back and stick Rimoth like the pig he was, but then what? The alarm would be sounded. The army would come. She couldn't fight them all.

She bared her teeth at him and growled. "You're going to pay for this."

"I already have."

She backed up, letting her weapons fade to nothing.

"Rimoth!" Garrot barked. Immediately, the sounds of struggle from the back stopped. Rimoth came back inside, muttering and readjusting his clothing.

Larkin had known Rimoth was slimy, but she'd never thought him capable of this. She shot him a dark glare, swearing she would kill him before this was all over. She took the quill Garrot offered her and looked at the map, surprised to find she recognized the landscape. She was shocked at the level of detail the druids knew—the river and the waterfall, the dense forest, even the Alamant, drawn in painstaking detail with its outer wall, the White Tree at the heart.

"How many people?" one of the druids asked as he leaned over the map. "How many men? Where? Landmarks on the way?"

She stared at the depiction of the White Tree. The cartographer had made it grotesque—all spidery lines and sharp angles with a bleeding skeletal face at its heart. The Alamant was the opposite of this. It was light and color and magic. She found Denan's tree, which had cradled her in its boughs. She'd slept and woken to the sound of Denan's pipes. *Wyn and Aaryn and Mytin and Tam and Talox. Denan.* She cared about them, about the Alamant. She didn't want to betray any of them. Tears pricked her eyes—tears she stubbornly blinked down.

"Perhaps we began with the wrong sister," Rimoth said. "The younger one, what was her name? Sela?"

"Start with the prince's tree," Garrot said. "Where is it?"

She bent down, marking the wrong tree, one near the wall. Garrot stared up at her. "Rimoth, I believe Nesha is still waiting for you outside."

Rimoth started toward the kitchen door.

"Wait! Why?" Larkin asked.

Garrot's hand flashed out, slapping her. She cupped her cheek, shocked. "We know much about the Alamant already," he said. "If I catch you lying to me again, I'll have her beaten. Lie to me twice, and Rimoth gets to have fun with her."

Larkin closed her eyes. The druids would never make it past the Forbidden Forest, not with the wraiths and mulgars in their way. So she began drawing, pleading ignorance as often as she dared.

Shortly after Larkin finished the list, the tailors came, fitting her in a rich red gown for her wedding, which they took away to make alterations to. She went to the window and caught sight of her sister working in the garden. Larkin watched her limp to the pump, fill a bucket, and carry the water to the new plants.

Worried sick for her sister, Larkin formed her sword and cut through the lock on the door. Slipping her shoes off, she moved soundlessly down the stairs, relieved the house seemed empty. That still left the guards at either side of the back door.

Larkin formed her sword and her shield and shoved the door open. The guards turned to her, faces going slack with shock. "Run and tell Garrot I escaped."

One of the men drew his short sword and swung it at her. Larkin's sword cut it in half. She slammed her shield into him, throwing him back a dozen paces. She glared at the other guard, who took off running without a word, the first guard scrambling after him.

Larkin stalked down the garden path. Her sister backed away, pale face terrified. No matter what Nesha had done, she was still her sister. She had to know Larkin wouldn't hurt her. She released the magic as her sister reached for the barn door and yanked it open.

"I'll cut it open," Larkin called after her.

Nesha hesitated a moment, and then her shoulders slumped. "What do you want?"

"I wanted to make sure you were all right after Rimoth ..."

Nesha chuckled without humor. "Garrot wouldn't let anyone hurt me. I came into the back with Rimoth, and he stood there while I screamed."

Larkin's mouth fell open. "Why would you do that?"

"To get you to tell us the truth!"

Larkin saw what she'd failed to before. First, because of Nesha's bulky apron, and then because of the angle and distance of the second-story window, but she could see it clearly now—the hard lump that was her sister's stomach.

Larkin gasped in shock. "How long have you been sleeping with him?"

"How long were you sleeping with him?" Nesha shot back.

Larkin half shook her head, not understanding. "I'd never let Garrot touch me!"

"Garrot?" Nesha laughed bitterly. "You think Garrot did this?" She wrapped her hands around her stomach. "No, this was months ago, Larkin, long before Garrot ever arrived in Hamel."

The boy Larkin had seen her sister with the nights the druids had come. But why would Nesha ask how long Larkin had been sleeping with him? "Why would I—" It all clicked into place. "Bane?"

Nesha shook her head in disgust. "Don't pretend you didn't know, little sister. You saw us together that night. And the very next day I find you in his arms. Then you convinced Mama to marry him to you instead of me!"

Larkin staggered back as if Nesha had slapped her. It couldn't be true. It couldn't. But then, Alorica had hated Larkin for the same reason. "I never saw his face. I didn't even know Mama was going to ask—Does Mama know?"

Nesha sniffed. "You were always her favorite. Sela's too."

Larkin spread her hands. "So you betray me instead of talking to me."

"You're the traitor, not me." Nesha spat to ward off evil. "You've chosen those cursed pipers instead of your own people—your own flesh and blood."

"What's going on here?" Larkin turned to find Garrot coming into the yard with a dozen druids behind him.

She turned back to her sister. "After he threatened to hurt Mama and the little ones, you're defending him?"

"Threats are different from actions. He took me in, gave me a job when everyone else would have watched me starve." Nesha straightened. "Garrot does what he has to in order to save the Idelmarch. If you weren't a traitor, he wouldn't have to threaten anyone."

"Larkin," Garrot barked. "You've caused your sister enough heartache. Back inside."

Hurt and anger and confusion roiled in Larkin, but the strongest emotion by far was loss. "What makes you believe him over me?"

"I was there, remember? I saw it happen."

Larkin shook her head. "You don't know what you saw. Garrot has warped your sense of reality." Larkin heard the soldiers spreading out around her, felt their unwavering gazes. She glanced sidelong, enough to note the drawn bows.

Larkin turned to find Garrot had halved the distance between them, hand on his sword. She hadn't even reached for her magic yet. "Since I've outlived my usefulness, do you plan to kill me?" She shook her head. "Tell me, Garrot, do you actually believe these lies?"

Garrot's eyes slipped past her to Nesha, and Larkin heard the slightest shuffling that told her Nesha had retreated. Garrot visibly relaxed.

"Did you really think I'd hurt my own sister?"

"Giving you a room in my own house was a courtesy. You were to stay there."

Larkin looked toward the distant forest. How far could she make it before Garrot brought her down?

"Don't make me do something we'll both regret."

Larkin worked her jaw. Without another word, she went back inside and up to her room. She stood before the largest window, overlooking the street. She saw Bane come. He hesitated and pulled his hands through his hair, hat in hand, before finally coming inside. She heard him climb the stairs, the door groan open, and his tentative footsteps as he approached.

She didn't turn to face him. She was too afraid she'd draw her sword and do something she couldn't take back. "Did you know Nesha's pregnant with your child?"

His steps stopped. She heard him turning his hat nervously in his hands. "My father wouldn't let me marry her."

"And Alorica?"

Bane huffed and started pacing. "Alorica wanted to be the next lord's wife. She didn't want me."

Alorica had implied there had been more to it than that. "It didn't stop you from sleeping with her."

His jaw hardened. "She pushed for that more than I did. It was before I knew what she was really like, and long before you and I ever started."

So, Bane *had* slept with Alorica … and Nesha. Who else?

Larkin gripped the windowsill, fingers aching. She forced herself to face him. "Did you ever love me at all?"

He ran his hand through his hair. "Not like that—at least, not at first."

She fought to keep her face from betraying the humiliation ravaging her. She hadn't thought Bane could hurt her any more than he already had. "When did that change?"

He sagged in defeat. "Do you really want to know?"

No. "Yes."

He slumped against the wall not far from her. "You were like a sister to me, but after your mother asked me to save you, I decided to try kissing you, to see if there was any spark at all. I was surprised when there was."

That day by the river. He'd been so hesitant and she so thrilled, then Nesha had seen them. "Ancestors." No wonder her sister hated her. She rubbed her eyes, wanting him to stop but even more desperately needing to know everything. "When did you find out about the baby?"

He was silent for time. "Not long after we kissed. She hid it from me because she didn't want me marrying her because of the baby. I tried to convince her that we could still be together. After all, I was marrying her sister to save her life. I wouldn't be the first lord to have a mistress."

She was going to kill him. "It doesn't work like that, Bane."

He spread his hands. "What did you want me to do? I loved both of you. You both needed me. Should I have abandoned one of you? I had the means to provide for both of you, and Nesha would never have been allowed to marry. You're sisters. You should want what's best for each other."

"By that logic, you shouldn't have a problem sharing me with Denan."

Everything in him hardened. "The situations are not comparable."

"Why did you trick me into coming back with you?"

"To save you," he said through gritted teeth.

"You still don't believe me when I tell you I could change things."

"Larkin ..."

Her eyes narrowed. "Say it, Bane."

He held out his hands in a gesture of helplessness. "You're just one girl."

His words shuddered through her. She backed away from him, leaning against the windowsill. "One girl can change everything."

His expression turned pitying. "He told you that to make you stay. He told you what you wanted to hear."

As if he had done any differently. "You should have believed me, Bane."

He took a step toward her. "You'll see. When the thrall fades and you're back to yourself, you'll—"

She drew upon her shield between them. "You don't want to see. You want things to be what they were, but they'll never go back to what they were—if that ever existed at all."

He swallowed hard. "Nesha won't speak to me anymore. It will just be you and me, like you wanted."

"I'm not under any thrall. Denan isn't—"

"Don't say his name!" He punched the wall, plaster falling around his hands. He groaned and pulled back, cradling his hand. "Why did you have to kiss him?"

All the blood drained from her face. "After what you did, you don't get to be angry about that."

Bane braced himself against the wall, eyes shut tight. "I spend a week chasing after you. I nearly died more times than I could count. I hid behind enemy lines and stole what little food I could find for days. I finally found you—and you're kissing him like he's life and you're dying."

Ancestors, this really was the end of her friendship with Bane. He'd been the very best part of her for so long. Pieces of

Larkin were flaking off, falling around her like a tree shedding its leaves before the killing frost.

Bane took a ragged breath. "You're telling me you weren't under his thrall. That means you meant to kiss him." A silent sob tore through Larkin. Bane moved slowly toward her, his gaze boring through her. "Which is it, Larkin?"

She closed her eyes, unwilling to watch the devastation play out across his features. "I meant to kiss him."

Bane turned on his heel and slammed the door after him. Larkin winced, the sound shuddering through her, and then the silent sobs became audible, tearing through her with the force of a blizzard.

CHAPTER 35

WEDDING

The door closed behind the tailor and his crew, finally leaving Larkin alone. One of the pins in her tightly curled hair dug mercilessly into her scalp. Trying to rearrange it, she approached the mirror they'd left for her. She looked abnormally pale; whether because of the powder they'd used to try to cover her freckles or because she was being forced to marry again, she wasn't sure.

The dress was a monstrosity, the gold bodice fitted over a corset and shift. The underskirt added a ridiculous amount of volume. The deep ruby overdress was like a coat, buckled snugly under her bust, surrounded by pleats. Shining beads caught the light and shimmered when she walked. But if it was a monstrosity, then Larkin supposed it was a beautiful one.

A song wove through the darkened streets, dancing across the rooftops before swirling around Larkin. She rested her forehead against the cool glass of her prison. It was her heartsong—hers and Denan's. He was here. He was calling for her, and she couldn't go to him. Longing and sadness swelled until it burst. She trembled with the effort of ignoring that call, and then it stopped. She rubbed at the ache in her chest—unsure if the pain was from loss of the song or hope for what that song meant.

From the heart of the town, torchlight wavered in a long stream. They were coming for her. A line of druids appeared—at least fifty of them. Their flickering lamps cast their faces in sinister shadows. Rimoth and Garrot separated themselves from the others and looked up at her, daring her to deny them.

She wasn't afraid. Denan was coming for her. Donning the wedding cloak, she tugged the hood over her hair and left the house without a backward glance, meeting them at the front door, but she faltered at the sight of Harben at the head of the group. He smiled at her—as if he hadn't abandoned them when they needed him the most, as if he hadn't beaten them and lorded over them her whole life. She marched up to him and slapped him hard across the face.

His head whipped back to her, his fists already clenched. She dropped into a fighter's stance, sword and shield springing into place. His expression went slack, and he took a step back. She glared at him, daring him to come at her, daring him to fight her.

"No!" a voice cried. Raeneth rushed out of the shadows, stepping between Larkin and Harben. "Leave him alone!" In her arms, she clutched a newborn baby with a shock of red hair the same shade as Larkin's.

And Larkin understood. Harben finally had his son. She let her shield and sword fade away. "He's not my father," she said to Garrot. "He doesn't get to walk me to my wedding." She turned her back on him and marched toward the town center on her own, head held high, never once looking back.

Garrot caught up with her, matching his stride to hers. She half expected him to berate her or insist Harben take his rightful place. He didn't.

"Why did you bring that man to me?" she asked simply.

"Because the coward deserved it."

She glanced at him in shock. "Why do you care what Harben does and doesn't deserve?"

Garrot's mouth tightened.

She made a sound of disbelief. "You're in love with Nesha." Garrot stiffened and remained silent, which told Larkin everything she needed to know. "She couldn't pick anyone worse than you."

She outpaced him, turning toward the town's center—a simple intersection, two-and three-story buildings on all sides. Her mother was waiting, along with all her sisters. Nesha held the baby and refused to meet Larkin's gaze.

Bane stood in the center of the street, a torch in one hand. The other he held out to her.

Larkin's step faltered for a moment. Ancestors, how could everything fall apart so completely? Taking a fortifying breath, she moved to stand before him and looked into his eyes. "Why are you still going through with this?"

His eyes softened. "I've known you for years, Larkin. I know the girl you really are."

The girl who'd been powerless and hungry and desperate for any way out. Bane had been that way out. She shook her head. "I never want to be that girl again."

As soon as the words left her mouth, music drifted down on them, falling on them like heavy snow. The melody reminded Larkin of Mama's lullaby. It had the same rises and falls, the same notes, the same gentle melody. Even with the amulet, the memory of sleep weighed heavily on her body. Her mouth fell open. It *was* the same song. But how could her mother possibly have learned it? Her eyelids grew impossibly heavy, her thoughts sluggish. She looked around, bewildered.

"It's the pipers," Garrot cried as he pulled a sword from his waist. The druids drew their weapons, searching the rooftops for the source of the sound.

"Where?" Rimoth staggered. His sword drooped before clanging against the cobblestones. When he bent to pick it up, he pitched forward. He was snoring before he hit the ground. More druids and guards fell. Garrot lurched to the side of a building and collapsed against it, his chin tipping down to rest against his chest.

Larkin reeled toward her mother and sisters. Denan was coming for her, as he'd promised, but she couldn't leave without her family. "Wait," she slurred, hoping he was close enough to hear her. "Denan, please." She was a couple steps away when her knees buckled and she sank to the ground amid the clang of falling swords and thunk of falling bodies. Her mother and sisters were already asleep. The last thing Larkin saw before her eyes slipped closed were pipers falling from the sky. Somewhere, Denan was among them.

She woke with a start to see Denan crouched before her, his face shadowed by fallen torches. Behind him, she could make out over a dozen pipers, all of them playing, but the music no longer affected her.

"If you want to stay"—Denan's voice shook, and he cleared his throat—"I'll go. You'll never see me again."

Her mother's words washed over her: *Choose the chains that bind you.*

Larkin had to choose between Bane and Denan—the man she'd known her entire life or the man she'd known for a few weeks. The Idelmarch or the Alamant—the land and people of her birth or the place she'd found her power and her happiness. Did she want a future with Bane as a lord's wife, where she would be just one girl, but a girl he could protect forever? Or did she want a life in the Alamant, a queen beside a man who believed she could do anything?

Larkin stretched up and hugged Denan hard, the smell of the forest and his own musk washing over her and giving her a heady sense of relief. "I choose you."

He sagged against her and wrapped her up tight. For the barest moment, there were no druids or pipers, no enemies or friends. It was just his arms around her. She was safe and loved.

"You have to take my mother and sisters with us," she said. "Garrot will kill them if you don't."

He released her, turning to his men. "Talox, Benick, take the women. Tam, scout ahead and make sure the path is clear."

Tam started out. Her family was still sound asleep. Denan pulled Larkin to her feet as Benick swung Sela over one shoulder and tucked the baby in his other arm. Talox hesitated, vacillating between Mama and Nesha.

Denan took a single step toward them. "I'll—"

"Now!" There was a sudden movement, a flash of black against the flickering torches. Someone screamed. Druids poured from the buildings. The pipers hesitated, two of them mowed down, their songs silenced before Larkin could draw breath to scream.

"To me!" Denan cried.

Flutes falling against their necks, the pipers pulled out axes or swords and shields. They moved as one, shifting to stand with their prince and make a circle around Larkin and her family, but they were outnumbered five to one.

Talox placed the children in Larkin's arms before taking his place at Denan's side. Somewhere, music must still have been playing because Sela slept on, ignorant to the carnage around her. The baby snored a little through her open mouth. Larkin placed her sleeping siblings between her mother and older sister and stood protectively over them, sword and shield out.

Denan gave a trilling whistle. From above, a rain of arrows sliced through the ranks of druids and dropped them in screaming, writhing masses. Denan pushed something into Larkin's hands—amulets with different kinds of leaves. "Dampeners for your mother and sister. They'll block the thrall."

She wore a similar amulet—Denan must have placed it around her neck right before she woke up. She lifted her mother's head, settling the cord into place. Immediately, Mama shifted and let out a moan. Larkin did the same for Nesha—the first time she'd touched her sister since before she'd been taken. Within seconds, both women were struggling to their feet.

Larkin handed Mama the baby but kept Sela for herself. She was so grateful the little ones were sleeping through this. "Mama, we have to go with the pipers."

"What?" Nesha cried. "They're beasts!"

The battle raged around them, pipers fighting against druids, arrows and men falling. Larkin locked gazes with her mother. "Garrot will never stop hurting us, Mama. The pipers will help us." Her mother hesitated. "Trust me, please."

Nesha gripped her arm. "Mama, you can't!"

Mama's mouth tightened. "I know the monsters the druids are. We have to trust Larkin."

"You always do," Nesha said bitterly.

Another round of arrows rained down. Garrot and his druids retreated from the onslaught. "Where did these archers come from?" His voice rang out. "Get the dampeners off the dead. Put them on our reinforcements!" Druids scrambled to obey. "Nesha!" Garrot cried.

Denan whistled three short blasts, and the pipers shifted, pushing through a gap the druids had left. Before Larkin could grab her, Nesha ducked between pipers, nearly taking an ax to the side before the piper could turn his swing.

At the head of a charge, Garrot stepped aside to let her pass him and said, "Run and hide! I'll find you later."

"Nesha!" Mama wailed.

Larkin swung her sleeping sister over her shoulder and

brought out her sword. "We have to let her go, Mama. Nesha's chosen her side." She hated how their family was being torn apart, that she was losing the people she loved the most.

"Where did they get the dampeners?" Talox cried.

"I don't know!" Denan ordered the vanguard out. He and Talox took up defensive positions around Larkin's family. They rushed through the deserted streets. Steps scuffed on the rooftops above, black shadows rose up and let arrows loose. With grunts and screams, druids went down behind them. Denan whistled again, and about thirty archers dropped from the rooftops, taking up the rearguard.

From the direction of the forest, music wove through the buildings. It must be working, for Larkin didn't see so much as a curtain shift in the windows. There was no sign they were being followed.

"He'll be coming for us," Larkin panted, her corset restricting her breathing.

"Yes," Denan agreed.

The eastern gate came into view, a shadow outlined by even darker shadows. Ahead of them, something lay in the middle of the street. They came closer, the details coming into focus. *Tam.* The vanguard passed over him, taking up defensive positions as Talox knelt next to his friend. "He's alive. But what—"

"Arrows out!" Denan cried.

"Now!" someone shouted. Light fell around them in the form of falling torches. From above, a contingent of two dozen druids stood on the roofs, sighted down their arrows, and released a volley. Larkin didn't have time to think. Those arrows would find their mark, strike the pipers and her family indiscriminately. She lifted her left arm, calling up her shield above them, demanding it grow larger. Bright gold in the center darkened to marigold on the outer rim, a dome with a tree in the center formed above those closest to her.

The arrows slammed into it, sending ripples of light and

color across the surface. Larkin staggered, dizzy. The shield fizzled out. She'd managed to protect those closest to her—Mama, her sisters, Denan, Tam, and Talox. But the rest ... Dozens staggered and fell. She cried out, hating that she hadn't been able to protect them all.

Talox held his shield over Mama as he ushered her toward an alleyway.

Denan gripped Larkin's elbow, dragging her toward one of the buildings. "Arrows!"

The remaining pipers returned fire with deadly accuracy, dropping all but a handful of druids. The rest swung up the sides of the buildings and climbed like only pipers could. More fell to the druids' second volley. The sounds of weapons clashing and men dying drifted down from the rooftops.

Larkin fought a wave of dizziness. Her knees went soft. Denan pushed her against the wall, eased her to a sitting position, and stood guard over her. "You drew too much magic. It will pass."

Her aching arms around Sela went slack, her sleeping sister slumped against her chest. Her gaze met her mother's, who was cowering behind Talox, her body curved protectively around Brenna.

A final cry sounded from above. Less than a dozen pipers came back. "Guard them," Denan commanded Talox.

Larkin tried to stand, but it was awkward with Sela. Mama hurried over to help. The dizziness had passed, leaving behind a heavy exhaustion. Huddled toward each other, they eased away from the building, shoes soaking through with blood.

Denan crouched beside Tam. Someone had dropped him in the melee. Larkin had the discordant thought that if Tam died Alorica would kill them all. Denan shook his shoulder.

Tam groaned. "What happened?"

Larkin's eyes fluttered shut in relief.

"Can you stand?" Denan asked.

Tam pushed to a sitting position and looked around, a devastated moan slipping from his lips. "No! I didn't make it back in time to warn you."

"Tam." Denan's voice shifted to that of a commander. "Get up!"

Tam straightened and pushed himself, wobbly, to his feet.

"Naven, Benden, get that gate open," Denan said. Two pipers sprinted toward the entrance and up the stairs built on the side. The rest spread out, checking those who'd fallen. The pipers propped up men who could walk. Those too injured to manage were swung over shoulders. The dead were left where they lay. The broken group hurried toward the gate, the heavy wooden doors swinging outward. The two pipers came back down the stairs.

"You see anything up there?" Denan asked.

"No movement," one of them said.

Denan didn't take his eyes from the fields lying between them and the forest. "We do what we must."

The pipers echoed the phrase back to him.

Larkin swayed on her feet.

"Talox," Denan called. "Carry the little one."

Talox wrapped his big hands around Sela. Mama made a sound of alarm. "It's all right," Talox soothed. "I'll guard her with my life."

Larkin released her sister reluctantly. Mama stuck to Talox's side like a burr. The group headed out. Larkin tried to keep up, but her steps were unsteady.

Denan hung back, looking at his shield and ax as if trying to figure out how to carry her and his weapons. "Come on, Larkin. You have to keep up."

He lunged. One second he was beside her; the next he was behind her. Something clattered. She spun. Fifty druids sprinted through the gate behind them.

"Run!" Denan cried. More arrows flew, hitting the remaining pipers one by one, until only Talox and her mama remained.

Larkin didn't know someone had caught up until arms wrapped around her waist. She went sprawling, the breath knocked out of her and her face stinging where her cheeks skidded across the dirt.

"Denan!" She twisted in her assailant's arms, coming face-to-face with Bane. "Let me go!"

"Larkin," he pleaded.

Then Denan was there, ax swinging.

"No!" she cried.

At the last second, Denan twisted his ax so the flat side slammed into Bane's shoulder, sending him sprawling off her. She scrambled to her feet, only to be knocked down again by someone else. Denan pivoted to meet first one, then two druids. Another druid grabbed her by the ankles, tying them. She tried to bring up her shield or sword. Light sputtered before her fingers before stuttering out, her magic spent. She kicked and fought as another pair of hands joined the first.

"Get her behind the wall!" Garrot cried. "And bring me the piper prince alive!"

Denan finished one druid, who was replaced by two more. He still had a clear path to the forest. He could outrun the druids.

"Denan, go!" she cried. "Leave me."

Denan growled in frustration. Larkin's hands were tied, and she was hauled back toward the town. Tears streamed down her face. "Denan, go! Please!"

Denan kept fighting toward her. Five men now. The sixth, Garrot, snuck up behind him and slammed the handle of his sword into the back of Denan's head. He dropped to his knees. He looked up at her, his gaze unfocused.

"Tie him up," Garrot ordered. "Take him with the girl."

"No," Larkin gasped. She could see no way Denan would survive this. Beyond, Tam slipped inside the forest with Mama and both her sisters. Where was Talox? She could only hope he'd reached the Forbidden Forest ahead of them.

If nothing else, at least her family had made it to safety. Then the gate slammed closed, blocking her view of what lay beyond.

CHAPTER 36

CHAINS

The druids opened a newly installed trapdoor at the ruins of a house that had burned to the ground decades ago and was never rebuilt. Below, there was only blackness. They shoved Larkin in first. She landed hard, feet stinging and shins aching. She rolled out of the way seconds before Denan hit with a muffled groan.

"Denan," she cried. "Are you all right?"

"I'll live," he rasped.

The trapdoor slammed shut, plunging them into utter darkness. Larkin made her way by feel to his side. She could feel sticky blood on his face.

"There's a knife they didn't find," he said, voice strained. "Sewn into the hem of my tunic."

She located it, tore it free, and cut through his bonds. He did the same for her. She called up her sword, using the light to peer into the crooks of an ancient cellar filled with tree roots and rot. A woman crouched in the corner, matted hair covering all but a sliver of her too-pale face. Larkin gasped, heart leaping in her chest.

Filthy with hollow cheeks and yellowed bruises, Maisy stared straight at Larkin. "It would have been better if they'd killed you."

How long has she been down here? Larkin wondered. She waited for Maisy to attack or break into maniacal laughter, but she only rocked back and forth. Hoping that meant she didn't plan to assault them anytime soon, Larkin turned her attention to Denan.

"Where are we?" he asked.

"An old cellar."

"But how did we get here?"

Her brow furrowed. "What?"

"I-I can't remember." Before she could answer, he rolled to his side and vomited. She got a good look at the back of his head, a swollen, bloody mass. He rolled back over with a moan. "Curses, my head hurts."

Larkin pulled off her wedding cloak and draped it over him. "You're trained for field injuries. What do I do?"

"There are some herbs." He blinked in confusion. "I don't remember them."

Ancestors, he's been hit harder than I thought. "We don't have any herbs anyway."

He grunted. "Just let me sleep."

She helped him to the opposite corner from Crazy Maisy and propped his head in her lap. She watched the other girl warily until her sigil ached from holding her magic for so long. "Are you going to do anything?" Larkin finally asked, exhaustion slurring her words.

"What would I do?" Maisy asked.

Larkin didn't know, and that's what scared her. She gave in to the inevitable darkness.

Wraiths glided over the elegant wall of the Alamant. Their
evil swords cut through the people like scythes through wheat.
Darkness trailed after them—a dark stain that spread like smoky
tendrils, reaching, grasping for the White Tree until it was no
longer white at all, but black as a night forsaken by stars.

Larkin struggled to be free of the dream, but it pulled her in
time and again. A song echoed through the carnage.

Within the shadows of the trees,
The beast doth live, the beast doth breathe.
When day dies and shadows grow,
The beast without his kingdom goes,
Shadows his cloak, magic his staff;
His snaggily claws reach 'n grasp
Snatching the virgins from their dreams,
Never a chance to voice their screams.
Back to the forest, he doth go
To nibble and dribble their bones just so.

Larkin gasped awake as Crazy Maisy began the song again,
her face tipped toward the strangled light seeping around the
corners of the trapdoor, providing dim illumination to the abandoned cellar. It must be morning. Surprised she'd slept, Larkin
checked Denan. His chest rose and fell evenly. She gently laid
her hand against his cheek, relieved he wasn't fevering.

Her backside and neck ached. Not wanting to wake him, she
settled for rubbing her shoulders. Surprisingly, Maisy had a pretty voice. Then the words caught her attention. "Within the shadows of the trees, the beast doth live, the beast doth breathe."
Larkin stilled. "When day dies and shadows grow, the beast
without his kingdom goes." Tears slid unheeded down Maisy's
cheeks. "Shadows his cloak, magic his staff."

"Wraiths," Larkin breathed. Maisy went very still. "The beast in the song—it isn't the pipers. It's the wraiths."

Maisy turned toward her, face cast in shadows.

"How do you know about them?" Larkin asked.

Maisy wiped her face with her sleeve. "The same way you do."

Larkin half shook her head. "You've been inside the forest?"

Maisy slowly peeled back her skirt, revealing jagged scars like the tines of a fork crisscrossing her legs, but the lines were not black, and Maisy clearly wasn't a mulgar. Larkin squeezed Denan's shoulder. He blinked up at her, and she nodded toward Maisy. His brows furrowed, and he sat up. Maisy dropped her skirt, but not before Denan got a good look at her legs.

"Ancestors save us," Denan breathed.

"Maisy," Larkin said gently. "How did that happen?"

Maisy's gaze went distant. "I used to hide in the forest—the one place I knew my father would never go."

How desperate had Maisy been to fight past the barrier's magic? "Did he hit you?" Larkin asked.

Crazy Maisy scrubbed at her arms. She shook her head over and over and over. Larkin understood. Her father hadn't hit her, but there were worse ways to hurt a child. Larkin's eyes closed in revulsion. Beside her, Denan swore softly.

Maisy sang, voice thick with sobs, "Reach 'n grasp … snatch … no one ever heard my screams …" She trailed into silence, her eyes growing unfocused.

"Ancestors," Larkin breathed. "What did they do to her?"

"Did she ever go missing?" Denan asked.

Larkin shook her head. "She went to live with the druids for three years. When they brought her back, she was like this."

"Did you just hear her? She wasn't with the druids."

Larkin looked at Denan, whose face was swollen from the fight. "Then where was she?"

Denan studied Maisy a long time. "What if they took her to Valynthia?"

"Valynthia?"

"The wraith city."

Shivers worked up and down Larkin's arms. "They have a city? I thought they lived in the shadows?"

"They travel by shadow. They live with their mulgars and slaves in the ruined city of Valynthia." He rubbed his face. "It was once the twin city to the Alamant. It fell when the wraith king came into being."

The markings on Maisy's legs … "Ancestors, she was their slave?" Larkin asked. He nodded. "This city has a tree?"

"A Silver Tree twisted into a perversion."

That explained where the wraiths' magic came from. "And their king?"

"King Ramass was chosen by their tree, as ours chose me, but he descended into evil, and that evil corrupted his tree and his people."

That meant the wraith king was nearly three hundred years old. The same time the women had lost their magic. "The wraiths created the curse." Denan nodded. Horrified, Larkin drew her knees to her chest. "What are we going to do?"

"My pipers will come for us. Tonight, when our magic is strongest. We're going to escape and meet them. After that …" His voice had turned hard.

"It's war, then." Larkin could only be grateful her mother and younger sisters had escaped. "Will your men be safe in the forest?"

He nodded. "We have wards to keep the wraiths away from our camps. They don't help with the mulgars, but we can drive them back." He pivoted, barely managing to cover a wince of pain. "Show me your sigils."

She held out her hand, his fingertips worked over a leaf, tracing the lines that circled her wrist. A band had begun to form around the sigil on her left arm.

Denan grunted in amazement. "Your magic will be so strong when they've completely formed."

Leaning forward, she lifted her hair to reveal the one on the back of her neck. "What is it?"

"So far, just random lines, but they're spreading down your back."

"I still don't know what it does."

"Have you tried drawing from it?"

She closed her eyes and pulled magic through it. A vision flooded her mind. The White Tree, its luster diminishing to nothing. She sat back. "I saw the White Tree fade away."

He held out his hands in a helpless gesture. "She is nearly five hundred years old."

They fell silent for a time. "Denan, I'm sorry for what I said about Serek. I was angry and lashing out. It wasn't your fault. You did what you could for him."

He had to clear his throat a few times before he could speak. "Tell Magalia that."

"She knows," Larkin said softly. "She just can't accept it."

Denan took a shuddering breath. He looked like a lost little boy. She wrapped her arms around him. He was incredibly warm, his arms gentle. Sudden light blinded Larkin. Holding her hand up to protect her eyes, Larkin made out forms dropping into the cellar.

Denan was already on his feet. Blinking, Larkin drew her shield. Together, they faced dozens of druids armed with bows and arrows. Larkin pulled more magic, expanding her shield around them both, her arm buzzing like a thousand angry bees were trapped inside it.

Garrot dropped down last. "Come quietly, piper prince."

"I see no reason to go anywhere."

Garrot's eyes narrowed. "I still have your sister, Larkin."

Larkin shook her head. "You won't do anything to hurt

Nesha."

Garrot's silence confirmed her suspicion. He drew his bow and aimed for her shield. The arrow shattered on impact, the barrier rippling like water hit with a scattering of stones.

Garrot didn't seem surprised. If anything, he expected it. He murmured something to a pair of his men, who disappeared into the darkness behind them and came back with Crazy Maisy, kicking and gnashing her teeth like a wildcat.

Garrot traded his bow for a knife, which he held at the other girl's throat. Maisy stilled, her eyes wide and nostrils flared. Larkin locked her knees to keep them from shaking.

"What about Maisy?" Garrot said. "Will you let me kill her to save your own life?"

Denan's head came up. "This is how you wage war, Garrot? By threatening women and children?"

"Isn't that the way you've always played it?"

Denan took an angry step forward. "That was our treaty! Women in exchange for protecting you! It's not our fault you let those women believe beasts took them."

Garrot sneered. "The treaty is over. Now make your choice."

Why break an over two-hundred-year-old treaty now? The wraiths and mulgars were still out there. Denan's gaze shifted to Larkin. She saw the anguish and grief there. Already, she was shaking her head.

"You can't hold your shield forever," he whispered. "And that girl doesn't need to suffer more than she already has."

"They'll kill you."

He took her face in his hands. "No. They'll use me as bait to trap my men—like they used you to try to trap us last night. My men won't know about the dampeners."

"Tam and Talox—" she began.

"Tam doesn't know about the dampeners. Talox didn't make it out. You have to break out of here and warn them before dark. If you hear pipe music, you'll know it's too late."

A well of grief opened inside her. Talox was one of the kindest men she'd ever known. He'd died trying to save her family. But she'd seen Tam carry Sela and Brenna out, Mama beside them.

"Denan, please," she whispered.

He pushed her against the wall and spoke low. "You have to find a way out of this cellar. You have to warn my men."

"Warn them? How?"

He tore something out of his tunic and pressed it into her hands—how many things did he have hidden in his tunic? "It's a distress whistle." It was thin, half the girth and length of her smallest finger, and attached to a thin cord. "Blow on it, and they'll find you."

She closed her fist around it. She had to find her way out of this cellar. She stared at the distance from the floor to the cellar door; it was easily twice her height.

"You can do this." He pulled away from her, his absence leaving her cold. He stepped to the edge of her barrier. When it didn't dissolve, he looked back at her. Though his face was now cast in shadow, she knew the determined set of his shoulders. "Trust me like I trust you."

After all they'd been through … She let the barrier dissipate. He stepped through the parting druids without looking at any of them and halted before Garrot, who released Maisy. She scuttled back into the recesses of the pit. Garrot snapped his fingers. A ladder was lowered.

"After you," Garrot said. Denan climbed without looking back, the rest of the men following. Garrot was the last to go, his gaze lingering on Larkin. "I gave you a choice, offered you everything."

Larkin didn't owe him anything. "If you hurt Denan, the Alamant will descend on you."

Garrot gave a hard smile. "I'm counting on it." He dropped

a water bladder and something wrapped in cloth. One hand on his bow, he climbed the ladder and slammed the door shut.

Larkin released the shield, her knees buckling, all the fight draining out of her and leaving behind dread. She looked at the whistle in her hand—carved from the wood of the White Tree. She held it to her chest a moment before slipping it around her neck. When she'd regained a little strength, she approached the water thirstily. She drank until she could hold no more, then unwrapped the old towel, revealing travel bread and some early berries. Leaving half of it for Maisy, she retreated to her own corner of the cellar and ate, knowing she would need her strength.

"Maisy," she called out. "Is there a way out of this cellar?" No answer. "Maisy!" she snapped.

"Don't you think I would have left by now if there was?" Maisy's voice sounded more herself.

Larkin knuckled her forehead. "Do they leave a guard? Lock the trapdoor?"

"They don't need to," Maisy said. "It's too high for us to reach."

Well, that would be the druids' mistake. Larkin gathered rotten bits of shelving and stacked it under the trapdoor. Hours passed as she worked. The shafts of light around the cellar door slowly shifted from one side of the room to the other, growing stronger and then weaker as the day moved toward night.

She heaved on a particularly heavy piece, her hands slipping. The wood bit into her. She cursed, pulling back to find a sliver lodged in the meat of her palm. Holding her breath, she jerked on it, hissing as the pain flared. She laughed—a high, maniacal sound—but she couldn't seem to stop. A sliver. A sliver had started all this. Only, now the villains and heroes had switched sides, and so had she.

The mound was high enough now she could reach the trapdoor. She pushed against it, but it didn't budge. It was locked. She called up her sword and thrust it through the wood.

"I have orders to shoot you on sight!" called a voice from above.

They'd left a guard? How was she supposed to save Denan if she couldn't even get out of this blasted cellar? She sank down on the top of her precarious structure. There had to be another way out. Perhaps she could tunnel? But she'd spent all her time trying to reach the trapdoor. There wasn't time to dig her way out—not before nightfall.

"Is this real?" asked a small voice. "Am I really here?"

She looked up to find Maisy standing at the edge of the light. "Yes, Maisy, this is all very real."

Maisy's brow furrowed. "Why did he help me? My own father wouldn't have helped me."

"Because he's a good person—too good, sometimes." Larkin sniffed, struggling against the ache behind her eyes that signaled tears were close.

Maisy stared off. Just as suddenly, her lost-little-girl look hardened, and her voice changed, becoming deeper. "Come with me."

She moved to her corner of the cellar, shifted aside some hanging roots, and slipped out of sight. Larkin hesitated, wondering if this was a trick, but she supposed she didn't have anything to lose. Denan's knife tucked in her palm, she followed, soon realizing this wasn't a corner at all, but an opening to another room.

Judging by the undercurrent of rotten fruit beneath the musty dirt smell, this had been a wine cellar. The space was filled with roots. Larkin parted them and step around ones that had found purchase on the soil below.

Maisy climbed a set of roots and pulled back a free board that had been fitted between them. "We would have died down here weeks ago if we hadn't found a way out."

Larkin looked up to see the peachy yellows and oranges of

approaching sunset. "We?"

Maisy grunted. "You met the sad one earlier. I come out when she needs something done."

Larkin had no idea what that meant. "What about the guards?"

Maisy pulled out a stick sharpened to a wicked point. "If they see us, we'll have to kill them."

Larkin balked. She was trying to save her people, not kill them.

"The druids never came after the Taken," Maisy said matter-of-factly. "They let us think there was nothing we could do, when all along, girls were being bought and sold by the very men charged with protecting all of us."

Larkin's resolve hardened. She would not leave Denan at the mercy of the druids. She would not abandon him as she had been abandoned. She pushed past Maisy, peeking out into the twilight. She found herself between the roots of a massive tree, the crumbled building's walls beyond. She didn't see a guard, which she hoped meant he couldn't see her.

She eased halfway out, keeping low to the ground, ready to call on her magic at a moment's notice. Seeing no one, she hauled herself out. Maisy came up behind her, her widening eyes all the warning Larkin had. She threw her hand behind her and called up her shield before she'd even managed to turn.

Dancing light alerted her that she'd been hit. She opened herself to the magic and turned to face the guard. He discarded his bow in favor of a sword and shield. "Get back inside."

In answer, she charged. A blow from her shield sent him flying backward. He landed with arms and legs splayed, but somehow managed to keep hold of his sword. She stood over him and stepped on his arm. Her glowing sword pointed at his vulnerable throat, she looked into his eyes. They were dark brown and wide, his jaw clenched. She hesitated. She didn't have to kill this man. She could tie him up. She drew back a little. "Roll on your belly and—"

He swept her legs out from under her. She landed hard on her side, her magic stuttering out. All the breath whooshed out of her, her lungs paralyzed. He jerked her up and slammed her against the wall, a knife to her throat. "You're all the same. Weak little traitors who turn your backs on your families for little more than a song."

His blade parted her skin. Blood dripped down her neck. She wanted to fight back, but the slightest movement would send the blade into her throat. Suddenly, she wasn't in the ruins of an abandoned house, but lying on a field, Hunter pinning her down, his knife at her neck. Hunter's face superimposed over the guard's before fading back into the recesses of her memories.

He licked his lips. "They won't blame me for killing you. After all, you tried to escape."

He grunted suddenly, eyes going wide. His hand on her shoulder went from pinning her in place to clutching her for support. He slowly slid down the length of her body, landing in a jumble, a large stick between his shoulder blades.

Maisy spat on him. "Hypocrite." She retrieved his discarded sword and shield for herself. She hefted the weight of the sword. "Mercy is a luxury we don't have time for."

Larkin pressed her hand to her throat, cooling, sticky blood seeping through her fingers.

She lifted the whistle to her lips and blew.

Maisy started. "Who are you calling?"

Larkin met her steely gaze. "The pipers."

The other girl pivoted and walked away.

"Maisy," Larkin called after her. "Where will you go?" She didn't answer. She didn't have to. There was nowhere Maisy could go where the druids wouldn't find her—at least, not in the Idelmarch. "You have to know the pipers aren't the monsters the druids have made them out to be. They would take you in."

Maisy paused. "You can't know that."

"Denan is their prince, and I'm his wife. I can know that."

Maisy half turned. "Why would you help me?"

Larkin cleared the emotion from her throat. "Because I know what it is to have a monster for a father."

Maisy wet her lips. "Swear you'll get me out of here."

"If you promise to help me, I'll swear."

Maisy slowly came back. Larkin looked around, getting her bearings. They were on the southwest side of town. The four-story wall wasn't far. She searched its length for a swarm of approaching pipers but saw nothing.

She glanced at the sky, at the sun sinking below the horizon. She blew the whistle again. As the note faded away, flute music rose up all around her, dancing on the breeze that played with Larkin's hair. The melody spoke of beauty and majesty and magic—*The Song of the Alamant*. Such beauty contrasted with the dread coursing through her. Denan had said if she heard the music, it was already too late.

She spun as another song entwined with the first, coming at her from all sides. Her mother's lullaby. Maisy crumpled to the ground, the sword and shield still gripped in her fists. Larkin groaned in frustration. The other guards had worn dampeners. Perhaps this one did as well. Larkin knelt over the body, finding one of the leaf amulets under his shirt. She pulled it gently over his head and placed it on Maisy.

Within seconds, the other girl stirred. She sat up, eyes squeezed shut and the heel of her palm rubbing her forehead. "What happened?" she asked.

"The pipers are playing, putting the town to sleep and calling the girls from their beds."

Maisy peered at her. "How did you stop it?"

Larkin held up her amulet. "Dampeners. They block the effects of the pipers' songs. I put the guard's on you." Larkin scanned the length of the wall surrounding the town, searching for any sign of the pipers. "They're walking into a trap. They're all going to die."

She helped Maisy to her feet. Ahead and to the left, the manor lorded over the hill. Her eyes narrowed at something built before the front door—a platform, a form spread between two poles. Larkin gasped in recognition.

Denan.

They'd staked him to a crucible—as they'd done to her. She took off running.

CHAPTER

WAR

The horizon devoured the last smudge of the sun as Larkin barreled into town. On the hill, she had a clear view of Denan, but she couldn't make out if he was alive or not. Something wrenched loose inside her. Ancestors, what if he wasn't? She held the whistle to her lips, blowing and blowing and blowing, calling the pipers to her.

A fist wrapped around her hair, jerking her into an alley. Through the pain screaming through her scalp, Larkin threw a blind elbow into the person's ribs. A grunt came from behind, and a shove sent Larkin sprawling onto her back. She twisted around, her sword appearing in her hand.

Maisy glared down at her. "Are you *trying* to die?"

Relief and confusion warred inside Larkin. She released her sword and sat up, resisting the urge to rub her stinging scalp. "What are you—"

Maisy pointed to the rooftops beyond them. "You can't go running into a baited trap. The druids will catch you."

Larkin pushed to her feet. "I have to save him!"

Maisy fisted her own hair and sawed it off with the guard's sword. It fell to the ground like a dead thing. She tucked the jagged remainder behind her ears. "No. You have to think. You have to find another way."

"Larkin?"

A shadow emerged from the alley behind Maisy. Her knees went weak. "Talox?" A bandage was wrapped around his head, blood crusting one side. She threw herself at him, encircling his big frame, surprised at the tears gathering in the corner of her eyes. "I thought you were dead!"

His large hand patted her back. "Besides the lump on my head, I'm fine. Tam saw your family to safety and came back for me."

Ancestors, her mother and little sisters were safe. She looked behind him as another man emerged from the shadows. Tam looked her up and down. From the building beside them came soft thuds. Exchanging nervous glances, they backed farther into the shadows.

"Isn't that the one Alorica called Crazy Maisy?" Tam whispered.

Maisy lunged and shoved him against the wall. "Don't call me that! I hate when people call me that!"

Tam lifted his arms, his eyes wide. "I'm sorry."

Larkin pulled Maisy back. "We have to be quiet."

Maisy shoved him once more for good measure and released him.

Larkin made a mental note to never call Maisy crazy again. "She saved my life. I promised her the pipers would take her in."

Tam studied Maisy. She glared defiantly back at him. "Where are the rest of you?"

His head fell. "Of the fifty we brought, only seven survived, including Denan. Four are playing their pipes in the forest. That left me and Talox to come rescue you."

Rescue her, not Denan. The world spun around her. Dizzy, she braced herself against a nearby wall. "Do you really think now's the time to kidnap girls?"

"We need a ransom for Denan," Tam said.

She rubbed her forehead. "The druids have dampeners."

"At least fifty of them, if I counted right," Talox said.

Fifty against four.

From down the street, the thuds continued. Larkin barely heard them. "And you're going to abandon Denan?"

Tam's shoulders tensed at the accusation. "We have to wait for reinforcements."

She struck the wall, welcoming the pain that flared in her already sore wrist. "They'll torture him, Tam." Her voice broke. "Until he tells them everything he knows about the Alamant, then they'll kill him."

Talox gripped her upper arms. "We'll come back for him, Larkin."

She shoved away from him. "No. No. There has to be another way." She paced the alley, the thumping nearly driving her mad. "What is that?" she exclaimed. Even as she said the words, she realized what the sound meant. She jogged to a window, stood on her tiptoes, and peered in.

Rimoth's young maid, Gilla, was tied spread eagle to a bed to keep the thrall from stealing her away. All her younger siblings slept soundly on the floor beside her. She fought the bonds, repeatedly kicking one of the bedposts with her heel.

All the breath left Larkin's body in a whoosh. "We have to turn them loose."

She eyed Maisy. A slow smile of understanding spread across the other girl's mouth. "I'll meet you in the forest by the thorn tree."

Larkin nodded. Maisy took off. Larkin pushed her way into the house, Talox and Tam right on her heels.

"What are you doing?" Tam asked.

She pushed into Gilla's room and stepped over the children. Gilla lay under the window. Larkin's sword sang through the bindings holding the girl to the bed. She stood without making eye contact and marched through the doorway, the men stepping aside to let her past.

"Larkin?" Talox asked.

"You can't get to Denan, but I can." Larkin unclasped her overdress and let it crumple to the floor. Maisy didn't hesitate to loosen the corset, releasing her from its too-tight embrace. Larkin kicked the underskirt off, which left her in her shift, just like all the other girls would be at this time of night. Larkin stole a cloak from a peg, tugged it over her traitorous hair, and pushed past them. "Maisy will set the girls loose and then wait for us in the forest. I'll hide among them, cut Denan free, and meet you on the north wall. You'll have to pull us up."

She stepped onto the street. The deepening twilight had leached the color from the world, leaving shades of gray. Gilla headed toward the north gate, which would take her right past the manor house. Larkin hesitated to follow. Bane's house had once been like a second home to her. And Bane and Nesha— once her dearest, most stalwart defenders—were now her enemies.

Tam grabbed Larkin's arm, his eyes full of worry. "If the druids recognize you ..."

She rested her hand over his. "Then you'll have your chance to rescue me."

"Larkin—" he began.

"Let her go," Talox said. "She can do this."

She nodded her thanks to him. "Just be ready to help us over the wall." Steeling herself, she forced herself to match Gilla's pace and strode down the center of the street as if she wasn't the least bit worried about an arrow lodging in her back. A door slammed behind her. She glanced over her shoulder. Two more girls followed, a third soon joining them. She made her way through the gauntlet of streets, feeling the presence of druids all around her.

As Larkin approached the edge of town, steps scuffed on a roof above—probably archers. Larkin resisted the urge to look up.

A muttered curse. "The girls have worked loose."

"Let them go," someone replied. "We have our orders."

Larkin's eyes fluttered in relief. They hadn't recognized her. She came to the edge of town and swallowed a gasp at the sight of Denan, his limbs spread out, the dying light casting his warm skin a sickly silver. From a street over, another girl stepped into view and then another after that. Good. More girls meant fewer eyes on Larkin.

Steeling herself, she left the town and started up the hill toward the manor. She knew druids lurked inside, ready to pounce on Denan at the slightest sign of trouble. Ignoring the prickling of sweat on her skin, she kept her face hidden in the shadows of her cloak and studied Denan askance.

He was naked but for a thin strip of cloth around his waist, his sculpted body sagging with obvious exhaustion. Jaw clenched, Larkin forced herself to slow her steps instead of run to him. "Denan," she said under her breath when he was seven or so paces away.

His head came up, though he didn't turn toward her. "Larkin?" His voice was muffled through a gag.

Relief washed through her—he was conscious, at least—followed quickly by dread. "Talox and Tam are waiting for us along the north wall." At least, she hoped they were. She hoped they had time to get into position and that guards weren't waiting for them at the wall.

"Your shield?" he managed around the gag.

She knew immediately what he meant. "I'm strong enough."

She kept walking as if she would move right past the manor

house. At the last moment, she darted toward Denan, her sword flaring to life in her hand. Her blade sliced through his ropes. Denan collapsed with a muffled groan before staggering to his feet. He yanked the gag out of his mouth. She positioned her shield between them and the house. An echo of alarm sounded from within. Torchlight flickered in the windows, and the house came alive, druids pouring from its mouth.

CHAPTER

RESTITUTION

Denan gripped her arm. "Run!" They tore past the house, sprinting toward the outer wall.

"No!" Bane cried. "Larkin is with him!" There was a grunt and a shout of frustration.

Garrot's voice rang above the rest. "Better dead than aiding the enemy!"

She glanced over her shoulder. Men backlit by hastily lit torches lifted longbows. Calling up her shield, she flung her hand back. Among the sound of splintering wood and clacking arrows, light rippled. The magic blasted through her. She staggered and went down to one knee. Denan whipped around, hauled her over his shoulder, and limped forward. She let him, putting all her energy into the shield. Denan stumbled under her weight before finding a steady rhythm.

"After them!" Garrot cried.

Putting away their bows, druids stormed down the hill—druids she and Denan were in no shape to outrun. She let her shield fade away, and immediately her strength returned. "Put me down."

Denan slid her to her feet. Side by side, they sprinted toward the rising wall. There was no cover, nowhere to make a defense—nothing but open ground and an impossibly smooth surface four stories high.

"Tam!" Larkin cried.

Feet pounded behind them. Someone reached for her. She turned to put her shield between herself and a reaching druid, when he went down hard and skidded to a stop. She didn't understand until another man went down, an arrow in his chest.

"Tam!" Denan cried.

She turned toward the wall and made out Talox's hulking form, and beneath him, a long, thin shape shadowed against the lighter wall. A rope. They came to a halt at the base of the wall. Denan grabbed a loop, wrapping it around both their chests as Tam loosed arrows from above.

"This is going to hurt," Denan said.

Larkin didn't have time to ask what he meant. The rope jerked around her chest, jerking her up and squeezing so hard she saw spots and her vision darkened. She came around on the stone walkway atop the wall. She blinked to clear her vision. She took a breath. Her ribs groaned in protest. For once, she wished she'd left her corset on to protect her from the worst of it. Facing town, Tam fired his bow in rapid succession. Denan crouched on the opposite side of the walkway, attaching a pulley to one end of the rope. Talox was nowhere to be seen.

Denan looped the rope around a crenellation. "You're going to have to hold on."

She forced herself to her feet and followed his line of sight. Talox must have jumped from the wall, using his weight to pull them both up. While she'd been unconscious, he'd run to the edge of the river and tied the other end to a tree.

"What if I fall?" she gasped.

Denan took her face in one of his hands. "Don't let go." He enunciated each word carefully. Shouts rang, druids working to open the gates. They weren't out of this yet. If they didn't beat those druids to the ground, they'd be surrounded.

I'm not going to throw up. She took hold of the pulley and jumped. She sped through the air. Wind whipped across her cheeks. For a single moment, she was free, her fear gone. Then the tree rushed toward her, and she had no way to slow down.

Talox caught her legs, slowing her. She couldn't hold on and ended up in a heap on the ground. She groaned as she sat up to assess if anything was broken. Her ribs pulsed with pain, but other than that, she seemed all right.

Talox rushed to help Denan, who'd managed to land on his feet and roll to a stop. Shouts and light came from Larkin's right. The druids had the gate open and were racing toward them.

"Talox!" Denan barked.

The big man handed Denan his bow and quiver and turned to grab Tam's legs. Denan let loose arrow after arrow. With Talox's help, Tam managed to slow enough to land lightly on his feet. They started toward the east, staggering to a halt as more druids appeared in front of them.

They were trapped.

"The bridge!" Denan cried.

They turned toward the newly made bridge that led to Larkin's land.

"Bring them all down!" Garrot screamed.

Arrows sprouted before them. Tam cried out and went down. Pivoting, Larkin held out her fist, the shield a glowing dome before her. Denan grabbed the whistle from around her neck and blew hard. More arrows rained down around them. Sweat ran down Larkin's temples. Her body quaked with effort. Another round of arrows hit her shield. She felt every one of the arrows as if they'd hit her. She collapsed, everything going dark. When she came to, three druids lay dead, their blood dripping through the fresh-cut boards. Another five fought the pipers.

"One of us is going to have to stay behind and hold them off at this bridge," Tam said through gritted teeth.

"I'll do it," Talox said.

Two more druids joined the fray. One shoved Denan's ax aside and slipped through, his gaze fixed on Larkin. His ax rose above his head. Denan turned, rushing toward her. He would be too late. She lifted her hand and tried to call up her shield. She managed a golden dusting that puffed away with the breeze.

The druid dropped to his knees. His eyes lost focus as he toppled forward, revealing an ax in his back. Behind him, Bane recovered from his throw—he must have been one of the two druids she'd seen coming in. The pipers finished off the other five men. Bane darted between the shocked pipers, yanked his ax free, and turned to face the coming druids. "Get her out of here."

Denan stared at him. Bane shoved him toward her. "She's chosen you. Get her to safety. I'll hold them off as long as I can."

Denan snatched her off the ground. She watched over his shoulder as Bane faced the oncoming druids. He ducked a swing and bashed a druid with his shield. His ax cut into another.

"We can't leave him!" Larkin protested. "They'll kill him!"

Denan didn't answer as they crossed her family's fields, didn't answer as arrows rained down around them, didn't answer as Bane fell beneath an onslaught of druids that rushed after them.

"Bane!" Larkin screamed.

CHAPTER 39

AHLEA

Larkin awoke in a tree pod. Midmorning sunshine filtered through the dark canopy. For a moment, she didn't understand where she was, then everything came back in a rush. *Bane.* She'd sobbed for hours until Denan had been forced to play his pipes or risk facing the entirety of the horrors of the Forbidden Forest at night. Her mouth had the medicinal aftertaste like when Magalia had treated her after the lethan attack, which meant they had drugged her too. She tried to sit up, but her ribs barked in protest. She gasped and lay back, panting as the pain flared. Denan appeared above her.

"You drugged me."

"You wouldn't stop screaming."

She screwed her eyes shut. "He's dead, isn't he?"

He was silent a beat. "Not yet."

Her head jerked up. "What?"

"They've tied him to the crucible. He's still alive."

Gritting her teeth, she pushed herself up. "Then we can rescue him." She swayed.

Denan steadied her. "You need to worry about healing a little first."

She hated that he was right. "Where's my family?"

"Foraging. Sela was driving your mother mad scampering about the tree boughs."

"And Maisy?"

Denan hesitated. "She disappeared this morning, but she slept in the same tree as your mother last night."

At least she made it out alive. She searched his dark eyes. She had chosen a side—his side. "I can never go back." Her voice wavered, and she fought to keep her tears at bay.

Denan wrapped his arms around her. "I'm with you. You are not alone."

Denan tied to the crucible ... She'd come so close to losing him. The tears she'd been fighting swelled and trickled down her cheeks.

His brow furrowed. "What is it?"

"Don't scare me like that again."

His expression softened, and his calloused hands took hold of her face, his thumbs wiping the moisture away. "You, Larkin, are a warrior. With you by my side, we will set this right." Despite all the evidence to the contrary, she believed him.

He is mine. He'd told her as much the first day they'd met. She'd been fighting him ever since. She didn't want to fight anymore. She reached up and ran her fingers across the soft hair bristling across his scalp. Her fingers trailed down his scarred cheeks and then, disobedient, strayed across his full lips. His eyes slipped closed. He took hold of her hand, kissing her palm. Honey warmth drizzled through her veins.

Her other hand circled around his neck and pulled him down to her, her lips replacing her fingers. The kiss was soft, full of sweet promises and trembling awareness. She'd kissed him before, a frantic kiss full of desperation and relief and another full of passion and want. But this ... Surrendering had never felt so much like winning.

Their lips parted, but their gazes didn't. Something shifted between them, golden and warm and safe. A giving and a taking in equal measure that created a connection as fragile as it was strong.

"What happens now?" she whispered.

Denan smiled, revealing dimples. "We should probably let your mother know you're awake. She's been worried."

That wasn't what she meant, and he knew it, but she was glad he was giving her space. Rising, he held out a hand to her. She let him help her out of the pod and down the tree, the tincture he'd given her helping with the pain that pulsed through her ribs with each step. When she finally made it safely to the ground, she found pipers everywhere, hundreds of empty pods dangling from trees. All the men wore weapons and armor—a military encampment.

"They arrived this morning," Denan explained.

The forest take her, this really did mean war, but it also meant she had the means to free Bane. And after ... *Wraiths glided over the elegant wall of the Alamant. Their evil swords cut through the people like scythes through wheat. Darkness trailed after them—a dark stain that spread like smoky tendrils, reaching, grasping for the White Tree until it was no longer white at all, but black as a night forsaken by stars.*

She let out a long breath. "After we free Bane, we'll plant a new tree before the barriers fail."

"And find a way to reconcile our peoples."

"Restore the magic."

"Break the curse."

Denan chuckled. "Can't be any harder than what we've already done."

She cocked her head to the side. "You mean sparking a war?"

He leaned in, resting his forehead against hers. "No. We found each other. You brought back women's magic for the first time in over two hundred years. We aren't bound by an archaic treaty anymore. It's time our peoples became one."

Denan tugged her forward, away from the pods and the men in armor, toward a small stream that gurgled toward an unseen rushing river. Her mother stood in the shallow water, gathering watercress into the pouch around her waist. She looked up as they came closer, ran through the water, and enveloped Larkin in her arms.

Larkin gasped in pain, and her mother quickly released her. "Where are Sela and Brenna?" Larkin asked.

Her mother wiped her hands on her apron. "Brenna is sleeping in one of those pods." She pointed to one hanging from a branch in a nearby tree. "And Sela ..." She turned in a circle, her expression shifting to panic. "Where did she go now?" she practically wailed.

Holding her ribs, Larkin turned in a circle and searched the ground for tracks. The three of them spread out, searching and calling. It wasn't long before Larkin found herself in an ancient part of the forest, not even a whisper to reveal the encampment somewhere behind her. The enormous trees gave off a sense of awareness Larkin had only ever experienced in the White Tree. She found little footprints, the toes digging deep where Sela had run. Trotting, Larkin followed them until they disappeared. She circled, looking for a sign that wasn't there. What if Sela had been taken by one of the gilgads? Or worse, a mulgar?

Heart racing, she forced herself to close her eyes and reach for her magic. "You've given me visions before. I need one now."

A bird called, trilling sweetly. She opened her eyes, the vision of the bird superimposed over the real world. It fluttered to her right. She ran after it, dodging branches and leaping over roots. It darted between two massive trunks. When she reached the other side, the bird was gone. Winded, she looked back. The trees stood equal distances apart, their boughs weaving together like a crown. Above her, the canopy was thick and nearly impenetrable. At the center was a tree so large it dwarfed all the others.

Standing at the base stood a little blonde girl, her head thrown back and streams of light curling around her. Larkin held her breath and approached slowly.

When Larkin was a few steps away, Sela looked over her shoulder, face lighting up. "I told you," she said, the first words she'd spoken since Larkin had been taken. "The trees are our friends."

THE END

Turn the page for exclusive bonus content of Amber Argyle's bestselling novel, *Witch Song*.

AMBER ARGYLE

WITCH SONG

Witch Song 1

Brusenna is the last free witch.

The others have all been imprisoned, their magical songs twisted from harmony and growth into chaos and death. With only her guardian by her side, Brusenna must free her fellow witches before their stolen magic destroys the world.

But freeing them won't be easy. The dark witch is cunning, cruel, and vastly more experienced. Brusenna must face magical storms, choking fog, and her own demons before she'd ever be ready to fight for the world that hates her.

With over 1,000 pages of adventure and romance, the acclaimed Witch Song Series will sweep you into a world brimming with magic.

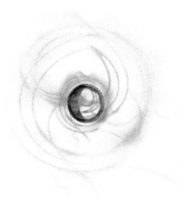

1

WITCHBORN

Brusenna's straw-colored hair felt as hot as a sun-baked rock. She was sticky with sweat that trickled down her spine and made her simple dress cling to her. Her every instinct urged her to run from the glares that stung like angry wasps. She had already put off her trip to the market for too long.

The merchant finished wrapping the spools of thread in crinkling brown paper. "Twelve upice," Bommer said sourly.

A ridiculous price, no doubt made worse by the drought. Had Brusenna been anyone else, she could have bartered it down to half that. Even though the villagers only suspected, it was enough. Careful not to touch her, the man's hand swallowed the coins she dropped in it. She wondered what marvelous things he ate to flesh out his skin that way. Things like the honey-sweetened cakes she could still smell in her clothes long after she'd left the marketplace.

As Bommer mumbled and counted his money, Brusenna gathered the packages tightly to her chest and hurried away. She hadn't gone five steps when a heavy hand clamped down on her shoulder. Fear shot through her veins like a thousand nettles. Here, no one ever touched her.

With a wince, she craned her neck back to see the merchant looming over her. "You tryin' to cheat me, chanter?"

This close, the smell of his stale body odor hit her hard. She swallowed the urge to gag. Her mind worked furiously. She'd counted twice. "I gave you twelve," she managed.

He yanked her around, grabbing her other arm and bringing her face next to his. She cringed as his large paunch pressed against her. Somewhere, a baby squalled. "You think I can't count?"

Brusenna tried to answer, but her mouth locked up. She should have been more careful. She should have stayed until he had finished counting her coins, but she had been too eager to escape. He shook her, his dirty nails digging into her skin. Her packages tumbled from her hands and hit the ground.

Taking shallow breaths and arching away from him, she squirmed, desperate to be free. "Please," she said, finally finding her voice. "Let me go!"

He laughed, his eyes gleaming with pleasure. "No. I don't think so. Not this time. You know what the punishment is for stealing?"

The stocks. Brusenna swallowed hard. Trapped for an entire day with the whole village taunting her. They'd throw things. Rotten food. And worse. She looked for help in the crowd that had eagerly gathered around them. Satisfaction shone plain on every face. She was suddenly angry with her mother for letting her face this alone. For refusing to come because someone might recognize her.

"I didn't steal," she whispered, already knowing no one

would listen.

"You callin' me a liar?" Tobacco spit splattered her face. He backhanded her. Her vision flashed white, then black with stars, then red. She tasted blood. Her eyes burned with tears. She clamped her teeth shut against the pain, refusing to cry out.

Bommer half-dragged her toward the center of the square, where two thin blocks of wood were connected with a hinge. Three holes, one for her neck and two for her wrists. Remnants of rotten food, manure and rocks littered the base.

The sight of the stocks shocked Brusenna into action. She squirmed and struggled.

His hand on the back of her neck, Bommer shoved her throat into the largest, center hole. She tried to rear back. He pushed harder. The wood cut into her windpipe. She couldn't breathe.

"You let that child go, or you'll sorely miss your brain, my friend," said a feminine voice that was somehow soft and commanding at the same time.

Brusenna felt Bommer freeze, his arm still pinning her neck.

She strained against Bommer to see who had spoken. In front of her, sitting astride a glossy black horse, a woman glared at the merchant down the barrel of an expensive-looking musket. The wind picked up and her gleaming hair shifted like a field of ripe wheat. The woman's cobalt eyes met Brusenna's golden ones.

Brusenna gaped. She'd hoped for help, but never imagined it would come from someone both rich and powerful.

"What'd you say to me?" he asked the stranger.

The woman cocked back the hammer. "You heard what I said." Bommer didn't respond. Brusenna felt him shift uncertainly. When no one moved to support him, he growled deep in his throat. He pushed once more on Brusenna's neck, hard. But then she was free. She collapsed, clutching her throat and coughing violently.

When the spots stopped dancing before her eyes, she glanced up. The woman was watching Brusenna, fury burning in her eyes. The stranger let the barrel drop. "Where I come from, merchants ask for the missing coin before they accuse their customers of stealing. Especially a child."

A child? Brusenna bristled as she rose to her feet. She was nearly fifteen. Then, from the corner of her eye, she saw Sheriff Tomack pushing through the crowd. All thoughts of defiance flew out of her head. She tried to slip through an opening, but the press of bodies tightened into an impregnable wall. Arms roughly shoved her back to Bommer.

She shuddered as his hand clamped down on her shoulder again. "Sheriff, this girl stole from me and this," he worked his tongue like he had a bad taste in his mouth, "woman is interfering."

"I already heard it, Bommer." Sheriff Tomack studied Brusenna with an unreadable expression. "You trying to cause trouble, girl?"

Digging her toenails into the packed dirt, she shook her head adamantly.

He grunted. "Well then, give Bommer his upice or spend your day in the stocks."

Anger flared in her chest and died like a candle flame in a windstorm. It didn't matter that she'd already given Bommer twelve upice. It didn't matter that he was lying. She couldn't prove it and her word meant nothing to the villagers. Scrabbling in her money bag, she found an upice and held it out for Bommer.

The merchant slowly shook his head. "I don't want her money. I want her time in the stocks."

Brusenna's hand automatically moved to her bruised throat. Tears stung her eyes. She quickly blinked them back.

"Why?" Sheriff Tomack asked.

Bommer snorted. "You know why."

"You got proof?"

Bommer spit in the dirt. "None of us needs it. We all know what she is."

No one said it, but the word echoed in Brusenna's head, *Witch*.

"Has the girl ever stolen from you before?" Sheriff Tomack asked cautiously.

Bommer took a deep breath. "Her punishment is my choice."

With a click, the woman on the horse released the hammer on her musket. Dismounting, she strode forward. The crowd parted, half in fear and half in awe. She threw a handful of coins at Bommer's chest. The gleaming silver bits bounced off and scattered across the ground. Brusenna's eyes widened in disbelief. The woman hadn't tossed a few dirty upices; the coins were silvers.

Looking both beautiful and terrible, the woman straightened her shoulders. "Take your money, merchant. If you give this girl more trouble, I'll see that no one ever buys from you again."

Bommer spit a stream of tobacco juice dangerously close to the woman's foot. "Who're you to make threats?"

She smiled, a mere baring of her teeth. "Would you like to find out?"

Glaring, Bommer rolled his chaw around his mouth. Finally, his glower shifted to Brusenna. "You ain't worth it, chanter." He scooped up the coins and stomped back to his booth.

Hate filled Brusenna. She hated that Bommer's lies allowed him to abuse her without cause—had earned him ten times his due. She hated the crowd for hating her. Still, it could have been much worse. She could be in the stocks. Grim relief washed through her, cooling her anger. It was past time to be heading home. She twisted to disappear in the crowd. But the strange woman gripped the back of her dress with an iron fist. Knowing better than to fight, Brusenna stifled a groan. *Not again,* she thought.

Sheriff Tomack gave the woman a small nod before moving away.

Brusenna turned a pain-filled glance to the marketplace. Though the crowd had grudgingly moved on, people still shot suspicious, hateful glances her way. Their tolerance of her had taken a dive since the drought had worsened. They blamed her and her mother for their dying crops, simply because they were Witches.

She forced herself to unclench her fists. The breeze felt cool against her sweaty palms. She turned toward the woman, though she dared not look at her face. "Thank you," she murmured.

The woman cocked her head to the side. "Why do you buy from him?"

Brusenna shrugged. "The others won't sell to me. And Bommer needs the money."

"So he resents you for it." She released her grip on Brusenna's dress. "What's your name, child?" Her voice was as sweet and lingering as the smell of the honeycakes.

"I'm not a child. My name is Brusenna."

The woman sighed in relief. "Ah, Sacra's daughter. I thought so."

How could this woman know Brusenna's name? Her mother's name? Her ears buzzed. She managed to bob her head once. She began gathering her scattered packages. The paper scraped loudly against the packed dirt.

The woman crouched beside her. Picking up the last package, she brushed it off and handed it to Brusenna. "My name is Coyel. Will you take me to your mother?"

Brusenna's stomach clenched. There were two iron-clad rules—one: never let them hear your song; two: never lead them home. She swallowed hard. "Thank you, Coyel, for helping me. But I'm not ... I mean, I shouldn't ... I mean—"

Coyel cocked an eyebrow and pitched her voice so no one else would hear, "I'm the eldest Keeper of the Four Sisters."

Brusenna blinked in confusion. Coyel's statement seemed to hold a deeper meaning, but for all her searching, she couldn't understand it. "I ... I'm an only child. My sister died before I was born."

A look of disbelief crossed Coyel's face and Brusenna knew she had missed the mark entirely. "Take me to your home. I must speak with your mother."

She bit her bottom lip. Coyel had saved her from the stocks, so if she wanted to speak with her mother ... well, Brusenna owed her that much. With a nervous glance at the townspeople, she nodded then scurried through the streets. Almost as soon as the village thinned behind them, they crossed into fields flanked by deep forests that grew over the gentle hills like a furry blanket over sleeping giants. Usually, those forests were deep green, but the drought had caused weaker patches to give up the season, trimming themselves in golds and reds.

Brusenna's shoulders itched for the cool, comforting shadows of the trees. She felt naked out in the open like this, where hateful villagers could scrutinize her. She felt even more vulnerable with the echoing clop of the horse's hooves to remind her of the woman and her cobalt eyes.

Nearly a league from the marketplace, Brusenna waited while Coyel tied her horse to a nearby tree. The path wound through thickets as dense and tangled as matted cat fur. She and her mother made it this way to keep strangers out.

Just as she moved to enter the forest, Coyel placed a hand on her shoulder. "This is your home. You should be the one to sing the song."

Brusenna's eyes widened in disbelief. Another Witch? It couldn't be.

Coyel lifted an eyebrow. "Unless you'd prefer me to sing?"

Brusenna didn't understand. Coyel was beautiful and powerful. Not skittish and weak. How could she be a Witch? "At the marketplace, you knew what I was. How?"

Coyel shot a glare in the direction of the village. "I heard someone saying the Witch was finally going to the stocks."

Brusenna folded her arms across her stomach. It made sense. Who else but another Witch would have helped her?

Coyel must have sensed her hesitation. "Are you unable?" There was simple curiosity in her gaze. As if she wanted to see if Brusenna could do it.

Of course she could sing the pathway clear. She'd been doing it for years. But Brusenna hesitated. It went against years of training to sing in front of a stranger. She was nervous to perform in front of another Witch who was everything Brusenna wasn't.

Before she could change her mind, she squared her shoulders and started singing.

Plants of the forest make a path for me,
For through this forest I must flee.
After I pass hide my trail,
For an enemy I must quell.

The underbrush shivered and then untangled like it had been raked through by a wooden comb. As they walked, Brusenna continued her song. As soon as their feet lifted, the plants wove behind them, tangling and knotting themselves into a formidable barrier nearly as tall as a man's chest.

What was nearly impossible without the song was fairly easy with it. In no time, they left behind the last of the forest. Brusenna stepped aside, giving the woman a full view of her home. Drought left the whole countryside brittle. And yet here, their lush gardens thrived. The house and barn were neat and well tended. The milk cow lazily munched her cud under the shade of a tree. With a fierce kind of pride, she watched for

Coyel's reaction.

Coyel took in the prolific gardens with a sweep of her gaze. But the woman didn't seem impressed. As if she'd expected no less. And maybe she had.

Brusenna wanted to ask why Coyel had come, but her tongue dried in her mouth. Her mind shouted it instead, *What do you want with us?*

Bruke, Brusenna's enormous wolfhound, noticed them from his position in the shade of the house and bounded forward, the scruff on the back of his neck stiff with distrust. They'd purchased him as a guard dog after someone had shot their old plow horse. His wary eyes shifted to Brusenna in question.

Brusenna blinked rapidly. She suddenly wanted to explain why she'd broken the rule before the stranger breezed into their house. She darted past Coyel and up the worn path. "Bruke, heel."

With a glare at the stranger, Bruke glued himself to Brusenna's side.

She pushed open the door to the house. "Mother!" she called, pulling some clinging hair off her sweaty forehead.

Sacra's head popped up from the floor cellar. "What is it, Brusenna?"

"A woman named—"

"Coyel," the woman finished as she stepped up behind her.

For the longest time, the two women stared at each other. The charge between them made the tiny hairs on Brusenna's arms stand on end. Coyel stepped into their home. To Brusenna's knowledge, she was the first outsider to do so.

"It's been a long time, Sacra," Coyel said.

Brusenna's gaze flitted back and forth between her mother and Coyel. That they knew each other went beyond her comprehension. In her fourteen years, Brusenna had never seen her mother converse with anyone other than an occasional trouble-making villager—usually one of the adolescent boys who had taken on the challenge to kill one of their animals as a dare.

Sacra stepped out of the cellar and lowered the door as gently as if it were glass. Slowly, she straightened her slender back. "Brusenna, leave the things on the table and go check the corn."

Brusenna's disbelief rose in her throat, nearly choking her. "But, Mother—" At her mother's glower, she swallowed her words, dropped her purchases on the table and ducked out the door. Bruke followed. Careful to keep her stride even, she waited until she had rounded the corner of the house before peeking back. The way was clear.

"Bruke, stay," she whispered. With a disappointed whine, the dog sat on his haunches.

Hunched over, Brusenna retraced her steps. The soft grass felt cool under her hands and the sun was hot on her back as she crouched on one side of the doorway. There were no sounds from within. She waited until her knees were practically numb. She'd almost determined to chance a peek through the window when their voices halted her.

"What brings you, Coyel?" her mother asked warily.

"The Keepers need you, Sacra. There are precious few of us left and signs of the Dark Witch increase daily. The Circle of Keepers must be complete if we are to recapture her and stop the drought."

Brusenna's eyebrows flew up in wonder. It had never occurred to her that Sacra could have been a different person before she became her mother. Mustering every ounce of bravery, she peeked through the corner of the window.

"Calling Espen the Dark Witch only increases her power over us." Sacra's gaze remained fixed on the floor. "Find another Eighth."

Coyel pressed her lips in a tight line. "The others are gone."

Her mother's head came up slowly; she blinked in surprise ... and fear. "I have a daughter. You have only yourself."

Coyel pointed toward Gonstower. "They call us Witches.

But long before that, the Creators named us Keepers. It's what we are. Keepers of the Four Sisters—Earth, Plants, Water and Sunlight. And as a Keeper, you can't deny that all are floundering. If we don't act now, it'll be too late."

Sacra stood rigid and immovable. "No."

Coyel's voice flared, "You know what the Dark Witch will do if she succeeds? Your daughter is Witchborn; even worse, she's the child of a former Head of Earth." She shook her head in disbelief. "She doesn't even know our signs."

Her mother turned away and stared blankly at the trees behind the house. "The less Brusenna knows, the safer she is."

"Safer?" Coyel spat. "You haven't taught her to protect herself. She's terrified of those *villagers*." The last word sounded like her mother's voice after she'd found rats in their oats. "What chance do you think the girl will stand when Espen finds her?"

Her head in her palms, a moan escaped her mother's lips. Coyel stepped forward and rested her hand on Sacra's shoulder. "I've heard her. When she's fully come into her own, I wouldn't doubt she'll be at least a Level Four. But right now, she's … immature. And not just her song. Keeping her isolated will only make it worse. She needs to be around other Keepers her own age. Learn."

Brusenna's cheeks flamed with shame, partly because she suspected Coyel was right about her immaturity. Whenever she was around strangers, her tongue dried up in her mouth and her stomach felt full of writhing snakes.

Her mother jerked away as if Coyel's touch had burned her. "Coyel, no. Espen won't find her. I've been careful. Gonstower is isolated. No one knows I'm here. And we're not completely without friends."

Friends? Brusenna mentally flipped through the faces of the villagers who would have gladly seen her in the stocks. What friends?

Coyel's gentleness vanished, replaced by disbelief and anger. "I found you. And if you think those villagers will protect her identity, you're deceiving yourself. The ignorant fools would gladly turn her over. Never understanding the very Keepers they hate are all that stand between them and—"

"I said no!" Sacra shouted. Brusenna jumped. She'd never heard her mother shout before. "Get out!"

Coyel backed away, her jaw working as if she might chew through Sacra's resistance and then her head dropped. "We're gathering at Haven. I'll wait in the village for three days." Her fervent gaze met Sacra's smoldering one. "Please, Sacra. We can't do it without you."

Not daring to linger another moment, Brusenna scampered away from the door and pressed herself flat against the smooth boards on the other side of the house.

"Please, Sacra," Coyel asked again. And then all Brusenna could hear was the sound of footsteps that grew fainter within moments.

She barely felt Bruke nudge her with his wet nose. Her chest rose and fell as her mind reeled with unfamiliar names. Circle of Keepers, Level Four, the Dark Witch? Surely her mother had no understanding of such things. Surely she'd lived here for generations.

Hadn't she?

Order your copy today!

Visit http://amberargyle.com/witchsong/ to order.

ACKNOWLEDGEMENTS

Thanks go out to my amazing editing team: Charity West (content editor), Jennie Stevens (copyeditor), Cathy Nielson (proofreader), Rebecca Belvins (proofreader), and Amy Standage (proofreader); and my talented design team: Michelle Argyle (graphic designer), Julie Titus (formatter), and Bob Defendi (map maker).

My everlasting love to Derek, Corbin, Connor, Lily, and God.

ABOUT THE AUTHOR

Bestselling author Amber Argyle writes young-adult fantasies where the main characters save the world (with varying degrees of success) and fall in love (with the enemy). Her award-winning books have been translated into numerous languages and praised by such authors as NYT bestsellers David Farland and Jennifer A. Nielsen.

Amber grew up on a cattle ranch and spent her formative years in the rodeo circuit and on the basketball court. She graduated cum laude from Utah State University with a degree in English and physical education, a husband, and a two-year-old. Since then, she and her husband have added two more children, which they are actively trying to transform from crazy small people into less-crazy larger people. She's fluent in all forms of sarcasm, loves hiking and traveling, and believes spiders should be relegated to horror novels where they belong.

To receive her starter library of four free books,
simply tell her where to send it:

http://amberargyle.com/freebooks/

OTHER TITLES BY AMBER ARGYLE

Witch Song Series
(http://amberargyle.com/witchsongseries/)

Witch Song
Witch Born
Witch Rising
Witch Fall

Fairy Queens Series
(http://amberargyle.com/fairyqueens/)

Of Ice and Snow
Winter Queen
Of Fire and Ash
Summer Queen
Of Sand and Storm
Daughter of Winter
Winter's Heir